SWIFT

'We're interested in your knowledge of SWIFT, doctor.'

'Which will be of no use to you. SWIFT III is unbreakable. I have already made that clear.'

'And I have made clear what will happen to your daughter if you don't cooperate with us.'

Crick's spectacles glittered. He spread his hands. 'Then you will have to kill us. There is no way that SWIFT III can be broken into by individuals with limited resources. A government – maybe – but only then with great difficulty.'

'Who said we were individuals with limited resources?'

SWIFT

James Follett

ARROW

A Mandarin Paperback

SWIFT

First published in Great Britain 1986
by Methuen London
Mandarin edition first published 1989
Reissued 1994
by Mandarin Paperbacks
an imprint of Reed Consumer Books Ltd
Michelin House, 81 Fulham Road, London SW3 6RB
and Auckland, Melbourne, Singapore and Toronto

Reprinted 1994

A CIP catalogue record for this title
is available from the British Library
ISBN 0 7493 1012 X

Printed and bound in Germany by
Elsnerdruck, Berlin

1: London

It was dusk when Dr Hans Crick flicked his main beam switch and so fired the detonator that blew the van's rear tyre. Traffic passed the crippled vehicle on both sides as he nursed the van to a standstill in the centre of the Mall – less than two hundred yards from Buckingham Palace. He flipped on the hazard lights, jumped out of the vehicle and ruefully examined the shredded tyre.

His timing was excellent; the manhole cover was right under Damion's nose when the van stopped.

Damion was a big man. His height – over six feet – gave him the appearance of lankiness; his powerful frame, spread prone in the back of the van, was nearly the length of the vehicle's floor. He reached through the hole in the floor and hooked a prybar under each of the cover's two lifting lugs. A decidedly unheady aroma of London's Victorian-built sewers bludgeoned its way into the van as he levered up the cover. The four-inch thick steel plate was heavy but Damion had little trouble lifting it. Thirty seconds later the replacement – outwardly identical – manhole cover was in place. Damion opened a polythene bag that contained a quantity of London dirt and dust, and worked the contents into the disturbed joint. He banged twice on the floor. Crick steered the van to the kerb and set about replacing the wrecked tyre.

Police constable Brian Ludham swung his motorcycle in a tight circle and pulled up alongside the van as Crick was cranking the jack. 'Quick as you can, please, sir,' Ludham requested politely.

'Yes – of course,' Crick grunted, without looking up.

Ludham noticed that the man spoke with a slight foreign accent – probably Dutch. 'Thank you, sir.' With that the police officer opened his throttle and roared off. He returned a few minutes later and was pleased to see that the offending vehicle had gone.

The two men dumped the van at a car breaker's yard and returned to their estate car.

'Are you sure he didn't see your face?' Damion persisted.

Crick sighed. 'It was getting dark and I didn't look up at him.' He glanced at the powerfully built man sitting beside him in the driver's seat. 'Listen, Damion. I do not like this. That bomb –'

'For Chrissake!' Damion snarled, blasting his horn at a cyclist. 'Will you stop going on about that goddamn bomb like a stupid old woman!'

'I think there might be another way –'

'There is no other way. And even if there was, it's too late to do anything about it now.'

Crick remained silent until they returned to their flat at Putney. The Belgian had experienced the big man's volatile temper on a number of occasions. Arguing with him was dangerous.

The two men had spent most of the day preparing for their departure from the country, so for once the flat was clean and tidy. There were three pieces of electronic equipment in the flat – reassembled now that the extensive modifications that Crick had carried out were complete. The two men carried the units carefully down to the estate car and packed them neatly with plenty of foam rubber around them for protection.

The last thing Damion did after a final check around the flat was to ensure that the backup power supply to the radio transmitter, hidden inside the telephone answering machine, was in working order. He locked up, checked the locks, and took the lift down to where Crick was waiting in the car.

'You know the way to Winchester,' he told Crick. 'You can drive for once.'

Crick obediently did as he was told. He drove steadily without exceeding any speed limits. They rarely spoke; Damion was not the sort of man who encouraged conversation. After an hour they were driving along the darkened stretch of the A31 between Farnham and Alton. It was a typical English trunk route: services for motorists after eleven o'clock at night were nonexistent.

'Pull in at the next lay-by,' Damion instructed. 'I want a pee.'

After another mile, Crick drew into a deserted lay-by and waited while Damion disappeared into the darkness for a few minutes.

Damion returned. Instead of opening the front passenger door, he climbed in the back and sat behind Crick. 'More room to stretch my

6

legs if I sit sideways,' he explained. He took a swig from a hip flask and pulled from his pocket a loop of plastic strapping attached to a miniature, plastic-encased servomotor. The tiny electric motor, with its built-in reduction gearbox and penlight batteries, was small – the size of two cigarette packets.

Crick started the engine.

'Don't switch the lights on yet,' said Damion quietly.

'What?' As Crick half-turned in his seat, Damion quickly slipped the plastic strap over his head and pulled it tight.

Crick gasped out a strangled protest but got no further. His fingers went to the strap that was cutting into his throat but he was too late; Damion had switched on the tiny motor. The servomotor's power was very little, but with the aid of its 100:1 reduction gearing, it possessed sufficient power to wind the strap into Crick's neck with an unstoppable thousand-pound force. He got out of the car and walked away a few yards and waited while his victim thrashed on the front seat, choking, kicking out wildly, and clawing dementedly at the deadly strap and the servomotor.

Damion took another draught from the hip flask and carefully replaced the cap. Eventually Crick's dying gasps were weak enough to be drowned by the whirring from the tiny electric motor. After four minutes Crick was sprawled across the car's front seats, not moving, not making a sound. The motor continued to pull the strap deep into Crick's neck – the whirring gradually slowed as the garrotting drained its two penlight batteries.

Damion opened the driver's door and pulled Crick's body upright. The strap had virtually disappeared into the deep furrow it had created in the Belgian's neck. He released the strap from the servomotor's drive capstan and pocketed the murder weapon. He was pleased with the tiny gadget which he had spent several hours making in the flat after Crick had gone to bed. It killed cleanly and quietly – the victim was unable to make a sound. Also there was no danger of being scratched during a struggle, with the attendant risk of traces of skin and blood left under the victim's fingernails for the forensic scientists to work on. And, of course, one did not have to be present to witness the whole distasteful business.

As Damion resumed the journey to Winchester, where a gas incinerator was waiting for the corpse in the back of the vehicle, he went over the design of the bomb in his mind. It was annoying to be plagued by the feeling that there was something he had overlooked. No, he told himself, he was worrying needlessly. Every detail had been meticulously planned. In any case, Damion had sufficient confidence in the late Hans Crick's expertise to be certain that the radio-controlled device that had been planted in the Mall would kill all the occupants of the target vehicle.

He ran his fingers through his mop of unruly hair. The bomb was small and yet its blast would shake the Western world. He chuckled to himself; the real irony was that the whole enterprise – what was certain to be the greatest crime of all time – had started a year previously as the result of a computer keyboard error by a New York bank clerk.

2: London

Anton Suskov lay back in bed and decided that there was nothing quite as sexy as a long-legged girl wearing a man's shirt and nothing else.

'Where do you keep your cereal, Tony?' the girl called over her shoulder.

'Top shelf on the right.'

The shirt rode up over the girl's buttocks, exposing a dark little scut as she reached up to the cupboard. Tony groaned inwardly with embarrassment – not at the girl's delightful revelation – but at the realization that he had forgotten her first name. Surely he hadn't called her Miss Fleming all evening? It wasn't his style. He had her business card but that was in his jacket in the wardrobe. Feigning sleep, he rolled onto his stomach, head and arm draped over the edge of the mattress, and deftly opened her handbag. A quick flip through her credit card wallet while she was struggling with the door of one of his temperamental cupboards answered the question.

Elaine Fleming . . . Elaine – that was it. The girl on the Keytech stand at the London Computer Fair. He had been drawn to the stand simply because Keytech were a company that he had never heard of. Elaine Fleming. A statuesque brunette with dazzling jade-green eyes that had looked right into his soul. No ordinary salesgirl but someone who knew her company's services inside out. Keytech provided banks with repair and replacement services for their computer

8

terminals. Banking was an area where Tony had few contacts therefore she was worth cultivating. She had glanced at his press card and invited him into the stand's office for a drink. After a brief chat she had accepted his suggestion for dinner that evening. Her outrageous personality had provided him with a memorably stimulating evening. When he had suggested returning to his studio apartment in Cork Street for coffee, she had fastened her incredible green eyes on him and said: 'Why are you inviting me back, Tony? Be honest with me. Is it because you want to screw me?'

Tony's smile had never wavered even though her directness had floored him for a moment. 'Of course,' he had replied, matching her candour, and hoping his voice sounded sufficiently casual to suggest that he was used to answering such questions.

Elaine had signalled the waiter.

'This is my evening,' Tony had protested.

Elaine had shaken her head and produced a gold American Express card. 'As you're a self-confessed Russian agent, I'd rather the evening ended with you owing me all the favours.'

'Hey! Wake up! Breakfast!'

Tony opened his eyes just as Elaine, armed with a laden tray, sat immodestly cross-legged on the bed. She brushed her long dark hair away from her face and proceeded to devour a slice of toast that was piled high with his Fortum & Mason marmalade.

'Coffee?'

'Please.'

Elaine poured with one hand and continued eating with the other. 'I always eat an enormous breakfast,' she explained, talking with her mouth full. 'And next to nothing for the rest of the day. I split with my last boyfriend because he couldn't stand breakfasts with me. What's the point of a relationship without shared breakfasts?'

'Absolutely,' Tony agreed solemnly, propping himself up and sipping his coffee.

'Breakfasts like this are sexy,' said Elaine, sinking her perfect teeth into another slice of toast. 'No one ever thinks that breakfasts are sexy. It's always evening meals in smart restaurants that get all the press. Don't you think I look sexy? Half naked? Hair all mussed? After all, you'd never see me looking like this in a restaurant.' She stopped eating and looked critically at Tony. 'I like blond men. I think you're my first Russian. You don't talk like a Russian and you don't look like a Russian. I always think of Russians as pudgy. You're much too tall and you're much too sexy.'

'I don't feel sexy.'

Elaine threw back her head and laughed. 'Oh yes you do, Anton Suskov. I've been watching your eyes. Riveted on it like it was about to leap from between my legs and bite your head off.'

Tony grinned. 'You don't miss much, do you?'

Elaine tucked into a generously filled bowl of muesli. 'Never. And you certainly don't either, do you? Mmm . . . This is good stuff. I hate muesli that looks like rats' droppings in sawdust. Why did you peek in my bag?'

The sudden switch in the flow of her idle chatter caught Tony off guard. 'I . . . er . . .' he floundered.

Elaine's smile was one of triumph at his embarrassment. 'For a spy you're a lousy operator. Mirrors on all your kitchen cupboards.'

'Please, Elaine – I keep telling you – I am *not* a spy.'

'Bullshit. I bet all Tass correspondents are spies.' She glanced around the tastefully furnished studio. 'If you've got a hidden video camera somewhere, I'd love a copy of the tape.'

'I'm a science correspondent.'

'Even worse.' Elaine decapitated a soft-boiled egg and spooned the contents into her mouth. 'Don't you think there's something faintly disgusting about eating a runny boiled egg? Explain your sordid prying into my handbag, you voyeuristic wretch.'

'I'd forgotten your first name,' Tony confessed, shamefaced, realizing that this extraordinary girl would see through anything other than the truth.

'You see? You're a lousy operator. A good operator would come up with a flattering lie. Jesus Christ – is that the time?' Elaine leapt from the bed and yanked Tony's shirt off, showering him with toast crumbs. 'Be an angel and call a taxi while I'm in the shower.' With that she darted naked into the bathroom.

Tony was clearing away the breakfast when she was ready to leave. She opened his dressing gown and pressed herself against him. Her arms went around his neck and she gave him a long, sensual kiss. 'Hell,' she muttered, drawing away and looking appreciatively at him. 'If I had the time, I might stay and have my wicked way with you. Will you do me a big, big, big favour?'

'If I can,' he said guardedly.

'Come round and see me Sunday afternoon. You've no idea just how much I loathe Sunday afternoons. You can get me worked up by telling me lots of lurid tales about your spying missions and about all the hapless confidential secretaries you've seduced.'

Tony grinned as he opened the front door for her. 'Of course – I'd love to. Where do you live?'

'Call me at the office. You've got my card.'

'Will your boss mind?'

She paused as if the question had annoyed her. 'I am the boss. Sort of . . .'

Tony was about to say something, but Elaine was gone, her expensive shoes clopping rapidly down the stairs. From the window he watched her climb into the waiting taxi. She must have guessed he was watching because an elegant arm waved from the cab's rear window as it moved off.

By the time Tony had washed and shaved, it was time to start work. He opened his bureau and sat staring at his reflection in his data base's monitor screen, while thinking about the twelve wasted hours in the company of the delightful Elaine Fleming. Wasted because he hadn't obtained any real information from her about her company's activities. No, he decided, the time had not been wasted; he had enjoyed every minute of the twelve hours. She was the most captivating girl he had ever met. To hell with his employers. He had not paid for the meal, therefore there was nothing to enter on his expenses claim. There was only one thing Tass resented more than their employees having private lives, and that was financing their private lives.

The circle of engineers, scientists, journalists and civil servants who were Tony's close contacts found it difficult to accept that he was a Soviet citizen. His taste for a Western life style and his warm, outgoing personality simply did not fit the popular concept of how a Russian ought to behave. Certainly he was very different from Tass' previous London-based science correspondents. The smiling Tony was a friend of everyone's. Scientists and engineers liked him because of his remarkable ability to grasp the essentials of their work and to produce good English and Russian copy from their turgid press releases; sub-editors and copy-tasters liked him because his material was always tailored to their house style; the British intelligence services liked him because he always cleared copy touching on military matters through the Ministry of Defence press office. In fact Tony was more cooperative than many Western science correspondents, and certainly more knowledgeable. The Foreign Office tolerated Tony because of the number of informal introductions he had arranged in the Soviet Union for British industrialists. Tony had been the unofficial go-between behind a number of lucrative export deals. When needed, permission from them for him to leave London to visit a trade fair was always forthcoming.

The Foreign Office's view was that of course Tony was feeding intelligence back to the Soviet Union: all Tass correspondents throughout the world were intelligence officers – 'legals' in espionage jargon. But if you were going to have spies in your midst, you might as well have useful ones. The people who had reservations about Tony were his own employers – ultimately, the KGB. Part of Tony's job was to glean and translate useful information from the outpourings of the Western technical presses in addition to maintaining close contacts with scientists engaged in 'interesting' work. His great value to them was the accuracy of his assessment reports. He had a rare ability to be able to separate essential information from the background 'noise'; it was unusual for Tony to be wrong.

He traded much of his information on Soviet research through the various computer data bases that he subscribed to. There were times when Tony's KGB masters wondered who benefited most from his all-round knowledge: Mother Russia or the West.

Tony pushed Elaine from his thoughts. Tass had asked for an analysis on the likelihood of British Airways ignoring government pressure and buying from Boeing, rather than Euro Aerospace, to replace their ageing long-haul TriStar fleet. No doubt his employers wanted advance information so that they could gauge the strength of the European aerospace industry in the decade ahead. Even so, their insatiable curiosity about the West was a constant source of surprise to Tony, although a KGB colleague had once pointed out to him that today's press releases were tomorrow's intelligence reports.

Tony had amassed all the information needed for the analysis: copies of Hansard, British Airways' policy statements, notes on his interviews with government and airline officials, and even transcripts from memory of his conversations with influential senators and congressmen during his visit to the United States the previous month.

He switched on his data base terminal and entered his personal identification mailbox access number. The usual collection of tickets, press hand-outs and invitations were downloaded onto his printer. A quick glance at his bank statement to make sure he was in the black. He was very much in the black.

$102,300 in the black more than he should be.

Tony stared at the statement in dismay and ripped it from the printer. Someone in New York had paid $102,300 into his account at the end of the month. The cryptic entry merely said 'sundries' in the credit column and showed the amount in pounds sterling after conversion from US dollars. A commission paid for a useful introduction? Tony searched his mind and could think of no one who had even hinted at the possibility of a payment. They had been offered in the past but he always refused them – including gifts. The standing joke among Tass personnel was that any member of the staff caught accepting outside payments ended up as a sub-editor on the weekly magazine *Siberia Today*. Suddenly it seemed like a very sick joke indeed, which was why he was experiencing a feeling of mounting panic over the mysterious $102,300 payment. It had been paid in a month previously during one of his visits to New York. Whatever it was for, he didn't want it. The time would come when there would be a payment that Tony would accept. A payment large enough to buy him a new identity in the West and set him up in luxury for the rest of his life. But it would have to be a very substantial payment indeed – at least seven figures.

Certainly not $102,300.

It was an embarrassment – an extremely dangerous embarrassment. He decided to get rid of the evidence by transferring the data to his private file on a Geneva data base that he subscribed to.

But first it was necessary to check his phone for intercepts or bugs. He dialled the speaking clock. While the masculine voice intoned the time, he switched on a broadband Trio scanner. The receiver's digits winked rapidly as it raced through the radio spectrum, searching for strong local signals such as might be radiating from a bug planted in the building. As usual, the only discovery the receiver made was when it locked onto a cordless Pokketfone telephone conversation from a nearby architect's office. Tony pulled the cover off the telephone's junction box and checked the line with a multimeter. Any form of connection to the line would alter its resistance.

13

Everything was okay. He would have been surprised if it had been otherwise. Having located several expensive devices in the past, including the one that was still operating in his car, they now tended to leave him alone.

It took him less than thirty seconds to transfer his bank statement details to the Geneva computer. All his files were stored on the data base: he even used its terminal as a word processor when writing his copy. He never kept material he had written in his flat. With the bank statement print-out safely shredded in the waste disposal unit he felt a little better, but he knew from his own experience just how easy it was to obtain information from British banks. The next thing was to find out who had deposited the money.

3

The bank's chief accountant was all smiles when he looked up from his computer terminal.

'I've found the problem, Mr Suskov. A discrepancy between the payment into the New York bank and the transaction they fed into the computer.'

Tony's relief did not override his journalistic instincts. He was curious to see what was on the accountant's screen.

'May I see, please?'

The accountant considered. The satellite access codes and the bank's authentication codes had been entered and were no longer on the screen. 'Certainly, Mr Suskov.' He swivelled the monitor. Tony's full name and address and other details were displayed along the top of the screen. He pointed to an account number. 'That's Tass' New York account number. They paid $1,023 into your account last month – not $102,300. Naturally the error would have come to light at the end of the week.'

'Naturally,' Tony agreed, remembering that $1,023 was his expenses claim for his stay in New York. 'Can you rectify the mistake now and mailbox me a revised statement please?'

'No problem, Mr Suskov.' The accountant turned the monitor so that it was facing him again and made some entries on the keyboard. A printer purred briefly and ejected a new statement.

Tony noticed that the name S.W.I.F.T. III and a logo of a globe were embossed on the printer and the computer terminal. The same logo had been marked on an identical terminal on Elaine Fleming's Keytech stand at the London Computer Fair. Odd that the same name should crop up twice in twenty-four hours.

'Thank you,' said Tony, checking the revised figures. 'That was quicker than I expected.'

'The New York banks and markets don't open for another hour,' the accountant explained. 'Once they do, even with the huge amount of traffic the SWIFT satellites can handle, it's sometimes necessary to wait as long as several minutes.'

Tony nodded knowingly. 'Do such errors happen often?'

The accountant checked that no one was within earshot. 'Officially – very rarely. Unofficially – all too often. Last month over half a million pounds was paid into a pet shop's account in Hendon.'

'Really? I hope they thanked you.'

The accountant gave a wry chuckle. 'They didn't have time to blow it on dog biscuits: big payments are automatically verified within an hour by another system.'

Tony had mentally composed the opening paragraphs of his article on the weaknesses of the Western banking system when the taxi dropped him outside his Cork Street flat. It would be the sort of article that Soviet weeklies liked: basically accurate, but with emphasis on the faults of the system and little mention of its merits.

The article kept praying on his mind while he was working at his terminal on the airline analysis. On an impulse, he entered SWIFT on his keyboard and sent it as an interrogation to the Geneva data base. Back came a menu – a long screen listing of all the references to SWIFT: the full names of several prominent people called SWIFT; cross-references to the entries in every telephone and cable directory in the world; the bird; and Operation Swift of World War II. 'Please enter your choice', said the screen. Tony scrolled through the menu and came to a line that looked interesting:

S.W.I.F.T. BANKING SYSTEM. ALL INFORMATION ACCESSES NOTI-
FIED TO SOCIETY FOR WORLDWIDE INTERBANK FINANCIAL TELE-
COMMUNICATION, BRUSSELS.

The clause amused Tony. It was typical of the Swiss to guard the interests of a banking system. He decided that he did not want

SWIFT, whoever they were, to know that a Tass correspondent in London was showing an interest in their organization. There was an English saying about there being more than one way of skinning a cat.

He called up information on Keytech. Registered office was the same address as Elaine's flat. The company's articles of association were interesting: Keytech held the United Kingdom repair and replacement franchise of SWIFT interface terminals from S.W.I.F.T. Terminal Services S.A. Directors of Keytech were named as Mark Fleming and Elaine Fleming. Mark Fleming? Her husband?

A Surrey home address near Woking was given for Mark Fleming. Tony accessed the United Kingdom Land Registry data base. Entering the Woking address provided him with details on the property. The freehold land area was less than one tenth of a hectare. A modest detached house. Mark Fleming had been its owner for twenty-two years. He had to be Elaine's father, unless she had married a man much older than herself.

A phone call to Mark Fleming might solve the problem.

'Hallo?' A woman's voice. Elderly. Cultured.

'May I speak to Mr Fleming's daughter please?'

'I'm sorry. Elaine now lives in London most of the time. Can I help?'

Having found out what he wanted, Tony was tempted to hang up, but there was a good chance that the woman had one of the new telephones that displayed on a miniature screen the telephone number and name of the incoming caller. Only payphones and Pokketfones were safe nowadays for making anonymous calls. He assured the woman that his call was not important, thanked her, and hung up. For the time being he was content. All the other things he wanted to find out about Elaine and SWIFT could wait until Sunday. He cleared his computer screen of the Land Registry data and returned to his work.

4

Two familiar combat jackets flashed across Tony's field of vision, but at that moment he was distracted by Elaine uttering a demonic whoop of triumph and accelerating into the inside of the bend. She

16

side-swiped Tony's car, making it skid off course. Tony spun his steering wheel so that the front of his car collided with her vehicle as she tried to overtake him. They raced along side by side at the maximum speed the bumper cars were capable of.

Admiring male eyes followed Elaine as she swept past the onlookers. She looked incongruously elegant in her wide-brimmed straw hat and Edwardian-style dress, although the effect of the latter was spoilt because it was hitched halfway up her thighs.

Tony pulled ahead and saw the two combat jackets again: two gangling youths dressed in cliff assault boots, combat fatigues and webbing army packs – the 'terrorist' look – the current vogue outfit of London's young unemployed. Their sneering faces had watched Elaine and Tony on the whip and the deathride.

Tony hooked his wheel. The collision jarred both cars. '*Now* you'll tell me about SWIFT!' he yelled.

'You haven't won yet!'

Tony wrenched his wheel again. He was ten yards ahead by the time Elaine had brought her spinning car back on course. Tony risked a glance back at her and drove into a car crewed by two teenage girls who had even less control over their car than their hysterical laughter. Elaine shot past – mocking fingers upraised. She was prevented from bumping Tony by the ride operator cutting power. All the cars on the circuit ground to a standstill and a fresh wave of customers charged onto the steel floor to claim vehicles. The two combat jackets did not join in the surge but continued to watch their objective, jaws champing on chewing gum.

Tony helped Elaine from her car. 'I won,' he boasted.

'Crap.' She brushed the creases from her dress.

Tony was indignant. 'You hit me twice. I hit you at least twenty times.'

Elaine wasn't impressed. 'Trust a Ruskie to twist the facts. Wasn't it a Russian general who once said that he was engaged in a triumphant retreat before an enemy advancing in utter disorder! Buy me a hot dog and stop griping and I'll whisper you my plans to restore your devastated masculine ego.'

There was no sign of the two youths when Tony sat beside Elaine on the park bench and handed her a hot dog. As they ate, he broached the subject of SWIFT again.

Elaine wiped her fingers clean with a tissue and regarded him steadily. Her green eyes made him feel uncomfortable but he met them without flinching.

'Why do you want to know about SWIFT?'

'I'm a journalist.'

'Lying toad. You're a KGB spy.'

'Elaine – how many times do I have to tell you? I am *not* a spy. Why? Is SWIFT a secret?'

'Sort of.'

Tony considered. When obtaining information on a sensitive subject, it was best to put the informant at ease by first asking questions on unimportant matters concerned with the main subject. 'What does SWIFT stand for?'

'There's nothing secret about that,' said Elaine. 'Society for Worldwide Interbank Financial Telecommunication.'

'SWIFT looks after all international financial transactions between banks?' Tony queried.

'Yes.'

'And SWIFT III?'

'That's the new system. SWIFT I was the first back in 1973 when the SWIFT society was formed. SWIFT II came into service between 1985 and 1987. Now we're phasing in SWIFT III.'

The questions could now become more pertinent. 'What's so special about SWIFT III?'

Elaine hesitated. 'Well – I don't suppose it'll hurt to tell you. It was publicized at the time. Basically, SWIFT was set up as a secure system to transmit financial transactions between member banks. It uses an unbreakable encryption for all messages. Originally data was transmitted over public telephone lines, leased line private circuits – and satellite networks. By the end of the eighties, the public networks were griping about the huge amount of traffic SWIFT II was generating. During hours when the New York and European banking hours overlapped, it was becoming difficult to make a transatlantic phone call because SWIFT was hogging so many lines.'

'Surely SWIFT uses high speed data transmission techniques?' Tony queried.

'That's right. In excess of quarter of a million baud – that's quarter of a million bits of information per second.'

Tony decided not to break Elaine's train of thought by telling her that he knew what a baud was. It would only start an argument.

'But it didn't matter how fast SWIFT sent its data,' Elaine continued. 'The system was gobbling up phone and satellite channels as fast as the commercial communication networks could expand.'

Tony finished his hot dog. They started walking towards the pleasure garden's exit. Neither of them saw the two youths emerge from the trees and follow them at a discreet distance.

'So what happened next?' Tony prompted.

'SWIFT launched their own satellites. Three of them to cover every square inch of the globe. They're supposed to have enough capacity to handle all their traffic way into the next century.'

'Are they large enough?'

'Even if I knew the answer to that, I wouldn't tell you.' The sudden curtness of her reply made Tony decide to drop the subject, but Elaine continued: 'But they're a success. Christ – that's an understatement. They're a super staggering colossal success. All the large banks now have a direct microwave link with a SWIFT satellite. I reckon it's only a matter of time before every little branch bank is hooked up to the system. Apart from the speed, it saves them a fortune in landline charges.'

'And makes their profits even more grotesque.'

'Absolutely obscene,' Elaine agreed cheerfully. 'It's cheaper for two banks a hundred yards apart to talk to each other via a SWIFT satellite than it is for them to use a phone line. Your place or mine?'

They were crossing the car park when Tony saw one of the combat jackets duck behind a Ford. He gripped Elaine's arm and stopped. 'Trouble,' he muttered.

'The two in camouflage jackets?'

'You noticed them too?'

'They were watching us on every ride,' said Elaine. 'Come on. They're probably harmless.'

'You stay here. I'll find out what they want.'

'Tony – don't go playing the hero.'

Tony ignored her and walked towards his car. The two youths appeared in front of him. The taller one propped himself against a parked van while his colleague sat on the bonnet of Tony's Skoda, idly swinging his legs. They watched his approach with vacant, disinterested expressions. As he drew near, Tony realized that they were older than they looked. Possibly in their late twenties. Not the age group that favoured the 'terrorist' look. They both faced Tony when he was within ten yards of them. The last time Tony had faced two men was during a training confrontation in the gymnasium at the KGB Central Training School in Moscow. His combat instructor had been particularly good, and Tony had been a particularly apt pupil.

He stopped within groin-kicking distance of the two men. They both moved back a pace. Professionals, thought Tony – not ordinary street muggers. He said mildly: 'Your luck's out. I lost all my money in the arcade.'

The taller of the two men grinned. 'That's okay, sir. We've already been paid. Well paid, in fact.'

He was well spoken. Tony watched him carefully, giving no indication that he had noticed the smaller man edging sideways.

'What do you want?'

The taller man's grin broadened. 'Just to give you a little lesson, sir. Nothing too violent just yet. Just enough to make you dwell on your sins for awhile.'

The second man was now nearly out of sight. He suddenly lunged at Tony but was not quick enough. Tony spun on one toe and lashed out with his other foot. His timing was brilliant: his flailing toecap steam-hammered into the thug's jaw. The man gave a gasp of pain and crumpled. As Tony recovered his balance, the knife edge of his outstretched palm smashed into the taller man's neck. For a second he stared at Tony in surprise before his legs buckled under him, pitching his body across his motionless colleague.

Tony stared down at the two still forms. Apart from the year before when he had surprised a burglar in his Moscow flat, it was the first time he had ever had occasion to put his training to the test. Elaine strolled unhurriedly to his side.

'I suppose I ought to rush up saying, are you okay?' she observed. 'But it's perfectly obvious that you are and they're not. Shall we call the police?'

'No.' He opened his car door and pushed her in.

'Now I know you're a spy,' Elaine announced, as they drove out of the car park. 'Only spies and film stuntmen fight like that. So – we know who you are. But who were those two?'

Tony hooted impatiently at a dawdling Datsun. 'I've no idea.'

'Tony.' Her voice was reproving.

'Elaine – I swear I don't know who they were.'

20

'I heard what one of them said. It sounded like they'd been paid to give you a working over.'

Tony nodded. 'That's what I thought. It must be a case of mistaken identity. Maybe I resemble someone who's run up a gambling debt?'

Elaine smiled and kissed him. 'And now you've run up a debt with me.'

'Eh?'

'As honest, law-abiding citizens – at least I am – you're a spy – it's my duty to report those two to the police.'

'I'd rather you didn't. My employers hate their minions mixing it with the natives.'

Elaine laughed at his phraseology. 'I bet they do. Can't have their spies brawling, can they? Hence the debt.'

'Which I have to repay?'

'Of course.'

An hour later they were lying quietly in each other's arms in Elaine's narrow divan bed.

'Penny for them,' Elaine prompted.

'Oh – thinking.'

'About me?' She snuggled closer, entwining a long, slender leg sensually around him.

'Of course.'

'Mm . . . I like you thinking about me. It makes me feel secure.'

Tony chuckled and stroked her hair. 'You're funny.'

She bit his chest, lightly and lovingly. 'Why?'

'This flat. I don't know what I imagined. Not great luxury, of course. But not this. Vinyl flooring everywhere. Pine furniture.'

'What's wrong with my flat? It's clean. It's simple. I like plainness and simplicity. I'm a plain and simple girl.'

'Who happens to enjoy fishing for compliments,' Tony added.

'I don't really like indoor luxury.'

The curious expression puzzled Tony. 'Only someone who is used to it could say that.'

'It's true, Tony. I like being out in the world. I want to be the dynamo behind a powerful organization. And the only way I can do that is by running my own business and doing things my way – even if it means being chained to a desk and a phone twenty-four hours.

What I don't want is to be tied down to people or possessions. I don't have to worry about this place. If I want to suddenly zoom off somewhere, I can. Or I like to imagine I can.'

'Does your job involve much travelling?'

Elaine's expression hardened sufficiently for Tony to guess that he had touched on a sensitive area.

'Occasionally daddy allows me to visit SWIFT's HQ in Brussels,' she said, not looking at him. 'But only when his precious general manager is busy with something else. Brussels has to be the most boring city in the world. Last year was a special treat – I was actually allowed to attend the SWIFT seminar in Nice.'

'Do I detect sour grapes?'

Elaine looked sharply at him and was relieved to see that he was serious. 'You really do speak good English, don't you?' she commented. 'Sour grapes . . .?' She hesitated, as if forcing herself to accept a suppressed emotion. 'Yes – I suppose I am bitter. Last year I came back from Nice with an extension to our franchise – the Channel Islands. I thought my father would be pleased. Especially as I had negotiated very favourable terms. But he was really livid – he raged at me – saying that I had no right to interfere.'

'But you're a director of Keytech?' said Tony, regretting having probed a wound while at the same time interested in what she had to say.

Elaine grimaced. 'Legally – yes. Look – don't get me wrong: daddy's very loving and kind and all that, but he sees me as little more than a pretty face at jamborees like the London Computer Fair. He won't let me play a really active role in managing the company. Christ knows why. Maybe he's unconsciously paying me out for not being a son – I don't know. What I do know is that what I want more than anything else in the world is to run my own business. I want that more than children, a home – everything. Not only for my own satisfaction, but to show my father that I can do it.' She stopped talking and looked guilty. 'Oh Christ. I've never gabbled on like this to anyone before.'

Tony smiled and stroked her hair away from her eyes. 'I don't mind,' he said quietly. 'I enjoy listening to you. What sort of business would you like to run?' –

'Terminal repair and servicing will do for starters because that's what I know about, and then I'd move on to the bigger stuff on main-

22

frames. But I'd have to take over an existing company. It's no good starting from scratch because all the existing companies have got all the franchises sewn up. That means buying a company. The ones doing well aren't up for grabs and no bank will loan money on the stragglers.'

Tony kissed her ear. 'Have you tried?'

'Several times.' She smiled mischievously at Tony. 'You don't have four million pounds you could spare for a dead cert, do you?'

Tony laughed. 'If I did, it would be yours. Why?'

'I know of a nice little company that's doing reasonably well but could do a whole lot better with a little imagination. The owner has told me that he'd sell up tomorrow for four million. Within three years I reckon it would be worth ten million.'

'And then you'd buy out your father's company?'

'That's not what I want. I don't want to spite daddy; I want to prove to him and myself that I can do it.' She suddenly laughed – making a determined effort to shake off her sombre mood. 'Now it's your turn. Tell me about all those hapless confidential secretaries you've seduced in the course of your spying career.'

The constant barbs were beginning to irritate him. 'Elaine – I am *not* a spy.'

'But you are a communist?'

'I'm a member of the party,' he admitted.

'I didn't ask you that.'

'I used to be but not now. I think living in the West has corrupted me.'

Elaine slid her hand between their bodies and caressed him gently while smiling mischievously. 'Have I corrupted you too?'

Tony grinned. 'Just a touch.'

She gave a gurgling laugh. 'Can they send you home?'

He didn't reply immediately. She sensed the sudden chill that her words had induced. 'Tony?'

'They can send me home any time. Once when I was working in New York, they gave me three hours to pack and catch the evening Aeroflot flight to Moscow. No explanation. Nothing. And then the British government and my government could get into a mutual expulsion brawl and I could be thrown out by the Foreign Office. That's why I stay out of trouble and try to make myself useful.'

'What's wrong with home?'

Tony hesitated. 'You live in the West. You could never understand.'

'Try me.'

His eyes became troubled. 'It's the mistrust you could never understand. It's something that I can't come to terms with. It's the sort of mistrust that crawls right into your soul and even makes me wary of talking to you . . . I'm sorry, Elaine.'

She detected the edge in his voice and decided not to pry further. She took hold of his hand and pressed it against her breast. 'Do you know something? I hardly know you and yet . . .' She fell silent, as if she was frightened of what she had been about to say.

'And yet, what?' Tony's voice was gentle again. His fingers teasing lightly at her nipple.

'Nothing.'

'I don't know much about you,' Tony pointed out. 'Except that you'd like to become a high-powered business tycoon.'

She laughed. 'A bloated capitalist grinding the face of the poor.'

Tony moved down and brushed her hardening nipples with his lips. 'With me as your right-hand man. Would you like that?'

She gave an involuntary shudder. 'God – yes – if you promise to do that every night.'

'You'd have to pay me a lot of money to tempt me away from the bright lights and the glamour of Moscow.'

Elaine laughed again. 'Anton Suskov,' she said severely. 'I do believe you're a capitalist at heart.'

'Let's say we both have expensive ambitions.'

Elaine ran her fingers through his hair and closed her eyes. 'I know. The other problem with daddy's company is that it will never make a fortune out of fixing dud SWIFT terminals.'

'Maybe there is a way of making a fortune out of SWIFT?'

'No one makes money out of SWIFT,' said Elaine. 'Not even SWIFT. It provides a nonprofit-making service to all its member banks. You go to their HQ and the integrity of that outfit borders on the boring.'

Tony pulled the bedcovers down. 'In the course of an hour,' he said, speaking slowly and deliberately, 'how much electronic money moves from Europe . . .' he kissed her left breast, '. . . up to a SWIFT satellite . . .' he kissed her on the mouth, '. . . and down to North America . . .' he kissed her right breast, '. . . and vice versa?'

24

He repeated the cycle of kisses in reverse.

Elaine giggled. 'You have a wicked way of mixing business and pleasure, Anton Suskov,' she reprimanded.

'I'm serious.'

Elaine frowned. 'Christ . . . All transactions between Europe and North America?'

'All transactions,' Tony affirmed, making circles around her navel with his forefinger. 'In a typical hour.'

'Well . . . The real peak is between 2.30 and 3.30 pm – that's when the banks are open on both sides of the Atlantic. London–New York traffic alone is about two billion dollars during that hour. Taking the whole of Europe – about twenty billion dollars.'

Tony's fingers ventured tentatively across her abdomen and into her dark cloud of hair as if uncertain of their welcome. She opened her legs slightly for him.

'So,' said Tony, looking into her jade-green eyes. 'Hijacking SWIFT for an hour at the right time could hardly be called nonprofit-making?'

Elaine suddenly pulled him very close. 'Tony, you stupid bastard.'

'Yes, my darling?'

'Right now I'm more interested in making love than money.'

Afterwards Tony lay awake while the first tenuous, crazy, impossible plans to make himself the richest man in the world took shape in his fertile mind.

What little charm Colonel Gregor Yuragi may have possessed as a baby had long deserted him by the time he was fifty-five. With his heavy jowls, unshaved, and wearing a coat that looked as though he had slept in it and an expression that radiated about as much peace and good will as a cruise missile, he was slouched in Tony's Skoda the following morning when Tony slid behind the wheel. Hardly welcome company. Tony spared his senior officer a cursory glance as he started the engine.

Forced cheerfulness: 'Good morning, Gregor.' He always used Gregor's first name because he knew that the familiarity irritated the KGB officer.

Colonel Yuragi pulled a UHF bug from his pocket and dangled it accusingly by one of its wires.

'I found this an hour ago in your car.'

'Congratulations,' said Tony, merging the car with the early morning traffic. 'I found it three weeks ago. The two extra wires are my addition. A permanent feed of Capital Radio from the car radio. You've ruined someone's morning entertainment. British-made, therefore my guess is that you planted it. The British plant Soviet-made bugs. We get the better of the deal – the lithium battery the British use outlasts ours.'

Gregor wasn't amused. 'Who's the girl?'

Tony shrugged. 'A girl.'

'Useful?'

'In what respect, Gregor?'

'You know what I mean,' Gregor growled.

'I don't know yet. I'm thinking of writing a piece on international capitalism. Banking. She has some useful contacts.'

'I'm to tell you that your work on the European aircraft industry has been well received,' said Gregor grudgingly.

'My God – praise! What's the bad news?'

'If you'd spent the night at your flat instead of fornicating, you would be checking your mail now and you'd know what the bad news is.'

Tony's bland expression concealed his anger. He was being recalled. Right when he was on the verge of something big. Damn! Damn! Damn! Another grey, soul-eroding six months back in his pokey Moscow flat while they discovered for the fifth time how useful he was in London and how incompetent his replacement was. 'Congratulations, Gregor. So you've got your way again? How much time do I have to pack this time?'

'You may have to be sent home permanently because of what's happened,' said Gregor. 'Remember the article you wrote last year on Carlos Rossini?'

'Carlos Rossini? You mean Charlie Rose – the motel chain owner? He hates being called Rossini. What about him?'

'He arrived in this country last week. The first thing he did was to tell his London lawyers to sue you for a million dollars. They sent a copy of their letter to you to the office.'

Tony nearly drove into the back of a taxi. 'He did what! Why?'

'He read your article in *21st Century Frontiers*. Mr Rossini doesn't like being called a gangster.'

'In that case there's been a mistake,' said Tony, thinking quickly. 'Firstly, the piece wasn't written for *21st Century Frontiers*. Secondly, I was careful not to call Charlie Rose a gangster. I said that his contemporaries were. Thirdly, I wrote the article in Russian. Fourthly, I never wanted to write the thing in the first place. I did it as a favour for Svendal when his wife was ill. I'm not a profile writer.'

Gregor appeared to be enjoying Tony's alarm. 'It was translated into English and reprinted in *21st Century Frontiers*.'

'Okay. So tell Mr Rose to sue the translator.'

Gregor pulled a magazine from his pocket and tossed it on the parcel shelf. 'Only your name appears against the article.'

Tony swore to himself. The two thugs who had attacked him yesterday would have been hired by Charlie Rose. That was his preferred method of operating: a frightener first, followed by legal action.

He dropped Gregor near a taxi rank and returned to his flat. The long white envelope was from Issac Meinken and Partners – one of the most expensive law firms in London. He opened the letter. Tony and *21st Century Frontiers* had, in the view of Issac Meinken and Partners, held Mr Rose up to hatred and contempt and that Mr Rose had instructed them to institute immediate proceedings to recover substantial damages.

Tony turned to the magazine. *21st Century Frontiers* was an English language weekly with a split personality because it purported to offer unbiased political insights into international affairs, and yet ninety per cent of its editorial content had a distinct left-wing slant. Its lack of advertising, good quality paper, and reasonable cover price suggested a hefty subsidy from somewhere. Tony's three-thousand word piece on Charlie Rose was the lead article. Worse – it had been entitled 'The New Hoodlums'.

He read it through twice – the first time in anger at the distortions the English translator had introduced; the second time in near panic when he realized the full extent of the trouble the distortions had landed him in. Officially he was a foreign correspondent. He had no diplomatic accreditation and therefore could not hide behind the privileges of diplomatic immunity.

Tony switched on his data base and printer and recalled copies of his original notes based on his two interviews with Charlie Rose, plus a copy of his original article in Russian. He read the magazine version for a third time and compared it with his original text. At least they hadn't tampered with the first few hundred words covering Charlie's background.

5: North Carolina

Carlos Rossini's mother died when he was ten minutes old. He emigrated from Spain to the United States with his father and sister in 1950 when he was twelve years and three months old. By the time he was twelve years and nine months old, he had a new name – Charlie Rose – and could speak perfect English. He and his older sister, Pia, worked all their spare time in the run-down twenty-room motel that his father had bought at Raleigh in North Carolina. In the evenings an exhausted Charlie watched the traffic hurtling south to Florida and gazed with envy at the smart cars that turned into the Rapids Motel two hundred yards further down the road. Smart cars didn't visit his father's motel. Their customers were faceless salesmen driving battered Buicks who swapped the forty-watt lamps in their rooms for hundred-watt lamps and sat up half the night filling in sales returns.

Occasionally Pia visited them in their rooms. Sometimes for a few minutes, sometimes for the night.

Charlie was an arrogant, ambitious seventeen-year-old when his father was killed making a careless left turn out of the motel's drive. The truck hauling steel girders south flattened the pick-up like a tin can in a steam press. Pia was twenty-two. She became Charlie's legal guardian but Charlie was the boss and she didn't argue. Just so long as she could continue making money on the side.

It was a hot Independence Day eve and Charlie was out with a local girl when the white Bentley Continental tourer pulled up outside the motel's office. Victor Salavante was hot and tired. He had driven the five hundred miles from New York and now the only goddamn motel he could find with a vacancies sign was this tumbledown joint. He brightened when he saw Pia behind the office desk. Tall and dark with flawless olive skin. Too tall for a Puerto Rican, he reflected.

'What happens round here at night?' he asked as he registered.

'Nothing,' said Pia, impressed by the stranger's car and expensive clothes. She put his age at about forty. 'A few drug stores in Raleigh
28

stay open late and there's the drive-in.'

'What do you do?'

'Watch television and play Scrabble in Spanish with my brother. Number twelve, Mr Salavante. It's our best room.' She noticed his manicured nails as he picked up his key.

Victor smiled. 'I can play in Italian. But not Spanish. Maybe you can teach me, huh?'

'Maybe,' Pia replied noncommittally.

'About eleven. When I've cleaned up and had something to eat. Okay?'

'Okay,' said Pia indifferently.

Charlie arrived home late in his Ford station wagon. He was in a foul mood. His charm and conquistador good looks had been wasted on the girl. Three hours in a drive-in with a girl who had let him play with her breasts. Nice breasts – not too big. She had returned his kisses – with genuine passion at times – but she had kept her knees locked tighter together than a terrapin's jaws. When he saw Pia walk along the breezeway to the room where the Bentley was parked, he put two and two together and made a fast four. He grabbed her by the wrist and pulled her through the office and into their kitchen.

'So who's the Bentley?'

Pia realized that the evening had gone badly for Charlie. A wrong word from her and he would fly into a rage. 'A Mr Salavante. That's all I know. New York.'

'And you're going to let him screw you for a lousy ten dollars?'

Pia went onto the defensive. It was an argument they had had many times. 'It's sometimes more. If they're feeling generous.'

Charlie stared at her. His eyes roved over her body in a way that she knew was wrong for a brother to look at his sister. 'Remember those nylon toreador pants you bought at the flea market last year? Go put 'em on.'

'They're too tight,' Pia protested. 'They cut me here.' She moved her hand to her groin.

Charlie took a threatening step towards her. 'You do as I say, bitch! Go put 'em on. And that nylon halter thing that went with them. And no pants or bra.'

'Charlie – they were for a fancy-dress party. I can't wear them here.'

Charlie raised his hand. Pia fled. She returned to the kitchen a few minutes later feeling embarrassed and self-conscious in the revealing outfit. Charlie glanced at her and pushed a bowl of crushed ice across the kitchen table.

'What's that for?'

'Get that halter off.'

Pia was about to protest again but changed her mind. Charlie had marked her face for a month the last time he had hit her. She removed the tight-fitting halter and stood facing him – hoping that her defiant expression concealed her fear.

'Now rub the ice into your tits,' Charlie ordered.

Without a murmur, Pia scooped up some crushed ice in her palm. She hesitated, bracing herself for the shock, and then worked the melting cubes against her breasts. Charlie used a towel to mop up the icy water that trickled between her fingers and down her stomach. After a minute he stood back and regarded her critically. The ice had darkened and engorged her nipples. He pinched them gently in turn, making them stand out even more.

'Okay,' he said curtly. 'You'll do.'

Victor was sprawled on the motel bed reading a magazine when there was a knock on the door. 'Come in, honey.'

Pia let herself in with a pass key. Victor gaped at her in disbelief and failed at first to notice Charlie who had followed her into the room.

'Mr Salavante? I'm Charlie Rose – the owner. I think you've already met my sister – Pia?'

Victor tore his eyes away from the vision for an instant. They immediately switched back to Pia as if they were spring-loaded. 'Yeah – sure,' he said weakly. Jesus Christ! This kid could make a fortune in New York.

'I'm sorry you've had to make a complaint about your room, Mr Salavante.'

'Complaint?' Victor echoed. 'What complaint?'

'If it's okay with you,' Charlie continued, 'Pia will stay and fix everything now.'

'Sure. Sure,' said Victor faintly, wondering if he really was in North Carolina.

'But if she does stay, that'll be an extra hundred and fifty on your bill.'

Mention of money provided Victor with an instant restoration of his reason. He looked at Charlie and smiled. 'Sorry, kid. I never pay for it.'

Charlie shrugged and took hold of Pia's elbow. 'Okay, Mr Salavante. I understand.'

'Hold it, kid. Hold it. One hundred.'

'One twenty-five,' Charlie countered.

Victor's eyes followed the seam down the front of Pia's pants to where it disappeared into the divine divide between her thighs. Hell . . . 'One twenty-five,' he agreed.

When Victor checked out the next morning, he paid his bill in full without argument and reserved his room on the same terms for his return trip in four days. Charlie watched the Bentley turn out of the drive and head south. He promised himself that he would own a Bentley Continental by the time he was twenty-five – in seven years' time. Never again would a chick refuse him like the one last night.

He went to Victor's room and woke Pia by brushing a hundred-dollar bill lightly across her cheek. She opened her eyes and focused them on the money. Her expression became incredulous.

'He paid?'

'One hundred and twenty-five plus his room,' Charlie affirmed with a broad grin.

Pia gave a shriek of delight, sat up in bed and threw her arms around Charlie's neck.

'I don't believe it! He *really* paid all that?'

'He sure did. You must've been real special.'

They stared at each other for a moment and then rolled onto the floor, entangling themselves in the sheets and laughing helplessly.

'One hundred and twenty-five dollars,' Charlie kept repeating. 'One hundred and twenty-five dollars!'

'I could've killed you last night, you bastard,' Pia declared, wiping her eyes and pulling the sheet up over her breasts. 'You've no idea how close you came to having a kitchen knife stuck in you.'

Charlie became serious. He held Pia's chin, forcing her to look at him. 'I made you do that because it's what I'd want, so I knew it was what he'd want. Women don't know what men like. They think they do, but they don't. In future you trust my judgement in everything. You understand?'

Pia looked into her brother's black, ruthless eyes and nodded.

Charlie relaxed and smiled. He held up the hundred-dollar bill. 'You do that, Pia, and this is only the beginning.'

Victor returned four days later and kept Pia in his room for ten hours.

'You're a day's drive from New York,' he told Charlie as he got in his Bentley. 'I've got friends who drive down to Miami pretty regular. Maybe I'll tell them about your place, huh?'

'I'd be very grateful to you, Mr Salavante.'

Victor laughed. 'Hell, kid. I don't want your gratitude. Just fifty per cent off my bill in future.'

'Twenty,' said Charlie promptly.

'Forty.'

'Twenty-five and it's a deal,' said Charlie.

Victor looked thoughtfully at the eighteen-year-old and started his engine. 'Know something, kid? You're gonna be big one day.'

'That's right, Mr Salavante. Very big.'

'Just so long as you stay out of New York, Miami and Las Vegas. I've got friends there who'd kill you.'

With that Victor slipped the gearbox into drive and left Charlie staring after him.

Six months and twenty stays later, Charlie felt that he knew Victor well enough to mention a subject that he had been nursing for several weeks. He tackled the New Yorker when he was eating a breakfast that Pia had cooked for him. He was now a favoured guest.

'Mr Salavante. I want to rebuild this motel and I need two hundred thousand dollars.'

Victor slowly lowered his coffee cup and regarded Charlie solemnly. 'Say that again, kid, but slowly.'

Charlie repeated his needs.

'What sort of motel, for Chrissake? That sort of money would buy a piece of a Hilton.'

'A motel with class, Mr Salavante. Real class. Fifty suites – not rooms. A swimming pool. A French restaurant. Turkish baths. A pool room. Two pool rooms. Landscaped gardens – we've got five acres here. The works.'

Victor laughed. 'Whoever heard of a classy motel? A motel is a cheap room for the night. If people want class, they shack up in a hotel.'

Charlie had all his arguments ready. 'Have you seen the hotels in Raleigh? There's a lot of rich people heading south on Highway 95. And, as you once told me yourself, we're a day's drive from New York. All the motels along this strip try to undercut each other on prices . . .'

'It's called competition,' Victor interjected.

'. . . and they end up cutting their services, and their guests don't come back a second time. I want to be the first luxury motel in North Carolina.'

'You'd be the first luxury motel in the whole of the United States,' Victor growled. 'For about a week before you went bust. Have you any idea what you'd have to charge for rooms?'

'Suites,' Charlie corrected. 'About ten times what I charge for a room now.'

With an effort, Victor kept a straight face. 'And you think people would pay that?'

'Why not? You do.'

Victor looked sharply at Charlie and could see that the kid was serious. 'I get a special service.'

'So would all my guests. Those that wanted it.'

'Hey, now wait a minute. What you're talking about is illegal. Especially in North Carolina.'

'Is it?' Charlie queried innocently. 'Have you ever paid Pia a cent?'

'Well – no.'

'Then it's not illegal. She's over age. Her private life is her affair. You've always been charged for your room and nothing else, Mr Salavante. I'd staff the motel with the best-looking chicks I could find and I'd pay them to look after the guests. A girl accepting as much as a cent from them would be fired on the spot.' Charlie paused and smiled at Victor. 'I've got this idea that my business would be a lot more legal than your business, Mr Salavante. Ten trips to Miami in six months? No one's that keen on sunshine or orange juice. What sort of hole would a $200,000 loan make in the profit on one trip?'

'I've got partners to think of,' said Victor evenly, not liking the turn the conversation was taking.

Charlie nodded. 'Yeah – I know. They've stayed here.'

'You talked this over with any of them?'

33

'No.'

'Just as well.'

'Why?'

'I like you Charlie. If I levelled with you, I'd hurt you.'

'Tell me what you have to, Mr Salavante. I'm always honest with you.'

Victor regarded the black-eyed boy standing before him. He sighed. 'You're a spic, kid. To a Sicilian that makes you shit. Something lower than a 'Rican street pimp.'

There was a brief flicker of suppressed rage in Charlie's eyes. He nodded and said in a soft voice: 'And you think the same, Mr Salavante?'

'No.'

'So will you help me?'

Victor was silent for a few moments. He could just about afford a $200,000 risk loan but he preferred to launder surplus capital by sinking it into one hundred per cent legal enterprises. Charlie's crazy scheme was dangerously near the fringe. On the other hand, the kid already owned the land, and property was always a sound investment. Maybe it wasn't such a crazy scheme.

'Well, Mr Salavante?' Charlie prompted.

Victor finished his coffee and stood. 'Gimme a few days to think it over and I'll call you.' A thought occurred. 'Hey. If I'm a partner, maybe I'd save on motel bills, huh?'

Charlie shook his head. 'No, Mr Salavante. If you stayed in the motel, you'd have to pay just like anyone else.'

It was that answer that decided Victor to help the kid. But it wouldn't hurt to let him sweat awhile. He called Charlie a week later and offered him the $200,000 in exchange for a fifty-one per cent stake in the motel. Charlie refused to share ownership. After an argument, they agreed on a straight loan, repayable over three years at twenty per cent per annum interest.

Charlie opened the Golden Rose Motel in 1958 – on his twentieth birthday. It was just as he had dreamed: fifty suites of unashamed luxury set amid five acres of lush, subtropical gardens. The motel had everything: even a movie theatre that ran the latest releases. But its greatest asset was its staff of twenty voluptuous Puerto Rican girls that Pia had recruited in New York. Their uniform consisted of very tight, crotch-seamed toreador pants and a sleeveless bolero style jacket. Charlie's eye for detail was such that the girls who worked behind the bar wore apparently modest, high-buttoned jackets, but cut extra low under the arms so that the guests crowding onto the stools and paying over New York prices for their drinks were treated to frequent glimpses of well-rounded breasts. The girls were managed by Pia who looked after them with almost motherlike devotion. The only girl she made a mistake over was Marie – a volatile nineteen-year-old pocket Venus who refused to oblige the more amorous guests. Charlie solved the problem by marrying her.

'Congratulations, kid,' said Victor, when he collected his first month's payment. 'Looks like you're gonna make it.'

'This is nothing,' said Charlie fervently. 'One day I'm going to own the biggest hotel in Las Vegas.'

Victor laughed. 'Stay east, Charlie. Stay out of the cities and you won't have no trouble.'

By 1960 Charlie had paid off his debt to Victor Salavante plus the interest, and was the delighted father of two boys with a third child on the way. In that same year he opened the second Golden Rose Motel near Columbus, Ohio, followed by three more before President Kennedy's assassination. He stuck to his formula of catering for the rich by providing them with luxury and sex a day's drive from a major city, and the formula never let him down. Several attempts by various states to nail him for running brothels failed through lack of evidence. All his girls were over age: if they took a liking to a guest, that was their affair.

When Neil Armstrong set foot on the moon, Charlie owned one hundred motels; the illuminated golden rose motif on its slender phallic column was becoming a familiar sight along the highways of the Eastern States. He left the running of them to Pia, preferring to operate a ruthless land-buying, planning and building machine based in New York whose sole object was to open a new Golden Rose Motel every three weeks. Officials and local politicians who opposed him were bought. If they couldn't be bought, they were compromised. And if that didn't work, a $250,000 cash payment to Victor ensured that they were dealt with by other means.

As Charlie's wealth and power increased, so did his burning ambition to own the biggest and best hotel in Las Vegas. His bid for a five-acre prime site when it came on the market was answered with the firebombing of his first motel at Raleigh.

'Charlie – for Chrissake leave LV alone,' Victor warned. 'A lot of the old timers are still holding the reins. They won't have what they see as spic shit on their patch. As far as they're concerned – you're nothing and you gonna stay that way.'

Charlie made another Las Vegas move in the mid-1980s. The mob retaliated by firebombing his Johnson City motel. Marie died in the inferno. For a year Charlie was heartbroken. He wanted war. The bloodier the better; but he was talked out of it by his three sons. Charlie could hardly credit their attitude; their own mother killed by those thugs and they weren't burning for revenge! Who were these men he had sired? He was ashamed of them. But they and Pia were now running virtually the entire organization. And so, to his undying shame, he was forced to bow to their will.

The years that followed had no diminishing effect on the desire that burned in Charlie to avenge Marie's killing, and show the business-suited murdering hoodlums of the West that he was not a Spanish shit for them to look down their noses at.

6: London

Tony guessed that Charlie might be staying at his private penthouse on the top floor of Winchester's Golden Rose Hotel, seventy miles southwest of London. It was where he had first interviewed the hotelier the year before for the article.

'I'm very sorry, Mr Suskov,' said the hotel's receptionist firmly. 'Mr Rose says that if you have anything to say to him, you're to say it to his lawyers.'

Tony thanked her and hung up. At least he now knew for sure where Charlie was.

It was while he was studying the notes he had made after his second interview with Charlie that Tony had an idea. He made a call to a contact in the Foreign Office and obtained permission to leave London. His third call was to Elaine.

'Remember our little enterprise, darling? I think I've found a backer.'

'Enterprise?' She sounded puzzled.

'My get-rich-swift idea.'

'Tony – you're crazy. It was a joke. There's no way –'

'Don't let's talk about it now. Are you free for tonight?'

'Well – yes.'

'How about spending a night of sin with me at the Winchester Golden Rose?'

Elaine laughed. 'Isn't that like taking sandwiches to a banquet?'

'There's a large blue book on your desk,' said Tony. 'The SWIFT directory. I had a peek in it. It lists all the member banks of SWIFT. Pack that as well.'

'I can't do that, Tony. It's confidential.'

'I'll make a reservation and pick you up at six,' Tony promised. 'Don't forget the book.'

In her flat, Elaine replaced the receiver and stood in thought for some seconds. She picked up the receiver and dialled the number of her father's home in Surrey.

'Hallo, mum,' she said brightly. 'Can I have a quick word with daddy, please?' A pause. 'Hasn't he got his Pokketfone with him?' Another pause. 'Be a darling and get him to call me back before six. Tell him I want to take a couple of days' leave. That'll please him.'

7: Winchester, England

The Winchester Golden Rose was Charlie's first venture in Europe and it was an instant success. His sons and accountants had advised strongly against it so he had gone it alone: setting up a separate holding company and personally supervising every aspect of its design and construction. The hotel had been a labour of love – something human-sized and manageable – far removed from his home empire of standardized menus, portion-controlled catering and bulk-purchased supplies. Not only was the Winchester Golden Rose Charlie's personal statement on what was a good hotel, it was also his home whenever he was in Europe, which, nowadays, was an increasing amount of his time.

'What a fabulous bed for breakfasting on,' Elaine exclaimed, delightedly torpedoeing herself onto the circular, emperor-size bed and bouncing on it as though it were a trampoline. She paused and poked her tongue out at her reflection in a black-tinted floor-to-ceiling mirror that covered the entire wall facing the bed. The mirror was at least thirty feet wide.

'A mirror that size in front of a bed is indecent,' she observed. 'And breaking it would bring an awful lot of bad luck.'

Tony studied the constant display information monitor and said in a clear voice, 'Rosa. Hologram scene twenty, please.'

'Hologram scene twenty coming up, Mr Suskov,' said a soft, alluring voice. It was a voice without the mechanical qualities of the early speech synthesizers.

The entire mirror brightened. The wall dissolved to reveal a magnificent tropical beach. The three-dimensional image was so startlingly vivid that it was possible to see tiny darkening patches on the rocks at the side of the picture where they were being splashed by the surf. The reality of the scene was heightened by the soft warmth of a glorious sunset radiating from the screen and a gentle hint of a warm breeze perfumed with the heady scent of exotic tropical flowers.

Elaine gave a squeal of delight. She looked at the monitor screen and called out: 'Rosa. Jacuzzi, please!'

They sat in silence and watched a partition slide aside to reveal a jacuzzi large enough to accommodate a football team.

'Seawater or freshwater?' Rosa inquired.

'Freshwater please, Rosa.'

The jacuzzi began to fill.

'My God, you need some high-power hardware and software to run a system like this,' Elaine commented admiringly.

'Charlie showed me over the place when I interviewed him,' Tony explained, pulling off his shirt. He removed his shoes and socks before rolling Elaine onto her stomach and unzipping her dress. 'He said that it's the most modern hotel in the world. Somehow, I don't think he was exaggerating. This is the most expensive suite in the hotel. I decided when I saw it that one day I would stay in it with the most beautiful girl in the world.'

Elaine entwined her fingers in Tony's hair and kissed him.

'The trouble is,' Tony added, 'I couldn't wait, so I brought you instead.'

Elaine smiled and kept entwining her fingers. She gave a sudden hard yank. Tony yelped.

'Bastard,' Elaine murmured. 'Kiss me.'

He kissed the nape of her neck. 'Where's the SWIFT directory?'

'In my bag. Tony – something's worrying me.'

He pulled her to her feet and fiddled with the fastenings on her dress. 'Yes, my darling?'

Elaine stepped out of her dress. 'Isn't it just a tiny bit possible that a night here is going to make a staggeringly enormous hole in your monthly pay cheque? I mean, don't you think you should economize for a week or two if Charlie Rose is going to sue you for a million or two?'

Tony unclasped her bra and guided her into the swirling pool. The water temperature was slightly above blood heat. They kissed, standing in the water. 'I think Charlie will be far too interested in our scheme to sue me.'

'Your scheme,' Elaine corrected.

They sat facing each other and kissed passionately.

'It'll never work,' Elaine declared, luxuriating in the warm water bubbling erotically around her.

'Why not?' Tony demanded.

Elaine slid her arms around Tony's neck and pressed her forehead against his forehead. Her devastating green eyes regarded him with great seriousness. 'Maybe someone could round up all the world's top cryptographers and set them to work for a million years to break the SWIFT encryption. Maybe. But whoever it is, it'll need organizing by someone with an incredible eye for detail.'

'Which you don't think I've got?'

'Nope.'

He began to get annoyed. 'Why?'

'Because, Tony – my sweet, precious angel – you've still got your trousers on.'

8

Tony darted across the rooftop helicopter pad and launched himself across the gap. He landed lightly on the inspection catwalk and spent a few seconds collecting his nerves. Despite his intensive KGB training, he was more at home in front of a keyboard than leaping around in the darkness on the roof of a hotel. The catwalk skirted the huge Plexiglas solar roof that enclosed Charlie Rose's private swimming pool adjoining his penthouse apartment. There were lights on in the pool hall and he could hear voices, but he was unable to see any details through the translucent roof panels. He started to circumnavigate the roof in the hope of finding a way into the penthouse. All he needed was five minutes of Charlie's time to whet the hotelier's appetite. Stuffed in his pocket were a few pages torn at random from the SWIFT directory. He inched along the catwalk, unaware that the infrared-sensitive buglike eye of a remote-controlled television camera mounted on the car park flagpole was following his movements with great interest. The lights in the pool hall suddenly went out and the voices fell silent. Tony prayed that Charlie wasn't going to bed.

The night was hot. Tony began to sweat. He leaned against a glass panel and would have appreciated there being a glass panel for him to lean against. But there was nothing. Nothing but space and his falling body and the force of gravity thrown in for bad luck.

The lights came on as he fell.

9

To his fellow Americans, it was not Charlie's fleet of forty assorted Cadillacs and Rolls Royces, 'Ten for each direction,' as he liked to remark jokingly, that told them he had made it. Nor was it his luxury homes and even more luxurious bank accounts around the world, or even the distinction of having a permanent army of Inland Revenue Service investigators trying to pry into those bank accounts. It was none of those things. What told Americans that Charlie Rose had arrived was Baldwin – his English butler. The thirty-year-old Baldwin had the sort of physique which made people realize that perhaps building the pyramids hadn't been such an impossible feat for mankind after all. Baldwin had muscles. Baldwin had height: at least six feet six inches of height. He also had brains: a degree in economics. But above all, Baldwin had style: with a flick of his wrist, he could break a collarbone or the seal on a champagne bottle with equal aplomb. He had another gift: a sense of humour. But that wasn't apparent as he watched the floundering apparition that had just had the temerity to fall into his master's swimming pool.

Charlie was stretched out on a lounger drinking a brandy. Now in his fifties, his body was still lean and hard and he had retained his conquistador good looks. 'Baldwin,' he said, gesturing to Tony floundering and spluttering in the water. 'Fetch.'

Being English, Baldwin did not ruin his thousand-dollar evening attire by plunging mindlessly into the rose-shaped pool and retrieving the hapless Tony. Instead he strolled to the pool ladder and beckoned to Tony with a finger that resembled an articulated broomstick.

Tony swam to the ladder. 'I'm very sorry about this,' he began. 'But –'

Baldwin grabbed a handful of Tony's jacket and lifted. Normally the butler would have had no trouble hiking a man of Tony's build out of the pool despite his waterlogged clothes. But Tony objected to being unceremoniously hiked out of swimming pools and unobligingly hooked his toes under the pool ladder's step. Baldwin was caught off guard and off balance. The inevitable happened as happens to all those who are caught off guard and off balance beside swimming pools.

'I said to fetch him! Not go swimming with him!' Charlie snarled, as the two men clambered out of the pool.

Tony felt that he had won the point, and so allowed Baldwin to frogmarch him across to Charlie.

'My apologies, sir,' said Baldwin blandly. Despite the fact that his hair was plastered over his eyes and his evening dress dripping all over the marbled floor, Baldwin managed to maintain some vestige of dignity as he frisked Tony. He found the sodden sheaf of the SWIFT directory pages which he tossed on the table before thrusting Tony into a chair.

The hotelier continued to sip his brandy while regarding his prisoner with black, fathomless eyes.

Tony felt that the meeting had got off to a bad start. 'Mr Rose. Please accept my –'

Charlie held up his hand for silence and got it. He spoke, choosing his words with great care. 'Who the hell are you?'

'Mr Rose,' said Tony, mustering what dignity he could. 'I am Anton Suskov. I interviewed you last year –'

Charlie gave an angry start when he recognized Tony. '*You*! This is the guy that libelled me, Baldwin.'

'If you wish me to deal with him, sir . . .'

The black, staring eyes were unblinking. Tony wondered how many of Charlie's enemies had known the same feeling of dread that he was now experiencing.

'Well, Mr Suskov?' said Charlie with unexpected calmness. 'Can you give me one very good reason why I shouldn't have Baldwin remove your liver to feed to my pet fish?'

Tony thought quickly. He was tempted to say, 'maybe they don't like liver?' But the circumstances suggested that it might be in his best interest to come straight to the point. 'Mr Rose – I've got an idea that will enable you to hack into the SWIFT international banking system and transfer billions of dollars into selected accounts.' It was about as straight to the point as it was possible to get.

Charlie's expression remained impassive. Tony pressed on. 'Naturally, it would be a huge operation that would cost several million to finance, but the rewards would be astronomical.'

'Baldwin.'

'Sir?'

'What can this guy get in this country for attempted murder?'

Baldwin thought. 'About ten years, sir.'

Tony was alarmed. 'I haven't tried to murder anyone. You were the one who set a couple of thugs onto me. All I –'

'You *haven't* tried to murder anyone?' Charlie echoed. 'You're a Russian agent that I'm about to sue. You come busting in here with a knife –'

'I haven't got a knife!'

'Baldwin – can we find the gentleman a knife?'

'No problem, sir.'

'Okay. So call the cops.'

'Certainly, sir.' Baldwin unfolded a Pokketfone. It refused to work after its immersion therefore he was obliged to pick up an ordinary phone.

'Please, Mr Rose,' Tony pleaded. 'Those pages are just a few from the SWIFT directory. I've got it in my room. It lists all the member banks in the world.'

Baldwin waited, his finger poised over the telephone's keypad, waiting for Charlie's signal.

'What banks?' Charlie queried, distastefully prodding the saturated pages on the table.

'All the banks that are members of the SWIFT society,' Tony

replied. 'That's just about every bank in the world.'

'What in hell is SWIFT, Mr Suskov?'

'A computerized banking system,' said Tony, talking quickly. 'It handles billions and billions of dollars' worth of transactions every day. I believe it would be possible to break into the system and transfer funds into any account.'

Charlie ran his fingertip absently around the rim of his brandy glass. 'What banks belong to this system?'

'All the world's major banks.'

Charlie sipped his drink. 'Even the Nevada banks?' he asked at length.

Sensing that he seemed to have caught the hotelier's interest, Tony nodded. 'The directory covers all the major banks in every state in the United States, Mr Rose.'

Charlie's eyes remained unblinking – staring hard and suspiciously at Tony. 'This crazy notion of yours. I want some more details before I call the cops. So talk.'

Tony talked for five minutes. When he had finished, Charlie remained deep in thought for a few moments. 'Do you and your girlfriend take breakfast?' he asked abruptly.

'Well – yes. And Elaine certainly does.'

'Okay. We'll talk it over tomorrow morning at breakfast. Eight o'clock. Bring that directory and anything else you've got. Baldwin – see if we can fix this guy up with some clothes.'

Later that night Charlie watched a hologram in the solitude of his magnificent bedroom but was unable to concentrate on the story. His thoughts kept returning to the crazy, impossible scheme that the young Soviet had outlined to him. The idea excited him. Life was dull. He had power but somehow that lacked the thrill of obtaining it. His empire was now run by Pia and his sons aided by a colourless army of charcoal-suited accountants and public relations men. He particularly disliked the latter because they had cleaned up the Golden Rose image and made it almost respectable. Girls in toreador uniforms still staffed his motels and hotels – he had insisted on that – but their pants weren't so tight, the material was slightly thicker, and the girls were now required to wear panties and bras. The mid-1980s had even seen the introduction of a knotted sash to cover the girls' bare midriffs. After that, the accountants and the PR men had

43

discovered a new word – diversification – and applied it to his business, making it even more complex than it should be. Charlie swore softly to himself. Goddamn it, his cherished golden rose motif now even adorned a home microcomputer. What particularly infuriated him was that the army of highly paid middlemen refused to expand his empire into Las Vegas.

'It would result in too many problems with established interests in the state, Mr Rose.'

'Too much hassle, Mr Rose.'

'Not cost-effective, Mr Rose.'

Charlie changed his tack. Okay then. How about moving into the gambling business in southern Africa? That was where the mob were now sinking money in a big way. Easy gaming laws. Millions of *nouveaux riches* Africans looking for somewhere to spend their money.

To Charlie's despair, the same negative, objecting voices trotted out the same lame excuses. Jesus Christ – no one wanted to fight any more whereas he wanted to fight above all else. He especially wanted to fight the mob. It was not only the savage killing of Marie that kept the flame of raw hatred burning; the humiliating words Victor had uttered all those years ago still rang as fresh in his mind as the day they had been said:

You're a spic, kid. To a Sicilian that makes you shit.

Suddenly a soft-spoken Russian who spoke perfect English had awoken in Charlie those aggressive instincts from the days when he had planned and schemed his rise to power and wealth. The staggering fortune that would result from Tony's idea was of little interest; he had amassed more than he ever needed anyway. Apart from the excitement the enterprise offered, what was particularly attractive was the prospect of becoming the man who had pulled off the greatest crime in history – a billion-dollar sting that would deal a body blow to the six-hundred-year-old Mafia from which it might never recover. Without its source of power – its money – the mob would be nothing, and Charlie Rose's name would go into the history books as a hero – as a part of the Great American legend.

10

'There're so many problems,' said Elaine, tucking into her second poached egg, 'that I hardly know where to begin. Could I have some more toast, please?'

Tony groaned. 'Elaine,' he muttered disapprovingly. Charlie and Elaine had hit it off from the moment they had met. Tony felt left out.

'Sure, sweetheart,' said Charlie, signalling to Baldwin who was hovering nearby.

'And another pot of coffee.' Elaine broke off and looked guiltily at Charlie. 'Oh dear. I hope you don't mind me giving your butler orders, Charlie?'

'Elaine – I hardly eat breakfast, so you're giving Baldwin some useful experience. Isn't that right, Baldwin?'

'An amazing amount of experience, sir,' said Baldwin drolly, deftly removing the silver toast rack.

'Oh good. And some more butter please, Baldwin.'

Charlie chuckled. 'Hungry for food – hungry for love, eh, Tony?'

Tony made a noncommittal noise and wondered what Charlie would say if he knew that Elaine had already had a starter in their room, which had consisted of a plate of mushrooms and three cups of coffee.

For the third time Charlie pretended to flip casually through the blue-jacketed SWIFT III directory. Nothing about his expression betrayed his innermost excitement as he studied the columns of small print that listed the Nevada banks. 'So what are the problems with this SWIFT thing?' he prompted.

'The first one is the encryption,' said Elaine, scavenging an untouched sausage from Tony's plate with her fork. 'It's unbreakable.'

Charlie tossed the directory on the table. 'But people are not. Someone must know the code.'

'No one knows it. It was written by a computer.'

'So who wrote the computer program?'

'The chief consultant was a Damion Silvester. He's now got his own consultancy – Software Science Incorporated in New York. English. He set up business in New York about ten years ago. He sometimes takes me out to dinner when he's in England.' Elaine refrained from adding that her last evening out with Damion had ended with him nearly raping her.

'Married?'

'Divorced.'

'Does he need money?'

Elaine's expression hardened. 'Damion always needs money. But not friends.'

'How old?'

'About thirty-five. There aren't many top computer scientists over thirty-five. And Damion won't be around for much longer if he's still drinking.'

'Reliable?'

Elaine considered. 'He's ruthless. He lets nothing get in his way once he's decided to do something.'

'Sounds useful,' Charlie commented.

'Also he's good with his hands. He's got a little workshop in his apartment. A watchmaker's lathe. That sort of thing. He likes making gadgets.'

'Who else will be needed?'

'Get Damion first and let him decide who he needs.'

'*If* we can get him,' Tony pointed out.

'You haven't got me yet,' Charlie observed. 'Just because I'm interested doesn't mean I'm going ahead. I want to know what return I'm going to get for what investment.'

'You won't know the answer to that until you've risked at least half a million dollars on a feasibility study,' said Tony. 'That would be the best way of tackling this, Charlie. One risk at a time; one problem at a time.'

'There's a lot of guys like you around,' Charlie observed. 'Great at spending other people's money. So let's assume that I'm spending money. What's the first problem?'

'Damion,' said Elaine.

Charlie nodded. 'Okay. You deal with him.'

'Oh Christ,' said Elaine, dismayed. 'Do I have to?'

Charlie's expressionless black eyes stared at Elaine and Tony in turn. 'I'm not committing myself just yet,' he warned. 'But if I do, I risk the money and you risk your necks. Okay?'

'Okay,' said Tony after a pause.

Both men looked expectantly at Elaine. Eventually she nodded her

46

agreement.

'One thing, Charlie,' said Tony. 'I want twenty per cent of the proceeds after expenses have been deducted and I don't see why Elaine shouldn't have the same.'

'You put money on the table then you can talk percentages,' Charlie rasped.

Tony stood. 'In that case, Charlie, there's no point in going any further. You're only risking money. I'm risking my career, my freedom – everything. It only needs a suggestion that I'm up to something and the British Foreign Office could throw me out of the country.'

'Siddown.'

'Twenty per cent, Charlie,' said Tony firmly.

'I said, siddown!'

The two men glared at each other. Charlie's iron will won. Tony sat.

'Firstly,' said Charlie, 'I haven't committed myself to this crazy enterprise. Secondly, if I do, I agree in principle that you two should have a percentage. What worries me is that we're gonna have to pull in a lot of people into this operation – key personnel already making big money. They won't be interested unless we can offer them bigger money. And we can't do that if everything is already sewn up. As I said – I agree in principle to the idea of you and Elaine having a slice of the pie. But first we find out how big the pie is and how much it's gonna cost to bake.'

11: New York

Ignoring the naked girl's pleas, Damion Silvester caught her by the wrist as she was about to escape from his bedroom.

'Please, Mr Silvester! she implored beseechingly. 'No more – please! I'm sore!'

Damion's answer was to drag her across the room and slap her with such force that she fell backwards across the rumpled bed where she had already endured an hour of near torture. She tried to struggle up but suddenly he was astride her, his knees pressing her arms painfully into the mattress, his genitals, like a separate living creature, sprawling pallid and demanding across her chest. She

47

looked pleadingly up into the merciless eyes, red-rimmed with drink, and wondered for the hundredth time what during that nightmare evening had persuaded her to accept his invitation to dinner. Perhaps it was because the big man was her first employer and because she had been flattered by his attention. She desperately wished that she had heeded the warnings of the other girls in the office.

Damion tried to force a hand between her legs. She locked her knees tightly together. 'Please, Mr Silvester – I'm very sore.'

He laughed and took his hand away. 'Okay, kid. So let's try something different, huh?' He grabbed a handful of her hair and jerked her head up. 'You hurt me, kid,' he warned, easing himself forward, 'and you'll wish you'd never been born.'

Too terrified of the consequences if she refused, the girl closed her eyes and forced herself not to think about the humiliating act that she was being made to perform on the big man. He pushed hard against her, causing her to choke and splutter. The bedside telephone warbled. She thought she was going to be reprieved but he kept thrusting, grunting occasionally when he forced himself deep. The telephone kept up its insistent summons.

Damion cursed softly. 'Okay,' he grunted, shifting his weight off the girl. He picked up the handset. 'Yeah?'

'Mr Damion Silvester?' A warm, seductive, feminine voice.

He noticed from the telephone's display that the call was coming from the United Kingdom. 'Yeah. I'm Damion Silvester. Who's this?'

'Congratulations, Mr Silvester. I'm calling from England on behalf of Golden Rose Hotels. You're our millionth call in our worldwide telephone survey and you have won quarter of a million dollars plus a two-week vacation at the Golden Rose Hotel, Winchester, England. There's an air ticket waiting for you at the TWA terminal at Kennedy.'

The girl slipped quietly off the bed and gathered up her clothes.

'I've what?' Damion yelled into the mouthpiece.

By the time the caller from England had repeated her message, the girl was tiptoeing furtively towards the door.

Damion was suspicious. There was something vaguely familiar about the caller's voice. He knew he had heard her somewhere before. A chick paying him out? 'Listen, kiddo. Is this some kind of joke?'

The girl soundlessly opened the door and was gone.

'It's no joke, Mr Silvester. I promise you. We'll leave our number in your phone's memory. Punch the zero key when you're ready to call us back. Just remember – you've won quarter of a million dollars.'

Damion returned the receiver to its cradle and sat on the edge of the bed, staring at it. He suddenly remembered the girl and turned around. He was alone. He heard the front door of his apartment click shut and was tempted to go after her. And then the full realization of the message sank in and the girl was forgotten.

Quarter of a million dollars!

He grabbed the telephone and punched the zero button.

12: London

Elaine was talking to her father on a payphone in the arrivals hall at Heathrow Airport when she spotted Damion after he had cleared customs and immigration controls. She hurriedly finished the conversation with her father and moved across the hall to intercept the big man. Nothing about Damion had changed: the same gangling frame; the same mop of unruly black hair; and the same cruel, sardonic expression as he looked around.

'Damion!' Elaine waved her purse to catch his attention. His eyes widened in surprise when he saw her.

'Elaine!'

Elaine's expression belied her dislike of the man. The time when she had escaped from his London hotel room after threatening him with a knife was still fresh in her mind. Her cheeks dimpled in a warm, welcoming smile. 'Hallo, Damion. How's things?'

'What the hell's going on, Elaine?' he demanded, as they sat in Tony's car and headed southwest out of London.

'Tony will explain everything,' said Elaine reassuringly.

'Who the hell's Tony?'

'You'll find out. There's nothing to worry about.'

Damion looked uneasily at her. 'Who said I was worried?'

'Damion. Will you please just sit back and savour my delightful company. All will be revealed just as soon as we get to Winchester.'

Damion wasn't reassured. He moved his lanky frame into a more comfortable position. He was now used to American cars. Most European cars weren't made for people over six feet. 'Listen,' he said. 'If this is some cheap trick you've pulled to pay me out, by Christ, girl – I'll tear you apart.'

Elaine glanced at her passenger. She had no doubt it was not an idle threat.

'It's not a trick, Damion.'

'You mean – I really have won quarter of a million dollars?'

'You'll probably end up with twenty times that if everything works out.'

The effect of the drinks Damion had consumed on the four-hour flight suddenly wore off. He stared suspiciously at Elaine. 'If what works out?' There was ice in his voice.

'I'm sorry to be such a bore, Damion, but Tony said that I wasn't to discuss it with you.'

13: Winchester

Elaine showed Damion into the hotel suite and introduced him to Tony.

'Good to meet you, Damion,' said Tony warmly, shaking the new arrival by the hand. 'Congratulations on your win.'

'So I *have* won something?' Damion queried, when Elaine had poured him a drink. Despite her frequent assurances, he was still disbelieving.

Tony gave an expansive gesture. He kept his other hand in his pocket and switched on his miniature tape recorder. 'Let's say you've won the chance to take part in the biggest money-making enterprise in history.'

Damion was unimpressed. 'What about the quarter of a million dollars?'

'How badly do you need it?'

'Very badly.'

Tony grinned. 'Let me guess. Quarter of a million will just about cover your debts. Yes?'

Damion licked his lips and glanced at Elaine. He didn't like the public discussion of his financial affairs. He nodded. 'I need nearer half a million.'

Tony sighed. 'It's amazing how banks will let high earners run up such debts. Mr Silvester – you can have the quarter of a million right now. But would you be interested in making twenty times that?'

'By hacking into SWIFT?'

The silence told Damion that he had scored a direct hit.

'I didn't say a word to him, Tony,' said Elaine quickly in response to Tony's raised eyebrow.

'I guessed what you wanted as soon as I walked in here,' Damion rasped angrily. 'I've been approached before.'

Tony looked interested. 'Who by?'

'A group of Harvard graduates. About a year ago. But they didn't offer me quarter of a million up front. Hasn't it occurred to anyone that I could hack into SWIFT and transfer funds into any account at any time?'

'But could you?' Tony asked.

'Sure. No problem. Give me a terminal and a radio teletype transverter and a broadband EHF transmitter with a dish antenna, and I could transfer a million or even ten million to my account any time. No problem. I know all the SWIFT access codes, protocols and authentication procedures.'

'So what's stopping you?' Tony inquired.

'The thought of about twenty years in prison. All transactions are re-encrypted automatically and batch-verified every hour. The really big transactions – ones that would be worthwhile – are authenticated by landline. If, say, a fifteen-thousand-dollar transaction pops up for authentication on a terminal that didn't originate the transaction, then – kerpow. Every ten-thousand-dollar-plus transaction made during the previous hour throughout the entire network is frozen. And the protocol echoes – that's the system verifications – are also routed through transatlantic telephone cables which means that you'd also have to bust into a PSTN system.'

'PSTN?' Tony queried.

'Public Switched Telephone Network,' Elaine explained.

Tony looked questioningly at her. 'But you said all SWIFT traffic now goes through the SWIFT satellites.'

'Ninety-nine point nine per cent of it does,' said Damion. 'But now we've got SWIFT III on line with encryption levels in the satellite. That's why all the major credit card companies now lease

SWIFT channels for day-to-day transactions. That's placed a fantastic load on the system.'

'That's something I didn't know,' Elaine admitted.

Damion shrugged. 'SWIFT's got the capacity. Their channels are cheap and secure. Also Reuters and FT have just started leasing them for money market information. And now the wire services – Associated Press and all the other news services – want to get in on the act because the wire services of Eastern Bloc countries are hogging all the high frequency radio teletype telex channels with nonstop propaganda. Everyone's trying to jump on the bandwaggon. With frequency multiplexing, the more users who cram onto the system, the more secure it becomes. Hacking into SWIFT is a bit like trying to eavesdrop on a conversation in Shea Stadium when the Giants score. Millions of minor transactions going back and forth across the Atlantic. What's going to screw up any plans you might have is that the authentications on all major banking transactions have PSTN landline routing options which are usually exercised if there's not too much voice traffic on the PSTN transatlantic phone lines.'

Tony's head swam as he tried to assimilate all the information that was being thrown at him. 'It all sounds hideously complicated,' he admitted.

Damion ran his hand through his mop of hair and helped himself to another whisky. 'It doesn't just sound complicated – it is complicated. Fucking complicated. To stop the landline authentications, you'd have to bust into the right central switching telephone exchange which is handling the right transatlantic lines and private circuits, and install your own multiplexer/demultiplexer, primed with the right protocols, connected to the right lines with the right routing onto your lines. If you can find a way of taking over an international telephone exchange for a week with no one noticing you'd only be halfway there. After that, you'd have to find yourself a rocket to take you up twenty-two thousand miles into a geostationary orbit alongside the SWIFT satellite to fix it to accept your originations. Do all that and maybe you're on your way. I don't know – I'm a software scientist – not a communications engineer.'

'Supposing we could get a communications engineer?' Tony suggested. 'There's got to be someone. Who designed the SWIFT III system?'

'Dr Hans Crick,' Elaine murmured.

Damion looked startled for a moment and then he threw back his head and laughed. 'Get him on your side, and I might be interested in joining you. But I'd still like that quarter of a million in advance.'

When the tape ended, Charlie increased the xenon lighting that bathed his swimming pool in artificial sunlight. He slipped his lean, wiry body into the water. 'So who's this Hans Crick?' he wanted to know, resting his arms on the pool's marble surround and running an appreciative eye over Elaine's lithe body. Her two-piece bikini was barely large enough to hide a sneeze.

'A Belgian,' Elaine answered, returning Charlie's gaze. 'I met him in France last year at a SWIFT seminar. He's the consultant head of the SWIFT III satellite design team. He's one of the world's top authorities on information and communication technology. Nuts on amateur radio. My firm used to send technical queries to his electronic mailbox in Spain where he lives. He invoices us a thousand pounds an hour for his time. Those sort of rates are more to do with plain, old-fashioned greed than a reasonable going rate for his expertise. We don't call him too often. There's a rumour going around that he's involved in a big row with the SWIFT board but I don't know the details.'

'We recruit him and we've got Silvester,' said Tony.

'Silvester's no problem,' said Charlie. 'He sounds tough and he needs money. He's interested.'

Tony spoke carefully. 'But are *you* interested, Charlie?'

Charlie thrust himself away from the pool's edge and swam slowly on his back towards the deep end.

'He does that when he's thinking,' Tony commented quietly to Elaine. 'Every time I asked him an awkward question when I interviewed him, he'd swim a couple of lengths.'

Charlie breaststroked back to the shallow end and stood, water streaming in rivulets off his matted chest, his black eyes on Tony. 'How tough are you?'

'I don't understand, Charlie.'

Charlie hauled himself out of the pool. 'For Chrissake – it's a simple enough question. How hard are you? Could you kill a man?'

Tony was at a loss. 'I don't know. Could you?'

The hotelier scowled. He was not used to receiving verbal parries. He was about to make an angry retort but Elaine quickly intervened.

53

'Is it important, Charlie?' she asked, while helping to towel him.

'Sure it's important. Pulling off a billion-dolar sting means it's gonna get rough somewhere along the line.' Charlie allowed Elaine to steer him into a lounger.

She stood behind him and gently massaged his neck muscles. 'I could kill a man, Charlie.'

Charlie grinned up at her. 'I bet you could, sweetheart.'

'And Damion could kill a woman.'

There was a silence. Tony caught Elaine's eye. She had told him about the time that Damion had nearly raped her. He finished his drink and stood looking down at Charlie. 'The question is, Charlie – does the operation go ahead?'

Charlie gave himself time to think by lighting a cigar. He exhaled slowly and regarded Tony through a cloud of blue smoke. 'You like living in the West, huh?'

Tony hesitated and then nodded.

Charlie gave a grunt of satisfaction. The threatened lawsuit he had hanging over Tony gave him a lever. He liked having levers on the people he was using. 'Let me guess. If I was to go ahead with this legal action against you – it doesn't matter about the rights or wrongs of the case – you'd be sent back to Moscow? Right?'

'It's likely,' Tony admitted.

Charlie grinned. 'You bet it's likely. You screw up on this and I pull the trap on my lawyers so they all fall on you like a pack of wolves. You understand?'

Tony could see that the American was deadly serious. As much as he hated being dictated to, he was forced to concede defeat. 'I understand.'

'Okay – call the Silvester guy. We'll do some hard talking.'

14

That night Elaine entwined a leg around Tony and drew him close, flattening her breasts against his chest. 'You know the trouble with these emperor-size beds? I can never find you when I want you.'

Tony drowsily encircled her waist with a limp arm and tried to feign sleep. Elaine responded by reaching down between them and grasping him gently.

'You're not asleep, Tony.'

'I'm not now,' he agreed.

'I've been thinking.'

'About breakfast? Or – in your case – breakfasts?'

Elaine's sudden squeeze made him yelp. 'Pig,' she retorted. 'I've been thinking about Charlie.'

'What about him?'

'I know why *you* want to go ahead with this crazy idea. And Damion. And me. But why Charlie? I bet he could spend a quarter of a million dollars every day for the rest of his life and he wouldn't notice it. So why is he so keen?'

Tony waved his hand in front of the wall panel that brought the bedroom lights on. 'But he's not that keen,' he pointed out.

Elaine looked contemptuous. 'He's keen all right. He was positively champing at the bit right from the word go. It amused him to have us massage his ego by letting us talk him into it. But *why* does he want to do it? He's got money – power – everything.'

Tony yawned and closed his eyes. 'I think he's interested in stinging the banks in just one state.'

'What state?'

A light snore answered her question.

'Tony! What state?'

'Nebraska.'

'Nebraska?'

'Or Nevada . . . Can't remember.' With that Tony drifted off to sleep and refused to be woken. Elaine lay awake. Nevada kept preying on her mind. Nevada? Why Nevada? She spent a few minutes fruitlessly worrying before her thoughts drifted to the day when she would be proving herself to her father and a critical world by running her own business – fuelling it with energy and imagination while her father's business continued to stagnate. They were pleasant thoughts to drift off to sleep to.

15: London

It was a warm June afternoon. Tony was drinking his second cup of coffee at an outside table at the Serpentine cafeteria when Gregor joined him.

'I may sit here?' Gregor's English was not good, but Tass preferred their staffmen in London to speak English to each other in public places to avoid attracting attention.

Tony smiled. 'Sure. Help yourself.'

Gregor plonked his coffee and his heavy frame down.

'Your English still isn't perfect, Gregor,' Tony commented teasingly. 'An Englishman would start off by saying, "is anyone sitting here?"'

Gregor's expression suggested that he did not appreciate Tony's lesson in vernacular English. 'A stupid question,' he observed, while glancing quickly around at the neighbouring tables to ensure no one was within earshot. 'You have been away for two days,' he said accusingly.

'Two and a half,' Tony amended. 'I notified the bureau. Didn't you check?'

Gregor grunted. Obviously he had not. 'You wanted to see me?'

'I need your permission to travel.'

Gregor emptied four packets of sugar into his coffee. His tooth was sweeter than his disposition. 'Where?'

'Spain. I want to interview someone about the Western banking system for an article. But it's very possible that I might find some useful intelligence.'

'How useful?'

'I don't know until I've carried out the interview.' Tony sat back and regarded his superior in amusement. He knew that he had a deserved reputation for being one of the KGB's best 'legals'. Some of the reports he had filed had reflected well on Gregor, therefore permission was unlikely to be withheld.

'Very well,' said Gregor after a face-saving pause. 'Five days. No more.'

'I'll take no longer than is necessary,' Tony promised.

Gregor lapsed into Russian. 'I don't want to find out that you've been lolling around on Spanish beaches.' He drained his coffee and stood. 'So don't come back with a suntan.'

'My dear Gregor,' said Tony mischievously, sticking to English. 'I could never bring myself to cavort with all those topless, decadent girls on Spanish beaches. If I wanted a suntan, I wouldn't dream of acquiring it anywhere but Odessa.'

Tony took a taxi to the Spanish Embassy in Belgrave Square and saw the press attaché who repaid a couple of favours by arranging a visa on the spot. 'You must stay in the province of Alicante,' said the embassy official as he authenticated Tony's passport card. 'And you must report to the Guardia Civil every twenty-four hours.' Such are the bureaucratic complications Soviet citizens must endure when they wish to travel within the EEC.

Elaine's voice answered the phone. Tony retrieved his telephone credit card. 'All fixed,' he announced. 'We leave from Gatwick at six this evening. I've got the tickets.'

'Gatwick! Yuk! A bucket-and-spade airport. Worse than Luton.'

'You, my angel, are a snob. I managed to get two cancellations on a B-Cal charter flight to Alicante.'

'You make us sound like a couple of members of the beer, bingo and Benidorm brigade,' Elaine complained.

'And you're also an incurable snob,' Tony replied cuttingly. 'That's exactly what we're going as – a couple of holidaymakers.'

'Oh Christ. Daddy's going to go mad. We're snowed under with work.'

'I'll pick you up at three-thirty,' Tony replied. 'Don't forget to pack that decadent bikini.'

'I won't need the top in Spain. Oh well – it could be worse – we could be going to France.'

'What's wrong with France?'

'They don't eat proper breakfasts. I had a miserable time at the Nice seminar on SWIFT last year.'

Tony laughed and hung up. His next call was to Damion at the Intercontinental Hotel.

'Shit,' said Damion when Tony finished talking. 'How the hell do you expect me to cope alone? I don't know anyone in London these days.'

'You've got that phone number Charlie gave you?'

'Sure.'

'Call him up, Damion. Tell him the story we agreed. If Charlie's used him, he's certain to know his stuff.'

'Yeah? And whose money do I use?'

'The money that's been paid you,' Tony replied impatiently.

'I need most of that.'

'Quarter of a million?' Tony was irritated by Damion's financial

57

problems.

'I owe the Internal Revenue Service two hundred grand.'

'For God's sake, Damion, you've been promised a refund on all your expenses, so stop complaining. I'll see that you get your money.'

'Okay,' said Damion after a pause. 'When will you be back?'

'With luck, in about a week. Should give you enough time to find yourself a flat and have a preliminary look around. Any more problems?'

Damion could think of thousands. 'Yeah. But they can wait.'

'Okay,' said Tony breezily. 'Good luck. Catch you further down the charge sheet.'

Damion did not appreciate the joke.

16: Calpe, Spain

The white-walled, Roman-roofed villas that dot the Spanish Costa Blanca between Calpe and Javea like acne range from modest two-bedroom apartments grimly clinging to the pine-clad mountain slopes for a better view of the Mediterranean, to massive phoney wrought-iron and turreted affairs built like miniature castles to satisfy the craving among the Teutonic *nouveaux riches* to own a private *Schloss*.

Of the latter, one of the most grandiose was Villa Katrina, which, together with its grounds, occupied an entire headland. The lack of beach that such a position dictated had been no deterrent to Dr Hans Crick when he had built his peninsular paradise: an artificial cove had been dynamited out of the rockface to provide a small harbour for his yacht. And the easy access to the sea enabled his eighteen-year-old daughter, Marianne, to indulge her passion for windsurfing without having to venture onto the nearby tourist-infested Playa Levante. A small outcrop of rock near the villa provided the mounting for a tall lattice mast that carried his complex arrays of amateur radio aerials.

Tony and Elaine had spent their first day in Spain trying to keep the villa under observation from the road. But that proved impossible: Calpe's millionaire villa owners used pines to shield their properties from landborne prying eyes and yet went to considerable trouble to ensure that they were well exposed on the seaward side. From a chartered thirty-five-foot Fairy Huntsman anchored three miles offshore – a vessel that had seen better days – Tony and Elaine were able to fish and sunbathe, and keep watch on Villa Katrina without arousing suspicions.

On the fourth day of their lazy vigil, the sea was sufficiently calm to enable Elaine to hold the binoculars steady so that she could see Hans Crick in his lounge working at his computer terminal. Had they been anchored another mile out to sea, Villa Katrina would have been lost in the haze. A movement caught her eye. She swung the binoculars in time to see Crick's daughter, Marianne, plunge into the swimming pool. There was no sign of her boyfriend's Ferrari. The girl's windsurfer, with its distinctive red and white striped sail, was propped against the wall of the private harbour where it had remained unused during the four days that they had been keeping watch.

The sun beat down. There was no breeze, and the haze hung low and heavy like smoke on a battlefield.

Elaine yawned. It looked like being another uneventful day. Tony was sprawled on a cockpit mattress, sleeping off midday wine and midnight lovemaking. Elaine looked worriedly at him.

'Tony.'

'Mmm?'

'Isn't there another way? Does it have to be like this?'

He didn't answer. She was about to prod him but decided against it. Instead she draped a T-shirt across his reddening chest and propped her head comfortably against him where she could see the villa.

Elaine was woken by the gentle flapping of a canvas dodger. She looked guiltily at her watch and wondered how long she had been dozing.

The villa was no longer where it should be. She sat up with a start and twisted around. There was now a brisk breeze blowing from the southwest. It wasn't strong enough to clear the haze that clung to the land but it had swung the cruiser about its anchor. There was something different about Hans Crick's artificial harbour. Elaine suddenly realized that the windsurfer was missing. She frantically swept the sea with the binoculars and picked out a tiny red and white

59

sail about three miles distant, scudding across the aquamarine surface towards the mist that hid Javea.

'Tony! Wake up!' Without waiting for a reply, Elaine scrambled along the narrow side deck and leaned against the pulpit while quickly hauling up the anchor. Tony was pulling on the foam rubber jacket of his midseason scuba diving suit by the time she jumped back into the cockpit.

'Where is she?' he demanded, swinging himself into the helmsman's seat.

Elaine pointed to the distant triangle of sail. Tony thumbed the twin Volvo Penta starter buttons in turn and gunned the engines without waiting for them to warm up. He spun the helm. The big cruiser heeled hard as it swept in a tight circle.

'What about the waterskis?' Elaine yelled above the roar of the two engines.

'Not enough time!' Tony yelled, pulling the jacket's hood into position so that only his face was showing. 'Get into your scuba jacket!'

The original plan had been for Elaine to be waterskiing behind the cruiser so that their intercept of Crick's daughter would, to a casual observer ashore, look like a mishap. She pulled on the foam rubber jacket and passed a facemask to Tony which he settled on his forehead. He slammed the Morse control levers fully open as soon as the bow was aligned on the sail that had nearly disappeared into the haze. The one hundred horsepower engines thrust the Huntsman's deep vee hull effortlessly onto the plane, accelerating the craft to thirty knots in a few seconds. Tony cranked the trim tab handle; the water speed indicator crept up to forty knots. Elaine glanced back at their wake. The Huntsman was carving a massive furrow in the water; she was certain that the clouds of spray thrown up by the pounding bow would be visible for miles.

'Tony! Ease up!'

'But those windsurfer things can move, can't they?'

'Not as fast as this, for God's sake! And the further offshore she is when we catch up with her, the better.'

Tony saw the sense in what she said and backed off the throttles. The engine note dropped and the Huntsman settled to a steady twenty-five knots. At least they could now talk. A minute passed. The gap closed to a mile. Elaine pulled her own facemask over her forehead. The windsurfer went about on a tack that took it further out to sea. It was now possible to see the diminutive figure of a girl in a speckled bikini bottom holding the bow-shaped boom. She was well-balanced, legs slightly bent, the sail perfectly filled so that it formed an efficient aerofoil.

'She's good,' Elaine commented. She had once tackled windsurfing and had given it up as impossible. 'Any ideas on how we stop her?'

'We'll think of something,' Tony answered, not taking his eyes off the windsurfer. 'Masks.'

They both covered their faces with the diving masks. They were five hundred yards from the girl when she became aware of the Huntsman bearing down on her. She expertly tacked the windsurfer and waved to Tony to keep his distance. Tony pretended not to understand. He waved back at the girl.

'An idea!' Elaine called out as she darted into the cabin. She reappeared holding the radio-telephone handset.

The girl tacked again, shifting her thin, well-tanned body on the narrow hull and slewing the windsurfer onto a fresh course. Tony payed the stainless steel helm through his fingers.

'Get in front of her!' Elaine yelled.

Tony increased power and circled sharply. The gap was fifty yards and closing fast. Elaine held the radio telephone handset above her head and waved it so that the girl could see it.

The girl stared at Elaine in surprise. Elaine glanced around. The coast was a smudge barely visible through the haze. There were no pleasure craft or swimmers about. She picked up the loudhailer microphone. Her amplified voice from the deck-mounted speaker boomed across the narrowing gap.

'Marianne! Are you Marianne Crick?'

The girl lowered the boom. She used a lanyard to hold the sail at an angle to the water so that she lost speed. She nodded in answer to the question. Tony throttled back the Volvos and slipped them into neutral. The Huntsman lost way. Its hull sank off the plane.

'Marianne,' Elaine continued. 'Your father spotted us and called us up. He wants to speak to you. It's urgent.'

The girl expertly steered her windsurfer alongside the Huntsman. She dropped the sail and mast onto the water and tossed a line to Elaine before jumping nimbly onto the side deck and scrambling into

61

the cockpit. Her hair was tied into a tight plait; the speckled bikini bottom – more a G-string than the essential fifty per cent of a swimsuit – was her only item of clothing. Her boyish, elfin features were pinched and drawn. Tony decided that she wasn't particularly attractive. She was far too thin.

'I don't understand,' said Marianne in good English. She stared at the couple, wondering why they were wearing their facemasks. She pointed to a waterproof Pokketfone clipped to the windsurfer's mast. 'I have a telephone if anyone wishes to speak with me.'

'Maybe it's not working,' said Elaine.

Marianne reached for the handset that Elaine was holding and then tried to cry out as Tony suddenly pulled a black bag over her head and clapped a hand hard over her mouth. He pushed her into the salon and threw her face-down onto a berth. Her screams choked against the gag that he knotted tightly in place outside the black bag. Elaine pinioned the girl's thrashing legs while Tony lashed a cord around her ankles. The young Soviet knew the excruciating pain that a skilfully tied short length of cord was capable of inflicting. While gripping the girl's neck with one hand, he managed to yank the free ends of the cord into the small of the girl's back so that her legs were bent backwards. Still maintaining his deadly grip on her neck, he quickly bound her wrists to her ankles.

Tony released the girl's neck and yanked at the speckled G-string, snapping its side laces.

'Is that necessary?' asked Elaine reprovingly.

Tony didn't answer. Without showing a trace of interest in the girl's nakedness, he snatched a silver crucifix from around her neck, breaking the chain. He straightened and studied the crucifix and the slip of material. 'We'll need these,' he said shortly.

Twice the girl tried to struggle up and twice her efforts led to her collapsing back on the berth with a gurgling whimper of pain. The piece of cord had been less than four feet long.

'Wow,' Elaine breathed in grudging admiration. 'Who taught you that?'

'Guess,' said Tony curtly, heading aft to the cockpit. Tying up the girl had left an unpleasant taste. 'Draw the curtains.'

As Elaine did as she was told, she noticed that the lashings were staining red where they were cutting into the whimpering girl's wrists. Elaine was surprised. She hadn't supposed that Tony – her gentle, loving Tony – was capable of such violence. The sound of the Volvo engines opening up intruded on her thoughts.

17

Two hours later, Tony drove slowly past Villa Katrina's imposing wrought-iron gates in a hired Mercedes. He had tied the girl's speckled G-string into a tight ball with the aid of her crucifix enabling him to lob it over the gates. He drove on and parked the car two hundred yards from the villa's entrance. A brief reconnoitre along the deserted road, overhung with pines, revealed the whereabouts of the villa's overhead telephone line. He followed the line through the trees to a spot where he could not be seen from the road. He knelt down and unpacked the small kitbag. The miniature grappling hook attached to a length of nylon cord snagged the telephone line on the third attempt. He heaved. Nothing happened. He heaved again, nearly lifting himself off the ground. This time the line parted. The broken ends fell snaking into the undergrowth. Tony selected the end that led to the villa. He stripped back the insulation from the two conductors and connected the line to a portable telephone. He held the handset to his ear and pressed the button that sent fifty volts down the line to operate the bell. A voice answered on the third ring.

'Ya?'

Tony pushed a miniature voice scrambler into the mouthpiece. 'Doctor Crick?'

'Ya?'

Tony answered in English. 'Doctor Crick. I wish to speak to you about Marianne.'

'She is out windsurfing,' the voice replied in clipped, carefully pronounced English. 'Please call back later.'

'It's very important.'

A muffled grumble. 'Your name please?'

'I'm a friend of Marianne's.'

'This is a bad line. I am not responsible for my daughter. Marianne is old enough –'

'Are you alone?' Tony interrupted.

A pause. 'Does it matter?'

'What matters, Doctor Crick, is that at this moment you *are* very much responsible for Marianne's safety.'

Another pause. 'I am sorry,' said the Belgian. 'I do not understand.'

'We are holding your daughter. Provided you cooperate, she will come to no harm.'

'But my daughter is windsurfing –'

'Go to your front gate,' Tony ordered. 'You will find the bottom half of her bikini and her crucifix. It was all she was wearing when we took her. Go and look now. I'll hold on.'

'But this is absurd –'

'Go and look,' Tony insisted.

There was a long silence. Three minutes passed and then there was the sound of the telephone being picked up. 'I do not understand,' said Crick's voice. He sounded more puzzled than alarmed.

'Really? I thought I made it perfectly clear.'

'You . . . You have kidnapped Marianne?'

'Congratulations, doctor. You are most perceptive.'

The Belgian suddenly sounded frightened and confused. 'I have very little money in Spain. A peseta account in Calpe for day to day expenses.'

'We're not interested in your money, doctor,' said Tony smoothly. 'What we're interested in is your brains – more particularly your knowledge of SWIFT III.'

There was a note of panic in Crick's voice when he answered. 'We cannot discuss this on the phone.'

'We can't be heard – I promise you that.'

'You want to break into SWIFT?'

'Exactly.'

'But it is impossible! Not even I could do that!'

Tony gave what he hoped sounded like a sinister chuckle. 'In that case, tomorrow we will send you Marianne's left ear.'

'It is impossible! I beg of you to understand – it is impossible to break into SWIFT!'

'Why?'

'Because I made it so.'

Tony's voice was brittle. '*Why* is it impossible?'

'I cannot tell you. I am sworn to secrecy.'

'Very well, doctor,' said Tony, speaking slowly and deliberately. 'Tomorrow you will receive Marianne's left ear. And the day after tomorrow, you will receive her right ear. Do you understand?'

The Belgian made no attempt to hide the panic in his voice. 'Please,' he implored. 'Breaking into SWIFT III is impossible. You must believe me. I beg of you.'

'Tell me why it's impossible.'

For a moment there was no answer. 'There are three SWIFT III satellites, you understand,' said Crick, his voice little more than a croak. 'They are in stationary orbit thirty-six thousand kilometres above the equator.' The Belgian paused, struggling to form the sentences in his confused mind. 'One is over India. One is over the Pacific and one is over the Atlantic. Together they cover the entire globe, although the Atlantic satellite is the most busy. It is the primary link between Europe and America. You understand?'

'Yes. Go on.'

'The SWIFT III system is heavily layered with protection passwords and user validations. This is very important. Radio signals – even the narrow beam microwave signals used for the satellite uplinks and downlinks – are vulnerable. Unauthorized interception is possible. You would not believe the sophisticated electronic equipment that can be bought in amateur radio stores today. Especially in America. This was a weakness that occupied me for many months when I was designing the new system.'

'So how did you get round it?' Tony prompted.

'Marianne –'

'Marianne will come to no harm if you cooperate. Please continue.'

Crick nervously cleared his throat. 'Most communication satellites are transponders – repeaters, you undersand. They merely receive signals on one frequency and retransmit them on another frequency. The SWIFT III satellites are more than repeaters; they add their own secondary encryption to the already encrypted signals they receive before retransmitting them. Very few know this – not even the world's governments. Everyone thinks that all the encryptions originate in our main-frame computers.'

'Why did you add a secondary level of encryption?'

Crick hesitated. 'Not only as additional protection against computer fraud – that would be impossible anyway – but to prevent governments from eavesdropping on SWIFT III satellite traffic.' The Belgian paused. Tony could hear his uneven breathing. 'There is no way that anyone can break into the SWIFT III system. Not even

I could do it. One would have to disable the existing satellite and simultaneously provide a duplicate satellite without the secondary encryption level. And that would cost millions. I beg of you to believe me – SWIFT III is unbreakable.'

18

That evening, with the Huntsman moored to a floating jetty in Calpe's yacht marina, Tony decided that it would be safer not to use the vessel's telephone. He left Elaine in charge of their captive and telephoned Charlie from the payphone outside the crowded, noisy Bar Bardel seafood restaurant.

'I've tried negotiating with the franchise owner under the circumstances you suggested,' said Tony as soon as he was through. 'We can't go ahead with the deal.'

'Why not?' Charlie demanded.

'There's no way we can get round the technicalities. I'm sorry, Char –' Tony checked himself; he had nearly used Charlie's name. 'I'm sorry, sir, but we will have to call it off.'

'What technicalities?'

'The franchise owner outlined them. They are insuperable.'

'And you believed him?' Charlie sounded angry.

'Yes, sir.'

'For Chrissake,' Charlie muttered. 'There's gotta be a way. There's always a way.'

'Not this time.'

'You agreed delivery terms with him for his goods?'

'Yes,' said Tony, guessing what was coming.

'Okay. No problem. Go ahead with the first delivery then see what he says.'

Tony decided that he disliked dealing with Charlie. 'There's no point. The technicalities –'

'Fuck the technicalities,' Charlie snarled. 'Just do as I say and watch him change his tune. Jesus Christ – if you don't carry out my orders –'

Knowing how impossible the hotelier could be when he didn't get his way, Tony slammed the handset back on its cradle and strode angrily out of the bar. He returned to the Huntsman. Elaine looked questioningly up at him when he entered the salon. Marianne was sitting at the table, struggling to drink a cup of soup through a slit in the black bag. She was wearing one of Elaine's beach dresses.

'She promised not to make a sound so I untied her,' Elaine explained.

Tony produced a knife. He yanked the girl's head back and pressed the point of the knife gainst her throat. 'We're taking you home,' he said, speaking very quietly, his mouth close to her ear. 'If you make trouble, you'll never see it or your father again. Do you understand?'

The terrified girl whimpered but was unable to speak.

'*Do you understand!*' Tony shook her head roughly to emphasize his point.

'Yes – I understand,' the girl whispered.

'Even so, we'd better put the gag back on her,' Tony commented.

19

There was no moon. Villa Katrina was still and silent. As soon as he had gagged Marianne and tied her securely by her wrists to the villa's gates, Tony left Elaine in the Mercedes to look after her and went to retrieve the portable telephone that was hidden in the undergrowth and still connected to Hans Crick's line. He found the instrument without difficulty and was about to call Crick when he was suddenly bathed in light from a powerful flashlamp.

'Please do not move,' said Crick's voice from behind the blinding light. 'I will shoot if I have to.'

Tony froze, his thoughts whirling.

'I've been waiting a long time,' said Crick. 'My patience is exhausted, therefore you have only five seconds to tell me where my daughter is.'

'We've brought her back,' said Tony calmly, avoiding looking into the light to preserve his night vision.

'Unhurt, for your sake?'

'Frightened but unhurt,' Tony confirmed. 'How did you find out about the telephone?'

Crick gave an arrogant chuckle. 'You forgot something. I guessed what you had done when I discovered I could not make or receive

67

calls. A resistance and impedance test on the line told me that the break was within one hundred metres of the house.' There was the metallic click of a safety catch being released. Crick's voice was suddenly soft and menacing. 'You were most stupid.'

20: Washington, DC

Jackie Morrison's Pokketfone buzzed just as she was paying off her cab outside the Department of the Treasury on Constitution Avenue. She pressed the key that transmitted a buffer store recording of her voice promising the caller to get right back to him or her, and hurried to her office. She glanced at the line printer that was busily churning out information on a certain Damion Silvester. She lit her tenth cigarette of the day and dropped into a swivel chair before thumbing the return call button on the telephone.

Jackie Morrison was a slightly built thirty-nine-year-old widow who looked thirty. She had fifteen years in the Internal Revenue Service to her credit – or discredit as her friends would joke. To the despair of her mother, Jackie had never remarried following the death of her husband ten years previously. To the amazement of her colleagues, she was now six months into a diet that had resulted in her shedding thirty pounds and gaining a figure that was the envy of girls twenty years her junior. She aimed to stay that way even though none of her clothes fitted any more. For two weeks she had been nerving herself to spend several thousand dollars on a new clothes shopping spree. She sometimes wished that she could divert some of the willpower that she had discovered during the diet towards kicking cigarettes. The trouble was that for every hamburger and spoonful of sugar she had cut out, she was now smoking an extra five of the damn things.

The telephone emitted a warning tone as the connection was completed. 'Harry Walsh – N Y C' said the handset's display. Walsh was based in a New York Internal Revenue Service field office and was in charge of an I R S special investigation team.

'Hi there, Harry,' said Jackie genially as soon as she was connected. 'Sorry about just now. How you doing? What's this stuff you're sending me on . . .' She ripped the first sheet off the printer, 'Damion Silvester? Who is he and why are you telling me about
68

him?'

'We had a notification from the local field office here,' Walsh replied. 'They've been after Silvester for a year now for just over two hundred thousand dollars unpaid tax. He finally paid out yesterday – in full.'

'Okay – fine,' said Jackie. While Harry was talking she was speed-reading through the information on Silvester as it rolled off the printer. 'So tip off the FBI,' she suggested. 'Let them worry about where our customers get their funds from – just so long as we get to grab that which belongs to Caesar.'

Walsh sounded aggrieved. 'I don't think it is an FBI matter. Silvester obtained the money outside the United States. He wired the payment from London. Listen, Jackie – he leaves the country broke – the rent on his apartment and his offices two months overdue – and now he's issuing drafts for two hundred thousand dollars.'

Jackie started to light her eleventh cigarette of the day and realized that her tenth cigarette was still half-smoked and smouldering in her ashtray. 'Maybe he's got property in England? He was British.' At that moment she saw on the print-out exactly why the New York team were worried: Damion Silvester was one of the country's top software scientists. General Electric had imported him from the United Kingdom and he had spent several years with them developing space defence software before setting up his own consultancy – Software Science – in New York. General Electric and a number of other major military equipment manufacturers were now clients of his company. Jackie swore. 'For Chrissake, Harry – I've just read your para six.'

'Not only does the guy know a helluva lot about space defence software – he actually wrote it.'

Jackie thought fast. The export of strategic software, like computer hardware, was prohibited. It was a customs matter but customs came under the Department of Treasury. It looked as if this particular buck was going to lodge itself firmly in her office. She lit her eleventh cigarette from the butt of her tenth cigarette and inhaled deeply. 'Have you talked to anyone about this?'

'No,' said Harry. 'Just passive snooping – collating all the keyboard data we could.'

'Okay, Harry. You've done a good job. Leave it with me.'

Two hurried conferences later, Jackie left the Department of the

Treasury with instructions to find out all she could about Damion Silvester's activities.

'Try not to alert him or his colleagues, Jackie,' Matt Fitzgerald, the director of I R S Special Services, had instructed her. 'Chances are it'll all add up to a big nothing. I don't want to go screaming wolf unless I'm a hundred per cent certain.'

That was funny, Jackie thought sourly. Matt Fitzgerald wouldn't even whisper 'wolf' – not even if he was a thousand per cent certain. Fitzgerald wanted an easy life and hated anything out of the ordinary. Jackie could think of several major tax evasion investigations that had come to nothing, simply because the prime suspects had political influence and because of Matt Fitzgerald's talent for getting nervous whenever something really big was thrust under his nose.

21: London

Damion's simple disguise consisted of blue overalls, a bulky toolbag, an electronic notepad, and a worried expression. It worked better than he dared hope. He entered the South Bank telephone exchange through the works entrance at the rear of the building.

'Had anyone screaming about water coming out the air conditioning ducts?' he asked the security man who was sitting behind a tiny window.

The security man looked up from his paper. 'No – why? What's happened?'

'Bleedin' dehumidifier's packed up,' Damion retorted over his shoulder as he hurried off. 'Tell 'em I'm dealing with it if anyone starts howling.'

No one challenged Damion during the very profitable hour that he spent in the building. While pretending to examine the overhead air conditioning ducts, he made his way through all the central switching areas – making floor plan sketches on his pad. On one occasion he even climbed on top of a System M power supply cabinet and pretended to take a close look at a duct. The position afforded him a panoramic view of the international switching room and enabled him to note the number and positions of the infrared-sensitive closed circuit television cameras.

Jesus Christ! There were ten of them!

'What's the problem?' a male voice asked when Damion was about to descend.

'Bloody dehumidifer's acting up,' Damion muttered ruefully, making a note on his pad without looking down at his questioner. His pulse rate climbed.

'Oh – not again?'

'That's right,' Damion agreed, hardly believing his luck. He loaded the latest sketch into the pad's memory and jumped down off the cabinet. 'Haven't seen any water coming through anywhere, have you?'

The questioner was a studious-looking youth. 'No.'

Damion grunted. 'Can take hours to come right through the system. Probably happen tonight. Anyone around at night?'

'A couple of switchboard operators downstairs. There's only a skeleton staff at night. All this area is unmanned after five-thirty. Automatic, of course.'

'Okay,' said Damion breezily, picking up his toolbag. 'Looks like I'd better have a word with the guv'nor.'

Damion's last find before he left the building turned out to be his biggest stroke of luck yet: it was a small room used for storing cleaning equipment and it had a fanlight. Albeit a fanlight in a robust steel frame. His attention was drawn to a number of co-axial cables that fed into a junction box mounted high on the wall. It was marked 'Labgear TV Surveillance Equipment Plc'. He stared disbelievingly at it, wondering what he had done to warrant such amazing good fortune. Ten minutes later he was sitting in a pub, restoring his shattered nerves with the aid of a double whisky while congratulating himself on a mission successfully accomplished.

22: New York

Jackie returned to her apartment and packed a few belongings. She left a terse teletext message on the kitchen television for her latest boyfriend, suggesting that now was as good a time as any for them to split. She nearly added she was better at producing meals than he was at providing orgasms but decided that that would be unnecessarily cruel.

The drive to New York took four hours and two packets of cigarettes. She found a parking space near Damion Silvester's apartment building in Queens and examined the exterior. It was an expensive place. A marbled lobby, a security guard, and a receptionist who looked like a Miss America contestant. She was presiding over a massive horseshoe desk with a battery of closed-circuit television screens set into its surface. The desk was completely devoid of papers. During her years at the Treasury, Jackie had developed a theory that desks expanded as their necessity shrank. The girl was very polite. Mr Silvester was not at home. No – she did not know when he was returning. She was sorry, but the management's rules forbade the disclosure of tenants' activities.

Jackie decided not to show her I R S card. The chances were that Silvester was keeping in touch with the front desk; news that tax officials had been sniffing around would soon get back to him. She thanked the girl and left.

She stayed the night at a TraveLodge and dined on two bananas. The following morning, after a customary light breakfast and the passing of a resolution to give up smoking . . . tomorrow, she visited the modern offices of Software Science on a twentieth floor overlooking Park Avenue. Security was tight: fingerprint recognition locks on the doors. She caught a brief glimpse of a main-frame computer as a door opened. A clean-cut young man appeared.

Jackie introduced herself as 'Mary' – an old buddy of Damion's from their days at General Electric. 'Damion told me to look him up next time I was in New York,' said Jackie, smiling cheerfully. 'So you tell Damion that Mary's here.'

'I'm sorry, but Mr Silvester isn't available.'

Jackie looked at her watch. 'Guess I can wait awhile.'

'Mr Silvester isn't in the country,' the young man explained apologetically. He was curious. It was rare for a young woman to look up his boss. One date was usually enough for them to show no further interest.

Jackie looked suitably annoyed. 'But he was expecting me. I called him some days ago.'

The young man gave an embarrassed smile. 'He was called away unexpectedly.' He hesitated and decided that there would be no harm in confiding in the visitor. 'He's won a prize.'

'You don't say?'

'It was amazing. Quarter of a million dollars.'

This time Jackie looked genuinely surprised. 'You're kidding?'

The young man laughed. 'We thought he was too, but he took us all out to lunch. Something to do with a Golden Rose Hotel survey. His name popped out of their computer. He's flown to England to collect the prize.'

Jackie was lost for words.

A girl put her head around a door. 'Jeff – Marius Hoffman of SWIFT.'

The young man held out his hand. 'If you're in New York for a few days, call us tomorrow – Mr Silvester said that he wouldn't be more than two or three days.'

A few minutes later Jackie was strolling thoughtfully along Park Avenue while musing on Damion Silvester's good fortune, and reflecting how often it was that seemingly suspicious circumstances had an innocent explanation. Golden Rose? Charlie Rose's hotel and motel chain. A curious coincidence, but at the last resources meeting, one of the items on the agenda had been the allocation of more funds to cover the cost of the Charlie Rose tax evasion investigation . . . Wheels within wheels . . . .

Most I R S agents would have left it at that but Jackie preferred to double-check. She called the Golden Rose central office and asked for their publicity department.

A woman's voice answered her.

'Can you tell me who won the big competition please?' Jackie requested.

'What competition is that, miss?'

'The one you've just paid out a quarter million prize to.'

A pause. 'I think you're mistaken, miss. All our promotional prizes are vacations at our inns. Never money.'

'I read about it somewhere. The winner gets a trip to the UK to collect the money.'

The woman sounded puzzled. 'We don't operate in Europe, miss. There is a Golden Rose hotel at Winchester, England, but that's Mr Rose's personal venture. It's nothing to do with us.'

'I guess that must be it,' said Jackie.

'But I still think you're mistaken. Mr Rose doesn't operate like that and we certainly don't. Try one of the other chains – Holiday Inns or Howard Johnson. Although if that sort of money was going as

73

a prize – we would've heard about it.'

Jackie thanked her and hung up.

Charlie Rose's 'personal venture'?

She sat on a bench and went over the recent events. Someone, somewhere, had dangled a quarter-million-dollar carrot to entice a top software scientist out of the country. Worse than that – the carrot had been accepted. Even worse: maybe it was only a stage payment? If so, Jackie reckoned she could make a shrewd guess as to the nature of the prize Damion Silvester had to offer, and the nationality of the buyers.

But a guess, no matter how shrewd, would not be enough to make Matt Fitzgerald take fast action. Nothing could achieve that. Jackie was no expert on military affairs, but what little she knew was enough to tell her that the passing of Space Defense Initiative software to the Soviets could seriously endanger the security of the United States.

Jackie started walking, hands thrust into the pockets of her now oversize jacket. To hell with Matt Fitzgerald.

She decided to blow hard and loud on a very large whistle.

23: London

Billy Watts guided his portable thermic lance along the edge of the skylight and reflected that there were some weird people in the world. He could think of no good reason for anyone wanting to break into a London telephone exchange even once, never mind every night for a week. Still, the lanky man with the slight American accent had already paid him a grand with the promise of another grand after each visit.

'For Chrissake hurry it up,' Damion muttered anxiously, glancing around at the surrounding, night-shrouded rooftops. His imagination created infrared surveillance cameras on every shadowy air conditioning vent. He took a swig from his hip flask.

'Can't hurry this, guv,' said Billy, intent on his work. 'Not if we're going to use this way in again. You said to leave no trace. You just worry about keeping the mask in place.'

Damion repositioned the welder's mask to screen the light that was flickering around the spluttering lance.

Billy reached the corner of the skylight and extinguished the lance. 'Okay – that's it. Catch hold of your end.'

The two men lifted the glazed panel to one side. Billy unpacked an aluminium and nylon rope ladder. He secured it to the skylight frame and dropped the free end through the opening. 'Seems okay, guv,' he said, after testing his weight on the ladder. 'I'll go down and hold it steady. Tricky things if you're not used to 'em.'

Damion grabbed his bulky pack and followed Billy cautiously down the ladder into the darkness. A brief survey with a penlight revealed the anti-room crammed with vacuum cleaners, floor polishers and brooms. 'Cleaners' room, just as you reckoned,' Billy commented admiringly, wiping the sweat that was trickling from under his Balaclava helmet. 'Now what?'

Damion removed a portable video recorder from his pack and checked the condition of its lithium battery. He reached up and removed the cover from the Labgear junction box and connected a recording lead from the box to the video recorder. A bright, clear picture of a corridor appeared on the video recorder's tiny monitor screen. After a few seconds the picture changed to the same corridor seen from a different position. Damion touched the record key to start the tape.

'Neat,' said Billy, when the picture changed again.

'The picture from each camera is automatically displayed for about three seconds at a time,' said Damion. 'There's three minutes of tape in the cassette on a continuous loop. We're now recording the output from all the cameras.'

The machine recorded for three minutes and switched itself off.

'Touch the play key when I say,' Damion instructed, his finger poised on a control button inside the junction box. 'Get ready . . . Now!'

The changeover from live pictures on the monitor to the recording was achieved without a flicker. Three floors below, the security man sitting before his bank of monitors was unaware that some of the pictures being fed to him were now a recording.

Damion tested the door. It was unlocked. He listened for a moment. 'Follow me,' he said.

Billy dutifully followed along a narrow passageway that had been created through racks of electronic equipment. The air was filled with the soft hum of miniature cooling fans. Occasionally relays in the cabinets would click furiously, making Billy jump. The letters and numbers stencilled on the cabinets were meaningless to him, but the lanky man seemed to know what he was doing. Occasionally he would pause and play the penlight beam on the legends. He stopped at one of the cabinets. Billy held the penlight steady while the big man released the turnlock fasteners on an inspection panel. Inside the cabinet was an incomprehensible mass of printed circuit boards, microprocessors, edge connectors, and cable harnesses.

Damion unpacked a Pentax and took several flashlight photographs of the cabinet's interior and of the schematic diagram thoughtfully provided on the inside of the cover.

'Okay,' Damion muttered quietly. 'Put the cover back.'

The process was repeated with several more cabinets.

'Fine,' said Damion, removing the third roll of film he had used that night from the camera. 'That's enough for now.' He flashed the light on a robust door marked:

TALL COMMS
STRICTLY NO ADMITTANCE
TO UNAUTHORIZED PERSONNEL

'That room will be the last on the agenda,' said Damion. 'I'll want to go in there on Friday night. So take a close look at it before then.'

Billy studied the two Chubb mortise locks. 'They're going to be a right pig, guv,' he confessed.

'Can you do it?'

Billy grinned. ''Bout thirty minutes each.' He looked at the notice. 'What does "TALL" mean?'

'Transatlantic leased lines,' said Damion curtly, returning the camera to his pack. 'Time we got out of here.'

24: Calpe, Spain

'Where is my daughter?' asked Crick, speaking very softly.

'Safe.' Tony tried to look beyond the blinding flashlight beam but it was impossible. With difficulty he could discern the muzzle of a double-barrelled shotgun beneath the beam as Crick advanced towards him. He guessed that the flashlight was mounted on the barrel, but he had to know for certain.

76

'I asked where she was – not how she was,' said Crick, his tone icy.

'She's tied to the front gates of your villa. She's come to no harm.'

'I hope for your sake that you are telling the truth. Start walking please.'

'Where?'

'Back to my villa.'

The swing of the beam as Crick gestured told Tony that the flashlamp was definitely mounted on the shotgun, which meant that he now knew exactly where the gun was pointing, even when he had his back to it. He led the way through the pine trees with the Belgian following closely behind. From his shadow cast ahead of the uneven, stony ground, Tony was uncomfortably aware that the shotgun was trained square on the small of his back. Crick's frequent stumbles on the rough ground had Tony worrying about the possibility of the shotgun being accidentally fired. And then Tony tripped on a pine root. He put out his hands to break his fall and his fingers encountered a large stone. He picked it up.

'Keep moving,' Crick ordered, his voice edgy.

Tony straightened and continued walking, keeping his hand holding the stone in front of him. He waited until the beam wavered and, with a flick of his wrist that he prayed Crick would not see, he sent the stone crashing into a nearby gorse bush. His timing was better than he had dared hope; the beam whipped to one side. Tony dived in the opposite direction. His shoulder hit the ground and he swept his feet round in an arc that connected with Crick's shins. The Belgian gave a grunt and fell backwards. Tony was on top of him immediately. He grabbed the shotgun by the barrel and tried to twist it out of the Belgian's grasp. The beam made a dancing spoke of light in the overhanging pine branches as the two men fought dementedly for possession of the weapon. Tony eventually wrenched it free and jumped to his feet, aiming the weapon at the figure on the ground.

'No please!' Crick implored. 'Don't shoot!'

Tony played the beam on the Belgian. 'Don't worry, Dr Crick. I think I can handle one of these things better than you. Get up but no sudden moves.'

The Belgian climbed shakily to his feet. For the first time Tony was able to get a good look at him. He was short and stocky with iron-grey close-cropped hair. He straightened his rimless glasses and stood blinking in the bright light – looking slightly ridiculous in an expensive tracksuit.

'You lead the way this time,' Tony invited.

The two men walked back to Villa Katrina where Elaine was sitting in the back of the Mercedes with Marianne. She lowered the window and looked questioningly at Tony and Crick as they approached.

'He was waiting for me by the field telephone with this,' Tony explained, indicating the shotgun.

'Marianne!' Crick exclaimed.

Tony made no attempt to intervene when Crick helped his daughter from the car and embraced her. They talked excitedly in rapid French. Marianne began to cry.

'Okay,' said Tony, now embarrassed by the fiasco. 'Let's go into the house.'

A few minutes later the four were sitting in Crick's living room. The Belgian had his arm around his daughter and was comforting her. Tony and Elaine were sitting opposite in separate chairs. Tony held the shotgun lightly across his knees. He noticed that Crick appeared to be self-conscious of the arm he was holding around his daughter – as if they rarely touched under normal circumstances. She was staring at Tony and Elaine with large, frightened eyes – her tiny form coiled protectively against her father.

'Take her to her room and keep an eye on her,' Tony instructed Elaine.

The girl shrank away when Elaine rose and held a hand out to her.

'Now don't be silly, Marianne,' said Elaine, surprising Tony with her good French. 'You know I won't hurt you if you're sensible. Anyway – I'd like to see your room.'

Crick spoke encouragingly to his daughter. She stood and moved reluctantly to the door with Elaine following.

'Don't forget your father's safety in case you think of trying anything silly,' Tony reminded her as they left the room.

There was a silence when the two men were alone. Tony spoke first. 'There's something you ought to consider, doctor. Both of you have seen our faces. It means that we have nothing to lose by killing you if we have to.' He hoped that the threat sounded convincing.

The Belgian inclined his head so that the light caught his glasses, making it impossible to see his eyes. He reminded Tony of a KGB

78

instructor who had a similar habit.

'I have seen the girl before,' said Crick calmly. His voice was surprisingly steady as if the shotgun no longer intimidated him. 'The SWIFT seminar at Nice last year. I have an excellent memory for faces.'

'We're interested in your knowledge of SWIFT, doctor.'

'Which will be of no use to you. SWIFT III is unbreakable. I have already made that clear.'

'And I have made clear what will happen to your daughter if you don't cooperate with us.'

Crick's spectacles glittered. He spread his hands. 'Then you will have to kill us. There is no way that SWIFT III can be broken into by individuals with limited resources. A government – maybe – but only then with great difficulty.'

'Who said we were individuals with limited resources?'

Crick gave a confident smile as if he were master of the situation. 'To even attempt a serious break into SWIFT III would cost many millions of dollars with no certainty of succeeding. Anyone with the business acumen to have amassed such a sum would not need to break into SWIFT to amass even more. And would not risk it on such an uncertain venture. It is all a matter of logic, you understand.'

Tony could think of nothing to say. He was too preoccupied with trying to think of a way of extricating himself and Elaine from what had become an impossible situation. Having to return to Moscow for an indefinite period was fast becoming a bleak reality. He doubted if Elaine would be prepared to return with him. And then Crick said something unexpected:

'So who are you working for?'

'Does it matter?'

'He or she has great wealth?'

'Perhaps,' said Tony cautiously, wishing he could see the Belgian's eyes. 'Why?'

'Is he in Spain?' There was the faintest hint of suppressed excitement in his voice.

'No,' Tony replied, wondering what the Belgian had on his mind. Nothing could have prepared him for what Crick said next:

'I should like to meet him.' The Belgian leaned forward. This time Tony could see his eyes. They were alight with anticipation. It was as if something of great importance had just occurred to him.

'Marianne will do exactly as I tell her. If I give you a guarantee of her behaviour and mine, would it be possible for me to meet the man you are working for?'

25: Washington, DC

Jackie spent ten minutes at the keyboard of her computer terminal, combing through the activities and functions of all the agencies within the Department of Defence. Of the department's one million employees, she was looking for the one man or woman who would be interested in what she had to say, and with enough political clout in the right places to do something about it.

Mike Randall of the Defence Intelligence Agency, listed as 'Director, Defence Software Security', looked a possibility. Jackie called his Pentagon office. He sounded young and friendly, and he listened attentively to what Jackie had to say about Damion Silvester.

'Don't you think you should refer this through your director?' he tactfully suggested.

Jackie snorted. 'Sure I should,' she agreed. 'But Matt Fitzgerald sits on reports and hopes they'll go away.'

Randall chuckled. 'Okay – I'm ready – give me a download on what you've got.'

Jackie operated the transmit control on her keyboard. She could hear Mike Randall's printer purring in the background.

'Software Science?' he mused, when his printer stopped. 'Okay. I'll check with contracts – find out what they're handling.'

'I want you to file a status two report on this one,' said Jackie grimly. 'I can only go to status five.'

'Let me check out Software Science first before we do anything drastic,' Randall suggested.

26: London

After their fourth clandestine night visit to the South Bank telephone exchange, the procedure used by Damion and Billy had become routine. But their fourth break-in was different in one respect: instead of photographing the interiors of the System M cabinets, Damion wanted Billy to open the door that led to the high-security transatlantic leased lines communication room.

Billy finished tracking his metal detector around the edge of the door. 'No separate alarm contacts, guv,' he stated. 'Unless they're built into the locks or hinges.'

'Is that likely?' Damion queried.

'Anything's possible,' said Billy, sorting through a giant bunch of adjustable keys. 'I don't know much about telephone exchange security systems. Least they're not electronic locks. They're bastards. Haven't cracked one yet. Even so – these are going to take a bit of time.'

In another part of the building the night security officer noticed something that he considered odd. The cycle of different views throughout the exchange that flashed on his surveillance monitor with boring regularity included a shot of a corridor with a wall clock that appeared to have stopped. All the clocks throughout the exchange were slaves, controlled by the country's atomic master clock at Greenwich. It was unheard of for one clock to stop. He watched the screen intently. The clock appeared again. It had definitely stopped. If one clock stopped, they should all stop. The officer decided to investigate. He reached for his two-way personal radio.

Billy gave a satisfied grunt and cautiously eased the door open to reveal a small room crowded with equipment cabinets similar to those in the main area. He checked the inside of the doorframe for concealed microswitches. 'There you are, guv. No alarms.'

Damion grabbed his bag. They entered the room. Billy closed the door while Damion carried out a cursory examination of all the cabinets and opened the one furthest from the door. He was busy with his camera when both men heard a burst of crackling outside the door. Damion recognized the sound as white noise from a two-way radio.

'It's Jeff,' said a voice. 'I'm at location twenty. I thought one of the clocks had stopped so I came up to have a look.'

A loudspeaker made garbled noises that the voice seemed to recognize as human speech.

'No – everything's okay. I must've made a mistake.' More garbled noises, then: 'I'm going back now.'

Footsteps receded into the distance. Damion breathed again. 'Any wall clock on the video loop is going to look like it's stopped,' he commented. He took a sip from his hip flask to steady his nerve.

Billy hurriedly gathered up his kit.

'Wait,' Damion ordered. 'We finish what we came for. I need only a few more pictures.'

Billy was horrified. 'But he'll yell when he gets back to his video screen!' he protested.

'That's a chance we've got to take,' said Damion, opening a cabinet that was standing separate from the others. The soft click of hidden microswitches closing as he removed the front panel warned Damion, even before he heard the shrilling of distant alarms.

The two men put everything back as they had found it, grabbed their kit and dashed back to the cleaners' room. They heard men running into the building just as they finished stowing the video recorder. They hauled themselves through the skylight and replaced the glass panel. Damion followed the roof-wise Billy. After a number of anxious moments that made Damion wish he had stayed in New York, they reached street level and the dubious sanctuary of their car parked several streets away.

Damion was about to start the engine but Billy stopped him. 'No, guv – driving this late after an alert – we'd be pulled by the law. We wait until after six when there's some traffic about.'

Damion nodded in agreement. Billy demanded to know what was in the cabinet.

'Christ only knows,' Damion admitted, removing the last roll of film from his camera.

In fact the cabinet that Damion had had the misfortune to open belonged to the Government Communications Headquarters and was one of the most politically sensitive pieces of equipment in the country. It contained some of GCHQ's 'Tinkerbell' switchgear that linked them with their leased transatlantic telephone lines. One of the features of 'Tinkerbell', apart from its eavesdropping capabilities on overseas telephone traffic, was that it enabled its users – not only GCHQ – to dial into the telephone systems of the United States and to monitor conversations on specific numbers without the consent of the US Department of Justice. It was telephone tapping by remote control. The version of 'Tinkerbell' that Damion had stumbled upon was used to listen in and automatically record the conversations of known IRA sympathizers and supporters in the United States. A subsystem known as TASI created sufficient spare capacity on the transatlantic line for 'Tinkerbell' also to monitor public telephones near the suspects' homes – just in case the suspects believed that their calls were being intercepted. Indeed, familiar voices identified by GCHQ's voice-recognition equipment and flagged as coming from public telephones near targeted homes usually warranted very close attention because they tended to be very fruitful.

27: Washington, DC

Mike Randall breezed into Jackie's office. He cheerily introduced himself, perched himself on the edge of her desk, and produced an evil-looking pipe which he proceeded to fill with a tobacco that looked and smelt illegal. He was a tousle-haired, clean-cut Harvard graduate whose charm was negated to a certain extent by his belief that he radiated sex appeal like a radio transmitter.

'I've checked out Damion Silvester and his Software Science outfit,' he told Jackie. 'I can't go into details, but you're right about Silvester being involved in SDI software. He personally wrote some high-power programs for the new Space Defence Command Centre at Colorado but that was three years ago. All the stuff he wrote has since been upgraded, but not by him or his staff.'

'But it's still sensitive?'

Mike Randall inhaled a lungful of smoke that could have zonked a gorilla. 'You're goddamn right it's still sensitive. But not as sensitive as the upgraded stuff. The trouble is, if Silvester *is* selling software to our friends, why draw attention to himself by going to Europe? He can squirt the programs down a line to them from any public telephone. Controlling the movement of software and computer data is next to impossible. The days of microfilms and microdots and all that garbage are over.'

'So what is Silvester involved with now?'

'He's a software consultant to SWIFT. Has done a lot of work for them.'

'SWIFT?' Jackie queried. She had heard the name before but could not remember where or when.

'Society for Worldwide Interbank Financial Telecommunication,' said Randall. He gave Jackie a brief outline of SWIFT and its purpose.

'Sounds dull,' Jackie remarked

'And not our concern,' Randall added.

Jackie had a thought. 'Silvester must have a lot of contacts in Space Defence Command? Maybe he's got hold of the upgrades on his programs?'

'It's possible,' Randall conceded. 'Listen, Jackie – I don't mind filing your report on a status two routing priority. That way, it'll go high – but not too high. But your director's name goes on the report as well as mine. I'm not carrying this one alone.'

'Put my name on it,' said Jackie firmly.

Randall removed his pipe. 'You *are* kidding?'

'Put my name on it,' Jackie insisted grimly.

Randall relit his pipe. 'Okay. I only hope for your sake that the fan isn't spinning too fast when the report gets back to your director.'

28: Winchester

Charlie was not impressed by Elaine's account of the abortive kidnapping. 'So where is this Crick guy now?' he demanded, idly dangling his feet in the swimming pool while Baldwin refilled Elaine's toast rack.

'Room 401,' Elaine replied, talking with her mouth full. 'Tony's with him now.'

'So is he gonna do what we want him to do?'

'He refuses to discuss it with anyone but you, Charlie,' said Elaine.

Charlie looked sharply at her. 'He knows my name?'

'We've only referred to you as the boss.'

'So he finds out who we are and then he goes yelling to the cops or SWIFT. Great.'

'No,' said Elaine firmly. 'It's not like that, Charlie. I made a few phone calls from Spain. Remember me saying that there was a rumour going around that he's been in some sort of row with SWIFT's board of directors? Well, it's more than a row – more like a war. A majority of the board want Crick off the payroll because they're fed up with his inflated consultancy fees. Crick reckons that because he's the best communications expert in the business, then

84

his expenses are very special. They've lopped a chunk off his last bill. There was some talk about him overclaiming on expenses. I don't know the details, but the row was enough for him to go storming out of a meeting in Brussels, quit SWIFT and head for Spain.'

Charlie considered the implications. 'No way do I want him to know who I am just yet,' he decided. 'Like I said – you're the ones to stick your necks out – not me.'

Elaine produced a passport card. 'This belongs to his daughter. She can't leave Spain. We've told Crick that we've got men watching her. Any trouble here and she's . . . .' She left the sentence unfinished.

The American nodded his approval. 'Okay. But how much do we really need him?'

'Charlie,' said Elaine. 'There are a thousand and one problems to overcome before we can break into SWIFT. Having Crick with us will solve about nine hundred of them.'

Charlie came to a decision. 'Baldwin – call 401. Tell them they can come up.'

Tony ushered Hans Crick into Charlie's presence a few minutes later. The meeting got off to a bad start due to Crick advancing across the penthouse floor towards Charlie, hand outstretched, and saying: 'How do you do, Mr Rose.'

Charlie scowled. 'Who said my name was Rose?' He glared at Tony.

Crick smiled blandly. 'No one said anything, Mr Rose. I read an article about you in a magazine. It said that you had made this hotel your home.'

Ignoring the outstretched hand, Charlie said: 'You say anything about this meeting to anyone, Crick, and my men will deal with your daughter.'

Crick gave a partial bow. 'So I understand, Mr Rose. I have given a guarantee which I shall keep. I hope you will do the same.'

Charlie's eyes hardened but he let the comment pass. 'My colleagues think you might be useful to us.'

The Belgian's glance took in the penthouse's luxurious interior and the sparkling, heated pool. He gave a bland smile. 'No. I think that is wrong. I think it is you who will be useful to me, Mr Rose.'

The comment did little to improve Charlie's temper. 'How much did you make last year?' he barked.

'Is it important?'

Charlie gestured impatiently. 'How much?'

Crick shrugged. 'The SWIFT organization owes me a great deal of –'

'How much?' Charlie snapped. 'For Chrissake, it's not such a tough question!'

'A little over four hundred thousand US dollars. How much did you make, Mr Rose?'

There was a crunch as Elaine bit into a slice of toast. Tony braced himself for the expected eruption.

Charlie balled his fists. He looked as if he were about to start shouting, but he changed his mind. 'No idea,' he said shortly. 'I've told my accountants to holler if my personal accounts drop below five million. So far, they've been as quiet as Grant's tomb. So . . . If you can make four hundred grand a year legally, why do you want to bust into SWIFT?'

Crick gave an icy smile and tilted his head up. 'Mr Rose. Considering your vast personal fortune, I believe I am entitled to ask you the same question. Why do *you* want to break into SWIFT?'

Elaine watched Charlie carefully. It was something she had often wondered herself.

'I have my reasons,' Charlie replied guardedly.

'As I have,' said Crick, smiling at the American. 'I think it best if we agree to respect each other's motives, Mr Rose. For my part, once we have broken into SWIFT, I wish only to make one transaction. I will provide you with my expertise – in return you will finance the operation.'

Charlie's scalp went back. 'God give me patience,' he muttered, deciding that he detested the smug little Belgian. 'So now you're saying that you *can* break in SWIFT?'

Crick maintained his infuriating smile. 'I believe so.'

'How?'

'It will cost you five million dollars, Mr Rose.'

Charlie's expression became dangerously mild. 'To be spent how?'

'Four million to launch a killer satellite to destroy the SWIFT III Atlantic satellite. That's cost price, Mr Rose. It will just about cover operating expenses. Naturally, the launchers of such a satellite will require to make their profit afterwards by carrying out their own SWIFT transaction.'

86

Charlie was suspicious. 'Did you have all this figured out before we approached you?'

'That would be telling.'

'So tell.'

Crick stared at his interrogator. 'I have given the matter some thought for the past month,' he said at length. 'A purely theoretical study, you understand. A lack of funds has prevented me from putting anything into practice.'

'A problem, doctor,' said Tony, speaking for the first time. 'How do we launch a satellite without involving a government?'

'There is a privately owned German company, *Verein fur Raumschiffahrt* – the Space Exploration Society – named after the rocket pioneer group that was formed in Berlin before the war. VFR operate in Central Africa. They launch satellites using Wotan – a simple but effective three-stage solid fuel rocket that they have developed.'

'I've heard of them,' said Tony. 'They're based in Chad. They've launched a few Earth resources satellites for the smaller oil companies.'

'That is correct,' Crick confirmed.

'And they're supposed to be testing a long-range rocket based on the Wotan for Libya,' Tony added. It was a subject that his job demanded he should know something about. 'There's been a lot of pressure on the Chad government – mainly from Israel – to throw VFR out of the country.'

Crick nodded. 'I doubt if the Chad government will take much notice. Their country is very poor. Mainly desert. VFR brings in much-needed currency.'

'They also bring in trouble,' Tony commented acidly.

'Why operate in a God-forsaken place like Chad?' Elaine asked.

'One needs plenty of land to test fire rockets,' Crick answered. 'Also, the Earth's spin of sixteen hundred kilometres per hour at the equator provides a useful kick when launching satellites. It is best for launching sites to be as close to the equator as possible, you understand.'

'Hold on. Hold on,' Charlie interrupted. 'Why do we need to knock out the SWIFT satellite?'

'To ensure that *all* SWIFT transatlantic traffic is routed by landline,' Crick explained. 'To break into SWIFT, it is essential first to ensure that all its traffic is forced to use either the satellite or

87

landlines, you understand. The satellite is its own telephone exchange – it adds an additional encryption level to the traffic it handles whereas the public telephone systems do not. When the SWIFT satellite stops functioning, it will be assumed that it has sustained a meteoroid strike and all traffic will be automatically switched into the telephone landlines until the stand-by satellite is launched.'

'How long will that take?' Charlie demanded.

'About twenty days.' Crick paused. 'Once the SWIFT III satellite is knocked out, we will need no more than twenty minutes to do what we have to do.'

'How do we know that this VFR outfit will want to be included in?' Charlie wanted to know.

'I've discussed the matter in roundabout terms with them. Perhaps I should say, with Walter Reinhart. Reinhart *is* VFR. A fellow countryman of yours, Mr Rose. He bought a controlling interest in VFR five years ago when he left the Marshall Space Center. I believe he wants to pull out now. The Libyans are unreliable customers and he realizes that it's only a matter of time before Israel persuade Chad to throw him out.'

'Meaning we can drive a tough bargain on the money he wants up front?' Charlie suggested.

'Perhaps,' said Crick. He looked at Elaine. 'Can you obtain a SWIFT III terminal?'

'No problem,' Elaine replied. 'There's usually two or three in working order in our workshop.'

'Excellent.' The Belgian turned his rimless glasses on Charlie. 'We will need to build our own encryption unit, you understand. I have all the specifications and the circuit diagrams, therefore it will be no problem for a specialist electronics company. I estimate it will cost between one hundred thousand and one hundred and fifty thousand dollars.'

Charlie regarded the Belgian coldly. 'Anything else?'

'Yes. We will need a suitable control computer. There are a number of micros on the market that can be modified. I will also need the circuit diagrams for the switching of the transatlantic System M telephone exchange. A London exchange most probably. That will entail a massive bribe.'

'That's been taken care of,' said Charlie, pleased at being able to score one over the self-assured Belgian.

Crick looked surprised. 'Very good,' he conceded. 'Also we will need a software scientist. I suggest someone who is familiar with the SWIFT system. Naturally, he or she will have to be paid a substantial sum. I can provide a list.'

'That's also been taken care of,' said Charlie triumphantly, doubly pleased with himself.

'It has?'

'Yep.'

'May I ask who?'

'Damion Silvester. Ever heard of him?'

'He was at the Nice seminar,' said Elaine.

'Yes,' said Crick slowly. He paused. 'I underestimated you, Mr Rose. Damion Silvester is the best . . .'

Charlie's expression became grim. 'Don't ever underestimate me again, Crick,' he said venomously. 'You louse up on this – you take one step out of line, and not only are you in big trouble, but your daughter as well. You understand?'

Crick's air of self-assured arrogance evaporated as he met the hard black eyes. He nodded. 'Yes – I understand, Mr Rose. You've already made that clear.'

29: Washington, DC

Matt Fitzgerald was apoplectic with rage. He waved the report under Jackie's nose and came close to pounding his desk.

'You know who this went to?'

'I saw the distribution list,' said Jackie, wondering if it was possible for anyone in a rage to fulfill a cliché by bursting a blood vessel. Right now it looked very possible.

'Right up to the defence deputy secretary! Do you realize the trouble that this has caused the department?'

'You mean, for you?'

'Goddammit – I *am* the department!' Fitzgerald raved.

'Matt – listen –'

'I've been made to look an idiot because I had no idea what the hell the guy was talking about!'

'Matt –'

'Jesus Christ, if I had gotten my way over this, right now you'd be busted right out of here.'

'So you didn't get your way?' Jackie inquired. She knew that Fitzgerald's powers were limited, but he could clobber her with a three-month suspension.

Fitzgerald calmed down. He regarded Jackie with undisguised loathing. 'I'll have my way when this is over. So help me God, I will.'

Jackie was puzzled. 'When what is over?'

'You're to go to the UK.'

Jackie stared. 'I'm to what?'

'You heard.'

'What for?'

'To find out what Damion Silvester is playing at, goddammit!' Fitzgerald shouted. 'That's what for! It's nothing to do with me. It's now out of my hands!'

'It was never in them, Matt,' Jackie observed in a reasoning voice.

'Get out!'

Once outside Fitzgerald's office, Jackie thrust her hands into the pockets of her jacket and fought hard against the temptation to burst out laughing.

The door flew open. Fitzgerald appeared. 'And Miss Morrison!'

'Mr Fitzgerald?'

'Buy some clothes that fit before you leave!'

Jackie's Pokketfone bleeped just as Fitzgerald slammed his door. It was Mike Randall. She took the call in her office.

'Hi, Angelica.'

'My name's Jackie.'

'I like Angelica.'

'Why the sudden familiarity, Mr Randall?'

'I've been looking at your file. You're not married.'

'Not now,' Jackie replied.

'How'd it go with Matt Fitzgerald?'

'To say that he was mad would be an understatement.'

'I did warn you. When do you plan on leaving?'

'I thought – tomorrow. Christ – I haven't had time to think.'

'Wrong, Angelica,' said Randall. 'You're leaving for London tonight on the Eastern Airlines SST.'

'Are you giving me orders, Mr Randall?'

'You bet, Angelica. As from fifteen minutes ago, you're working for me until this thing is resolved. If you don't believe me, check your printer.'

'What about your own agents?'

'What about them?'

'Well – I'm not on your payroll. I've been with the Treasury all my –'

'Exactly,' Randall cut in. 'You've got a ready-made cover. Tax officials don't get involved in military intelligence. Also you've proved that you're a good snooper. So – your flight leaves at ten. That'll give me enough time to pick you up and take you somewhere.'

'What did you have in mind?' Jackie inquired cautiously.

'A meal followed by some sexual harassment.'

'Really? Suppose I don't feel like sexually harassing you?'

Randall laughed. 'Yet you do though – every time you speak. See you in an hour, Angelica.'

Later, over an early meal in a bar, Randall checked that no one was within earshot and toyed absent-mindedly with Jackie's fingers. It seemed such an innocent action that Jackie was loathe to remove her hand.

'One last thing, Angelica,' he said earnestly. 'The real reason behind all this panic is that the UK have agreed in principle to buy an SDI laser beam projector system. We don't want anything to get out right now that might give the British the idea that there's been a leak of vital software data to the Soviets. The deal is to be signed in London in the next few months. A visit by the President or the Vice President. Real top level stuff – that's how important it is. So keep everything low key. Don't draw attention to yourself. Don't do anything illegal and above all, don't involve our London embassy or anyone else. Report to me every day through my PCC mailbox number. Sign yourself as Angelica. Understood?'

'Understood,' said Jackie.

'Fine.' Randall dumped a shabby leather travel bag on the table. 'There's a few things in there that you might find useful, like a microdisk for your PPC computer that contains hacking information on a lot of useful computers in Europe. There's also full data on Damion Silvester plus instructions on how to use the items in the bag.'

'Hacking is illegal,' Jackie pointed out.

'Use the passwords on the disk to look at data but don't tamper with it and no one will know you've been snooping around inside their main-frames.' Randall unexpectedly leaned forward and kissed Jackie on the cheek. Late afternoon and he smelt of aftershave. And his disgusting tobacco. 'Good luck, Angelica . . . Goodbye.' He placed his finger on her lips. 'Don't say anything. And don't worry. You'll cope. God bless.'

With that he stood and walked out of the bar without looking back.

Jackie cautiously opened the bag. The first thing she noticed was a set of photographs of Damion Silvester.

30: Winchester

Photographs were also being studied on the other side of the Atlantic in Charlie's penthouse suite at the Winchester Golden Rose Hotel. Over two hundred numbered pictures were spread out on Charlie's huge glass-topped dining table.

'These are superb,' said Crick admiringly, pouring over the dozen or so pictures that Damion had taken of the first cabinet in the telephone exchange.

While Charlie looked on, Damion removed more photographs from an envelope and slid them across the table to Crick. 'And these are all the circuit diagrams. They were on the inside of each inspection panel.'

'Excellent. Excellent,' said the Belgian, making no attempt to conceal his excitement. 'These are first class.' He picked up a magnifying glass and peered closely at a particular print. 'Ah, yes. It is even possible to read the type numbers on the microprocessors.' He beamed at Charlie and Damion. 'With these pictures I can make an immediate start on the design of a demultiplexer and its wiring harness. I shall make the unit so that it fits unnoticed at the bottom of one of the cabinets.'

'How long do you need?'

'To make the demultiplexer? A month from now, it will be ready.'

'In that case you'd better get moving,' said Charlie dismissively. 'Like now.'

'Yes – of course.' Crick nodded vigorously and gathered up all the photographs. Before Baldwin showed him out, he paused at the door and said: 'Of course – it will be necessary for me to get into the exchange to install it.'

'One problem at a time,' said Charlie. 'First you build the gizmo. Okay?'

'Okay,' Crick agreed.

Once they were alone, Charlie poured whiskies for himself and Damion. 'You did well.' Compliments from Charlie were rare but he had a sneaking regard for the big man.

'So long as Crick's happy.'

'No – so long as *I'm* happy,' Charlie corrected. 'Which I am. Who processed the prints?'

'I bought some gear and did it myself.'

'In a hotel room?'

'No. I've rented an apartment in south London – Putney. Chambermaids are too nosey.'

Charlie nodded. As a hotelier, he had an innate prejudice against guests messing about with chemicals in their rooms.

'You owe me for all the gear I've had to buy and the money I've paid Billy,' said Damion.

'See Baldwin. He'll see you're okay. How did you make out with Billy?'

'He was pretty good,' said Damion, finishing his drink.

Charlie nodded while regarding Damion steadily. 'Yeah. I've always found him useful. Do you need him again?'

'No. I can get into the exchange any time now. There was a panic last time we left but no one will find out how we got in.'

'Let's hope not,' Charlie murmured. He ran his fingertip idly around the rim of his glass and regarded Damion steadily. 'If you've finished with Billy, you'll have to deal with him. He knows too much. And no arguments. No one argues with me. Okay?'

Damion met the black eyes. 'You don't have to give me orders on that Charlie. I'll be happy with him out of the way. But what about the body?'

'No problem. We've got the latest argon gas incinerator in the rear service bay. It destroys everything – even steel – and there's no staff on duty in there after midnight so you can drive your car right in. After that, you'd better get back to your apartment and lay low. Stay outta circulation until you're needed.'

'Okay. But Crick goes with me, Charlie. I don't trust that little creep to be by himself.'

'Who else don't you trust, Damion?'

'The Russian.'

'He's okay. I've got a lever on him. The whole thing was his idea anyway. What about the Fleming girl?'

'No way.'

Charlie was interested. 'Why not?'

'She once tried stringing me along. Why is she in this, Charlie?'

'She told me she's ambitious. She wants to start up her own business.'

Damion gave a cynical sneer. 'The Elaine Flemings of this world say one thing and mean another.'

Charlie was a shrewd enough judge of character to guess that few women would rank very high in Damion's estimation. 'Maybe,' he said noncommittally. 'Is there anyone you *do* trust?'

Damion leaned forward and said earnestly, 'There's going to be aspects of this operation – like what we were discussing about Billy Watts – that you and me are going to have to keep to ourselves, Charlie. Crick is just a cunt who wants to get even with SWIFT over something – I can deal with him any time he steps out of line. Suskov – maybe he's okay. But of all of us, the Fleming girl is the one with the least motive for wanting us to break into SWIFT.'

The hotelier finished his drink. 'Your trouble is that you hate women, Damion. Me – I love 'em.'

Two hours later, Charlie had another visitor. Jim Hoffman was a New York private investigator who had often worked for Charlie. He was a tall, spare man in his early fifties. He and Charlie shook hands warmly. The hotelier was genuinely pleased to see him. They had known each other a long time.

'Came as quickly as I could, Charlie,' said Hoffman. His eyes roamed around the penthouse's interior. 'Hey – no wonder we don't see so much of you these days. And the chicks in the lobby. Wow.'

Charlie grinned and poured his guest a drink. 'How's your room?'

'Unbelievable.' Hoffman took the drink and settled back in a chair.

The two men chatted about old times for a few minutes, until Charlie changed the subject.

'I've got a job for you, Jim. A big one.'

'Go ahead.'

'I want a listing of all the Mob's bank accounts.'

Hoffman's face remained impassive. 'Worldwide?'

'Worldwide. The whole goddamn lot. Particularly that country in southern Africa where they're going in big.' Charlie snapped his fingers impatiently as he tried to remember the name of the country.

'Transkei?' Hoffman suggested.

'That's it – Transkei.'

'The whole thing's a big job, Charlie.'

Charlie shrugged. 'So it's big. So I'll pay.'

'You mean all the accounts of their legal activities? The electronics companies; the hotels –'

'Everything,' Charlie interrupted. 'Every little niche throughout the world where they've got it stashed – I want to know about it. Account numbers. Names of holders. The works.'

Hoffman was too much the professional to ask why Charlie should want such information. Instead he mentally clicked up the fee that such a task could command. He would have to put a full-time investigator into southern Africa. 'Anything else?'

'How much is in the accounts if that's possible. But it's the numbers that are important. You've got three months.' Charlie poured the detective another drink. 'You don't have to tell me that it'll be dangerous, Jim. I've tangled with them. Will you do it?'

Hoffman sipped his drink and considered. Astute keyboard research – some judicious hacking would uncover sixty per cent of the information. Getting hold of the other forty per cent – especially the southern African data – would involve old-fashioned methods. Dangerous old-fashioned methods. He nodded. 'Sure, I'll do it, Charlie.'

31: Chad, Central Africa

Elaine and the Central African country of Chad did not get on even though they had known each other for less than two hours.

'Any country,' Elaine declared in a loud voice that carried across the restaurant at Ndjamena Airport, 'that has the misfortune to receive its official language from France, *and* its monetary system, *and* its independence, *and* its breakfasts, is doomed.'

Tony was tiring of making sympathetic noises. He wasn't having much success: Elaine without a breakfast inside her was proving an extremely difficult creature to pacify. Their journey to Chad had involved flight changes and long delays at Paris and Tunis; they were now waiting for word from the Red Cross that they could hitch a lift on a supply flight heading north.

They were drinking their fifth cup of coffee each when they were approached by a short, perspiring man dressed in khaki drill with a red cross sewn on his patch-pleated blouse pocket. He was holding a clipboard.

'You are the couple that wish to visit Oberth?' He spoke slowly with a strong French accent.

'That's us,' said Tony. 'Any news?'

'My name is Paul,' said the man enigmatically. 'I am the co-pilot. We are flying to Tshama in one hour but the captain has agreed to make a detour to Oberth. We cannot charge you a fare, of course, but a donation to our funds would be most acceptable.'

'Okay,' agreed Tony. 'Is a thousand francs acceptable?'

Paul gave a little bow. 'A thousand francs each will be most acceptable. We would not wish for you to pay more. The aircraft is an unsoundproofed and unpressurized DC-5. For freight only. It will not be a comfortable flight.'

'Just so long as it flies,' said Tony cheerfully.

32

Despite the heat, noise and vibration, Elaine managed to sleep during the flight, stretched out on the floor with her head propped against one of the giant bales of dressings – the only medical supplies that were not lashed to the floor of the ancient twin-engine aircraft.

Upon boarding the DC-5 she had directed a number of very pointed remarks at Tony about unfeeling people who were prepared to jeopardize her precious life by making her fly in an aircraft that belonged in a museum.

She was woken by Tony shaking her.

'We're landing in twenty minutes!' he yelled above the roar of the Wright Cyclone engines. 'You've been marvellous company!'

Elaine looked at her watch and found it hard to believe that she had slept for nearly three hours. She shouted a sarcastic remark at Tony and moved to a window. She peered down at the burning hills of the southern Sahara three thousand feet below, shading her eyes against the blinding glare of the sun reflected off the white-painted wing. Like the fuselage, the upper and lower surfaces of the wings were emblazoned with giant red crosses.

The DC-5 banked. The harsh yellow-brown landscape seemed to tilt and pivot about an unseen axis. They were flying over a featureless plain hemmed in by weather-eroded barren hills. Elaine caught a glimpse of distant buildings, shimmering mirage-like in the haze. She shouted to Tony and pointed. He joined her and cupped his hands near her ear.

'That must be Oberth!'

The DC-5 began to lose height. The temperature in the cabin rose. Elaine flattened her cheek against the vibrating window and could see a lane of white markers pegged out on the ground indicating an airstrip that was nothing more than a cleared stretch of bush. There was a rumble as the DC-5 lowered its main gear.

Two miles beyond the cluster of blockhouses and low buildings, Elaine spotted the lattice framework of what could only be a rocket service tower and gantry.

There was an unnerving jolt when the DC-5 touched down. It was followed by a series of stomach-churning lurches. The cabin floor tilted back and there was another, lesser jolt when the tailwheel bit into the dust. The spinning airscrews kicked up clouds of sand that streamed over the wings and whipped past the windows. The aircraft came to a standstill and the engines died to an idle.

'That,' said Elaine, now able to speak in a normal voice, 'has to be the worst landing I've ever experienced.'

'You've never flown with Aeroflot,' Tony commented, helping her to her feet and holding her steady on the steeply sloping floor.

Paul appeared. He opened the door and extended the folding ladder. 'A truck is on its way out to you,' he said, shaking hands with the two passengers. 'You will be in the sun for only two minutes. Our ETA tomorrow is fifteen-fifty. Please be ready.'

Tony and Elaine jumped down from the aircraft and waved to Paul. He acknowledged and pulled the door shut. The midday sun struck them as soon as they had moved clear of the wash from the propellers. The heat from the ground was already burning through the soles of their shoes by the time the aircraft had turned and was trundling down the airstrip, gathering speed.

The couple stared across the bush at the distant group of block-houses. Rising above the buildings was a water tower, and beyond that were the spherical shapes of giant liquid fuel tanks. The rocket gantry was too far away to be visible through the heat haze. 'Not my idea of a spaceport,' Elaine commented.

All that could be seen now of the DC-5 was its tailplane protruding above a cloud of dust as it lumbered down the airstrip. The roar of its engines faded. Tony was about to speak when he heard another sound: the unmistakable whine of jet engines. He gripped Elaine's forearm and pointed northwards at three dots skimming low above the hills.

'Fighters!'

Elaine shaded her eyes. 'Whose?'

'I don't know.'

The three aircraft wheeled as one, exposing their silvery, dagger-like swept-wing silhouettes. What appeared to be bombs detached themselves from the fighters' wingtips.

'Long-range fuel tanks,' Tony muttered, perplexed.

The three fighters levelled out and hurtled themselves low and incredibly fast across the plain towards the buildings. At that moment Tony suddenly realized what was going to happen even before the first salvo of air-to-ground rockets streaked away from the lead fighter. A series of blinding flashes. Then more silent explosions as the second and third fighters launched their missiles into the blockhouses.

Tony threw himself and Elaine to the ground just as the thunderous roar and shockwave from the first explosions reached them. Despite the distance, the ground seemed to heave beneath them and the terrifying concussion knocked the breath from their bodies. Tony raised his head. The fighters had separated as if each one had been assigned specific targets. There were more explosions from the direction of the rocket launching pad. Suddenly one of the liquid fuel tanks erupted, voiding a massive fireball skywards that one of the fighters actually seemed to fly through. The explosion was followed by several more as the rest of the globular tanks were hit in succession. One of the fighters banked hard, pirouetting on a wingtip as it turned. Its nose went down like the beak of a bird of prey closing on its kill and it howled towards some trucks that were speeding away from the systematic devastation. A staccato rattle of cannonfire, spurts of dust stitching across the ground followed by the trucks bursting into flames. Men could be seen leaping from the blazing vehicles – their clothes burning. Despite senses numbed by the cataclysmic events he was witnessing, Tony was certain that he could hear the anguished screams of the doomed men above the deafening roar of jet engines.

Suddenly a fighter was swelling rapidly as it thundered towards the terrified couple lying in the dust. Tony pulled his body on top of Elaine to protect her from the inevitable cannonfire. Sobbing in terror, he clenched his teeth – waiting for the hammerblows that heralded the tearing apart of his body when the shells ripped into him.

33: London

Jackie's temper and her tweed skirt travelled badly. She arrived at Heathrow with her nerves shot to pieces. The only available seat in the aircraft had been in the nonsmoking section; she had had to endure nearly four hours of gut-gnawing misery. Had her flight been nonsupersonic, the chances were that she would have slashed her wrists in the toilet. Her bad luck held long enough for her to find a taxi with a sign inside that thanked her for not smoking. Jackie decided that she could manage without the cab driver's thanks and lit up. She had smoked six cigarettes by the time the disgruntled driver deposited her at the Mercury Hotel.

Once in her room, Jackie wasted no time. After a shower and a smoke, she first checked the contents of the special travel bag that Mike Randall had provided. Its contents tended to duplicate her own possesions except for items that looked like a cordless shaver and charging pack, and a man's hairbrush kit. Like the camera and various other items, none of the contents of the bag were what they appeared to be. The travelling clock was particularly interesting and caused Jackie to smile to herself. It was a magnetic radio bug for attaching to vehicles. The associated receiver looked like an ordinary miniature radio. Whoever had prepared the items had been influenced by too many second-rate spy movies. Still, the gadgets looked businesslike and effective.

Next she unpacked her portable personal computer. There were millions of the IBM briefcase PPCs in the world, but the models issued to US government agents differed internally in a number of respects: the most important being their ability to transmit data over the world's telephone networks using noncommercial encryption.

She loaded into the computer the microdisk that Randall had put in the bag and scrolled through the telephone numbers and passwords that appeared on the computer's miniature screen. There were hundreds of them. It was as well that British customs were obsessed with searching for drugs and paid no attention to microdisks, because the listings gave Jackie the means of hacking into just about every government-owned and commercial computer in Europe.

She moistened the rubber sucker of the computer's induction modem and clamped it on the side of the hotel room's telephone. Dialling the number of the British Home Office computer produced a request for a password. Praying that the list was not out of date, she entered the appropriate password on the keyboard. The host computer's main menu appeared immediately on the computer's tiny screen. Moving the cursor to IMMIGRATION on the menu led her to the various submenus. Luckily the Home Office's program was user-friendly, therefore she had no difficulty keying through the data levels until she arrived at the passenger listings for Heathrow arrivals. She located Damion Silvester's entry. Silvester was no longer a British citizen, and therefore had been required to furnish a considerable amount of information including his UK address which he had given as the Golden Rose Hotel, Winchester.

Jackie was surprised; Damion was keeping up the deception, but was he actually staying at the hotel? She copied the screen data onto a microdisk for future reference and checked Randall's microdisk information. Sure enough, the telephone number of the Winchester Golden Rose management computer was listed together with several passwords. Jackie guessed that the computer had telephone access for the benefit of travel agents wishing to make direct bookings. It took her less than four minutes to break into one of the computer's restricted levels and access reservation and room allocation information. She soon found Silvester's entry. Damion had checked into the hotel two hours after he had cleared UK immigration. That meant that he had gone directly to the hotel. He had taken a taxi or someone had met him; it simply was not possible to clear airport formalities, hire a car or use public transport and be in Winchester in two hours.

No one else was listed as sharing his room. More out of curiosity than the playing of a hunch, Jackie called up the guest list for the date of Damion's arrival and scrolled through the names. Full passport card details were included for every guest of non-EEC nationality. Like many international hotels, the Golden Rose merely fed guests' passport cards through a reader that automatically dumped the magnetic strip data onto their own permanent mass storage. Jackie spotted something unusual among the entries that were rolling up the screen like movie credits. She quickly reverse scrolled and gazed in amazement at the entry that she had stopped in the centre of the screen:

    SURNAME: SUSKOV.
    FORENAMES: ANTON.
    NATIONALITY: CCCP.
    OCCUPATION: TASS SCIENCE CORRESPONDENT.

Jackie could scarcely credit her luck. She had hardly been in the country five hours and yet already she had established that Damion Silvester had stayed – and maybe was still staying – at the same hotel as a Soviet citizen. And no ordinary Soviet citizen either, but one who would be certain to know the value of SDI software.

Another check revealed that Anton Suskov was sharing a room with a certain Elaine Fleming – whoever she was.

Jackie sat on her bed and considered. Of course, it could all be a coincidence. After all, New York had Soviet citizens coming out of the woodwork and so did London. Damion could have got in touch with any number of them in New York instead of flying to England. Maybe Anton Suskov was just another Russian enjoying a Western lifestyle and an illicit affair. Maybe . . . Maybe not. She decided to send a report to Randall.

34: Chad, Central Africa

The scream from the aircraft's engines numbed Tony's senses as the fighter roared over them at a height of less than forty feet. He rolled off Elaine in time to catch a glimpse of the blue and white Star of David insignia on the underside of the fighter's wings. He gaped in astonishment – the holocaust that the fighters had unleashed was momentarily forgotten. The aircraft were Mark Ten Lavis of the *Chel Ha'Avir* – the Israeli Air Force.

One of the fighters closed on the DC-5 then sheered away – possibly because the pilot had spotted the red cross markings when the ancient aircraft shook off its enveloping cloud of dust and became airborne. The three fighters regrouped and swept over the hills. Then they were gone – the roar of their engines dwindling rapidly as they headed for home – sixteen hundred miles and thirty minutes' flying time to the northeast. Within seconds the only sound was the crackle of blazing buildings and the dull drone of the DC-5's engines.

That the DC-5 had been airborne for only a few moments brought home to Tony the awesome truth as he surveyed the appalling devastation and columns of black smoke spiralling lazily into the impossibly blue sky: the entire brilliantly executed attack had been carried out in less than sixty seconds.

35: Wimbledon, England

Billy peered out of the car window at the house beyond the trees.

'Is that it, guv?'

'That's it,' said Damion. He took a swig from his hip flask and returned it to his jacket pocket. As he did so, his fingers closed in anticipation around the tiny servomotor and its length of plastic strapping. 'What do you reckon?'

Billy was doubtful. 'Well – it's lonely, guv – not that that means anything. I'd rather come back in daylight.'

Damion withdrew the servomotor from his pocket. 'Fair enough, Billy. We'll come back tomorrow morning if that's okay with you.'

'That's fine, guv,' said Billy, grinning. His good-humoured expression changed to one of surprise when Damion slipped the plastic strap around his neck. 'Hey? What's this, guv?'

Damion yanked the strapping tight and started the servomotor.

'Guv?' Billy's fingers went up to the tightening strap.

Without even looking at his victim, Damion got out of the car and slammed the door shut. He walked a few yards along the deserted lane and waited. He felt for his hip flask and took a long pull. The whisky was a welcome scald at the back of his throat.

A minute passed.

Two minutes . . . How long did a man take to die? There was the sound of frantic kicking from the car but no other noises. No obscene gurgles. No sounds of death.

Damion waited five more minutes to be sure and returned to the car. Billy's body was slumped across the driver's seat. He turned the body over and looked dispassionately at the hideously contorted features. The motor was still whirring at the nape of Billy's neck, but quieter now under the enormous load. The strapping had pulled right into the flesh. Damion stopped the servomotor and pulled the strap clear with some difficulty before bundling the body into the back of the car and starting the engine. He set off for Winchester where the gas furnace was waiting to dispose of Billy Watt's body.

36: London

Jackie ventured into London and treated herself to new skirts and blouses. They were tighter than she would have preferred but, at the rate she was losing weight, they would be a perfect fit in a few weeks. The whistles she attracted in her new attire provided her ego with a considerable boost.

She dined early at a fish restaurant near Leicester Square and returned to her hotel. There was no message for her from Mike Randall in response to her report. There was nothing to do with the rest of the evening except smoke and watch television.

BBC Television's Nine O'clock news carried an update report on the Israeli attack on the rocket test centre in Chad.

'Two surviving witnesses of the air raid are shown here arriving at Paris' Charles de Gaulle airport this afternoon,' said the newsreader. 'The girl is believed to be English – Elaine Fleming of London. She was visiting the centre as an assistant to a Soviet journalist . . .'

Jackie forgot to inhale on her cigarette. She reached for the wall panel and turned up the sound.

'The couple were unwilling to discuss their experiences,' the newsreader's voice continued over a shot of the couple scurrying past journalists and filmcrews. Both were holding hands up to their faces.

They jumped into a taxi which moved off before its doors were slammed shut.

The story changed to coverage of a London demonstration against government plans to buy the American SDI anti-missile laser projector system.

Jackie kept the set on. She hoped to see the film clip again on the late-night news bulletin but was disappointed.

37

The passport officer's monitor was carefully concealed from passengers but Tony knew that trouble was looming even before the girl fed his passport card through her reader. Upon their arrival at Heathrow thirty minutes earlier, he had warned Elaine to be on her guard before he left her to go through the non-EEC passport control.

'Just a minute, Mr Suskov,' said the girl.

A man in plain clothes sitting beside the girl glanced at the hidden screen and at Tony. He took the passport card and came round from behind the desk. 'Please come with me, sir,' he requested.

Tony was shown into a small room, bare except for a table and two chairs. A large, florid man was sitting in one of the chairs. He invited Tony to occupy the other one.

'An amazing coincidence you being at Oberth when the Israelis attacked it,' the florid man observed.

'We had just arrived,' said Tony. At the florid man's request, he described exactly what had happened during that fateful sixty seconds.

'Very interesting, but why did you go?'

'I wanted to write a piece about the place. It had already received extensive coverage in the press here.'

'Why take Miss Fleming?'

'We met recently in London.'

'And now you're just good friends?'

'No,' said Tony evenly, staring the florid man straight in the eye. 'We're much more than that. We make glorious love at every opportunity.'

The questioner unwrapped a strip of chewing gum and bit on it. 'Don't mess with me, Anton.'

'I'm not messing with you or anyone,' said Tony calmly. 'I always obey the rules. We got to Oberth just as the Israelis decided to blow it up. We'd only just got off the aircraft – a Red Cross supply flight. Check with them if you don't believe me. The flight turned round and landed right after the attack. We did what we could for the survivors.'

'You knew in advance about the attack?'

'Of course I didn't know about it. Do you think I would've risked Miss Fleming's life if I knew what was going to happen?'

'You're a journalist. A nice little coup for you.'

Tony smiled. 'Had I known about the attack, I would have taken a video camera – or even an ordinary camera.'

The questioning went on for fifteen minutes and kept covering the same ground.

A Pokketfone bleeped. The florid man took a handset from his pocket and unfolded it. 'Collis . . .' He listened for a few moments. 'Yeah . . . I agree.' He snapped the handset shut and regarded Tony thoughtfully while champing on his chewing gum. 'We've been talking to your girlfriend.'

'She will confirm everything I've said.'

'All right,' the florid man said abruptly. 'You can go. Wait in the arrivals hall for Miss Fleming. We'll soon be through with her.'

Tony waited an hour. He was very worried about what sort of ordeal she was being subjected to, when she appeared, looking pale and drawn.

'What happened?' Tony asked.

'The same questions over and over again. At first they refused to accept that it was a coincidence that we should arrive at Oberth when the raid started. They went on and on at me.' She took his hand. 'Tony – I'm scared.'

'There's nothing to worry about,' he said, kissing her on the tip of her nose. For once she did not respond. 'Their questions were just routine. They had to ask them because we happened to witness something that's caused an international row.'

They left the terminal building.

'But they know I'm a director of Keytech,' Elaine pointed out while they waited for the car park courtesy bus. 'Supposing they put two and two together?'

'That's hardly likely,' said Tony. 'And besides, now that Oberth has been blown to glory, we'll have to forget the entire operation.'

38: Winchester

'We forget nothing!' said Charlie angrily, his black eyes blazing across the table at Crick and Tony in turn. 'When I set out to do something – I do it. And I don't let nothing stand in my way! Nothing!'

'This is very different, Mr Rose,' said Crick.

'Different – nothing! What's the matter with you guys? Okay – we've had a setback. So we think of another way of licking this thing. We don't give up – not when I've already sunk half a million bucks into the project.'

'Mr Rose. I understand how you feel,' said Crick. 'There is only one way of breaking into SWIFT, you understand. We have to do it through landlines – through telephones – which means knocking out the satellite. And that we cannot do. It is in a geostationary orbit thirty-five thousand kilometres above the equator. That is its security – no one can reach it. This is something you must accept.'

For a moment it looked as if Charlie was going to reach across the table and inflict violence on the Belgian. 'Don't you use that patronizing tone on me, Crick, or I'll –'

'Hold on,' Tony interrupted. 'Could we reverse the process? Could we forget the transatlantic cable method, and control the satellite? There's got to be a way of controlling it.'

'It is impossible,' said Crick flatly. 'As I have explained many times, the satellite introduces a secondary encryption level to the traffic before relaying it.'

'Maybe we could intercept the signals traffic ourselves?' Charlie suggested. 'Using an aircraft or something?'

Crick looked exasperated. 'It is impossible! All the SWIFT III earth stations on both sides of the Atlantic use narrow beam microwave signals aimed precisely at the satellite. It is impossible to intercept them.' The Belgian had an unfortunate habit of sounding like a schoolmaster talking down to a class of particularly dense pupils.

Tony saw that Charlie was about to explode. 'Doctor Crick,' he intervened quickly. 'If you had unlimited funds, how would you carry out the operation?'

Crick shrugged. 'It is an academic question.'

'So give us an academic answer.'

The Belgian thought carefully. 'With unlimited funds, the problem becomes much easier. I would use two satellites. One to disable the SWIFT satellite, and a duplicate of the SWIFT satellite but without the internal encryption circuitry. I would destroy the real satellite and, at precisely the same time, bring the duplicate satellite on line. The duplicate satellite would handle all the SWIFT traffic in the normal manner so that no one would realize what had happened, and, of course, I would have total control over it by means of a radio uplink and downlink. That way I could break into SWIFT at any time I wished. I would also have to blow up the international telephone exchange to ensure that all verifications for large transactions were routed through the duplicate satellite and not sent by landline.' Crick smiled benignly at Tony. 'Does that answer your question?'

'How easy would it be for you to build a duplicate satellite?'

Crick gave a patronizing smirk. 'Once I had the drawings and specifications, it would be very easy.' Crick's smirk broadened. 'As for destroying the real SWIFT satellite and replacing it with my own – no problem. I would merely go along to NASA with ten million dollars and my killer satellite and my duplicate satellite, and rent cargo space on the next shuttle flight. Of course, NASA might prove a little reluctant to accept the contract; they like to know the precise purpose of every payload they carry.' The Belgian was barely able to suppress his laughter when he looked at Tony and added: 'But there's always your countrymen, Tony. There's always the Russians. Ever eager to help.'

Tony had been thinking along similar lines but not in the same humorous vein as Crick. He jumped to his feet and moved to the door. 'Charlie,' he said earnestly. 'Keep the team together for a few more days. At least until I've had a chance to sound out some contacts.'

'What contacts?' Charlie demanded suspiciously.

But Tony had gone.

The unashamed decadence of the lobby at the Winchester Golden Rose did not equate well with Jackie's strict Methodist upbringing. Viewed from the plush main entrance, the giant hologram wall murals looked innocent enough, but as one approached the main desk, so the bronzed young people depicted in the pictures shed more of their clothes and adopted more erotic postures. God knows what they were up to on the way to the elevators.

The hotel receptionist was dressed in a toreador outfit that had to be the ruin of imaginative masculine thinking – especially when she bent over a computer terminal to deal with Jackie's query.

'No, miss,' she said. 'Mr Silvester left a few days ago. But we're still holding his suite for him.'

Jackie knew that from her hacking into the hotel's computer. 'Did he leave a forwarding address? I'm supposed to look him up.'

The girl checked the bank of pigeonholes. 'No, miss.'

'Can you fix me up with a room please? One at the front?'

'We have only suites, miss.'

'Okay – a suite for . . . four nights.'

The girl bent over the keyboard again. 'Yes, miss. Suite 277. It's the only one we have free. Two hundred and seventy pounds per night.'

'What!'

The girl smiled. 'The suites at the front are our economy accommodation, miss.'

'What's your idea of an uneconomical suite?'

'It is a beautiful suite. I'll show you what it looks like.' The girl's fingers danced over her keyboard. A hologram monitor glowed and depicted a wide-angle shot of a hotel room. A female voice-over extolled the virtues of the accommodation. A series of close-ups started with the bathroom and ended with a panoramic view of the hotel's car park and gateway.

'That's definitely the view from the window of Room 277?' Jackie queried.

'Yes, miss,' said the girl, sounding slightly apologetic.

'I'll take it.'

'May I have your passport and a charge card please? We accept all cards.'

'One thing,' Jackie instructed, handing over the cards. 'If Mr Silvester shows up, please don't mention me. I want to give him a surprise.'

'Very well, miss. That's no problem.'

Jackie was shown to her suite by a smiling young lady who introduced herself as Emma and who insisted on placing Jackie's travel bag and briefcase computer on an electric cart. On the way to the lifts, Jackie discovered what the young people in the holograms were doing, and following Emma's swaying hips along a corridor made her realize why Golden Rose hotels attracted noisy, feminist demonstrations.

Once in her room, Jackie offered Emma a tip.

'Oh, no, miss,' she said, giving Jackie a smile that contained more promises than a wedding ceremony. Clearly the hotel's staff had a degree of versatility inasmuch that they seemed prepared to cater for either sex. 'We're not allowed to accept any money from guests – no matter what services we provide.'

'Or what sex the guests are?' Jackie queried.

The girl giggled and explained the features of the room. She gave Jackie a key card and left. Jackie gazed speculatively at a vast round bed with its black silk sheets. The hologram recording in the lobby had not done the room justice. *Black silk sheets!* She preferred not to think about the pleasures available on the giant wall screen facing the bed. As soon as she was alone, she waded through the shaggy carpet that resembled the pelt of a woolly mammoth and positioned a reclining chair so that she could keep the hotel's front entrance under observation in comfort. She wondered if there were likely to be awkward questions when she filed her expenses. Two hundred and seventy pounds per night!

She lit her first cigarette. Just as she was exhaling for the third time, a distant alarm started howling. Running feet in the passageway. Her door buzzer frantically sounding off. Jackie glanced at the closed-circuit security monitor. Emma was standing outside in the corridor. Jackie opened the door and was confronted by the girl clutching a lethal-looking fire extinguisher. At first Jackie thought it was an overture that heralded the start of an interesting sexual escapade.

'Oh, Miss Morrison,' said Emma reproachfully, when she saw Jackie's smouldering cigarette. 'This is a nonsmoking floor. Didn't you see the signs in the corridor? The smoke alarms are very sensitive on this floor. It's lucky you didn't set off the sprinklers.'

Jackie muttered a hurried apology and returned to her seat. Two hundred and seventy pounds a night and she couldn't smoke!

She called the front desk and asked them to fix her up with a rented car. 'And not a nonsmoking car,' was her caustic, parting instruction to the receptionist.

The coming and going of guests during the following three hours was of no interest, although she did sit up and take notice when Elaine Fleming and Anton Suskov walked across the car park, deep in conversation, their expressions serious. They climbed into a red Skoda and drove off at speed.

Jackie noted down the car number. Mike Randall had advised her in answer to her last report that Anton Suskov's presence at the hotel was certain to be coincidental. Suskov was a 'legal' – a resident in the UK and subject to strict controls by the British Foreign Office. If Silvester was passing information to the Soviets, it was unlikely that they would use someone as obvious as Suskov as a go-between. It had to be someone else. The trouble was, the trail had gone cold. Damion Silvester had disappeared.

Jackie resigned herself to a long, cigaretteless vigil in surroundings she did not wholly approve of.

40: London

Despite the fine weather, Penn Ponds in the centre of Richmond Park were deserted. Tony pointed through the car windscreen to a short, thickset shape that was making its way from the car park to the edge of the larger of the two lakes. 'That,' he said to Elaine, 'is my boss.'

'Why don't you meet him in the Tass office in town?'

Tony laughed. 'Gregor watches too many spy movies. Also, this way he can claim a day's travelling expenses.' He kissed her lightly and opened the car door. 'This won't take long.'

Tony walked up behind the unsuspecting Russian and clapped him heartily on the back. 'Good morning, Gregor. For a man with no soul, you pick some delightful places to meet.'

Gregor scowled. 'I thought you might have trouble finding this place,' he commented icily in Russian.

'Oh. Why?'

'I saw you on television. Geography is not your strong subject. Most people know the difference between Africa and Spain.'

'But you gave me permission to travel,' Tony protested.

'I said you could go to Spain.'

Tony decided not to argue the point. He needed Gregor's cooperation. He picked up a stone and sent it skimming across the lake. 'I'm sorry about the misunderstanding, Gregor.'

'Is it true you saw the Israeli raid on Oberth?'

'Yes. That's why I need your help.'

'Why?'

'I want you to arrange a meeting for me with Academician Yuri Grechko.'

Gregor looked sharply at Tony. Yuri Grechko was the director of the Leibenov Institute. More importantly, he was chairman of the Council of Ministers Scientific Advisory Commitee and, as such, held an ex-officio seat on the Supreme Soviet and the Politburo. With his access to the Chairman himself, Academician Grechko was one of the most influential men in the Soviet Union.

'Why do you want to see him?'

'Because of what I saw at Oberth, I believe it imperative that I report to him direct.'

'I doubt it,' Gregor remarked drily. 'And what did you see?'

Tony sent another stone skipping across the water. He had rehearsed himself for this moment. The slightest miscalculation in the delicate gauging of Gregor's reaction could ruin the whole thing. 'I mean no disrespect, Gregor, but this thing is so sensitive, I think it best if I reported only to Comrade Grechko.'

'I have a right to know the subject matter,' said Gregor tartly.

Tony hesitated for what he prayed was just the right length of time. 'Somehow the Israelis have got hold of our latest SA-20 air-to-surface missiles.'

Gregor looked scathing. 'That is not possible.'

Tony looked his superior straight in the eye and said softly, 'I saw them, Gregor. I saw them mounted on the underbelly of a fighter as it flew over me. They were so close, I could virtually reach out and touch them. They were SA-20s. Someone, somewhere in a high position has made a monumental error. How else could the Israelis have laid their hands on such a missile? Can you imagine the reaction among our allies if this leaks out? It could undermine the Warsaw Pact itself. We can't go to the Ministry of Defence because it could well be a defence minister who is to blame. There will be a cover-up. That means going to the top.' Tony paused and glanced sideways at his chief. It looked as if the story had been swallowed but one could never be sure with Gregor. Now for a little bolstering of Gregor's ego. 'It's a very serious matter, Gregor. It will reflect well on you if you refer me direct to Comrade Grechko. A report sent through the normal channels would be seen by too many people.'

Gregor was deep in thought for some moments. He kicked absent-mindedly at a pebble. Eventually he nodded. 'Very well. You had better leave for Moscow immediately and wait at your apartment while I make the necessary arrangements. You realize that if this goes wrong, you're finished?'

'Yes,' said Tony seriously. 'I realize that only too well.'

41: Winchester

Jackie watched Tony drive away from the hotel. Elaine Fleming wasn't with him this time. Jackie had a sudden thought. Angry with herself for not thinking of it before, she opened her PCC, hooked it up to the telephone and dialled into the hotel's computer. Within three minutes she established that Suskov and the English girl had been staying at the Golden Rose for two weeks. Two weeks in a suite that was double the price of her suite? How much did Tass pay their correspondents? Or was the girl paying? If so, who was she and how could she afford that sort of money?

42: Moscow

Tony took an Aeroflot flight from Heathrow that afternoon and was back in his apartment overlooking Zukov Square by 9.00 pm. As expected, the place had been broken into. Everywhere was a mess; his portable television stolen. Soviet television used the French outmoded SECAM colour system instead of the European Super PAL system with the result that compatible sets were unobtainable in London. Televisions capable of receiving world satellite broadcasts were available only to a few privileged party members. This time Tony didn't care about the robbery. Instead he experienced a curious sense of detachment as he surveyed the mindless damage that the burglars had causd. They had taken most of his clothes – not that it mattered: his best stuff was in London as were his compact disk albums and his tapes, and nearly everything else he valued. Moscow was no longer his home. He no longer even felt that he was a Soviet citizen. God willing, he wouldn't be one for much longer.

There was nothing for him to do except wait for a telephone call. His country didn't even have a cellular radio Pokketfone network. It meant that he would have to remain in his flat. He made a start on clearing up the mess.

43

Tony's telephone rang. It had to be the long-awaited call. He snatched up the receiver.

'Anton Suskov?' A man's voice.

'Yes.'

'I am sorry to call you so late, comrade. You wish to see Academician Grechko. I am his secretary. A car will call for you at 8.30 tomorrow morning. Please be ready.'

'I will be,' Tony promised. The line went dead. No chance to say thank you or goodbye.

At 11.00 pm a party of drunken soldiers on leave began brawling on the communal lawns ten floors below. In an effort to cut down on the injuries among soldiers, all liquor sold in Moscow was now supplied in plastic bottles, but that did not stop them half-killing each other in hand-to-hand combat.

Tony listened to the sounds of battle while lying in bed. Eventually he drifted off to sleep and dreamed of Elaine and the high-flying life style that they would soon be sharing.

44

The car, an official Zim, arrived for Tony on time and whisked him through the southern suburbs of Moscow. After a thirty-minute drive, they stopped outside the front gates of an imposing nineteenth-century redbrick mansion set amid well-tended lawns and flowerbeds. The place was as beautifully kept as it had been during the days when it had been the Moscow home of Czar Nicholas II's Minister of Agriculture. Now it was the headquarters of the prestigious Leibenov Institute – the centre that carried out assessments on every item of Western technological hardware that the Soviet Union could get her hands on. Here was where the contents of diplo-matic bags from Soviet missions all over the world ended up: new micro-processors, video cameras, even entire defence systems in those cases where the KGB had pulled off a major coup. All were grist for the Leibenov Institute's laboratories and workshops that were staffed with some of the best scientists, technologists and instrument-makers in the country. No matter how sophisticated the equipment that was passed on to the Leibenov Institute, it could be duplicated and sometimes improved on.

Two guards carefully checked Tony's identity cards by feeding them through a reader before opening the gates and waving the car forward. The clang of the gates closing behind the car caused Tony to give an involuntary shudder. If this business went wrong, there would be gates slamming shut behind him for many years to come.

After more identity checks, Tony was shown by a male secretary into an austere office on the ground floor.

'Anton Suskov, Academician,' said the secretary, and promptly departed.

Yuri Grechko pushed aside his electronic memory pad immediately. He was a man who had no need to inflate his ego in the presence of visitors by continuing to write. He was a large, donnish-looking man with a deceptively warm smile and a powerful handshake.

'Please, Comrade Suskov,' he said, waving a huge hand genially at an empty chair. 'I know who you are and you know who I am. So let us not bother with introductions and such. You have precisely fifteen minutes of my time. Please start talking.'

Tony talked. He talked for ten minutes. Nervously at first and then with mounting confidence when Grechko didn't interrupt him and yell for the guards. Instead the Soviet scientist listened intently to Tony's story – his chair tipped back, fingers steepled together. Occasionally he made a note on his memory pad but he made no attempt to interrupt.

Tony told Grechko everything: his meeting with Charlie; the

kidnapping of Hans Crick's daughter; the planning of the SWIFT break-in; the abortive visit to Oberth. He told the truth although he was careful not to mention his motives for wanting to get involved in the enterprise – an omission that he felt certain would not escape the scientist's notice. He finished the account by outlining why the project had ground to a standstill.

The academician regarded Tony for some moments without speaking. He looked at his watch and picked up his telephone. 'Peter – my appointment with First Deputy Minister Mikolovitch in thirty minutes. Cancel it.' Grechko replaced the telephone and continued staring at Tony.

Embarrassed, Tony blurted out: 'If I have done wrong, comrade, then I am prepared to face the consequences of my actions.'

Grechko grunted and allowed his chair to tip forward. '*If* you've done wrong, Suskov? *If*? There is no *if* about it. I'm not a judge, but I should imagine that this can earn you at least ten years in the East. Possibly more. What I want to know is, why have you done this incredibly stupid thing?'

'I wanted to learn all I could about the weaknesses of the Western banking system,' Tony answered. And then he took a gamble by saying: 'SWIFT dominates the entire banking system of the West and yet we know virtually nothing about it. Knowledge is power, Comrade Grechko, as I'm sure you will agree, otherwise there would be no Leibenov Institute. I have found out more about SWIFT in a few weeks than all our operatives put together in as many years. I can let you have full details – even photographs of the leased line switching systems *and* their circuit diagrams, and a lot more besides.'

For a few moments there was silence. Tony had no idea how much his country knew about SWIFT; he had guessed that it would be very little.

'I agree we know very little about SWIFT,' Grechko conceded. 'Simply because we do not need to know. It is an electronic mail system. So what if it handles billions of dollars' worth of transactions in a working day? It is of little interest to us. There is Western information much more important than SWIFT which concerns us. It is essential that all efforts to obtain such information are properly coordinated and that individuals do not operate on their own initiative, squandering the state's resources, obtaining information on what they *think* is important.'

'May I speak freely, Comrade Grechko?'

The scientist made an expansive gesture.

'I believe that we should help Charlie Rose's group,' said Tony earnestly. 'We should launch a killer satellite to knock out the SWIFT satellite and launch a duplicate SWIFT satellite. I believe that we should allow Charlie Rose and Crick and the others to help themselves to funds – just enough for the SWIFT authorities to think there's been a mistake and for them not to suspect that there is anything wrong with their satellite. But *we* retain control of the duplicate satellite until such time as it is needed.'

'Why?'

The question annoyed Tony. The answer should have been obvious to a man of Grechko's intellect. 'It would be an incredibly powerful weapon in our hands, comrade. We could exercise control over world finances at any time that suited us. We could even wipe out the overseas currency holdings of any country. I believe the scheme should at least be considered.'

For some seconds Grechko stared at the inevitable picture of Lenin on his wall as if it could provide inspiration. His gaze switched to Tony. There was a decided chill in his voice when he finally spoke. 'Your passport please, comrade.' The scientist took the plastic card from Tony and noted down its number. 'A block will be placed on your passport. You will not be permitted to leave the country until it has been lifted. For the time being you will return to your apartment and stay there until further notice.'

45

To the accompaniment of screaming rubber, the Chairman's car bounced off the crash barrier and spun on a patch of oil like a wind devil before hurling itself back into the crash barrier.

'You have crashed!' grated a crude electronic voice in English, stating the obvious.

'Five hundred points less than my score,' Grechko announced.

The Chairman chuckled delightedly and climbed out of the ancient arcade booth. 'Very well, Yuri. But you can drive. I cannot. Come and try my latest acquisition.' The Soviet leader took Grechko by the arm and steered him past the private collection of vintage arcade video games to a large, gaudily decorated unit with a small screen and a single joystick control.

'The original Space Invaders,' said the Chairman proudly. 'The game that started it all back in the seventies. A secretary found it in a bar, would you believe. All these years it's been right under my nose.'

For the next five minutes the two men happily zapped away at the rows of marching electronic aliens. Grechko's score was lagging badly when he decided to resume the conversation. 'Well, Constantin? What do you think?'

'About the SWIFT business?' The Chairman chuckled. 'As a weapon, having control of the SWIFT system is useless.' The party leader thumped the games machine triumphantly when he cleared the screen of aliens and went into a third round.

'Oh?' said Grechko guardedly. 'Why?'

'The days of secret weapons are over, Yuri. A weapon one has to be secretive about is a useless weapon. One cannot use it as a bargaining chip. The merest hint to the SWIFT society that we have control of their precious satellite and they will stop using it immediately. You see the problem?'

Grechko nodded. 'I understand, Constantin.'

The Chairman stopped playing and straightened. He smiled at Grechko. 'But as a tool – it is superb. Exactly what we need.'

Grechko frowned. 'I don't follow you.'

The Chairman gestured impatiently. 'I am thinking about grain and all the millions of tonnes we are certain to need from America next year, and all the unpopular austerity measures that we will have to introduce yet again to pay for it. You say that this SWIFT satellite is now used by the London and New York money markets for the exchange of information on price movements?'

Grechko nodded. He had a sudden inkling of what was coming.

'So,' continued the Chairman. 'We use SWIFT – not to move money but to feed false information into the Western financial system. News reaching London that the dollar is plunging in New York will start a wave of panic-selling; the almighty dollar will suffer a catastrophic crash. We trade gold for cheap dollars, so that by the time the value of the dollar has returned to normal, we will have sufficient dollar reserves to buy back the gold *and* finance our grain purchases.'

'The break into SWIFT is certain to be discovered,' Grechko pointed out.

'Of course it will be discovered, Yuri. Of course.' The Chairman started a new game of Space Invaders. 'But if what you say is correct, we need only a mere sixty minutes. Perhaps not even that. We all know how quickly a currency can crash. The collapse of the dollar in London will lead to genuine panic-crashes on all the European markets. Panic breeds panic, Yuri. In fifteen minutes we could net billions of dollars.' The Chairman cleared an entire screen of aliens. He paused and looked reflective. 'There will be a huge row afterwards. Smaller countries will lose everything. If the operation goes ahead, there will have to be very positive safeguards to protect the good name of the Soviet Union.'

Grechko considered the implications and chuckled. 'I think the go-between has a much more modest operation in mind.'

'Let him go on thinking that. A double double-cross has a certain appeal, don't you think, Yuri?'

46

The following day, Tony was taken to the Leibenov Institute and given very precise instructions by Grechko. At the end of two hours' intensive briefing, the academician was satisfied that Tony had memorized every detail.

'The yacht is most important,' stressed Grechko, gathering up the papers and sketches that littered his desk and pushing them into a file marked 'SWIFT'. 'We need six point two metres' clearance between the underside of the deck and the keel to accommodate the rocket launcher in the retracted position.' The scientist held out his hand. 'Good luck.'

The two men shook hands. Hardly able to believe that his incredible gamble looked like paying off, Tony was then driven back to his apartment. The car waited while he packed his few things and then took him direct to the airport. He had just enough time to make a hurried call to Elaine before his flight was called. A prearranged phrase let her know that everything was okay.

47: London

Elaine was waiting for Tony at Heathrow. She threw her arms around him. The passionate nature of her kiss caught him off guard. He disentangled himself and smiled into her jade-green eyes. 'I bet you greet all your men like that provided they treat you to a decent breakfast. Or better still – several breakfasts.'

Elaine clung happily to Tony's arm as they walked to the short-term car park. 'All I want to have with you,' she said impishly, 'are indecent breakfasts. Thousands of them – stretching into a dim and distant and very decadent future.' She kissed him again when they got into the car. 'I thought I'd never see you again. I thought maybe they'd send you to Siberia.'

Tony laughed and started the engine. 'Those days are over,' he said, wishing that they were. 'There's some ultra-modern cities in Siberia where no one wants to live. Have you got your overnight things?'

'In the back.'

'I think,' said Tony, as he drove out of the car park, 'that we ought to see Charlie immediately.'

On the drive to Winchester, Tony outlined to Elaine the nature of the deal that the Soviets were prepared to enter into with Charlie.

'Christ,' Elaine muttered. 'I wonder how he'll react to the idea of collaborating with the Russians?'

48: Winchester

Charlie's black eyes blazed fury. 'No! No! No!' He strode across his penthouse living room and stood threateningly over Tony. 'No way do I do a deal with the Russians. No way. And who the hell said you could go to them?'

'I thought it was clear that I was going to approach them,' Tony stated.

'Like hell it was. Baldwin! Throw this creep out. And his girlfriend. I don't want to see them again.'

'Now just a minute –' Crick began.

'You stay out of this!' Charlie snarled, rounding on the Belgian.

'What are you scared of, Charlie?' asked Elaine.

'I'm not scared of nothing! I just don't do no deal with the Russians.'

'Is it because you don't understand them, Charlie?' Elaine queried, wondering if she was going too far. 'Or because you don't trust them?'

Surprisingly, Charlie did not lose his temper. He stared at Elaine and appeared to calm down. 'I just don't like them. This bust into SWIFT. What I want when we've busted in, is to do America a service. A big service. Now I know you Europeans don't understand patriotism. That's your problem. But it just so happens that I love America. It's done okay for me. We bring in the Russians on this and you can bet your life they don't want in for the excitement – they want to screw America. Well, I ain't helping anyone do that.'

The impassioned statement aroused Elaine's curiosity. 'How can you hope to do America a service by breaking into SWIFT, Charlie?'

Charlie realized that he had said too much. 'Forget it,' he muttered.

Elaine was not prepared to forget it. She wanted to know. 'But –'

'I said forget it!' Charlie snapped.

'Just a minute please,' Crick interjected. 'I would like to ask Tony something. Why do the Russians want to help us?'

Tony cleared his throat. 'They will give us all the help we need subject to certain conditions. Their interest in the operation is simple: they want two hundred million pounds transferred from the Bank of England to one of their accounts in Switzerland.'

Charlie was suspicious. The amount seemed ludicrously small compared with the transfers that were possible. 'Two hundred million? Is that all?'

'The two hundred million represents the money plus interest that Czar Nicholas secreted away in London before the revolution,' Tony explained. 'Money that belongs to the Soviet people.'

Crick nodded understandingly. 'Ah, yes. Of course. The dispute over the Czar's fortune has been dragging on for nearly a century now. It is entirely in accordance with the Soviet character that they would wish to do such a thing.'

Charlie was puzzled. 'Now just wait a minute. Hold on. Are you telling me that the Russians just want to get their own money back?'

'That's right, Charlie,' Tony commented, watching the hotelier carefully.

'Two hundred million pounds? And in all these years they've done nothing about getting it back? Jesus. If someone owed me a thousandth of that . . .' He left the sentence unfinished.

'I think,' said Crick, judging Charlie's mood extremely well, 'that it would be a good idea if we listened to the conditions that Tony was about to mention.'

Charlie sank into a chair and waved a hand disinterestedly. 'Go ahead. But I don't do no deal with the Russians.'

'Tony?' Crick prompted.

'Condition One,' said Tony. 'The Soviets do not want their part in the operation to become known.'

'That's fair,' Crick commented, looking keenly at Charlie.

'Condition Two. They'll move an existing killer satellite already in geostationary orbit near the SWIFT satellite to destroy it.'

'That sounds feasible,' Crick agreed. 'The geostationary satellite belt is already crowded with communication satellites. And despite international agreements, the belt is infested with Soviet killer satellites. Timing will be crucial, you understand. The duplicate satellite will have to be activated at the precise second that the real satellite is destroyed.'

'Condition Three,' Tony continued. 'The duplicate satellite must not be launched from Soviet soil.'

Crick frowned. 'Then how is it to be launched? Ah. From a Soviet submarine? Yes?'

'I'm coming to that,' said Tony. 'Condition Four. The duplicate satellite must not contain any Soviet-made components or materials. It has to appear to be of Western design and manufacture.'

'Why?' Charlie wanted to know.

'Simple. At a later date the duplicate is likely to be recovered by a US space shuttle. There must be nothing about the satellite's design and manufacture that implicates the Soviet Union in any way whatsoever.'

'The conditions are not unreasonable,' said Crick excitedly. 'Mr Rose. We must go ahead.'

'Goddamn Ruskies,' Charlie growled. 'They'll zap the SWIFT gizmo for us and that's it. They don't give us nothing else.'

'On the contrary,' said Tony, laying a slip of paper on the table. 'They've given us quite a lot.'

'What's that?' Charlie demanded.

'A bank draft for two million dollars.'

The hotelier and Crick looked surprised.

'The ironic thing is,' Tony continued, 'this draft will be processed by SWIFT III when we use it.'

'Use it for what?' asked Charlie.

'To buy a luxury yacht. A large one, Charlie. Somewhere in the region of a thousand tonnes.'

'Two million dollars won't be enough,' Crick commented.

'That's right,' said Tony carefully. 'Condition Five, Charlie – you're to match this draft with your fifty per cent share of the cost of the operation, less what you've already spent. If you decide not to, then this amount will be doubled and the operation goes ahead without you.'

'Jesus Christ!' Charlie snarled, his black eyes blazing. 'No one blackmails me. No one!'

Tony controlled his temper. Charlie's reaction was what he had been expecting. 'No one's trying to blackmail you, Charlie. It's a straightforward business deal. You have until midday tomorrow to think it over.'

49: London

Radio surveillance mobile tracers – known in the trade as buggy bugs – work brilliantly well in fiction and hardly at all in reality. The London Metropolitan Police discovered this during the mid-1980s when, to keep up with their fictional TV image, they started experimenting with bugs planted on suspects' cars. The experiments were an expensive failure. The main problem being that bugs invariably have to be attached to the underside of vehicles which is just about the worst possible position to install a radio transmitter. The other problem is size: to avoid detection, buggy bugs have to be small. This limits their antenna size which means that they have to operate on UHF frequencies. At such frequencies, radio signals tend to behave like light – that is to say, decent reception is only possible on a line-of-sight basis: the signals bounce off buildings rather than carry through them. Also, the higher the frequency, the more power is required for a given output. Bugs, by their very nature, have to transmit a continuous signal which entails a heavy drain on batteries.

Even bugs fitted with the latest lithium batteries have an effective life of only a few hours before the signal is so weak, it can be detected only by a receiver in a vehicle within a few yards – a factor which makes the original planting of the bug somewhat pointless. One solution the police tried was to power the bug off the vehicle's battery. This worked amazingly well but not in the way that the police intended: in one notable case, they knew exactly where a suspect's vehicle was because their bug had flattened his battery so that he was unable to start his car. Refusing to be defeated, the police then resorted to bulky external battery packs which, like the bugs themselves, were magnetically attached to the underside of a vehicle. The first car they tried the battery pack idea on was a Rolls Royce belonging to an industrialist who was suspected of breaking the United Nations' embargo on the supply of arms to South Africa. His chauffeur discovered the battery pack and called the local police, who called the Army bomb disposal squad who, with their motto 'if it sprouts wires – blow it up', did just that – Rolls Royce included. After paying out compensation, the Metropolitan Police decided that they had had enough of buggy bugs.

US law enforcement agencies were not so easily discouraged because America, with its long, straight and usually solitary highways, made buggy bugs a more practical proposition. Indeed the bug that Jackie had clipped to the underside of Tony's car was the latest product of the very best of American technology. The receiver, beside her on the front seat of her rented car, had a pair of automatic phasing antennas which provided continuous information on the direction of the bug. Unfortunately, neither it nor the bug worked too well; as soon as the red Skoda she was following disappeared over the brow of a hill, the receiver stopped buzzing. The wretched equipment only worked provided she kept the Skoda in sight. This was easy enough on the A31 trunk road, but she eventually lost track of the Skoda and its two occupants in the melee of West London's traffic.

By the time she was stuck in a Brompton Road snarl-up, the receiver was totally silent. She drove past Harrods and tried to double back using side streets. After ten minutes of confrontations with one-way streets and no entry signs, she was lost and the receiver beside her silent. She spent a frustrating hour cruising the streets of West London, but there wasn't even the faintest of buzzes from the

123

receiver.

Eventually she parked in a side street in Fulham and had lunch in the first public house she could find. She was angry: angry with herself and angry with the bug that had failed to live up to expectations. She had decided to follow Anton Suskov and Elaine Fleming purely on a hunch. And now she had lost them. With her luck, she thought ruefully, the chances were that the elusive Damion Silvester had probably turned up at the Golden Rose Hotel in her absence and then promptly disappeared again.

50

Had Jackie managed to keep track of Tony and Elaine, she would have been even angrier with herself at first because the purpose of the couple's London trip seemed to be nothing more incriminating than a shopping expedition for clothes. But, after the third expensive store they visited in Knightsbridge, Jackie would have had her naturally suspicious nature aroused by the amount of money they were spending. By early afternoon, after a further five visits, they had got through nearly twenty-five thousand pounds on clothes and jewellery. Tony's gold Rolex alone cost five thousand pounds. They laughingly piled into the illegally parked Skoda, and hugged and kissed each other while the taxi they had commandeered and loaded to the headlining with a cargo of parcels waited patiently. Eventually the convoy moved off.

Jackie's streak of bad luck continued. The sudden shock of the cool air and bright daylight that was lying in wait for her outside the pub at chucking-out time brought home to her that maybe, just maybe, three whiskies was a touch over the top when it came to driving. She had forgotten that one result of her diet, as well as a figure that she was proud of, was that she could no longer hold her liquor like she used to. Not that there was much danger of her driving because she couldn't find her rented car anyway. After thirty minutes of unsteady walking around backstreets that all looked the same, she was in danger of committing the ultimate crime for an agent of drawing attention to herself. She sat on a bench and smoked a cigarette. When she had calmed down, she realized that her search was not helped by the fact that she didn't even know the car's registration number, nor was she certain of its make. Also her memory was hazy as regards to its colour. Maybe enlisting police help to find it was not such a good idea. Perhaps she'd have better luck finding it in a couple of hours when the effect of the drink had worn off.

51

Elaine kicked aside some empty boxes and paraded into the middle of the living room of Damion's Putney flat. She spun around, impersonating a simpering photographic model, and blew kisses at a nonexistent camera. Her gauze-like De Vere evening dress floated around her, following her body like a cloud of gossamer smoke. Damion and Tony enthusiastically applauded her performance. She laughed at the two men's expressions and tried to dance a few steps but the floor was too crowded with parcels.

'What do you think?'

'Fantastic,' said Damion, shaking his head.

'Five hundred pounds,' said Elaine proudly.

'Jesus Christ! Charlie will go nuts.'

'It was his idea,' said Tony. He twisted his lips and, in a good imitation of Charlie's bark, snarled, 'If you kids are gonna front for me, you gotta do it proper.'

'He was hard to talk round?' Damion asked.

'You could say,' said Tony.

Damion's eyes were suddenly hard. 'Yeah – well I don't like the idea of having the Russians in as partners either. If they double-cross us in any way, I won't hesitate to kill you, Suskov.'

There was an embarrassed silence.

Elaine broke the tension with a light laugh. 'There's no double-crossing involved. We're partners with the Russians. They're sharing fifty per cent of the cost.'

'That sort of money's nothing to them,' said Damion sourly.

Elaine flounced her dress. 'And the cost of this thing is nothing compared with what his lordship spent on that suit,' she said airily, to change the subject. 'And have you seen the rings? Where are the rings, Tony?'

Tony took hold of Elaine's left hand and slipped a diamond

125

engagement ring and a wedding ring on her finger. 'I now pronounce us man and wife,' he said solemnly, kissing her hand and cheek in turn. He encircled an arm around her waist. 'Mr and Mrs Anthony Karn,' he said proudly.

Elaine smiled happily. 'Do we look the part, Damion?'

Damion's expression was cynical. 'Yeah – you look like you've been married for years.'

Tony was serious. 'Yes – but do we look as if we're used to wealth?'

'As if you were born to it.'

Tony examined his immaculate reflection in a mirror and thought of the drab suit that two months' salary would buy in Moscow. 'If my boss could see me now.' He gave Elaine a playful dig. 'Come on – put on something devastating, my angel. We've got work to do.'

'What's next on your agenda?' Damion asked.

'The boat,' said Elaine.

'Not the boat,' Tony corrected. 'The yacht.'

Damion was surprised. '*You* two are handling that as well?'

'Sure. Charlie wants to stay well in the background.'

'For Chrissake don't make a mess of it.'

52

Although Price, Kenton and Partners were not London's largest yacht brokers, they were certainly the most bent. They had a number of suspect yachts on their books and, because of their strange accountancy practices, they kept a number of suspect books on a yacht where they could be disposed of in a hurry. Young Oliver Kenton – 'Oily' to his few friends and many enemies – had fought his way from the bottom in his business using his special skills in arranging insurance fires, dubious Lloyds A1 certificates, and handsome bribes for those marine architects who were not fooled by the practice of adding sawdust to the sump oil of expensive diesel engines with buggered main bearings. An above-average number of motor yachts on his books had blown engines as a result of being chased in the Caribbean, sometimes for days at a time, by US Coastguard cutters anxious to find out why the yachts were so reluctant to be searched for drugs. Other yachts that Price, Kenton and Partners were responsible for were in such a state of neglect that no reputable broker would touch them.

But there was nothing about their plush Park Lane offices to suggest that they were anything other than models of probity and prosperity.

Tony and Elaine were shown into Kenton's panelled office whose walls were liberally decorated with prints of famous yachts that had no connection whatsoever with Price, Kenton and Partners. Kenton beamed warmly at his guests – especially at Elaine who was wearing an outrageous body-hugging Pony suit under her summer cloak. He plied them with sherry in Brierley lead crystal glasses. He caught a glimpse of Tony's Rolex wristwatch with a bracelet that represented a sizeable chunk of the gold reserves of a small country. The sight had the effect of widening his welcoming smile and causing him to fill the sherry glasses to a more generous level than usual.

The yacht broker listened carefully as Tony and Elaine outlined their requirements, occasionally making notes on a memory pad.

'At least a thousand tonnes,' said Tony.

'With an aft deck for parties under a tropical moon,' Elaine specified.

For the next hour, Kenton was kept busy showing his guests photographs and plans of the various vessels on his books. To his surprise, Tony produced an engineer's scale which he used on the profile plans to check carefully the dimensions of each yacht. Kenton noticed that Tony always scaled the lower deck clearances last; that almost certainly meant that those particular dimensions were the most important. In all cases the yachts were too small.

'I'm sorry, Mr Kenton,' said Tony, folding his scale. 'But it looks as if we're wasting each other's time.'

Kenton was not going to let the couple go that easily. The careful checking of dimensions suggested to him that these two wanted a yacht for a one-purpose trip – probably for arms or dope running. If he was right – and Kenton prided himself on being a sound judge of these things – it meant that they might not be too fussy about the yacht's general condition. If so, there was a chance that they would be interested in a particular vessel that was running up spiralling harbour dues in Spain.

'A moment, Mr Karn,' said Kenton quickly. 'I have one more vessel that could be exactly what you are looking for. The *Sarania*.' He removed a photograph folder from a drawer and passed it across to Tony.

'Four hundred feet LOA,' said Kenton expansively. And then he reeled off the *Sarania*'s features as if he had done it many times before: 'Two thousand tonnes gross registered. A large yacht – you will agree. But not too large for most Mediterranean harbours; twin General Motors diesels that give her a top speed of twenty knots and a cruising range of ten thousand miles at nine knots; a magnificent owner's stateroom and bedroom suite; accommodation for twenty guests; a swimming pool; a worldwide satellite TV system; two full-size motor launches. She was originally built in Amsterdam for a Dutch tulip grower. A welded steel hull. Only the Dutch know how to build steel hulls. A well-found ship, Mr Karn. She's lying at Alicante.'

Tony studied the photographs critically. The *Sarania* had a look of faded elegance about her. Her high clipper bow, having gone out of fashion twice, was now back in vogue, and the tiered superstructure, with its rows of distinctive raked windows, had an over-sleek appearance as if the yacht's designer had suddenly become obsessed with streamlining late in his career. Over-sharp lines on some of the shots of the *Sarania*'s art noveau interior suggested that the pictures had been retouched. The owner's stateroom looked like the foyer of a well-preserved 1930s cinema.

Tony passed the photographs to Elaine. 'How old is she, Mr Kenton?'

'She was launched in Amsterdam in 1950,' said the broker glibly.

'Don't you mean relaunched after a refit?' asked Elaine. 'She looks a bit nineteen-thirtyish to me. Look at this bathroom!'

'Launched,' Kenton emphasized. 'Her registration documents give her full history.'

'Where is she registered?' Tony inquired.

'Panama.'

Tony smiled. 'I don't know much about yachts, Mr Kenton. But I do know that the Panamanian authorities have a reputation for being . . . helpful . . . when it comes to registering shipping.'

'Very helpful,' Kenton replied, matching Tony's bland smile as he rose. 'I expect you would like to see the plans?'

'Please.'

Kenton produced a set of plans which he unrolled in front of Tony and weighted with ashtrays. Tony checked the overall length and beam with his scale before taking the important measurement: the distance from the top of the keelson to the underside of the foredeck. The *Sarania* had a small, circular swimming pool set into her foredeck, but there was still a little over seven metres clearance provided a lower deck could be removed.

Tony looked up from the drawings. 'How much are the owners asking?'

'Two million dollars,' Kenton replied, not even blinking. 'That, of course, will buy the charter company that owns her. The *Sarania* is the company's only asset. You buy the company who then lease back the yacht to you at a peppercorn fee. The charter company will require cash injections from you to pay for the running of the yacht. This means that the charter company will always show a loss which you can use to reduce your tax liability. It's normal practice.'

Tony drummed his fingers on the desk – the signal to Elaine that the yacht was exactly what they were looking for. 'What do you think, darling?' he asked her.

'It's not bad,' said Elaine doubtfully. 'I like the aft deck. Let's at least take a look at her.'

Tony looked quizzically at Kenton. 'Okay. We'll fly out tomorrow. Supposing we like the *Sarania*, Mr Kenton? Can we fix up the purchase in Spain? My time is valuable.'

'That will be no problem,' said Kenton, mentally rubbing his hands in glee while beaming at his visitors. 'I can also let you have a video recording that covers the entire yacht.'

'Excellent,' said Tony briskly. 'Right now we'd like three copies of these photographs and plans.'

'One more visit,' said Elaine, as she and Tony climbed into the Skoda.

'Where?'

'My flat.'

Tony held Elaine gently by the chin and kissed her. 'Elaine – my sweetheart. I think you're the most adorable, most fascinating, most beautiful girl in the world. But couldn't it wait until tonight? Please?'

Elaine returned Tony's kiss. 'No, Tony,' she said, her voice soft and husky. 'It can't wait.'

'*Please*, my darling?'

She nibbled his ear and then seemed to melt as his arms went

129

around her. 'Tony,' she said in a dreamy, faraway voice. 'Can I tell you something about you?'

'What's that, my darling?'

'You are one of the most conceited, self-opinionated men I have ever met. The reason we have to go to my flat is to collect the SWIFT III terminal I promised Crick. I've transferred one from our stores to my flat.' With that she bit Tony's ear very hard and made him yelp.

53

It was late afternoon when Elaine and Tony returned to Damion's flat with a large, cardboard packing case lashed to the roof of the Skoda. They manhandled the case up the lift and into Damion's flat.

Charlie and Hans Crick had already arrived, having driven up from Winchester in Crick's car.

'Excellent. Excellent,' breathed the Belgian as he examined the unpacked SWIFT terminal. 'This is exactly what we need.'

'And there's the control computer,' Damion reminded him.

Crick shrugged. 'That is no problem. We can buy that as off the shelf unit which I can modify.' He patted the terminal. 'But having this solves many, many problems.'

The five conspirators ate a light meal that Damion had prepared and got down to business as soon as the table was cleared.

'Okay,' said Charlie, examining the photographs of the *Sarania*. 'She looks smart enough. But no way is she worth two million bucks. Even if I'm only paying half.'

'That we can negotiate,' said Tony.

'If it's suitable, you're goddamn right we negotiate,' Charlie growled. 'I'll go with you to Alicante tomorrow.' He gave an unexpected grin. 'Be a chance to find out how much Spanish I've forgotten.'

'You'll need a marine architect to survey her,' Damion pointed out.

'That won't be a problem in Alicante,' said Tony.

'We take our own,' said Charlie firmly.

'At such short notice, Charlie?' Elaine queried. 'Will we find anyone?'

'A free trip to Spain? Sure we'll find someone. We'll go through

130

the classified teletext pages.' Charlie looked speculatively at Crick and Damion. 'Buying a yacht isn't the problem. You two guys have got the real problem. Somehow you've got to lay your hands on the drawings of the SWIFT satellite.'

'Over four thousand piece-part drawings, assembly drawings and parts lists,' said Crick, with what appeared to be misplaced pride. 'Plus all the circuit diagrams and test specifications.'

'We know what,' Charlie growled. 'The big question is, how?'

'I am giving the problem some thought,' said Crick. 'The master drawings are held on Winchester disks at SWIFT's headquarters at the World Trade Centre in Brussels. Breaking into there would be impossible. But a set of secondary master disks containing all the satellite's documentation is held by the original contractors who built the satellite. Microtech Instruments of Daytona in Florida. I worked there for several weeks when we were building the prototype satellite. I am certain the problem can be overcome.'

Damion snorted. 'I wish I had your confidence, Crick.'

'You broke into the South Bank telephone exchange,' the Belgian pointed out. 'I would have thought that that was a much bigger problem. And yet you solved it. And, of course, we will have to break in again when the blocking module is ready. The manufacturers say next week.'

'Okay, okay,' said Charlie. 'We deal with one problem at a time. That's sensible. But just how do you aim to get the drawings? By walking up to the front entrance of this Microtech outfit – whatever they're called – and asking for them?'

'Yes. I know Jeff Hunter, the owner of Microtech, extremely well,' said Crick dispassionately. 'Therefore I think the direct approach might work if we go about it in the right way.'

54

Jackie's luck improved. She found her car and sat in it, wondering what to do next. It was late: 6.00 pm. She decided to return to Winchester. She joined the traffic exodus heading south and drove over Putney Bridge into Putney High Street. Suddenly her improving luck took an even more dramatic turn for the better: just as she drove past a junction, the surveillance receiver emitted a buzz of such short duration, it was little more than a squawk. The noise surprised Jackie: she had forgotten that the thing was still switched on. She turned the car around at the first opportunity and approached the junction slowly – to the annoyance of following traffic. The buzz from the receiver lasted long enough for the direction indicator on its display to glow. Oblivious of the hooting of cars behind her, Jackie swung into the side street. The buzz became continuous. She worked her way around the maze of Putney's residential roads; sometimes losing the buzz and then regaining it again. It rose to a shriek when she turned into a pleasant road lined with high-rise apartment blocks. She was about to reduce the receiver's volume when she spotted the red Skoda parked outside the highest and smartest of the blocks. She parked a safe distance away and returned on foot to the apartment block. There was one label on the bell push speaking porter panel for a top floor flat that was recently printed and had not faded like the others. It bore the legend: D. SILVESTER.

Jackie returned to her car. Her hunch that there was a link between Damion Silvester and Anton Suskov had paid off. It was time to send another detailed report to Mike Randall in Washington.

55: Alicante, Spain

The sun was setting behind the mountains that overlooked Alicante harbour by the time Charlie, Tony and Elaine had freshened up at their hotel and taken a taxi down to the waterfront. The fourth member of their party was Rupert Owen – a broad, muscular marine architect in his late thirties. He had received a call from Tony the previous evening.

Owen had proved to have above average greed. As soon as he sensed that his services were urgently needed, his fee had gone up fifty per cent. He had also insisted on a chauffeur-driven car to take him to Heathrow Airport.

'Don't let it worry you,' Charlie had told Tony when he learned of the cost. 'I like dealing with men who have a price.'

The cool of the evening had brought Spanish families out for their evening strolls along the palm-tree-lined *ramblas*. The trio joined the casual sauntering crowd, and soon came upon the *Sarania*, her graceful clipper bow protected by coir fenders as she nudged restlessly against the quay. Her raked superstructure towered high above her neighbouring pleasure craft. The yacht was the largest vessel in the harbour; had it not been for the presence of the Alicante trawlers, she would have qualified as the scruffiest.

'Two million dollars for *that?*' Elaine queried.

'Ignore the paintwork,' Owen advised.

'Tell me how to and I will,' Elaine retorted.

'Dutch,' said Owen, running an experienced eye over the yacht. 'Not bad but certainly not worth what Oily Kenton is asking.'

'Hi there!' a voice called out.

'Talk of the devil,' said Owen.

Tony groaned when he saw Kenton striding down the gangway. 'The crook I told you about,' he muttered to Charlie.

The yacht broker advanced towards them, his hand outstretched, a well-rehearsed, welcoming smile firmly in place like a theatrical mask. 'Mr Karn. Mrs Karn,' he said affably. 'How nice to see you again.'

'We didn't expect to see you here, Mr Kenton,' Elaine remarked, when the introductions were over.

'I didn't expect to see Rupert Owen,' said Kenton, adding airily: 'I haven't seen the *Sarania* for a while, so I thought I'd fly out and take a look at her.' He omitted to say that he had flown out the previous evening within two hours of Tony and Elaine leaving his office, and had spent most of the day frantically bullying a team of dockyard workers into cleaning up the *Sarania*. Apart from the paintwork, he had had some success. The teak decks were clean and the raked superstructure was no longer encrusted with guano. Every window and porthole that could be opened was open.

'Shall we take a look around, Mr Karn?' Kenton suggested, standing aside.

'By ourselves, please, Oliver,' said Owen pleasantly.

'Of course, Rupert,' Kenton replied with mock graciousness.

'You two know each other?' said Charlie, as they made their way up the gangway, leaving Kenton watching them with a suspicious expression.

'We all know Oily Kenton,' said Owen, scribbling on a memory pad. 'It was sensible of you to bring me out. Knowing our Oliver, he'll have most of the local architects in his pocket. As you're proposing an extended open ocean cruise, I think we'd best start with the engines.'

The party entered the yacht amidships and descended a companionway. A watertight door at the foot of the narrow steps opened onto a walkway between two massive marine diesels. The heat and humidity in the enclosed space was not helped by the fact that the engines had been running recently. Owen made approving noises as he examined them. 'Not bad. Not bad. Closed circuit keel cooling – fresh water circulating through the engines' cooling jackets instead of seawater – always the sign of a quality ship.' He moved to the engineer's control panel, flipped the main switches and examined the various digital displays that came to life.

'What do you think?'

'I'd rather not say just yet,' Owen replied, while busily making notes.

'Risk it,' Charlie invited. 'A gut reaction.'

Owen considered. 'She's certainly worth a million, even if she needs new engines – which I doubt. She's not a bad vessel despite what I might say to Kenton. How about upping my fee a hundred for every per cent I knock Kenton down?'

'That's not in the deal,' said Charlie.

The marine architect looked at Tony and Charlie in turn. 'Exactly which one of you two is in charge?'

'I'm his financial advisor,' Charlie explained.

They spent an hour going over the craft, with Owen making detailed notes on his pad. Although there was a dank smell throughout the vessel despite all the open windows and portholes, Elaine was impressed by the six comfortably appointed cabin suites and the owner's dining saloon with its seating for twenty guests. The *Sarania*'s former splendour was still in evidence despite the faded carpets and curtains, the threadbare furniture fabric, blistered varnish, and flaking paintwork. The yacht was like an elderly dowager – not yet aged – who, given a facelift, had several more years' service in her as a glamorous socialite.

Elaine switched on the wall screen television and scanned through the channels. The number of programmes seemed endless. Every European and American service was available. There were even a number of Australian channels coming through with strong signals. 'Oh great,' she said delightedly. 'A satellite television system.'

Charlie laughed. 'You'll be able to watch breakfast television all day.'

Tony checked the two deck levels beneath the foredeck. The upper level was used for the storage of victuals, and the bilge area contained stacks of rusting paint drums – all unopened. Everything was as per the plans except for the circular swimming pool which had been enlarged. Even allowing for the loss of clearance caused by the pool, once the lower deck was removed, there would still be plenty of room between the underside of the foredeck and the keelson for the installation of the rocket and its launcher.

The inspection tour included lowering one of the motor launches on its davits so that Owen could take a close look at it, and ended on the spacious bridge; a pleasant area with excellent fore and aft visibility. There were comfortable chairs away from the helm and the navigation equipment so that the bridge also served as an observation lounge.

'This bridge has been added, Mr Karn,' said Owen, switching on the radar and studying the outline of Alicante harbour that appeared on the screen. 'She used to be a motor sailer. The removal of the mast and rigging has made the additional top hamper possible. I can't give a full report until after my detailed survey tomorrow. But, subject to that, I don't see why you shouldn't start negotiations for around one million dollars. Repainting and refurbishing her throughout is going to cost at least another million.'

'Is she seaworthy as she is?' asked Charlie.

'Unless I find something seriously amiss tomorrow – I should imagine so,' was Owen's careful reply.

'All right,' said Tony, catching Charlie's almost imperceptible nod. 'Let's call Kenton in.'

The yacht broker was a good actor; he looked suitably shocked at Tony's opening offer of eight hundred thousand dollars. 'We're asking for two million, Mr Karn,' he said reproachfully. 'There's nothing else like her in her price bracket in the Med.'

'She's been on the market a year,' Owen observed cryptically. 'And my guess is that she's at least fifteen years older than her papers say she is.'

'At least she's survived longer than the *Ikon*,' said Kenton tartly. 'Have you told your clients about the *Ikon*, Rupert?'

If the comment was designed to annoy Owen, it didn't work. The

135

marine architect merely shrugged and said mildly: 'The *Ikon* was a J Class yacht I was skippering in a tall ships' race a few years back. She was lost in a gale.'

'Have you got a master's ticket, Mr Owen?' asked Charlie.

'Sure. But that's nothing to do with this floating junkyard that Oily here thinks is a yacht.'

Charlie chuckled.

'Mr Karn,' said Kenton emphatically, giving Owen a withering look. 'The *Sarania* is the best craft of her type afloat in the Med.'

'She might be with another million spent on her,' Tony answered caustically.

'I agree there will be some expense to bring her up to standard,' Kenton conceded. 'Fresh paint throughout will transform her and won't cost anything like a million. I think one point eight million is a realistic figure.'

The haggling lasted fifteen minutes with Charlie appearing to take no part in the proceedings. In fact he stood a little way behind Kenton so that the broker could not see his frequent signals to Tony as the bargaining progressed. A provisional price of $1,300,000 was eventually agreed upon, subject to the owner's acceptance and the results of Owen's survey.

Afterwards Charlie took Tony to one side. 'We're gonna need a skipper. Someone we're gonna have to deal in on the operation.'

Tony nodded. It was something they had discussed in England. Charlie had promised to probe his many contacts. 'Do you have anyone in mind, Charlie?'

'Yeah. Owen. He's got a ticket.'

Tony was doubtful. 'But is he . . .?'

'Crooked?' Charlie grinned. 'Given the chance – you bet your ass, he is. If a man's greedy – he's crooked. Believe me – I know.'

Tony didn't doubt Charlie's judgement for an instant.

56: Winchester

Jackie was in a quandary. She had risen early in her suite at the Winchester Golden Rose only to discover that Tony and Elaine had gone. There was no sign of the red Skoda in the hotel car park. A check on the computer showed that their suite was still being held.

She dialled into Mike Randall's security mailbox in Washington and left a message for him to call her. She showered, ate her normal starvation breakfast, and drove to Damion Silvester's flat in Putney. No one answered the bell. She returned to Winchester. Luckily there were no reservations on her suite, therefore she was able to extend her booking by a further four days. Again she called Randall's mailbox. There were no messages for her even though it was now mid-day in Washington. She decided that she would return to Washington if she heard nothing from Randall within the next four days.

57: New York and Florida

Damion and Hans Crick arrived at New York's J F Kennedy Airport late that afternoon. They paid cash for a two-year-old Buick – Damion gave the dealer a false name and address – and stayed overnight at a small Manhattan hotel, well away from Damion's haunts because he had no wish to run into any of his employees. The next morning the two men went shopping. Damion had learned well from Billy Watts and knew precisely what was needed in the way of sophisticated equipment for breaking into protected premises. Also he knew New York, and where certain items could be obtained.

They started their expedition among the many electronic shops around Times Square; their purchases included a logic tester that could read the circuits of electronic locks. Next they visited several computer stores in turn in order to spread their purchases. At the first store they bought a set of four Winchester computer disks. According to the gaudy labels, each of the metal disks contained over a thousand 'absorbing and educational games that will keep the kids happily occupied for hours'. At the second store they paid cash for a battery-powered IBM personal portable computer that was complete with a Winchester disk reader and a modem for the transmission of computer data over telephone lines. Their last visit was to a large machine tool retailer in Greenwich Village where they obtained a portable thermic lance and a spark erosion machine. Damion brushed aside Crick's protests that they were unlikely to have to break into any premises therefore the machines would not be required; Damion said that he wanted them in case they were needed. After that they headed south for Florida on US95. Crick had

137

not liked the idea of the thousand-mile drive but Damion had overruled him on the grounds that they could not risk the possibility of a baggage search if they flew.

Stopping only to eat and stretch their legs, the two men took it in turns to drive. They covered the thousand miles to Daytona in less than thirty hours, arriving at the outskirts of Daytona Beach during the middle of a hot, humid Saturday afternoon.

'Ah, yes,' said Crick, as they drove past towering apartment buildings lining the oceanfront. 'This I recognize. I worked here for three months when we were building the SWIFT III satellites. But there was never time to visit the beach.'

'So where does Hunter live?' Damion wanted to know.

'I think before we do anything, we should rest,' Crick advised.

'We do what we have to, we get out of the country on a flight from Miami – then we rest,' said Damion curtly. He hadn't enjoyed the two days in the Belgian's company and was anxious to get the business over and done with.

Crick didn't like Damion's tone. 'I don't understand you, Damion. If we follow my plan, there won't be any need to leave the country in a hurry.'

'There will be if the goddamn plans go wrong. So where does he live?'

As Crick gave Damion the necessary directions, he suddenly realized that he was very afraid of the big man beside him.

58: Winchester

There was a sharp rap on Jackie's door.

'Wait a minute!'

She hastily exhaled her cigarette into the air conditioning inlet grille and stubbed the butt in the packet – ruining the remaining cigarettes. She touched the door monitor wall key. Mike Randall's face appeared on the screen. He was grinning up at the camera. She opened the door on the security chain. 'Hi there, Angelica,' said Randall breezily. 'Thought I'd better hop across and help you out of the mess you've gotten yourself in.'

Jackie threw the door open. Randall ambled in, still grinning. His gaze took in the luxurious decadence of the room. 'Well, well,' he

138

said, sprawling himself on the bed and hooking his hands together at the back of his neck. 'There's me thinking you're working your ass off and all the time you're living it up on Uncle Sam's account – sleeping in a bed that was designed solely for fornication. Have you gotten round to actually sleeping in it?'

Jackie kicked the door shut. She marched across the room and stood menacingly over Randall. 'Gimme three very good reasons why I shouldn't kill you. Slowly and painfully.'

Randall considered the options. 'Firstly – I'm the most devastatingly charming man that's ever entered your humdrum little life. Secondly – I thought I'd honour you by sharing this incredible room with you for a few days –'

'Thirdly – you didn't answer my last report!' Jackie snapped angrily. 'Why not?'

Randall patted the bed. 'I'll answer it now if you're nice to me.'

Jackie perched on the edge of the bed, pointedly ignoring Randall's invitation to move closer. 'Well?'

'You've done very well, Angelica,' Randall admitted. 'The trouble is, we're not too sure what it is you've done well at.'

'Thanks.'

'We've still no evidence that Silvester has been passing SDI software to the Soviets, and we still don't know where he got the quarter million dollars from. What is interesting is your establishing a definite link between him and Anton Suskov. Suskov's girlfriend – this Elaine Fleming – is even more interesting. Have you found out anything more about her?'

Jackie shook head.

'Remember what I told you in Washington about SWIFT?'

'Sure.'

Randall ran a finger idly up Jackie's spine. 'Elaine Fleming is a director of a little company called Keytech,' he said, unconcerned when Jackie moved out of reach. 'They hold the UK franchise from SWIFT Terminal Services S.A. of Brussels for the supply and maintenance of the terminals used by SWIFT's subscribers. So, we have a link with Damion Silvester – who's written SWIFT software – and the Fleming girl.'

'You think they could be planning some sort of operation involving SWIFT? How secure is the system?'

'A hundred per cent and more unless you can dream up a way of physically tampering with a satellite strung up twenty-two thousand miles above the equator. Which raises the one question that makes me nervous: what were Suskov and the girl doing at a privately owned rocket firing range in Central Africa?'

Jackie shook her head. 'Does it matter now that the Israelis have wiped the place out?'

Randall produced his pipe and proceeded to fill it with a tobacco that looked like shredded horse blanket. 'Mm . . . I'd like to know more about our Miss Fleming and Mr Suskov. And certainly we have to find out what it is they were up to before the Israelis screwed it up for them.'

'I did think of trying to search their room,' Jackie admitted. 'But you told me not to try anything illegal.'

Randall set fire to the tobacco and exhaled a cloud of heavy yellow smoke that looked like mustard gas. 'Just as well you didn't,' he commented. 'Hotels like these have all sorts of intruder detection systems that sound off whenever someone tries to tamper with the electronic door locks. Isn't modern technology just wonderful?'

Jackie was irritated by his patronizing tone. She was about to make a suitably cutting observation concerning the arrogance of certain men when an alarm suddenly went off.

Randall looked startled. 'What in hell's that?'

'This room has ultra-sensitive smoke detectors,' Jackie explained, giving Randall a sweet smile. 'We're on a no-smoking floor. Isn't modern technology just wonderful?'

59: Florida

'That's Jeff!' said Crick suddenly, pointing through the windscreen.

Damion drew slowly into the kerb some way from the house so as not to attract attention. They were in a broad, palmetto-lined residential street near New Smyna Beach, a few miles south of Daytona. Most of the decidedly up-market houses were hidden from the road by rich, subtropical vegetation. Crick was pointing to a man who had just dropped a suitcase into the boot of a Jaguar. He crouched and waved to two children in the back of the car. They waved back as the woman driving the car reversed out of the driveway.

'And that's his wife Joanna,' said Crick. 'She must be taking the kids to see her sister at Jacksonville. She used to go virtually every other weekend.'

Damion gave a satisfied grunt. 'Lucky timing for us.'

Crick was about to wave as the Jaguar swept past the parked Buick but Damion grabbed his arm. He held onto it until the man had returned to the house.

'The less people who know we're here, the better,' Damion growled.

'But what does it matter?'

'It matters if things go wrong!' Damion snapped. 'We do this my way or not at all.' With that he drove a little way past the house, snicked the Buick into reverse and backed up the double-width drive. 'Is anyone else likely to be with him?'

Crick looked doubtful. 'Not unless they now have an au pair. They used to talk about it.'

Jeff Hunter opened the front door before Crick rang the bell. He was a tall, studious-looking man aged about thirty-nine. 'Hans!' he said in surprise. 'Hey – this is a surprise!'

The two men shook hands warmly. 'Good to see you again, Jeff,' said Crick, returning Hunter's affectionate shoulder clasp. 'How are Joanna and the children?'

Hunter smacked a fist into his palm. 'Hell – you just missed her by a few minutes. She'll be real mad.' He looked curiously at Damion. In that instant, both men realized that they had met before. 'I know you,' said Hunter, offering his hand to Damion. 'Nice, France – last year – the SWIFT seminar. No – don't say who you are – let's try out the photographic memory. Your badge – Silver? David Silver? Something like that.' He suddenly snapped his fingers. 'Damion Silvester! Right?'

'Right,' said Damion. He sounded genial and yet his eyes were hard and unsmiling as he shook hands with Hunter.

'Should've got your name right away,' said Hunter, grinning. 'Age creeping up, I guess. Glad to meet you again, Damion. Come on in.'

Hunter showed his guests into a cool, air conditioned living room. He apologized for the toys scattered everywhere and busied himself producing tall lagers at an elaborate bar.

After a few opening pleasantries, Crick got down to business. 'Jeff – we've got a problem in Brussels. A big problem.'

Hunter looked concerned. 'At SWIFT HQ?'

Crick nodded. As he had hoped, the news that he and SWIFT had parted company had not reached Hunter. 'The integrity of the SWIFT III system is at stake. That is how serious the problem is and why we have come in person. We could not trust any other means of communication. What I have to tell you is in the utmost confidence. We cannot possibly risk jeopardizing the confidence of SWIFT subscribers in the system.'

'Sure. Sure,' said Hunter, his face serious.

'Two days ago a supposedly trusted employee removed from the records vault the Winchester disks that contain all the drawings and specifications of the satellites. It means that we won't be able to service the satellites on a shuttle mission or even manufacture replacements.'

Hunter's eyes widened, his drink forgotten. 'Jesus H,' he muttered.

'No doubt you can guess his motives,' said Crick.

'How much is he asking?'

'Ten million dollars.'

'Holy shit.'

'Only myself and Mr Silvester and the board executive group know about this,' Crick continued. 'Normally we would pay out and keep quiet. Obviously we cannot risk involving the police until we have the disks – or good copies of the disks – back in the vault. Until then – under no circumstances can this thing leak out. But the president has decided this time to take a stand.'

'The blackmailer doesn't know about the duplicate Winchesters we're holding?' Hunter ventured.

'Exactly,' Crick confirmed.

Hunter thoughtfully sipped his lager, and carefully replaced the glass on the coffee table. 'I can't do it, Hans. I can't release those disks. My contract with SWIFT –'

'We don't want you to release them. We want to copy them.'

'They're uncopyable.'

Damion snorted. 'There's no such thing as an uncopyable disk. There are disks whose operating system makes them difficult to copy. And other operating systems that make disks bloody near impossible to copy. But not impossible.'

Hunter looked keenly at Damion. 'And you can break their

protections?'

'Mr Silvester wrote the protection software,' Crick explained. 'That's why he had to come with me.'

'You want to make copies now, Hans?'

'There's an eleven o'clock flight from Miami tonight,' said Crick. 'We want to be on it with copies of the disks.'

Hunter drained his glass and stood. 'Okay. We'll use my car.'

'What about the security men at your plant?' asked Damion. 'Won't they think it odd? You turning up on a Saturday afternoon?'

'Not with me, they won't,' Hunter replied, grinning. 'I work the weirdest hours sometimes. You should hear Joanna beefing.'

'Jeff – we must not be seen,' Crick insisted. 'One of them might recognize us from our pictures in the house journal.'

'The guy in the gatehouse never looks in the back of my car,' Hunter stated confidently.

The Winchester disk drive whirred softly as Damion displayed its sectors on a visual display unit in Microtech's drawing office. He found the final protection byte he was looking for – innocently buried in a mass of other data – and deleted it. He looked up from the keyboard and nodded to Crick. The Belgian inserted in a drive the last of the games disks they had purchased in New York. Damion entered an instruction on the keyboard. The backup process began. Both drives purred softly as information was copied from the master disk to the games disk – the original games being erased in the process. At the end of thirty seconds the games disk had become a perfect copy of the master disk.

'Okay – that's it,' said Damion.

'Hell,' Hunter breathed admiringly. 'I never dreamed I'd ever see those hard disks copied.'

Crick removed the master disk from the drive and returned it to Hunter. 'Thanks, Jeff. This won't be forgotten. You will be receiving a letter from the board very shortly.'

Hunter laughed good-naturedly as he returned the disk to a fireproof box. 'Just so long as we receive the servicing contract for next time a satellite is recovered.'

Damion carried out a random verification of the disk by reproducing a drawing on a plotter. The pen whipped back and forth across the platen – automatically reproducing a dimensioned manufacturing drawing of part of the satellite's outer casing. 'Looks good,' he commented, switching the machine off.

It was dark when the three men returned to Hunter's house. They had a beer each, but Crick politely declined the American's offer that they should stay for a meal.

'We must be getting to Miami, Jeff. I won't be able to relax until these disks are back in our vault.'

Hunter nodded understandingly and showed his guests to the door. He watched as Damion prepared to reverse out of his drive.

'We could use his phone to transmit the disks,' said Damion abruptly to Crick, switching off the ignition and opening his door.

'It would be far too dangerous,' Crick protested. 'We must use a payphone.'

'I'll make it undangerous,' said Damion curtly.

Hunter watched expectantly as Damion got out of the car and walked towards him. 'Forgotten something?'

Damion produced his hip flask. 'Would you fill this with water please, Jeff? I have to take pills every few hours.'

'Sure,' said Hunter, taking the flask.

The two men entered the house. Damion closed the front door behind him and followed Hunter into the kitchen.

'How about some ice in this, Damion?'

'Please,' said Damion.

Hunter held the hip flask under an ice-cube dispenser. The clatter of ice cubes prevented him from hearing Damion creep up behind him. As he turned, Damion slipped the plastic strap noose around his neck, pulled it tight, and flipped on the servomotor. There was a cry of surprise from Hunter but Damion did not stay to witness the execution; he darted up the stairs and ransacked the bedrooms – strewing the contents of drawers on the floor and hastily cramming a few valuable-looking items of jewellery into his pockets. He used a handkerchief to avoid leaving fingerprints on the furniture.

Hunter was still alive when Damion returned to the kitchen. The computer engineer was lying on the floor – clawing weakly at the narrow strap that had sunk so deeply into his neck that it was no longer visible. Damion avoided looking at his victim's face. He stepped over the dying man and retrieved the drinking glasses that they had used from the sink. By the time he had carefully washed and polished them, Jeff Hunter was dead.

Damion knelt down by the body, switched off the servomotor and returned the murder weapon to his pocket. He filled his hip flask with whisky, took a long pull to steady his nerves, and returned to the car. 'Bring the disks and the computer,' he ordered.

Crick struggled into the house with the equipment. He saw Hunter's body on the kitchen floor. 'What's the matter with Jeff?'

'He's dead,' said Damion. 'Get that gear hooked up to the phone.'

'Dead?' Crick's eyes widened in alarm. 'But that wasn't necess . . .'

'It was if I say it was!' Damion snapped. 'Even if we make a billion each, it won't be any good to us if he blows a whistle. I don't give a damn about him knowing you, but he recognized me.'

'But the risk –'

'No one else knows we're here, so the risk is worthwhile. Now get that stuff hooked up.'

Crick busied himself with the computer while Damion went around the living room, polishing with a handkerchief any surface that was likely to bear incriminating fingerprints.

'Ready,' said Crick quietly, plugging the computer's telephone modem into a spare telephone socket.

Damion opened his pocket address book and found the Moscow telephone number that Tony had given him. He punched it out and waited, not certain what to expect. When the connection was made, he felt self-conscious about using the prearranged code name. 'This is Mr Hine calling from overseas. I have some market information for you.'

'Ah – Mr Hine,' a voice answered in perfect if stilted English. 'We have been waiting for your call. We are ready when you are.'

'Fifty thousand baud dump rate,' said Damion. 'Handshakes every ten seconds.'

'We are ready,' said the voice.

Damion nodded to Crick, who loaded the first games disk into the portable computer's disk drive. He checked the instructions on the computer's screen and pressed the key for the data transmission to begin.

It took ten minutes for the information on each disk to be sent to the computer that was on the other side of the world. Every ten seconds the process was automatically checked: the Moscow computer would send back for verification the data it had received during the previous ten seconds – the 'handshaking' process. If a segment of data did not agree – usually as a result of the corrupting influence of unwanted noises on the line – the data transmission would be repeated until it did. At the end of thirty minutes, every piece-part drawing, assembly drawing, component list and test specification for the manufacture of a duplicate SWIFT III satellite had been copied onto the computer of Moscow's Leibenov Institute. The equivalent of five tonnes of classified documentation had been despatched over five thousand miles for the price of a long-distance telephone call.

'That's it,' said Damion into the telephone.

'Excellent,' said the voice. 'It took less time than we expected. A clear line does speed things up. Good luck.'

'Okay,' said Damion to Crick, looking at his watch. 'We've got four hours to get to Miami Airport. Let's get moving.'

60: London

Mike Randall reset the tiny plastic toggles on the adjustable key and tried it in the lock again. This time the door to Damion's Putney flat opened.

'*Voilà*,' he said, holding the door wide for Jackie. 'You see how useless it is for virginal females to try locking me out of their rooms at night?'

'With your ego, I'm surprised you're not boasting about them locking you in,' Jackie commented tartly.

'That happens too,' said Randall, closing the door and glancing around the flat. 'You check the living rooms. I'll look at the bedrooms.'

Jackie found a set of photographs of the *Sarania* in a sideboard drawer. She called Randall. They spread the prints out on the table and studied them carefully.

'The *Sarania*,' Jackie remarked, peering closely at a print that showed the yacht's name. 'If he's thinking of buying this, then he's being paid a lot more than quarter of a million dollars. This little toy looks as if it's worth ten times that.'

'Exactly what I was thinking, Angelica,' Randall agreed. He turned one of the photographs over. The name, address and telephone number of Price, Kenton and Partners, yacht brokers, was stamped in the centre of the print. He picked up Damion's telephone

146

and punched out the number. He gave Jackie a wink while waiting for the connection to be made. After a brief conversation with the receptionist he replaced the receiver and looked speculatively at Jackie. 'Fancy a trip to Alicante, Angelica?'

61: Moscow

Academician Yuri Grechko strode into the panelled conference room of the Leibenov Institute at 10.00 am sharp. He nodded in turn to each of the assembled heads of departments and took his seat.

'Good morning, comrades,' he said briskly. 'You've read my brief and you've seen samples of the drawings. Our aim is to build a duplicate of the SWIFT III satellite and have it tested and working within thirty days from tomorrow. All work on other projects will cease forthwith. There are no budgetary restrictions. Initial reactions please, starting with you Valentina.'

Valentina Korcheva was the head of procurement: a forthright young woman with a remarkable ability for locating materiel supplies. She asked, 'What is meant by a duplicate satellite, comrade? Do you mean a performance duplicate? A physical duplicate? Or both?'

'Both,' said Grechko. 'If it is ever recovered from orbit, there must be nothing about it to indicate that it is of Soviet manufacture.'

'So it's actually going to be launched?'

'Oh yes.'

Valentina nodded. 'I've done some random sampling of the component lists. The active devices are all proprietory items in the West. I estimate that we have ten per cent of what is needed in our stores – preferred value subminiature semiconductor and resistors and capacitors and so forth. But the rest will have to be acquired in the West. From amateur radio and electronic specialists; mail order companies –'

'Let me have a list by tomorrow.'

The woman looked concerned. 'We're talking about ten thousand components, comrade. Possibly more. Such orders are certain to attract attention.'

'We'll spread the purchases across as many embassies and trade missions as possible,' said Grechko. 'You let me have the list tomorrow and we'll get the diplomatic bags moving. Mikhail?'

Mikhail Grovanich toyed with a drawing of a printed circuit board. He was the head of electronics development – the largest department in the institute. He was a man of few words but plenty of energy. 'Now we have the Canon microlithographic printer,' he said, 'we will have no problems reproducing these circuit boards and their associated dynamic RAM chips. I do not foresee serious problems, Comrade Grechko.'

Grechko nodded. The printer was the latest and most sensitive of the Leibenov Institute's acquisitions from the West. With the export difficulties faced by US manufacturers of equipment to make microprocessors, Japan had stepped in and grabbed the world market – destroying America's lead in the industry. Obtaining highly specialized equipment from Japan was not proving overly difficult. The moves by successive US presidents in the 1970s and '80s to deny such equipment to the Soviet Union from American sources had had the reverse effect and made it easier for them to obtain.

Similar positive reports were forthcoming from the heads of the various engineering departments. So total was the documentation on the satellite, that no one could foresee any insuperable difficulties in reproducing a perfect working replica within the thirty-day time scale.

'Excellent, comrades,' said Grechko, closing the meeting at 10.45 am. 'We will meet again on Monday at the same time to review progress.'

62: Hertfordshire, England

Two days later, Alex Tchaikov, a junior official at the Soviet Embassy in London, drove twenty miles from central London to Watford in Hertfordshire. He entered the large redbrick building of Watford Electronics – one of the largest electronic component mail order companies in the country – and placed an order for over two thousand electronic components: the part numbers neatly listed on a computer print-out. Watford Electronics were able to meet nearly ninety per cent of the order from their remarkably comprehensive stock. A grateful Alex Tchaikov paid cash. That night the components, sealed in a diplomatic bag, were on their way to Moscow on the evening Aeroflot flight.

Throughout the following week, similar scenes were repeated in New York, Washington and Tokyo – in fact in virtually every Western city. Upon arrival at the Leibenov Institute, the components were subjected to rigorous testing. The failure rate was unexpectedly high, but Valentina Korcheva had had the presence of mind to order five of everything. By the end of the week she was able to report to Grechko that the procurement of all the required electronic components – even down to reels of multi-core solder – was complete.

63: Alicante, Spain

After a week of eating beneath the *Sarania*'s afterdeck awning while moored in Alicante's harbour, Rupert Owen still found that having breakfast in Elaine's company fulfilled a cliché by being a meaningful experience. Although he understood the mechanics of ships perfectly, the workings of the human body – Elaine's body in particular – defeated him. It seemed incomprehensible that anyone could sustain such a massive daily cholesterol intake and yet maintain such a stunningly beautiful figure.

The week of frantic cleaning and painting by a small gang of hardworking Spaniards had transformed the *Sarania* into an immaculate craft that any self-respecting millionaire could be proud of. The outside work was finished. The interior workers were now mostly electricians – busily rewiring their way through the vessel with a posse of cleaners and decorators following in their wake. As Owen had predicted, the engines had required little attention. The biggest single task had been the installation of air conditioning on the bridge.

Each morning the three – Owen, Elaine and Tony – gathered for breakfast on the afterdeck to review the previous day's progress. Charlie and Kenton had returned to England the day after the yacht's purchase had been concluded.

'The engines are now perfect, Mr Karn,' Owen was saying as Pepe served greasy bacon and broken fried eggs onto Elaine's plate. 'Wednesday's shakedown revealed a few minor faults that have now been put right. Are you still serious about starting on a cruise next

149

Monday?'

'Yes,' said Tony. 'Will the weekend be long enough to sort everything out?'

'Should be,' said Owen. 'We've already made a start on victualling. Bunkering with fuel is routine. I'll see the agents today about hiring a skipper. Shouldn't be any trouble – there's plenty of Greek freelancers hanging around Alicante who know the Med inside out.'

'We'd like you to skipper for us,' said Elaine, drinking her fifth cup of coffee.

Owen looked surprised. 'Me, Mrs Karn?'

'Why not? You've done marvels with the *Sarania* and you've got a master's ticket.'

'Well – yes,' said Owen doubtfully. 'But you want the *Sarania* for Med cruising. I'm an ocean man. You really would be better off with a local. Especially someone who knows the Aegean as you're planning on going East. Although it's only about two hundred miles by four hundred, it takes a lifetime to get to know.'

'We'd like you to do it,' said Tony firmly. 'An old lady like this needs an engineer first to look after her. Say – ten per cent above the going rate?'

Owen pursed his lips at the mention of money. 'I've got my regular clients back home, Mr Karn. Shall we say . . . fifteen per cent to compensate me for the loss of good will?'

'Okay,' Tony agreed.

Owen looked carefully at Tony. 'And another five per cent to keep my mouth shut, Mr Karn.'

Tony kept his voice steady. 'Keep it shut about what, Mr Owen?'

Owen gave a lazy smile. 'I don't know yet. Something to do with installing something on the bridge – something that likes to be kept at a uniform temperature – a computer – or specialized communication equipment? Otherwise why go to the trouble of installing air conditioning on the bridge and not elsewhere? I can't believe you're that concerned for the crew's wellbeing.'

'The bridge is also the observation lounge,' Tony pointed out. 'It's where we'll be spending a lot of time. Two per cent.'

'You're on, Mr Karn.'

The two men shook hands on the deal.

'That's that problem sorted out,' said Elaine contentedly.

'Mister Owen!' Pepe called out. 'A truck come.'

Owen wiped his lips with a napkin and stood. 'Mr Karn. Mrs Karn. Please excuse me but there is much to be done. I'll start hiring a crew today.'

When they were alone, Tony smiled at Elaine and said softly, 'Another problem solved, sweetheart.'

'One problem – one solution,' she agreed. 'The next one will be: when and how do we tell him the truth? We'll have to, sooner or later.'

64

Jackie took her eyes away from the tripod-mounted binoculars. 'I don't believe it,' she declared, stubbing out a cigarette.

Randall joined her on the hotel's balcony. The balconies of their adjoining rooms had panoramic views of Alicante's harbour. The *Sarania*'s mooring was within four hundred yards of the hotel. Had they arrived a day earlier, they would have seen Charlie.

'You don't believe what, Angelica?'

'Elaine Fleming. It's not fair – being able to eat like that and have a figure like her's.'

'Life can be harsh,' Randall observed unsympathetically, dropping himself into a plastic lounger and stretching luxuriously. All he was wearing was a pair of underpants. 'But you're right – three days of Spanish food is showing on you already.' He produced his pipe.

'Skunk. And you can beat it back to your own balcony if you're going to smoke that thing.' Jackie rubbed her eyes. 'Another thirty minutes and it's your turn to cook your eyeballs with this thing.'

Randall's answer was a snore.

Ten minutes later Jackie woke him with a kick on the shin.

'Activity,' she announced.

'What sort of activity?'

'Unloading food from a truck activity.'

'Did you have to kick me so hard?' Randall complained, as he looked through the binoculars. 'Ah . . . A load of fruit.'

'Fresh fruit,' said Jackie pointedly.

Randall did not answer. As he watched, another truck drew up on the quay in front of the *Sarania*. Two harbour workers helped the driver and his mate stack crates of fruit on the yacht's foredeck. And then a third truck arrived. Suddenly the *Sarania* was at the centre of considerable activity as food and supplies were manhandled through the yacht's freight hatch.

Jackie could see what was happening without the aid of the binoculars. She stood and pulled on a floral cotton dress over her swimsuit. 'Come on,' she ordered.

'What?'

Jackie jammed her feet into a pair of sandals and headed for the door. 'It's time for action, Mike. We're not going to learn anything stuck up here, peering through those things. The way things are moving down there, we could blink and that yacht's gone.'

Mike grabbed a pair of shorts and half-hopped, half-ran along the corridor to the lifts while trying to climb into the shorts and keep up with Jackie at the same time.

'Listen,' he panted, when the lift doors slid shut behind them. 'All we can do is keep them under observation.'

'Which we can't do if the *Sarania* is a thousand miles away,' Jackie retorted. 'Fresh fruit going on board, Mike – it's only a matter of two days at the most before they sail.'

'So what do you suggest we do?' Randall demanded, as they crossed the hotel lobby and emerged into the bright sunlight. 'Alert the Sixth Fleet?'

'No – get us crewing jobs on board.'

'What! Are you crazy!'

'No – just practical.'

'But you know nothing about crewing a yacht, for Chrissake! And maybe they've gotten themselves a crew?'

'They've only got that cabin boy,' said Jackie, as they crossed the *rambla*. 'My guess is that a yacht that size is going to need at least a crew of six.'

'But –'

They were passing a restaurant that had tables and chairs set out on the *rambla*'s marbled surface. Jackie grabbed Randall's arm and pushed him into a chair. The *Sarania* was close – less than fifty yards away.

'You have a coffee while I find out what's what. And quit worrying – Suskov and the Fleming girl never saw me at the Golden Rose.'

With that Jackie left before Randall had a chance to protest further.

'Hi there!'

Owen was supervising the loading of crates through the *Sarania*'s freight hatch. He looked up. A woman in a print dress was hopping about on the quayside, trying to keep out of the way of the men who were human-chaining supplies onto the yacht's foredeck.

'Good morning. Are you the captain?'

'Yes – I'm the skipper.'

'I'm Jackie Morrison. We're looking for a crewing job.'

Owen leaned on the rail and regarded the woman. She looked about thirty to thirty-five. Attractive. A determined stance.

'Miss or Mrs?'

'Miss,' Jackie answered. 'I don't go for that mizz stuff.'

Owen gestured to the gangplank. 'Come aboard, Miss Morrison.'

Jackie trotted nimbly up the gangplank as if she had been trotting up gangplanks all her life.

'What part of America are you from?' Owen inquired when they shook hands.

'Washington, captain. Do you have any vacancies?'

'Do you have any nautical experience, Miss Morrison?'

Jackie had once taken a three-hour Circle Line trip around Manhattan. 'Sure,' she said breezily.

'Well,' said Owen doubtfully. 'We'll be looking for someone to take charge of the galley.'

'You mean, you need a cook? I can cook. Clean. Just about anything.'

'Do you have a work permit? I can't hire anyone without a work permit.'

'Just my ID and my passport card,' said Jackie. 'Hey – look – we don't want a job with pay or nothing. Me and the guy I'm with like bumming around the Med. We'll just work for our keep.'

Owen wasn't surprised by the proposed conditions; the Mediterranean ports were thronged with people of all nationalities who worked for their keep and little or no money. They were usually students and were invariably younger than the American woman confronting him.

'What can your boyfriend do?'

'Oh, he's not my boyfriend. Not like that. He's just a guy I bum around with. There's less hassle that way. He's strong. He can do

153

just about anything. Painting. Cleaning. The dirtier and messier, the better he likes it.'

'A general hand might come in useful but I wasn't thinking of taking one on,' Owen admitted. 'But someone in the crew who speaks English would be an advantage. You'd have to share a very small cabin with him. We're short on crew accommodation.'

Jackie thought quickly. Life was complicated enough as it was; the last thing she wanted were the added problems of having to share a cabin with Mike Randall and his disgusting pipe. There had been a battle with him over her insistence on separate rooms at the hotel. 'In that case I'll dump him,' she decided aloud. 'He'll make out okay without me.'

Owen laughed. He decided that he liked her. 'Okay, Miss Morrison. We sail on Monday. You can start work today. And if you poison us between now and Monday, I'll kick you off the ship and find someone else. Is that a deal?'

'It's a deal,' said Jackie eagerly, wondering what she was letting herself in for.

Randall was horrified when Jackie broke the news to him.

'Angelica – you can't do it! It's crazy!'

Jackie finished packing her travel bag. She zipped it shut and lit a cigarette. 'Why?'

'Because it is, for Chrissake.'

'Listen, Mike – whatever it is they're up to – and we don't really know if they are up to anything because there's been no sign of Damion Silvester – we won't learn anything stuck in this hotel.'

'Don't be naïve – of course they're up to something,' said Randall impatiently. 'A Tass correspondent buying a yacht like the *Sarania*? All Tass "legals" are KGB. And for the sort of money they've spent buying that yacht, they're not going to hesitate to toss you overside if they find out who you are. This game's gotten a little too big for us to handle. We ought to turn it over to –'

'Whoever takes over is not going to get the sort of break I've gotten right now to infiltrate the crew. Right?'

'Maybe,' Randall conceded. 'But –'

'So I get on the yacht. I find out what's going on, and I report to you.'

'How? Pokketfone calls would be routed through the yacht's main

154

transmitter.'

'Christ – I don't know.' Jackie hoisted her bags onto her shoulder. She paused at the door. 'The *Sarania* doesn't sail until Monday. You've got two days to think of something.'

Randall saw the uselessness of further argument. He lit his pipe and exhaled a cloud of riot-control gas. Suddenly the hovering mosquitoes lost interest in him. 'Okay, Angelica. Go ahead. I've got to go to Madrid. I'll be back tomorrow or Sunday.'

'Why Madrid?'

'I've got to report this in person.'

'Report what?'

Randall was at a loss. 'Christ – I don't know.'

'Just so long as they don't come crashing in and screw everything up.'

'They won't,' said Randall. 'Good luck, Angelica. See you at that café when I get back.'

'If I can get the time off,' said Jackie over her shoulder as she left the room.

65: Winchester, England

Charlie hauled himself out of the swimming pool and stretched out on his stomach on a massage couch. A Golden Rose girl wearing only a rose-shaped loin cloth knelt over him and began working her fingers expertly into his shoulder muscles.

Baldwin approached. 'Mr Crick and Mr Silvester to see you, sir.'

'Great, great,' said Charlie enthusiastically. 'Drag 'em in.' He sat up and slapped the girl playfully on the bottom. 'Okay, honey – that's fine. Take the rest of the day off, huh?'

The girl muttered her thanks and passed Crick and Damion as she left the penthouse. Crick was carrying a small suitcase. Baldwin busied himself at the bar, pouring drinks for the new arrivals.

Charlie waved to some chairs. After an exchange of greetings, Baldwin served the drinks and withdrew.

'So what's new?' Charlie asked.

Damion briefly outlined the salient points of their trip to the USA. He omitted to mention that he had killed Jeff Hunter.

'So the Ruskies now have a complete set of manufacturing

155

drawings of the SWIFT satellite?' Charlie queried.

Damion nodded. 'That's right.'

'He killed Hunter,' Crick blurted out.

Charlie raised an eyebrow at Damion. 'Is that right?'

'He recognized me from a SWIFT meeting a year back.'

'It was unnecessary,' said Crick vehemently. 'I had no idea that there would be a killing involved.'

Charlie caught Damion's eye. Both men immediately guessed what the other was thinking.

'I made it look like his place had been broken into and robbed,' said Damion boredly. 'There's no risk of anything being traced back to us. What about the *Sarania*?'

'She's now ours,' said Charlie expansively. 'She's been cleaned up and she sails on Monday. No problems there. So what's next on the agenda?'

Crick opened his suitcase and produced a small electronic unit the size of a cigar box. 'This is the telephone exchange module I was telling you about.'

Charlie glowered at the device. '*That's* what I paid nearly quarter of a million bucks for?'

'The central processor had to be specially made,' said Crick defensively. 'It's a thirty-two bit chip. The mask alone –'

'Yeah, yeah, yeah,' said Charlie impatiently. 'Spare me the details. So what does that thing do?'

'In fact the module is now much more complex than was originally anticipated,' the Belgian explained. 'Since studying the circuit diagrams of System M's central switching in the South Bank telephone exchange in detail, I have had to devise a different method of blocking SWIFT's transatlantic cable traffic. The main logic unit can now handle –'

'Just tell me what it does, for Chrissake!'

Crick inclined his head and pushed his rimless glasses more firmly into place. The gestures were the nearest to an expression of irritation that he permitted himself. 'As you know, all SWIFT transatlantic authentications for the transfer of large amounts of money are sent by landline – by transatlantic cable. Once installed in the telephone exchange, this unit will trap those authentications and send "line overloaded" signals back to the SWIFT central processing computer. The authentications will then be routed through the

156

satellite – giving us total control.'

'It works,' said Damion. 'We've tested it with several computer simulated runs.'

'When are you going to install it?' Charlie wanted to know.

'We can get into the exchange any time,' said Damion, crossing to the bar and pouring himself another drink. 'We can't install it too early in case it's discovered.'

'Which is unlikely,' Crick interjected.

'And we can't leave it too late in case there are problems. We thought around two weeks before the operation goes ahead. *When* it actually goes ahead now depends on our Russian friends.'

'That is the one big advantage of this operation,' said Crick. 'Once we are ready – we can strike any time. One banking day is just like any other.'

'How about the control computer?'

'We are still working on it,' said Crick. 'Damion's preparing the software and I'm modifying the SWIFT III terminal that Elaine provided, and preparing the control computer. We do not anticipate any serious problems.'

Late that night Charlie had another visitor.

Baldwin showed Jim Hoffman into the penthouse. The New York private investigator looked tired and worn.

'Hey, Jim,' said Charlie in concern when he had dismissed Baldwin. 'You don't look so good.'

'I don't feel it, Charlie,' said Hoffman, accepting a whisky and sinking into a chair.

'But you've done it?'

Hoffman set his drink down, removed a sheaf of documents from his briefcase and passed them to Charlie. 'It's all there. My guess is that there's more information in that report on the Mob's bank accounts than they know themselves.'

Charlie leafed through the pages of typescript. Every sheet was filled with neat columns of bank account numbers and their owners. There were several hundred entries ranging from major accounts in the world's capitals to small day-to-day trading accounts in obscure towns. Estimates of the average amounts held in each account were also shown. All the accounts had one thing in common: they were all owned or controlled – directly or indirectly – by the Mob. In many cases individual accounts were shown for a number of notorious big names.

'Holy shit,' Charlie muttered under his breath as he ploughed through sheet after sheet of information. An appendix listing the accounts of holding companies ran into six pages. And another appendix highlighted the Mob's hideously complex chain of inter-locking companies and trusts.

'The more I dug, the more I unearthed,' said Hoffman. 'Every door I opened led to several more.'

Charlie grunted. 'I guess you've earned your fee for once, Jim. How accurate are these amounts?'

'Pretty accurate,' said Hoffman. 'From what I could make out, those accounts in Mexico are used for narcotics payouts – they're the ones subject to the biggest fluctuations.'

'Where's the information on their south African accounts?'

'The last two pages. The information only came through yesterday.'

Charlie turned to the end of the report. The huge sums of money being injected into Transkei confirmed Charlie's belief that southern Africa had been earmarked by the Mob as their scene of major expansion in the twenty-first century.

'I lost an agent in Transkei on this operation,' said Hoffman softly.

Charlie stopped reading. His black eyes stared unblinkingly at his guest. 'You what?'

Hoffman outlined the disappearance of a young employee.

'You sent a kid into Transkei!'

'No, Charlie. I sent her to Durban. Keyboard research only. She went into Transkei against my orders to chase up a lead.'

'What happened to her?'

Hoffman looked down at the carpet. 'She drove from Durban to Transkei and just vanished. I don't know what happened to her. I flew out to find out and I couldn't get past Transkei immigration. And they tagged my passport card data to make sure I'd never get into their country. I had no choice but to use a south African agency to check up. They had no luck either but they did manage to dredge up that information on the Mob's money in Transkei and south Africa.'

'So the kid blabbed and now I've got the Mob onto me?'

'She didn't know who I was working for. You're safe, Charlie.'

Suspecting sarcasm, Charlie treated Hoffman to an icy stare and returned to the report. He made a rough mental total of the amounts and swore softly to himself. A name against a private account number caught his eye. A name from the past: Victor Salavante. Hell – Victor must be well over eighty now. Not only was Victor still alive, but all he had in the bank was a lousy three thousand bucks.

'Does this guy have any other holdings?' Charlie asked.

Hoffman leaned forward so that he could see the entry Charlie was pointing to. 'Victor Salavante?' The private investigator searched his memory. 'I don't remember, Charlie. Hold on.' He produced an electronic memo pad and keyed in Victor's name. 'Yes – Victor Salavante. No income for ten years. No other accounts that I could trace. And that account has gone steadily downhill. Monthly payments to the Saint Bernadette Senior Citizens' Care Village on Long Island for the past five years. I've got a note here – says that Salavante appears to have fallen from favour and on hard times.'

Charlie's black eyes were expressionless. 'Okay, Jim – you've done a good job.'

'Do you want me to stay with it? There's still a few big accounts to be tracked down.'

'Yeah – why not. Let me know what you find. You invoice me and I'll see you're paid right away. And, Jim – I'm sorry about the kid.'

When he was alone, Charlie put through a call to one of his sons in New York. He hardly ever spoke to them these days. Charlie cut short his son's protestations of affection and concern.

'Listen, Philip. I've gotta small job for you. Take this down: Victor Salavante, care of the Saint Bernadette Senior Citizens' Care Village on Long Island.' Charlie read out the name of Victor's bank and his account number. 'Have you got that . . .? Good. Now listen. I want Golden Rose to make a quarter of a million bucks payment into that account and I want a letter to go to Victor Salavante on headed notepaper telling him that the payment is a settlement for an accounting error we made on the repayments on the original loan he made to Golden Rose Motels. You got that?'

There were protesting noises from New York.

'Don't argue with me, son – just do it,' Charlie rasped. He listened for a few moments and said in a more conciliatory tone, 'Yeah – it's a long story, Philip. I'll tell you about it some time. But don't tell nothing to Pia – you understand? That's very important. You can fix the books – you're good at that sort of thing.'

Charlie made certain that his son had got the instructions right and hung up. He went back to studying the sheaf of papers. His original estimate that he would be cleaning out the Mob to the tune of a billion dollars was wildly inaccurate:

It was going to be a ten-billion-dollar sting.

66: Moscow

The first SWIFT satellites, built nearly twenty years earlier, had one tenth of one per cent of the signals traffic handling capabilities of the SWIFT III satellites. Each one had been the size of a small delivery van and weighed several tonnes. The duplicate SWIFT III satellite taking shape in a sterile assembly room at the Leibenov Institute measured a metre high by half a metre in diameter. When completed, it could be carried by two men.

As Yuri Grechko and the head of the assembly department watched, a girl laboratory technician carefully positioned a light-sensitive photovoltaic cell onto the satellite's outer frame and used a laser micro-welder to secure it permanently in place.

'Those cells have given us some problems,' said the department head to Grechko. 'It seems that the Americans are well ahead of us in selenium purification techniques.'

'But the duplicate cells perform well?'

'Oh yes,' said the scientist. 'Our cells will deliver all the solar energy that the satellite needs. Our part of the work will be finished tomorrow.'

'Very good,' said Grechko. 'Very good indeed.'

The academician had received similar reports from all the other departments who were engaged in producing the satellite. He returned to his office and called the Chairman to inform him that the satellite would most likely be ready ahead of schedule.

67: Alicante, Spain

Despite her initial trepidation, Jackie succeeded in preparing several meals for the crew and the new owners of the *Sarania* without poisoning them. In fact, the general reaction to her meals had been very favourable despite her unfamiliarity with the *Sarania*'s temperamental cookers. By Monday morning she had learned that the simple culinary rule as far as Elaine Fleming was concerned was 'quantity in the morning, quality in the evening'.

The *Sarania*'s cramped galley was not particularly well equipped – most of the money spent on refitting the yacht had been spent elsewhere – but it was adequate, and Jackie soon had it organized to her liking. Pepe, the diminutive cabin boy, eagerly followed her instructions to the letter provided he understood them, which wasn't often. Her cabin was only slightly larger than a broom cupboard, but it had its own shower and lavatory. It was located along the passageway from the galley – mercifully separated from the other crewmen's cabins, although the six Spaniards that Owen had taken on had shown her considerable respect. She gave up trying to remember their names.

Late on Sunday morning, she was sitting on the weatherdeck, smoking a cigarette and watching innumerable Spanish families in their Sunday clothes returning from mass, when she spotted Randall taking a seat at the nearby pavement café and lighting his pipe. She finished her cigarette, told Owen she was going for a stroll, and walked down the gangway.

She walked past Randall. He followed her. They ordered drinks at the *Kon Tiki* – a yacht that had been converted into a floating bar. It was moored a safe distance from the *Sarania*.

'How you doin', Angelica?'

'No problem. Everything comes out of a tin or the freezers.'

Randall grimaced. 'Remind me not to propose to you.'

'Remind me not to accept.'

'When does she sail?'

'In six hours.'

'Any idea where?'

'Eastwards.'

'Where eastwards?'

Jackie shrugged. 'I don't know. The skipper doesn't know either. Wherever the whim of the owners takes her. He says it's not unusual for owners to make up their mind only after they've sailed. How did Madrid go?'

'So so. I've brought you this.' Randall slid a hand-held two-way radio and several spare battery packs across the table. 'Ever used one

161

of these things before?' he asked, snapping the radio's tiny stub antenna into place.

'Not one like that.'

'It's easy.' Randall showed her the various controls and how to replace the battery packs. 'It works on the UHF band – well away from the marine bands so there's hardly any danger of us being overheard,' he explained. 'Also the output is scrambled on a frequency-hopping sideband. Only one watt output. Range over water is about fifty miles. It's got a sensitive microphone and a pull-out earphone so that you can talk quietly. It's waterproof but it's no good for playing in the bath because it doesn't float.'

Jackie slipped the radio and the batteries into her shoulderbag. 'One problem,' she said. 'The *Sarania* has got a steel hull. How will that affect the signals?'

Randall looked dismayed. 'Shit. I thought she was timber?'

Jackie shook her head. 'Steel. You wouldn't believe the condensation problems I've got in the galley.'

Randall thought for a moment. 'Has your cabin got a porthole?'

'Yes.'

'Okay – stick the antenna out of the window when you want to call me. Someone will be monitoring the frequency all the time. Always call me Mike when everything's okay. If you use my second name, I'll know something's wrong and that you can't talk freely.'

'And what *is* your second name, pray tell?'

Randall reddened slighty. He hesitated. 'Do you promise not to laugh?'

'I promise not to laugh.'

'Solemnly promise?'

Jackie held up her right hand. 'I do solemnly promise not to laugh, so help me God.'

'It's Horace.'

Jackie's hoot of laughter had other people in the floating bar staring at her.

Randall pressed his lips together. 'And you'd better use Angelica as your callsign,' he said tightly. 'Okay?'

Jackie forced herself to look serious and repeated the instructions. She made a strange noise at the back of her throat but managed to keep a straight face.

'You must keep me posted on everything,' Randall insisted.

'Anything out of the ordinary – you call me up and tell me about it.'

'Where will you be?'

Randall grinned and chucked her under the chin. 'Out of radar range but within radio range.'

'All the time?'

'All the time, Angelica.'

68: London

Damion and Crick were on foot – reconnoitring the route they would be taking during their forthcoming break-in of the South Bank telephone exchange.

'What the hell's that thing on the roof?' said Damion abruptly. 'Don't make it too obvious that you're looking at it.'

Crick risked a glance up at the roof of the South Bank telephone exchange. 'Do you mean the mast?' he ventured.

'What is it?'

'It is too far away to say,' said Crick. 'Is it possible to get nearer?'

'This is the nearest we can get without losing sight of the roof.'

'Was it there when you entered the exchange before?'

'No, it bloody well wasn't.'

Both men crossed the street to a roadside stall and propped themselves against it, sipping coffee so that they could keep the telephone exchange under observation without arousing suspicions.

'Perhaps it is on the roof of a neighbouring building?' Crick suggested. 'The perspective from here makes it difficult to see properly.'

'We need to get a decent view,' said Damion grimly. 'From somewhere high up. I'm not going near that goddamned place until I know exactly what that thing is.'

Crick gazed in turn at the high buildings lining the South Bank of the River Thames. He pointed to an office block that towered over its neighbour, the National Theatre. 'What's that building?'

Damion had lived a long time in the United States and was not familiar with all London's large buildings. He pulled a street map from his pocket. 'London Weekend Television.'

Crick looked surprised, and then amused. 'Ah yes – the site of the LW amateur radio seventy centimetres repeater.'

It was Damion's turn to look surprised. 'The what?'

'During lift conditions, I have often talked through the repeater from Spain to radio amateurs in London. I remember a London operator telling me that the repeater was sited on the roof of the London Weekend Television building.'

Damion was immediately interested. He knew from his own experience that most of the problems associated with gaining unauthorized access to buildings were solved if one had the right pretext. 'These repeaters – they're unmanned?'

'Oh yes. They're looked after by local repeater groups. Volunteers. Repeaters need only occasional attention.'

'How often?'

Crick looked doubtful. 'It is hard to say. Once – perhaps twice a year.'

Damion finished his coffee. 'Good,' he said.

Crick showed the security officer his International Amateur Radio Union membership card. 'We have come to look at the repeater,' he explained. 'There have been complaints that it is drifting off frequency.'

The security officer glanced at the two respectably dressed men. One was carrying a small toolbox. He indicated the visitors' book. 'Sign here please, gentlemen. I'll get someone to show you up. It's on the roof.'

Damion and Crick signed the book using false names. A second security officer accompanied them in the lift to the top floor of the building and showed them onto the flat roof. He pointed to a waterproof steel case and a colinear antenna array that was secured to the parapet. 'There she is, gentlemen.'

'Thank you,' said Damion. 'It'll only take about five minutes.'

'I'll leave you to it then,' said the security officer. 'I'll be waiting inside.' With that he left Damion and Crick alone.

The view of London and the Thames was superb, but Damion was only interested in the view of the South Bank telephone exchange. Inside the toolbox was a pair of binoculars. He focused them on the skylight where he and Billy Watts had broken in. It had been replaced with a heavy grille which had been set into the masonry. The mysterious mast was planted squarely in the centre of the roof. On the top of the mast was a suspicious-looking black box. He passed the binoculars to Crick. 'What do you make of that?' he demanded.

Crick studied the mast for some moments. 'Mm . . . There's not much doubt about it, Damion. It's a three hundred and sixty degree infrared surveillance camera. An expensive one, too.'

Without saying a word, Damion took the binoculars from Crick and resumed his study of the roof. He spotted three more cameras that definitely had not been there when he had broken in with Billy Watts. There were even strands of electrified razor wire running around the roof's parapet. It was obvious what had happened: the skylight had been discovered and security had been subjected to a massive tighten-up all round.

Damion lowered the binoculars and stared at the distant building. 'So that's it then,' he said slowly. 'There's no way that we're going to get in there again. The whole thing's off.'

69: Winchester

'Off!' Charlie exploded, when Damion and Crick broke the news. 'Off?' His black eyes blazed at the two men standing before him in his penthouse.

'It's true, Charlie,' said Damion heavily. 'We'd never get back into the exchange now. The place is sewn up tighter than Fort Knox.'

'Do you have any idea how much I've sunk into this operation! Over two million bucks! Two million! And now you come waltzing in and tell me it's off because you're now shit-scared of breaking into a telephone exchange that you've already broken into a dozen times.'

'Charlie,' said Damion evenly. 'It makes no difference if you'd sunk two hundred million into the operation: I'm telling you – there's no way that we're going to get into that exchange. Not any more.'

'Well, I'm ordering you to fucking well find a way!'

The two men squared up to each other – Damion's lanky figure towering over the hotelier.

'Please, Mr Rose,' Crick intervened. 'You must understand – we cannot plant the module in the exchange. Damion is right – it will be impossible. And if we cannot plant the module then we cannot transfer large amounts of money through the duplicate satellite. We have to block all the SWIFT authentications by transatlantic cable, otherwise the system will not accept our transfers as genuine.'

'All I understand,' Charlie grated savagely, 'is that you mother-fuckers have conned me out of two million bucks. Well, no one does that to Charlie Rose – no one!'

'For Chrissake face up to reality, Charlie,' Damion muttered. 'You're going to have to put this one down to experience and call the whole thing off.'

Suddenly Charlie was unnaturally calm. 'No,' he said. 'No – I'll do the telling of what I'll have to do. If you don't come up with something by this time tomorrow – I'm gonna make use of a few contacts I've got on the West Coast that I'd never thought I'd have to use. Maybe it'll cost me another million but it'll be worth it.'

Damion returned Charlie's icy gaze. When he spoke, his voice was soft and dangerous. 'Like what do you have in mind, Charlie?'

'I'll leave you to figure that out. You have until this time tomorrow. Now get outta here before I throw up.'

'What did he mean?' Crick asked Damion when they had returned to Crick's suite.

'What do you think he meant?'

The Belgian hesitated. 'There is an English term I have heard. About a hit team or squad.'

'It's not an English expression – it's American,' Damion replied casually. 'And you got it in one.'

70: The Mediterranean

Alicante was in the shadow cast by the mountains behind the ancient walled city when the Spanish customs officers completed their inspection of the *Sarania*. Luckily, they were not interested in Jackie's shoulderbag where she kept the two-way radio.

The yacht's diesels coughed into life. Once they had warmed up and were running steadily in neutral, Owen called down orders from the bridge to cast off. The propellers churned the water white around the yacht as she went astern. Once clear of the quayside, the yacht turned in a tight circle and headed for the harbour entrance. The tempo of the twin diesels increased. Jackie emerged on deck. She leaned against the rail, smoking while she watched the Moorish city receding astern. She felt the movement of the vessel quicken beneath her feet as the fine clipper bow cleaved through the long, languid swell of the Mediterranean. After thirty minutes, the *Sarania* emerged from the shadow of the mountains. The yacht's wake was a sparkling essay in blue and white in the bright sunlight.

'A magnificent evening,' said a voice at her elbow.

She turned. It was Anton Suskov.

'Yes – magnificent, Mr Karn,' Jackie replied, smiling. She looked keenly at the good-looking Russian. It was the first time she had ever spoken to him, and the first time she had ever spoken to a Russian.

Tony leaned casually on the mahogany rail. 'You must be Miss Morrison? Captain Owen told me about you.'

'Nothing too derogatory, I hope?'

Tony laughed easily. 'Oh, no, Miss Morrison.'

Jackie was uncertain how to maintain the conversation. She wanted to ask him where they were heading for, but decided that that might be dangerously presumptuous. She moved along the side deck to the galley door. 'If you will excuse me, Mr Karn, I must see about dinner.'

'What is it to be tonight? Something special for our first evening at sea?'

'It'll have to be whatever comes out of the freezers first until I get them organized,' said Jackie apologetically. 'Tomorrow I'll have proper menus prepared.'

Tony laughed good-naturedly. 'Please don't worry on my account, Miss Morrison. I would not have thought it possible for you to improve on last night's meal, and Mrs Karn is very happy with her breakfasts.' He gave Jackie a conspiratorial wink.

There was another departure from Alicante harbour when the *Sarania* was a speck on the Eastern horizon. Outwardly, the sleek, 150-foot Chris Craft was yet another of the many millionnaires' toys that wandered the Mediterranean during the summer months. In fact, the craft was operated by the United States National Security Agency and was crewed by a team of highly trained radio operators. Its normal task was eavesdropping on low-power high-frequency radio traffic emanating from Albania. Now, following Randall's visit to Madrid, and after much argument, it had been assigned to the task of shadowing the *Sarania*.

The Chris Craft separated from the tangle of masts lining the northern end of the harbour, and nosed towards the entrance. The note from the vessel's two powerful Caterpillar diesels was a muted burble. It seemed in no hurry. Only when the vessel was ten miles out to sea did the engine note increase and a number of its complex antenna arrays appear. But the wave that appeared beneath the graceful flared bow was insignificant. The Chris Craft seemed happy to plod along at a steady six knots.

But its course was the same as that taken by the *Sarania*.

While struggling to read a Spanish label on a large packet of frozen food, Jackie decided that Anton Suskov was a very attractive young man. His command of English was amazing. The packet turned out to be a fine middle-cut of beef which she served up in a red wine sauce, complete with small, top-quality new potatoes – out of a tin – followed by ice cream and thawed-out raspberries.

'They like,' Pepe announced, after one of his frequent trips between the dining saloon and the galley.

'What direction are we heading, Pepe?'

'Pardon?'

'Direction. What is our course?'

'Oh – *si*.' Pepe nodded enthusiastically. 'I just serve the last course.'

Jackie gestured impatiently and pointed out of the window at the darkening sea. 'Our direction, Pepe?'

'We sail southeast.'

'And our speed?' She searched for an alternative word. 'Our velocity?'

'We make a good eight knot. Maybe ten.'

Jackie had the rest of the evening to herself once she and Pepe had eaten and cleaned up the galley. She locked herself in her cabin and removed the two-way radio from her shoulderbag. She knew that she would have to find a more secure hiding place for it. Holding the antenna near the open porthole, she cautiously switched the set on and pushed the earphone into her ear. She pressed the talk key and said in a low voice: 'Hallo, Mike. This is Angelica. Do you read?' There was the faint hiss of white noise in the earphone. She pressed the talk key again and checked to see that the red transmit light was glowing. 'Hallo, Mike. This is Angelica. Do you copy me?'

A click, then Randall's reedy-sounding voice in the earphone. 'Hallo, Angelica. This is Mike returning. Anything to report?'

Nothing in Jackie's voice betrayed the relief she felt when she heard Randall's reply. 'We're heading southeast at about eight to ten knots. Nothing else to report.'

'Okay, fine, Angelica. We knew that. Going clear now. We'll be listening all the time. Don't waste your batteries.'

Jackie switched the radio off. There was a padded backrest panel at the back of her bunk so that the berth formed a settee. She hinged the panel down by prising it out of its clips with the aid of a galley knife. There was a surprisingly wide gap behind the panel due to the curvature of the hull – wide enough to accommodate a person. She wondered if it had ever been used by stowaways. She wrapped the radio in a T-shirt and pushed it down inside the gap where it was held in place by a frame. She felt better with the set safely hidden.

Later, as she tried to sleep, the same worrying thoughts kept returning unbidden to her mind: it now seemed more than likely that there was an innocent explanation for the whole affair. Perhaps it was just possible that Suskov had purchased the *Sarania* on behalf of an influential senior official in the Soviet hierarchy who did not wish his or her purchase to become widely known. Such occurrences were not unknown. But whatever the reason, it was beginning to look as if Damion Silvester was not involved. Jackie felt guilty about the mounting cost of the operation to the US taxpayer and more than a little worried about the damaging effect on her career that the debacle was likely to have. She knew Matt Fitzgerald well enough to know that it would be a long time before he forgave her for going over his head with her original report.

It was with these thoughts plaguing her that she finally drifted off to sleep.

71: Winchester

Crick spent most of the morning after the explosive interview with Charlie sitting at the desk in his hotel suite, trying to devise a way around the problem of blocking the SWIFT transaction authentications even though he had no access to the telephone exchange. As he entered one logic diagram on his electronic pad, so the uselessness of his previous idea would become apparent and he would have to clear the pad and start again.

Damion looked in at midday. 'Any luck?'

'It's useless,' Crick complained. 'I was tasked with designing an unbreakable system, and that is exactly what we have.'

'Seems a pity,' Damion commented boredly. 'Having got this far.'

'Why won't Charlie accept the inevitable?'

'The Charlies of this world are used to having inevitable situations swept away by a combination of bluster and money.'

'For once, neither will work,' said the Belgian morosely, deleting yet another logic diagram from his pad. 'He will have to accept that.'

'He will,' said Damion. He operated the control pad and scanned idly through the world's television channels. They were cluttered with endless movies – dubbed into every conceivable language and a few inconceivable ones. And there were dozens of the inevitable game shows. The UK programmes weren't much better: an Open University film on structural engineering that was twenty years out of date; the news; and a thirty-year-old Richard Burton movie. He returned to the news and turned up the volume. 'But I'd rather you told him.'

Crick grunted and went back to work.

Damion yawned and watched the news, one leg hooked over the arm of his chair and swinging boredly. The main news item was about the forthcoming twenty-four-hour visit to London in a month's time by the Vice President of the United States, Howard Penn; and the new Secretary of State, Carol Weismann. The American politicians were to visit London to conclude the Space Defence Initiative deal for the supply and citing of anti-missile laser projectors in the United Kingdom. Although it was a working visit and not a state visit, the American politicians were to be accorded state visit hospitality – complete with afternoon tea at Buckingham Palace.

'Does SWIFT still have its London–New York leased transatlantic lines?' Damion asked. His leg was still swinging.

Crick looked up from his pad. 'Not now that SWIFT III's handling the bulk of the traffic. There was no point in paying the ruinous rental charges. Why?'

'So the authentications are routed through the ordinary PSTN lines?'

'If there's routing space available.'

170

'Supposing there isn't?'

The Belgian was puzzled. 'But you know the answer to that. If the lines are already overloaded – which hardly ever happens – then the authentications are automatically re-routed through the satellite.'

'Ah – but suppose we made it happen?'

Crick was still none the wiser. 'Made what happen?'

Damion's toe was brushing the carpet as he swung his leg. 'Supposing there was a momentous event in London a few minutes before we busted into SWIFT? An event of such importance that it had every wire service and about a million journalists in the States trying to get through to London?'

'A lot of wire service copy is sent by RTTY,' Crick pointed out. 'By radio telex teletype.'

'I thought all the high frequency RTTY channels were hogged by Eastern-bloc wire services churning out endless propaganda? Also, not all journalists and editors have immediate access to telex, but they can always find a phone or dial overseas on a Pokketfone.'

'Well – yes – that's true,' Crick conceded.

'So – if the lines were blocked, the authentications would be routed through the satellite where we would have control over them.'

Crick looked sharply at Damion. Since the killing in Florida of Jeff Hunter, he hated and mistrusted the big man. 'It would have to be an extremely momentous event,' he said.

The picture on the television changed to a close-up of the United States' Vice President. Howard Penn was telling the White House press corps just how much he was looking forward to his London visit.

Damion stopped swinging his leg. He grinned. 'Yeah,' he said, in answer to Crick's comment.

72: New York

It was after midnight when Jim Hoffman locked his Tenth Avenue office and crossed the street to the multistorey car park. He was unlocking his car when headlights blazed out from a car parked in an opposite bay. The car surged forward. Its wing hit his half-open door. Before he could recover his balance, the car had pinned him by the knees against the concrete wall. The agonizing pain made him scream out. He wanted to claw out his automatic but he needed both hands on the car's hood to prevent himself falling sideways. So intense was the pain that he was certain his legs would break at the knees if he lost his precarious balance.

The man in the car's passenger seat slid his bulk out of the car and dispassionately regarded the private investigator who was clawing at the car's hood. He was fat but wore an expensively tailored lounge suit. His double chins spilled over his collar like a stack of tyres on the tailboard of a truck. 'How'ya doin', Jim? A few questions we wanna know some answers to.'

Hoffman mouthed an obscenity.

The driver of the car gunned the engine on a signal from the fat man. The car pressed forward. The sound of Jim Hoffman's shin bones splintering into greenstick fractures was drowned by his scream. He collapsed, sobbing, his arms spread across the car's hood.

'Now, Jim,' said the fat man in a reasoning tone. 'You've been poking your nose into a whole lot of things. Asking questions. Now it's our turn. Who yah working for?'

'Go fuck yourselves,' Hoffman choked out.

The fat man gave a sorrowing sigh. The car backed off a foot, releasing Hoffman's body. He slipped to the ground, supporting his weight with his arms while sobbing in agony – a shattered shin bone protruding raw white through the fabric of his trousers. The car suddenly lunged like a wild beast. The fender crushed Hoffman's rib cage as though it were a Chinese lantern. The car backed off a few inches. The fat man shook his head sadly as he stood staring down at Hoffman. The New Yorker was writhing on the ground, blood frothing from his lips. The fat man lifted the private investigator's head with the toe of his polished shoe and nodded to the driver. The car surged forward for the last time, crushing Hoffman's skull between the fender and the concrete wall.

73: Winchester

Charlie was alone when Damion went to see him. He surprised Damion by not being wildly enthusiastic about the scheme.

'Now just listen,' Charlie growled. 'I didn't get into this to go

172

assassinating presidents or vice presidents. 'Specially as they're Republicans. You're gonna have to come up with something else.'

'There *is* nothing else, Charlie,' Damion answered. 'And I'm not talking about assassination but attempted assassination. Something to get the lines humming just before we bust into SWIFT.'

There was a silence. 'No – I don't like it,' Charlie muttered.

'I'm not too keen myself,' Damion admitted. 'But I've stewed my brains since yesterday over this. There is no other way. At least this puts us back in business, otherwise we're finished: I might as well pack my bags and you can kiss two million plus goodbye.'

Charlie crossed to the bar and poured himself a drink to give himself time to think. He came to a decision and then spoke quickly, as if he were afraid of changing his mind. 'Okay then. How do we do this thing?'

'For Chrissake, Charlie – I've not had time to give it much thought. A shooting. A bomb. Just so long as there's an attempt.'

'Yeah? And supposing it goes wrong?'

Damion grinned. 'It's assassinations that go wrong, Charlie – attempts always succeed in being attempts.'

Charlie saw the sense behind the contorted logic and gave a rare smile. 'When is the visit?'

'June 3. Four weeks tomorrow.'

'Will the duplicate satellite be finished in time?'

'Not only has it got to be finished, it's got to be launched and in orbit and tested, and the real SWIFT satellite knocked out.'

'Do our friends know?'

'I'm sending them the data this evening to enable them to prepare their own program for their accessing of SWIFT. I'll give them the times then.'

'Christ – I hate dealing with them,' Charlie muttered. 'I don't trust the bastards.'

Damion remained silent.

Charlie looked hard at him. 'Do you believe this crap about them only wanting the Czar's money?'

'I find it hard to believe, but I don't know the Russian mind, Charlie.'

'Jesus Christ – if they're double-crossing us . . .' A thought occurred. 'They don't have to know about the assassination attempt?'

173

Damion considered. 'No. If we say that we can only block the telephone exchange on June 3, they'll have to accept that. I'll have to tell them when.'

Charlie nodded. 'Okay, Damion. Don't tell them how.'

'That's one problem solved,' said Damion. 'But there's another one.'

'What?'

'I don't trust Crick. He won't go along with the bomb idea.'

Charlie met Damion's gaze. 'Do we still need him?'

'He's nearly finished the control computer and the modifications to the SWIFT terminal. Say – another week.'

Charlie broke the long silence that followed. 'I never did like the little creep anyway. Okay – I'll leave you to deal with him.'

74: London

Crick watched Damion prepare the control computer and the telephone modem.

'I don't like this,' he declared.

'Whether you like it or not is beside the point,' said Damion, checking the connections and switching on the control computer. 'We have a deal with the Soviets.' Damion loaded the disk he had prepared into the computer and transferred the disk's files ready for transmission.

'We're putting a powerful tool in their hands,' said Crick. 'With that information, they could destroy the Western banking system.'

Damion remained calm. It required an effort. 'The whole point of them becoming partners is so that they can write their own control program. I've got to send them these instructions. I doubt if they're stupid enough to destroy something they need. Anyway, you were the one who was happy with their story about them just wanting the Czar's money.'

'I've been thinking about that. Now I'm not so sure.'

Damion ignored the Belgian and dialled the Moscow number that he had last called from Jeff Hunter's house in Florida. The same voice answered:

'Da?'

'This is Mr Hine calling from overseas,' said Damion. 'I have some more market information for you.'

'Good evening, Mr Hine. We are ready.'

'The same protocols as before,' said Damion. 'Fifty thousand baud dump rate. Handshakes every ten seconds.'

'Please go ahead, Mr Hine.'

Damion pressed the key for the data transmission over the telephone line to begin. The process lasted less than a minute. The computer's monitor screen signalled that the 'handshake' information echoed back from the Soviet computer agreed with the original data.

'You've got it,' said Damion.

'Excellent, Mr Hine,' said the Russian voice.

'One thing,' said Damion. 'This is very important. The transaction must be carried out on June 3.'

There was a long pause. 'June the third? That gives us very little time. Why the rush?'

'Various market force factors,' said Damion. 'You will find details at the end of the program I've just sent you. But that date is extremely important. I'll give you the exact times when we've got more information.'

'I will pass on what you say,' said the voice. 'Good day, Mr Hine. And good luck.'

Damion grunted and cleared the line.

'Why June 3?' Crick wanted to know.

'You'll find out,' was Damion's cryptic reply.

75: The Mediterranean

By her third evening at sea, the *Sarania*'s eastward distance made good was eight hundred miles. Malta was visible through the dining saloon's port windows when Pepe was clearing away the remains of the evening meal. Tony waited until the cabin boy left and invited Owen to help himself to a cigar.

Owen lit the cigar and regarded Tony and Elaine through a cloud of blue smoke; a hint of a cynical smile on his face. 'Well, Mr Karn. Mrs Karn. Have you decided yet on our first port of call?'

Tony played a table lighter flame on the end of his cigar. He nodded to Elaine.

'Istanbul and then Odessa,' said Elaine.

For once the normally phlegmatic Owen looked surprised. 'Odessa!' he echoed. 'You mean Odessa on the Black Sea?'

'Is there another Odessa?' Tony inquired.

'But it's a Soviet port,' Owen protested.

Elaine smiled. 'We wouldn't be going there if it wasn't.'

'So I was right. You are up to something.'

Tony laughed. 'That's one way of putting it.'

'I think,' said Owen, speaking slowly and deliberately, 'it's time you told me exactly what is going on.'

'I agree,' said Tony. 'How would you like to make some money? Some real money?'

'That depends on how much and what the risks are.'

'Amount – half a million sterling. Risks – none.'

Owen's cynical smile returned. 'There's no harm in me listening.'

'Once you've listened, you're in it up to your neck,' Tony warned. 'Whether you like it or not.'

'And what if I don't like?'

'Why not tell him first?' Elaine suggested.

Tony talked for five minutes, outlining the basics of the operation but without going into great detail and without mentioning names. When he finished talking, Owen was gaping disbelievingly at him.

'You're crazy. You're both completely and utterly mad.'

'Why?'

'Oh – for God's sake. Isn't it obvious? Even if you got away with it – you'd be hounded around the world. Nowhere would be safe.'

'Assuming we'd be caught, which we won't be,' said Tony, 'the hounding would have to be done through national courts. As the offence will be committed in international waters, we'd be beyond the jurisdiction of any court. As this is a Panamanian registered craft, maybe we could be tried in Panama.' Tony broke off and grinned at Owen. 'Somehow I don't think any of us will find not being able to visit Panama too much of an inconvenience.'

Owen opened his mouth and shut it again. He shook his head. All he could think of to say was: 'Crazy . . . Absolutely bloody crazy.'

'There's another consideration,' said Elaine. 'I doubt very much if the international banking community will say anything about the hack. They've kept quiet when they've been stung before for fear of confidence being lost in the banking system.'

176

'But they've never been taken before for the sort of amount that you have in mind,' Owen pointed out.

'Exactly,' Elaine agreed. 'And that will make it even more unlikely that they'll scream.'

Owen relit his cigar and inhaled deeply. He seemed at a loss for words.

'Well?' Tony prodded.

'What about the crew?'

'We'll have to pay them off at Istanbul and take on a new crew on the return trip.'

'Leaving only the three of us on board to take the *Sarania* from Istanbul to Odessa?'

'Correct,' said Tony. 'It is, of course, vital that no one sees what happens at Odessa. Can the three of us manage the *Sarania* alone?'

Owen considered. 'It's about a twenty-hour run across the Black Sea from Istanbul to Odessa. We've got direct control of the engine room from the bridge and the engines should be fine without anyone in the engine room for that period . . . We can all take a trick at the helm. The weather's settled. Yes – we could manage.'

Tony looked pleased. 'Excellent, Captain Owen. You will find us obedient crewmen.'

Owen stared suspiciously at Tony. 'Look – I'm not committing myself, you understand, but supposing this lunatic plan works? How do I get paid?'

'Simple,' said Tony confidently. 'Most of the Swiss banks have branches in Istanbul. You open an account there, and then your account number is included on the control computer's program disk. Once we've broken into the SWIFT system, the transfer of funds will be automatic.'

Owen still hesitated. 'How do I know I can trust you?'

'You don't,' said Tony. 'How do we know we can trust *you*?'

'Why should you doubt us, captain?' Elaine asked in a reasoning tone. 'After all, it's not our money we'll be paying you with.'

'In that case, you can make mine a million,' said Owen shortly.

'I can't see any problem about that,' Tony agreed cautiously, thinking that Charlie was a shrewd judge of character.

The press officer at the American Embassy was surprisingly forth-coming about the Vice-Presidential visit to London. Over the telephone, she provided Damion with an outline of the US Vice President's and the Secretary of State's schedule.

'Will it be covered live on television?' Damion asked, as he made notes in the telephone box.

'Not all the visit will be covered, sir,' she said. 'But certainly the British Prime Minister meeting Air Force Two at Heathrow and the afternoon tea at Buckingham Palace will go out live – that's the drive to and from the palace. Negotiations are still going on for the deployment of cameras inside the palace.'

'What time is tea at the palace?'

'3.15 local time. That's 2.15 GMT. Does that help you, sir?'

Damion assured her that it helped him very much. He thanked her and hung up. He left the call box and strolled casually along the Mall towards Buckingham Palace. It was a beautiful spring morning. Tourists were thronging St James' Park; lying on the grass; talking in small animated groups; or feeding the wild fowl.

An assassination attempt along the Mall when the motorcade was on its way to Buckingham Palace for the tea would be the ideal place at the ideal time. Live television coverage on both sides of the Atlantic. Perfect timing for Central America's breakfast television. The assassination attempt would be seen by millions. Also the East Coast banks would be open and trading at that time. The reaction would be thousands of hands grabbing thousands of telephones and frantically trying to put calls through to London. A complete snarl-up that would effectively block the SWIFT authentication traffic and force its routing by satellite.

But there was a snag. Several major snags. The Mall was out of the question: there were no buildings and there was no cover unless one hid in a tree – and that would be courting certain suicide. Damion tried crossing the Mall and was forced to wait in the centre of the road for a gap in the traffic. As he did so, a circular steel manhole cover in the middle of the traffic lane on the approach to Buckingham Palace caught his attention. The road was clear. He dropped a couple of coins. Stooping to recover them gave him an opportunity to study the cover more closely. He memorized the pattern number that was cast into it and got a rough idea of its diameter against the span of his hands. He even noted the position of the cover's recessed lifting lugs.

Damion had realized that he was clutching at straws: the security surrounding the visit of US Vice President would be such that every inch of the route would be checked – including the lifting of manhole covers and the inspection of sewers to ensure that no bombs had been planted. They might even be temporarily spot-welded down.

He returned to his flat in Putney and found Crick busy with a soldering iron, carrying out modifications to a printed circuit board that he had removed from the SWIFT terminal. The living room had become a small workshop and was a mess. Every available piece of furniture was piled high with hard disk drives and assorted test equipment. The small control computer that would be used to process the messages before they were transmitted to the duplicate satellite was a disembowelled mass of wires and circuit boards on the dining table. On the floor was a Westinghouse wideband EHF radio transmitter of the type used by well-heeled radio amateurs for communicating through satellites. The kitchen was dominated by a folding dish antenna that was standing on a temporary tripod so that Crick could work on it.

'How's it going?' Damion inquired, flopping into a chair and yanking the top off a can of beer. He had walked several miles around central London.

'So so,' Crick answered, without looking up from his work. His face was bathed in the green glow from an oscilloscope screen. 'There are no significant problems with this equipment. Not that I can see any point in continuing, of course.'

Damion took a long draught from the can. 'We agreed that we would carry on. Something might come up.'

'Nothing will come up,' said Crick categorically.

Damion was getting tired of the pedantic Belgian's company.

'Once I have finished this and have the control computer working,' Crick continued, 'I see no point in my staying in London any longer. Already I am missing Spain. I shall need you to write a dummy program disk so that we can carry out some simulated transactions.'

'I'll make a start on it this evening,' said Damion, thinking that Crick was really going to miss Spain by the time he was through with him.

77: Moscow

There was a loud roar of air venting into the environmental test chamber. Once the air pressure was equalized, two technicians in sterile coveralls entered the chamber. They carefully lifted the duplicate SWIFT III satellite off its hoist and lowered it gently onto a specially shaped trolley. They were watched through a glass panel by Yuri Grechko and Mikhail Grovanich, the head of electronics development at the Leibenov Institute. Grovanich closed down the test console and examined the results of the space simulation on a print-out. He turned his swivel chair so that he was facing Grechko. He looked too exhausted to show any sign of elation at the successful conclusion of the final and most gruelling test that the satellite had just come through.

'Well done, Mikhail,' said Grechko, giving his colleague a warm handshake. 'You've done brilliantly.'

Grovanich smiled and nodded. 'You know something, comrade? That satellite is better than the original. We used the purest gallium arsenide semiconductors in the amplification stages. Look at these signal-to-noise figures.'

Grechko studied the columns of figures on the print-out and agreed that they made remarkable reading.

Grovanich stood and yawned. 'All that remains is to see that it fits into the SS-49A's dummy nose cone and then I hope that we can get back to our normal work, comrade.'

'It's been a strain, Mikhail. I realize this better than anyone.'

'How is the satellite to be'delivered?' Grovanich asked. 'By air?'

'Yes.'

'Tell the air force that if they drop it, I shall probably shoot myself.'

Grechko laughed good-naturedly and clapped Grovanich on the back. 'If they drop it, Mikhail, we'll invite you to shoot the air force. The club is still open – I shall buy you a drink. Two drinks. And then I am giving you a few days' special leave. Your fare and hotel and all expenses will be paid for by the institute.'

Grovanich looked interested. 'A paid holiday, comrade? Where?'

'Odessa,' Grechko replied abruptly. 'I want you to supervise delivery of the satellite and the installation of the rocket in the yacht.'

The responsibility that had been thrust upon him did not please

Grovanich. 'Why me, comrade?'

'Simple. I trust you, Mikhail. There is another problem. Time is now a crucial factor. According to the operator in London, the date of the operation has to be brought forward to June 3.'

'June 3!' Grovanich stared aghast at his chief. 'You mean the yacht has to be in launching position in mid-Atlantic by June 3? But it has not even reached Odessa yet!'

'That's why you're going to have to move fast, Mikhail,' said Grechko seriously. He smiled and clapped the younger man on the back. 'Come. We will discuss it over a drink.'

78: The Aegean Sea

It was another perfect day. The *Sarania* was heading north, threading a course through the myriads of Greek islands of the Aegean Sea, when Pepe approached Tony and Elaine who were sunning themselves on the aft deck. The Spanish lad was holding a Pokketfone. 'Señor Karn.' He touched Tony's forearm. 'Señor Karn. *Teléfono*.'

Tony was dozing. He took the handset. 'Hallo?'

'Mr Karn? Damion.'

Suddenly Tony was wide awake. The arrangement was that Damion would only attempt to contact him if the matter was serious. 'Hallo, Damion. How's London?'

'Sorry to disturb you, Mr Karn. We've got a problem. The deal has to be concluded on June 3.'

Tony sat up. His mind raced. 'June 3? But that's impossible!'

'It's got to be June 3,' Damion insisted.

'But why?'

'I can't say over the phone. But you know the problems I've got in London so I'll leave you to figure it out. But it has to be June 3. If I could make it later, I would, but I can't.'

The two men talked for another minute. 'Okay, Damion,' said Tony. 'I'll speed things up here.' He cleared the line and called Owen to the bridge.

A few minutes after Owen's PA announcement, Jackie locked herself in her cabin and recovered the radio from its hiding place. Already the *Sarania* had increased her speed to about sixteen knots.

'Mike – this is Angelica. Do you copy?'

There was more background noise than usual on Randall's signal when he replied. 'We copy you, Angelica. Go ahead.'

The sound of activity in the passageway outside Jackie's cabin made her hold the radio closer to her lips. 'Nothing much to report, Mike, but we've increased speed and we're putting into Istanbul for three hours.'

'Three hours? Are you sure of that?'

'Just enough time to take on fresh water and do a bit of shopping.'

'Roger on that, Angelica. We'll be . . .' The signal faded right out. Jackie experienced a twinge of alarm. 'Mike?'

'We're here, Angelica. Go ahead.'

'Why are you weaker than usual?'

'Could be signal absorption due to all the islands around . . . parts . . .'

There was a sudden banging on Jackie's door. 'Miss Morrison.' It was Pepe's voice. 'Capt'n Owen compliment. All crew on foredeck.'

'Coming!' Jackie said a hurried goodbye to Randall and quickly returned the radio to its hiding place. She went on deck and made her way to the foredeck where the hands were gathered around the empty swimming pool. They were looking expectantly up at Owen who was leaning on the bridge rail. The Sarania was still making a brisk sixteen knots through the narrowing Dardanelles Straits. Through the wheelhouse window Jackie could see Tony standing at the helm. The sun almost directly overhead, beating down on a cobalt blue sea.

'Sorry to disturb you, Miss Morrison,' Owen called down. 'What I have to say to you all won't take long. Pepe – you will translate for me – yes?'

'I try, Capt'n.'

'We have never been happy with the port engine,' Owen began. 'We know of a replacement, identical engine that's available at Odessa. Mr and Mrs Karn have decided that the Sarania should put into Odessa to have the engine replaced. Odessa is a Soviet port. None of you have visa authentications on your passport cards which is why we have to put into Istanbul – because we will have to pay you off there.' Owen paused to allow Pepe to catch up.

There was a murmur of dissent from the crew. 'We sign on for two month,' a seaman protested.

182

'And you'll be paid for two months,' Owen promised. 'You will have no problem finding other ships in Istanbul. We will be gone a week. If you are still in Istanbul when we return, we will be happy to sign you on again.'

Despite the muted grumbles, the seamen generally seemed happy with the arrangement.

'I'm very sorry about this, Miss Morrison,' Owen continued. 'I've spoken to Mr Karn. Your cooking has been excellent. Under the circumstances, he thinks it only fair that you should receive two months' pay so that you're not stranded in Istanbul.'

Jackie realized that she had no grounds for argument. 'Thank you, Captain.' She joined the exodus from the foredeck and returned to her cabin to decide what she should do about this latest unexpected turn of events.

79: London

Having exhausted just about every method of carrying out an attempted assassination that he could think of, Damion made a return visit to the vicinity of the South Bank telephone exchange in search of inspiration. He propped himself against the roadside coffee stall while sipping his drink and studying the surrounding buildings. The new mast was still in place. It appeared to have gained yet another camera. The visit was a waste of time: there was absolutely no way that he would be able to get into the exchange undetected.

As he returned his cup to the stall owner, he spotted a manhole cover set into the pavement right under his feet. He deliberately dropped a teaspoon, bent down to recover it and saw to his surprise that the circular cover was identical with the cover in the Mall. Even the pattern number was the same. He hailed a taxi and returned to his flat.

As usual, Crick was poking about inside the control computer with logic probes and a test meter. 'I'll be finished tomorrow,' the Belgian announced.

'Good,' said Damion, rummaging in a toolbox. He held up two prybars. 'Will you be needing these?'

'No. What do you need them for?'

'Trouble with the car.'

At 2.00 am the next morning, Damion parked his car beside the boarded-up coffee stall and pretended to consult a road map. All the car windows were open so that he could hear the slightest sound. A few vehicles passed by; and a couple of stumbling pedestrians, the worse for drink, singing lustily. A passing police car ignored them and Damion. Soon all was quiet. With a quick look around to make sure there were no police about on foot, Damion opened the nearside door and jumped out. The car screened him from the road. He hooked the prybars under the manhole cover's lifting lugs and heaved. It was much heavier than he had expected. It came free on the third attempt. The second surprise was that the cover was about four inches thick. Much thicker than he had dared hope. It was a neat, sliding fit in its sleeve. He dumped it on the floor of the car and positioned a heavy metal plate over the resulting hole in the pavement so that it would not attract immediate attention in the morning.

He took a pull from his hip flask and drove back to the flat, well satisfied with his night's work.

80: Istanbul

As soon as the *Sarania* was tied up, she was besieged by a noisy clamour of customs officials, harbour workers, chandlers and agents. Owen was near the gangway, using a fruit crate as a desk while simultaneously trying to deal with freshwater and fuel bunkerage, sort out a complaint from a hand who claimed his payoff money was short, and sign the multitude of forms that the customs men were waving under his nose.

Jackie waited her turn in the queue. So absorbed was she by her surroundings that she even forgot to smoke. The atmosphere of the capital of the once-mighty Byzantine Empire – and latterly of the Ottoman Empire – was irresistible. The buildings and golden domed palaces climbing the hills bore witness to a glory that was still very much in evidence. Once Istanbul had been the centre of the world. To Jackie it still seemed to be as ships, flying the flags of every maritime nation on earth, nosed and hooted their way along the Bosporus – the narrow straits that separated Europe from Asia. She was even treated to the incongruous sight of the *Minsk*, a Soviet

'Moskva' class helicopter cruiser, passing the towering moored bulk of the United States' aircraft carrier *Enterprise* as it passed through the Bosporus on its way to the Mediterranean. The two warships exchanged a flurry of courtesy signals.

'Ah, Miss Morrison,' said Owen, deleting Jackie's name from a memory pad and handing her an envelope. 'We've paid you in US dollars. I think you'll find the amount adequate. Would you sign here please? Thank you. And thank you for looking after us so well.' Owen shook her hand and turned to the next problem – a fuel agent who was demanding payment in cash.

Jackie returned to her cabin and locked the door. Her bag was already packed. She recovered the radio from its hiding place behind the bunk panel and tried to contact Randall, but the proximity of the quayside – virtually hard against her porthole – must have had a screening effect on the signal because there was no reply.

It was as she was pushing the panel back into place that she suddenly had an idea. It was such a ridiculous notion that her first reaction was to dismiss it from her mind. She stuffed the radio into her shoulderbag and moved to the door. She hesitated. Was it such a stupid idea? The whole point of her being on the *Sarania* was to find out what she could. And she couldn't do that stuck in Istanbul while the *Sarania* was five hundred miles to the north on the other side of the Black Sea at Odessa – assuming the yacht was going to Odessa as Owen had said.

She came to a decision, and acted upon it immediately by going to the galley. Luckily the suffocating conditions below decks, with no air conditioning and no ship's motion to force air through the ventilators, meant that the passageways were deserted. She collected enough tinned food from the galley stores to keep her going for a week and hid it down the back of the bunk in her cabin, together with plenty of toilet paper and other essentials. Fresh water was a problem; she decided that she would have to risk venturing out of her cabin at night. After all, it was only a short distance to the galley and there would only be Owen, Suskov and Elaine on board. The chances were that they would only go near the galley when they wanted something to eat.

Next she practised rolling herself quickly behind the padded panel and pulling it into place behind her. After two minutes in the darkened, airless compartment, her body was drenched in sweat.

She thankfully emerged from the claustrophobic hiding place and tried calling Randall again on the radio to let him know her plans but, as before, there was no answer.

81: London

Damion's patience snapped. He grabbed Crick by the lapels, thrust him into a chair and stood over him.

'Now you listen to me, Crick,' he grated. 'I've had it up to here with your constant griping. The only way we're going to snarl up the exchange is with a pound of plastic going off under the Vice President's car. Jesus Christ – a pound isn't going to hurt anyone – those diplomatic Cadillacs carry more armour than a Sherman tank. You have a choice. A very simple choice. Either I wring that miserable, scrawny neck of yours or you build the radio-control gear. Which is it to be?'

Crick swallowed nervously. He was no coward, but the memory of Jeff Hunter's brutal murder was still hideously fresh in his mind. He had no doubt that the big man had every intention of carrying out the threat. He nodded.

Damion slowly released his grip and straightened up. 'That's more like it.'

'But there are obvious problems,' said the Belgian. 'The police are certain to lift all manhole covers along the route. They would find the bomb immediately.'

'But they won't check the covers themselves,' said Damion. 'They'll lift the cover and replace it and weld it down if they find nothing suspicious underneath.' He gestured to the cover that was lying on the floor. That cover is big enough to be modified to contain a bomb.'

Crick did not reply immediately; he realized that Damion had a point. 'So how do you wish to activate the bomb?' he asked at length.

'From the *Sarania*.'

'When it's in mid-Atlantic? How?'

Damion produced a device that looked like an oversize pen. 'You know what this is, don't you?' he said. 'If I dial my home number from anywhere in the world, when my answering machine answers, all I have to do is send a coded audio signal down the line from this

186

gadget and the answering machine plays back its tape.'

Crick looked at the gadget and nodded. 'Of course I know what it is. It's a transducer. It sends a coded sonic signal down the telephone line. I use such an answering machine myself.'

'Right,' said Damion. 'Now it occurred to me, that instead of setting off a tape recorder, a device like this could be adapted to trigger a pulse-coded radio signal to detonate a nearby bomb. I could be anywhere in the world. All I've got to do is dial the number of this flat, send the tone down the line and . . . bang.'

The Belgian thought quickly. Damion's suggestion was perfectly feasible. 'But you want to detonate it from the *Sarania*?'

'Yes. That doesn't present a problem, does it?'

'Well – no. One could merely hold the line open to this flat through the ship-to-shore telephone link and send the activating pulse from the answering machine transducer whenever you wish. But how would you know the exact moment when to detonate the bomb?'

Damion gave a sudden laugh. 'You're the communications expert, Crick. Think. The answer's very simple.'

Crick thought. The answer came to him within two seconds. 'The visit is to be covered by British television and the pictures are to be sent live to America via satellite?'

The big man gave Crick a playful punch on the shoulder. 'You've got it, Crick. The specification for the *Sarania* says she has a full direct broadcasting satellite television receiving system. That means that I can be sitting in the comfort of the *Sarania*'s saloon watching the programme live on television while holding open the telephone line to this flat. The crowds lining the Mall; the motorcade of Cadillacs driving towards Buckingham Palace. And at the right moment, all I have to do is hold this thing to the mouthpiece of a Pokketfone and press the button. That's possible, isn't it?'

Crick nodded. 'Yes,' he said slowly. 'It is horribly possible.'

Damion laughed good-naturedly. 'You know something, Crick? Using modern technology to assassinate someone at a distance of six thousand miles has a certain style, don't you think?'

'No,' said Crick coldly. 'I don't think.'

Damion's smile vanished. With those four words the Belgian had determined his own future . . . Or rather, lack of a future.

82: The Sea of Marmara and the Bosporus

After six hours, the *Sarania* was still moored in the inner harbour at Istanbul.

Alone in her cabin, every nerve in Jackie's body was screaming for a cigarette but she knew that she dare not light up in case the fumes aroused suspicions when the cabin was checked before departure.

She heard voices approaching along the corridor. Doors were opening and closing. She unlocked the door. After a quick look round to make certain that the cabin bore no signs of occupation, she pulled back the padded panel and rolled into her hiding place, pulling the panel firmly into place behind her. She lay quietly in the humid darkness; beads of sweat prickling her forehead and running into her eyes; her heart pounding so hard that she was certain anyone entering the cabin would hear it.

The cabin door opened. Heavy footsteps within a few inches of where she was lying. Men's voices speaking Turkish. Laughter. A few sentences, and then the sound of the door closing and the footsteps receding. She waited a few more minutes to be certain that all was clear before emerging from her sweltering hiding place. She was soaking her face in the washbasin when the *Sarania* cast off. After a few minutes, she risked peering cautiously around the porthole curtain. The gleaming dome of the magnificent Sta Sophia mosque crossed her limited field of view. The *Sarania* was turning, bringing old Stamboul into sight.

There was little chance of anyone coming below until they were well clear of Istanbul. Fresh air wafted through the ventilators as the *Sarania* got under way. Jackie stretched naked on her bunk and let the welcome draught play on her body while she smoked a long-overdue cigarette. There was nothing else to do except wait, and wonder what the future held in store for her.

Breakfast and sex were Elaine's favourite pastimes. After that, the most recently discovered pleasure of them all: steering the *Sarania*.

She derived a curious, almost sexual pleasure in feeling the powerful yacht responding to her wishes as she held the helm spokes lightly between her fingers. Once they had passed through the Bosporus and were into the Black Sea, Owen had set her a course – virtually due north – and had shown her how to read the gyro-

188

compass and the plan position indicator radar. He had watched her for a few seconds, offering occasional words of advice, and had suddenly said: 'Okay – you're doing fine. Hit the alarm button and close down the throttles if anything comes within a kilometre on the PPI. I'll be asleep in the day cabin below, so don't worry.'

For the first hour Elaine had done nothing but worry. And then she had got the feel of the helm and began to enjoy herself. After several more minutes she felt exhilarated. She even swung the *Sarania* in a wide circle for the sheer hell of it without bothering to reduce the yacht's considerable speed. The sharp heeling and the change of course brought Tony onto the bridge.

'Bugger off,' she said cryptically, spinning the helm.

'We're off course.'

'No we're not. I'm just messing about.'

'My darling,' said Tony patiently, 'we cannot afford to lose any time.'

'One little circle's not going to make any difference.' She looked mischievously at Tony. 'Looking forward to being back in Mother Russia?'

Tony circled his arms around her waist. 'There's lots of things I'm looking forward to. But being in Russia isn't one of them.'

Elaine laughed and pushed his hands away. 'You behave yourself or I'll have you walking the plank. When I've got my own business and we're rich and infamous, I shall insist that we have a yacht like this.'

Tony held her tightly. 'We shall have a much better yacht than this with its own berth at Monte Carlo.'

'Monte Carlo's a ghastly French cliché,' Elaine wailed. 'Full of anorexic plastic proles. Won't it be wonderful to be rich enough to afford not to have to go to France. There're so many other places: America – Fort Lauderdale; Palm Beach. The Americans have a sensible attitude to breakfasts, and a sensible climate in the South to go with it. Now bugger off and leave me to finish my spell at the helm.'

83: London

Willard Machine Tools was one of those innumerable small jobbing engineering companies that had, with the encouragement of British Rail, leased railway arches in south London's Earlsfield area and turned them into workshops.

Joe Willard had been a toolmaker for forty years. He had had some weird propositions over the years but none as strange as the offer from the big man with the mop of dark hair.

'You want to rent my machine shop for three hours?' he queried. He was just about to lock up when the big man had approached him.

'That's right,' said Damion. 'I want to use that big Harrison.' He gestured to an ancient but very large lathe standing against the far wall.

'What for?'

'To finish the turning on some model locomotive wheels. All I've got in my workshop is a three-inch lathe. No good for what I want.'

Realization dawned on Joe. 'Oh – you're a steam freak? You should've said. Do you know how to use a Harrison? It's a big bastard.'

'No problem,' Damion assured him. He produced his wallet. 'I need about three hours. Shall we say . . . a hundred?'

'Done,' said Joe, taking the money. 'Three hours. I'm going down the pub. I'll be back at nine.' He waved his hand at the machines. 'Help yourself, guv. She's all yours.' He went out, leaving Damion alone.

Damion had used lathes before – he enjoyed any opportunity to use his hands – especially turning, but he had never used a machine as large as the Harrison. It took him fifteen minutes to centre accurately the heavy manhole cover in the giant four-jawed chuck. Once the cover was spinning true, he took an experimental skim off the manhole's underside with the cutting tool. Luckily the cover was steel and not cast iron – cast iron was a bastard to turn and required a continuous flow of kerosene as a lubricant for the cutting tool.

Satisfied that everything was correctly set up, Damion began the laborious task of machining a hollow in the underside of the cover that would be large enough to hold a radio receiver, an electric detonator and battery, and about two pounds of plastic explosive. The work took two hours and resulted in a small mountain of swarf

190

on the workshop's floor. He removed the much-lightened cover from the chuck and studied his handiwork with considerable satisfaction. The last task was to machine a disk from a piece of thick steel plate so that it would be a tight fit inside the hollow when driven home with a hammer.

Joe returned just as Damion was slamming the boot of his car.

'Everything okay, guv?' Joe inquired, glancing around the interior of his workshop to make sure that nothing had been taken. His speech was slightly slurred.

'Fine thanks,' said Damion. 'I owe you for a piece of five mill plate I used.'

Joe grinned. 'Forget it, guv.'

Damion looked up as Crick entered the flat. 'So what did Charlie have to say?'

Crick removed his jacket and dropped into a chair. Temperatures in London were edging into the thirties, and yet he insisted on wearing a jacket. 'He's not happy about the idea.'

'So what?' said Damion. 'None of us are. But it just so happens that we don't have much choice. Did he give you a contact?'

'Yes. A London number. The trouble is, the person may have moved by now or been caught by the police.'

'Only one way for you to find out,' said Damion, nodding to the telephone.

Crick looked alarmed. 'Surely you don't expect me to deal with it?'

Damion treated the Belgian to a menacing smile.

The narrow Limehouse streets were deserted. Crick hurried along, hands thrust in his jacket pockets. He felt uncomfortable – this was not the sort of area he would ever think of entering of his own accord during the day – never mind at night. He glanced at a street sign at a junction and turned left, slowing his step and looking anxiously at the names on the brooding, silent warehouses.

Suddenly he was grabbed from behind and yanked backwards into a darkened doorway. A powerful hand clamped over his mouth prevented him from crying out. Another pair of hands pinioned his arms behind his back and pushed him forward so that his face was flattened against a wall. His first thought was that he was being mugged, and then a voice said:

'Are you the guy that phoned?' Surprisingly, it was a cultured voice.

Crick made an affirmative noise.

'Make a sound and you're dead,' the voice warned. 'You may say one word and one word only. What's your name?' The hand was removed from his mouth.

'Crick . . .' The Belgian's voice was a frightened tremble. He felt a hand reach from behind and remove his wallet. A flashlight snapped on. They were studying the wallet's contents.

One of the men grunted. 'You'd be dead by now if we'd found a warrant card.'

Crick did not doubt them.

'Okay,' said the voice. 'We're taking the money out of your wallet. Two grand. The going rate. Not a penny more. Not a penny less.'

Crick heard the rustle of banknotes and felt the wallet being returned. A heavy weight was thrust into his jacket pocket.

'Now start walking back the way you came,' said the voice, pushing Crick back onto the pavement. 'Just keep walking and don't look back.'

The Belgian did exactly as he was told. He reached a busy road and hailed a taxi. Only when he was back in the safety of the Putney flat did he dare take the package from his pocket.

Damion unwrapped the brown paper and examined the package's contents. 'Just the job,' he remarked, grinning at Crick's worried expression.

Crick looked down at the electric detonators and the slab of grey, putty-like substance.

It was the first time he had ever seen plastic explosive.

84: Odessa

The SS-49A was a three-stage solid fuel rocket that had been developed at the Soviet's vast space research and vehicle launch complex at Tyuratum, halfway between Tashkent and the Caspian Sea. It was a relatively small rocket – ten metres long, including its launcher – because it was primarily designed for the launching from small research ships of geostationary satellites used for the testing of particle beam weapons.

The sight of the rocket on its articulated transporter driving through the entrance to the naval dockyard at Odessa was an immense relief to Mikhail Grovanich.

The dockyard superintendent entered the office where Grovanich was standing at the window, watching the rocket's team of civilian technicians inspecting their charge. The team had arrived earlier by helicopter.

'Your missile has arrived,' the superintendent announced.

Grovanich frowned. 'It's not a missile, comrade. It's a rocket.'

The superintendent shrugged. He was a naval man: anything with a pointed nose was either a ship or a missile. He handed a signal to Grovanich. 'An intelligence report from Istanbul. The *Sarania* sailed ten hours ago. It will be here at zero six tomorrow.'

The scientist thanked him. 'It will be a relief to start work. The last few days have been a considerable strain.'

85: The Black Sea

Jackie awoke and looked at her watch.

It was 5.30 am. The best time of day because the temperature in the cabin was tolerable. She felt for her cigarettes in her shoulderbag.

Only one packet?

She removed a precious cigarette from the packet and sat looking at it.

She was bored.

Bored. Bored. Bored.

During the thirty hours since the *Sarania* had left Istanbul, she had even found herself looking forward to the breaks in the monotony when the sound of someone approaching the galley obliged her to hide behind the panel.

She postponed lighting the cigarette by attempting to contact Randall yet again on the radio. Nothing. The indicator on the set showed that the battery was fully charged, and the red transmit light glowed brightly when she pressed the transmit key. She even risked holding the set out of the porthole at arm's length.

It was then that she saw the great forest of shipyard cranes and derricks edging above the horizon and into the early morning light.

Odessa.

Damion walked along the Mall by St James' Park towards Buckingham Palace. He was certain that he now knew every inch of the great thoroughfare. The sky was grey and overcast. A chill northeasterly wind was blowing. The sudden drop in London's temperature was an unwelcome reminder that winter had not long departed.

He reached the spot parallel to the manhole cover, took a Pokketfone from his shoulderbag and called the flat. Crick answered.

'Yes?' The Belgian was expecting the call.

'In position,' said Damion cryptically.

'Testing now,' Crick replied.

As Crick spoke, a muted buzzer sounded in Damion's shoulderbag. The buzzer was temporarily connected to the miniature radio receiver that would eventually be installed in the bomb to trigger the detonator.

'It's working fine,' said Damion, pleased. 'I'm coming back.'

'I said the test was unnecessary,' said Crick primly and cut the line.

Damion reflected that Crick was a pain. He hailed a taxi. Everything was going extremely well. The purpose of the experiment had been to ensure that the miniature radio receiver was working and that the pulse-coded transmitter in the flat at Putney had the necessary range to reach central London. Despite his satisfaction, Damion had an uneasy feeling that there was something he had overlooked – something incredibly minor and yet something that a sharp-witted schoolkid would spot immediately. He pushed the thought from his mind. Every detail had been carefully worked out: he was worrying needlessly.

When he returned to the flat, Crick was finishing clearing up. His work on the equipment to break into SWIFT III was finished. The three units: the SWIFT III terminal; the control computer; and the radio transmitter with its satellite dish, were ready for despatch. The SWIFT logos had been removed from the terminal. Altogether, the equipment could be carried in the back of an estate car.

'This came today,' said Crick, handing Damion a form.

It was the authorization from the Spanish Embassy, permitting the import of three listed items of amateur radio equipment.

'Fine,' said Damion. He lifted the manhole cover onto the table and took the radio receiver from his shoulderbag. 'Your last job is to fix this up.'

Crick made two final connections with his soldering iron while Damion packed the plastic explosive into the hollow. The lithium battery that could power the receiver and detonator for up to a month was pushed firmly into the explosive, followed by the receiver itself. Crick arranged the components so that the detonator switch was sticking out of the explosive.

'What about the antenna?'

'The cover itself forms the antenna, you understand,' said Crick coldly. He looked up at Damion. 'It is ready to test.'

Damion moved to the telephone and switched on the answering machine. There was nothing about the machine to suggest that it now also housed a pulse-coded radio transmitter. 'Make sure the detonator switch is off,' he ordered.

'It is off,' said Crick. 'I checked.'

'Well check again! I don't want to be blown to glory because you've made a stupid mistake, for Chrissake.'

Crick double-checked the switch. 'It is definitely off,' he confirmed.

Damion walked across the room holding a Pokketfone. He sat in an easy chair, grinned amiably at the Belgian and unclipped the answering machine's transducer from his breast pocket. 'Imagine I'm six thousand miles away in the middle of the Atlantic.'

'I will try,' said the Belgian indifferently.

Damion rested the transducer on the arm of the chair and punched out the flat's number on the Pokketfone. Two seconds passed. The flat's telephone bleeped. The answering machine opened the line on the fifth bleep and started the buffer store recording. A synthesized voice regretted that the flat was empty and invited the caller to recite his or her message after the tone.

Damion's face was tense as picked up the transducer. He held it near the Pokketfone's mouthpiece with his thumb resting on its switch. He waited for a minute and thumbed the switch without warning. As he did so, the receiver imbedded in the plastic explosive emitted an audible click from an internal relay.

'Bang,' said Damion softly, and then he laughed at Crick's disdainful expression. He crossed the room and switched the detonator on. 'Let's get it finished.'

'There is a problem with the transducer and the answering machine,' said Crick.

'Oh? And what's that?'

'The sonic pulses from the transducer will also start the answering machine's tape in the normal manner,' said Crick. 'Once that happens you won't be able to use the transducer again until the tape has stopped.'

'Meaning?'

'Meaning that you will only have the one chance to detonate the bomb.'

The beginnings of Damion's scowl changed to a grin. He clapped Crick on the back. 'One bomb. One chance. And that's all I need. Just the one chance.'

The remaining work to be done on the bomb was simply a matter of cutting out disks from a small roll of builders' sheet lead and packing them down on top of each other into the cavity. Finally Damion gently tapped the cover plug into the hollow with a hammer. He was particularly careful to ensure that the plug finished flush. He weighed the manhole cover experimentally in his hands.

'Brilliant,' he said. 'The same weight as it was before we altered it.' He turned the cover over and examined it critically. It bore no sign of having been tampered with. He picked up one of the spare detonators and held it under Crick's nose. 'Just one more little job with one of these, Crick, and your work is finished.'

'What do you want me to do with it?' the Belgian demanded suspiciously.

'Make a van blow a tyre at the right moment so that I can swap manhole covers. A simple job like that shouldn't give a clever man like you any problems.'

Crick took the detonator. 'Very well. But no more after this. Already I have done far more than my share of work on this operation. I have had little sleep for three weeks.'

For once Damion did not get angry. Instead he merely smiled and said: 'I give you a solemn promise, doctor – after tonight I shall not ask you to do anything else.'

Again the irrational feeling returned that he had overlooked something important. It made him angry with himself.

87: Winchester

It was 2.10 am, and Hans Crick had been dead for an hour when Damion turned the laden estate car through the entrance of the Golden Rose Hotel. He drove around to the rear of the building and reversed up to the service entrance. The folding doors were already open as Charlie had promised.

Damion checked the utility room to make certain no one was about before he swung open the door of the argon gas incinerator and pulled out the ceramic loading pallet. He went back to the estate car and returned with Crick's body slung over his shoulder. He dumped the body on the pallet, rolled the pallet back into the incinerator and closed the door. He selected the highest temperature on the control panel to ensure that even Crick's teeth were destroyed in the inferno, and pressed the start button. There was a muted roar from within the incinerator as the oxygen-fuelled gases burst into flame. An incandescent white light blazed through the inspection window. The incinerator burned for fifteen minutes and cut out. Damion peered through the window. The remains of a skull was sitting on the pallet. The same thing had happened when Damion had disposed of Billy Watts' body. Another burn, this time for five minutes, and there was no sign of the skull. The incinerator was empty. All that was left of Dr Hans Crick was a fine molecular dust that the extractor fans were sucking into the incinerator's filters.

Satisfied that all was well, Damion parked the estate car in Charlie's private garage.

88: Odessa

Jackie was lying on her bunk when the hammering started. It was no ordinry hammering. The appalling racket reverberated through the *Sarania* as if her steel hull was being ripped apart by pneumatic drills. She clapped her hands over her ears in anguish. Such a noise could not last long – the entire yacht would fall apart. But it did last. The frightful uproar went on and on. The porthole was no use in finding out what was going on because it was hard against a dockside wall.

After an hour, with her nerves screaming, she realized that she

197

would have to hide behind the panel because there was no chance of her hearing anyone approaching her cabin above the frightening din.

She pulled the panel closed behind her and lay in the darkness with her hands pressed hard over her ears. Instead of being quieter, as she had hoped, the noise was even worse. The temperature in the confined space rose rapidly, adding to her misery. After fifteen minutes of the seemingly unending torment, she did something that she had not done for ten years since her husband had died:

She began to cry.

Tony, Elaine and Owen leaned on the dockside wall and watched the assault on the *Sarania*.

'My God,' Elaine muttered. 'They don't care, do they?'

'It looks alarming,' Owen agreed as four Soviet technicians cut around the *Sarania*'s empty swimming pool with pneumatic chisels. 'But they know what they're doing.'

The team leader used a radio in his helmet to talk to the crane operator. The crane's hoist was lowered until it was hovering above the swimming pool. While the men continued cutting around the pool, the leader shackled the pool to the hoist by passing chains around its boarding ladder and safety rail. The crane operator, high above the dockyard, worked his levers and took up the tension in the hoist.

The men completed cutting around the pool. When they turned off their chisels, it was possible to hear the rest of the sounds of the Soviet navy's busiest and largest warm water dockyard. All around was a confused mass of cranes, warships and activity on such a scale that it was difficult to pick out details of exactly what was going on: the grey-painted bulk of cruisers merged with the outlines of frigates and helicopter assault craft. Every now and again there were bursts of brilliant blue lights from welding guns. It seemed to Elaine that half the ships were being torn apart rather than repaired.

One of the technicians signalled to the leader, who then spoke to the crane operator.

Elaine's eyes widened in surprise as the *Sarania*'s entire swimming pool was lifted as a single unit and swung clear, leaving a gaping, circular hole about fifteen feet in diameter in the *Sarania*'s foredeck. 'Hey – I hope they put it back,' she complained.

'They will,' Tony replied. 'But it'll be much smaller.'

The team leader shone a powerful lamp around the interior of the hole. He gave orders. A steel tape measure was produced. The leader disappeared into the hole down a ladder for a few minutes.

Mikhail Grovanich appeared on the foredeck. He waved to the trio and held a brief conference with the team leader. The scientist seemed satisfied. He left the *Sarania* and joined the group by the dockside wall. As when he had first introduced himself shortly after the *Sarania* had docked, he spoke English for the benefit of Elaine and Owen.

'Everything is going excellently well,' he said. 'There is plenty of room for the rocket and the launcher. Of course, the swimming pool provides an excellent hatch.'

'How long will it all take to install?' Owen wanted to know.

'We need two more clear days.'

'Have you decided on the launch position?' Owen asked.

'Not yet,' the Soviet admitted. 'It will have to be at least five hundred miles out to sea, of course, so that the rocket will not be seen from the land. Possibly off the west coast of Africa.'

'But the Americans will plot it, won't they?' said Elaine.

'They're almost certain to,' Grovanich replied. 'But as we often launch satellites from our research ships, they won't attach much importance to it. Especially as it is an extremely small satellite.'

Owen did a rough mental calculation. 'We're going to be hard pushed to reach a point five hundred miles off West Africa by June 3,' he observed.

'You can maintain fifteen knots?'

'Yes.'

Grovanich gave an expansive gesture and smiled. 'Then I don't think there is anything to worry about. You will be notified by radio of the launch position once you have sailed. I am sorry, but installation cannot be completed in less time. There is much work to be done besides mounting the rocket. There is the radio telemetry equipment to be installed and tested.' He steered them towards the administrative building. 'Now please. You must not worry. We have booked you into the best hotel in Odessa. Anton will tell you that Odessa is the finest coastal resort in the Soviet Union.'

'It's the only one,' Tony commented acidly.

In the chauffeur-driven car taking them to the hotel, Elaine gave Tony a sharp nudge in the ribs. 'What are Russian breakfasts like?'

she wanted to know.

'Huge,' Tony replied. 'Really enormous.'

Elaine gave a satisfied nod. It was the only thing that had been worrying her.

89: Winchester

'*Drive* to Spain?' Charlie queried, taking a drink from Baldwin. 'Why the hell should we drive?'

'After all the work that's gone into that equipment, I'd be a lot happier if it's never out of my sight,' Damion replied. 'I have nightmares about taking it to Gatwick and having the freight carriers dropping it, or sending it on the wrong flight to Japan or somewhere. We don't have the expertise of our Belgian friend any more, remember.'

Charlie looked reflective. 'We never did learn why he was so anxious to bust into SWIFT. The guy had money.'

'So do you, Charlie.'

Charlie gave Damion an icy look. 'What does that mean?'

Damion looked carefully at the hotelier. 'I want to break into SWIFT because I'm broke and I like money. Elaine because she wants to run her own business. Tony because he wants to quit the Soviet Union and live in style. But why you, Charlie? What do you hope to gain?'

Surprisingly, Charlie did not get angry as Damion had expected. Instead he picked up the sheaf of papers that Jim Hoffman had given him. He leafed slowly through them. 'Satisfaction,' he said shortly. 'That's all I want. Satisfaction.' He gave Damion the papers. 'Those are all the accounts I want cleaned out.'

Damion looked through the columns. He noticed that one name had been deleted: Victor Salavante. Damion was puzzled because the names of companies and individuals did not seem to have anything in common. 'Are these all your enemies, Charlie?'

'You could say that.'

'Jesus – don't you have any friends?'

Charlie's black eyes hardened. 'Why? Any problems with that list?'

'No problems at all, Charlie,' said Damion hastily, realizing that he had touched a nerve. 'I'll make up a separate program disk for your transactions.'

Charlie relaxed and nodded. 'Maybe I'll tell you about it some day. Okay – I agree with you about driving to Spain. How long will it take?'

'Three days. Two nights on the road.'

'We'll take my Rolls,' Charlie decided. 'It'll be more comfortable. My back isn't too good these days in small cars.'

The two men drank to the success of the operation.

90: Odessa

Jackie had smoked her last cigarette the day before. As a consequence, and because she had had to endure two days of almost nonstop, mind-shattering noise, her nervous system was in a state of collapse to a point where she could hardly think straight without an effort.

One thing she was certain of: whatever it was that was being done to the *Sarania*, it was not the fitting of a replacement engine. She refused to believe that replacing an engine in a yacht could be so important that a shipyard would work round the clock on the project for forty-eight hours. Especially as, during the lulls in the clamour, none of the other normal sounds of the dockyard could be heard at night. So why should a Soviet naval yard lavish such attention on a private yacht?

Conditioned by a habit of twenty-five years, Jackie's hand reached automatically for the cigarette packet beside her. The packet was empty. In anger and frustration she crushed the packet and hurled it across the cabin.

And then the hideous clamour of the pneumatic chisels started again.

The three technicians lowered the *Sarania*'s port motor launch on its davits to deck level and carried out a repeat of their performance on the starboard motor launch: they removed all the launch's buoyancy blocks from the fore and aft compartments and added sugar to the full fuel tanks. Two of them drained the two-hundred-litre fresh-water tank and refilled it with sea water, while the third unscrewed the cover from the radio transceiver and removed a few essential components. Finally they wheeled a spark erosion machine alongside the launch and used its gun to riddle the launch's steel hull with thousands of almost invisible perforations. They concentrated the gun along the inside of the rubbing strakes where the holes would not be seen when the launch was hoisted into place above the side deck. They then relashed the vinyl covers over the launch and cranked it back into position, suspended from its davits. The launch bore no outward signs of their handiwork. Their final task was to remove all the inflatable liferafts from their ready-use lockers that were dotted around the *Sarania* and slash them with sharp knives before restowing them. They did the same with the lifejackets.

Apart from a new dish antenna on the bridgehouse roof, there was little about *Sarania*'s external appearance to suggest that the yacht had been subjected to a number of major alterations. Closer inspection would have revealed that the swimming pool was a foot shallower, and that the billiard room portholes had been blanked off. Certainly, there were no obvious signs pointing to the fact that she now housed below decks a three-stage rocket mounted on a launcher.

Below decks the signs were more apparent: forty feet aft of the bow was a new beam to beam steel bulkhead that completely isolated the bow section of the yacht. The billiard room, with its gyro-stabilized billiard table, was no more.

Elaine surveyed the shortened dining saloon in annoyance. 'You've ruined it,' she said reproachfully to Grovanich.

'It was necessary to remove a metre,' the Soviet scientist replied. 'But the bulkhead panelling has been replaced exactly as it was.'

'But it's all out of proportion,' Elaine protested.

'What does it matter?' said Tony impatiently. 'It had to be done.'

The inspection party moved to the bridge where Owen was arguing with the leader of the Soviet technicians. He broke off and said angrily to Grovanich: 'So where are the launching controls for the rocket?'

Grovanich looked nonplussed. 'I don't understand.'

Owen pointed to a plain steel electronic cabinet that was bolted to the roof. The small unit was a new addition. It was fed by cables that were clipped neatly to the underside of the roof beams. 'From what this buy's been telling me, that's the control box for launching the missile.'

'That is correct,' said Grovanich. 'Why? Surely it is not in the way up there?'

'In that case, where are the controls?'

'At the launch control room, of course,' said Grovanich, clearly puzzled by Owen's anger.

'And where's that?'

'Somewhere in the Soviet Union. As soon as you are in position, we shall launch the rocket by remote control.'

It was Owen's turn to look puzzled. 'By remote control? From a distance of several thousand miles?'

'Why – yes.'

'But what about your crewmen?' asked Elaine. 'Won't they launch it?'

'What crewmen?'

'But surely you're providing us with some technicians?'

'That is not possible,' said Grovanich.

Tony realized what had happened. 'I think,' he said slowly, 'that we've assumed all along that there would be Soviet technicians on board to look after the rocket.'

'That is not possible,' Grovanich repeated.

'For God's sake' said Owen. 'Surely you're providing someone? There's only the three of us. We don't know anything about launching rockets.'

Grovanich shook his head. 'I am very sorry. I thought you knew? We have strict instructions that no Soviet technician must sail on the *Sarania*. Launching the rocket via the satellite link is very simple. You don't have to know anything about launching rockets. All you have to do is be in the right position –'

'We don't even know the position yet!' Owen interrupted.

The Soviet scientist was unperturbed. 'You will be told when you have sailed.' He pointed out a new radio transceiver that was mounted alongside the navigation equipment. 'We will be in constant touch with you through that set.'

'Christ,' Owen muttered. 'You mean that the opening of the hatch and the elevating of the launcher and the firing can all be controlled from Moscow or wherever?'

The Soviet scientist smiled. 'Thirty years ago we landed a probe on the moon. It collected some lunar samples and returned to Earth. All done by telemetry over quarter of a century ago. Believe me, captain – launching an SS-49A from the *Sarania* to inject a satellite into a geostationary orbit is no problem at all for us today. And nor will it be a problem for you.'

'What about when we've taken over the SWIFT traffic?' Elaine asked. 'How will you carry out your transactions?'

'Thanks to the information you have sent us, those too will be controlled from the control room,' said Grovanich smoothly. 'The duplicate satellite has ample multi-tasking facilities for all of us to carry out what transactions we wish at the same time.'

'The crewing was a misunderstanding on my part,' Tony admitted.

'Well – it's not a problem,' said Owen. 'What is a problem is we have to put into Istanbul to sign on another crew, and Alicante to pick up two other members of our team, and we're badly pushed for time. And on top of that, you won't be giving us our launch position until after we've sailed. Great.'

Grovanich gave a little bow. 'I fully understand your concern, captain. We will complete all our tests as soon as possible. There is no reason why you should not sail before dusk.'

91: Moscow Sunday, May 19

The Chairman annihilated a whole row of American tanks while he listened to Academician Yuri Grechko's report. He pressed a red button on the vintage arcade machine. A new company of tanks advanced across the video monitor and turned to face their inevitable electronic destruction.

'So,' said the Chairman when he had despatched the last tank. 'The *Sarania* has sailed. I suppose I should say well done.' He looked speculatively at Grechko. 'But there is one thing you have not mentioned.'

'There was not enough time to place explosive charges against the *Sarania*'s hull and to test them, Comrade Chairman.'

'You should have made time, Yuri.' The Chairman's tone was mildly reproving.

'I did consider attaching limpet mines to the outside of the hull,' Grechko explained. 'But there is always the risk that they might be spotted. Also, one can never be certain of the reliability of the radio control receivers after a long sea voyage. As for explosive charges on the inside of the hull – as I said – there was not enough time for the tests. Also, the *Sarania* has a steel hull. There would be difficulties with the radio control receivers. It would be embarrassing for us if the charges went off prematurely in the shallow waters of the Mediterranean where the *Sarania* could be salvaged or visited by pleasure divers. The discovery of the SS-49A –'

'Yes, yes. You don't have to spell it out,' said the Chairman testily. 'I suppose you did right. We will have to ensure that we have a surface craft or a submarine in the launch area to dispose of the *Sarania* by more direct means. When she's done what we want her to do, of course.'

'That's what I thought, Comrade Chairman,' Grechko murmured. 'For that reason we still have not decided the position that the *Sarania* should launch the missile from until we know the likely position of a suitable naval unit.'

The Chairman gave a frosty smile. 'I have discussed the matter with Admiral Kalinovitch. He has already sent a Moskva class helicopter-cruiser to a mid-Atlantic station. I do not think destroying a yacht will pose any problems for him.'

92: The Black Sea Sunday, May 19

Jackie woke with a guilty start.

Something was different. It was some moments before her befuddled mind interpreted the pounding as the *Sarania*'s engines. The *Sarania* was under way! She tried to move but her joints were locked with cramp. She had hidden behind the panel in case her cabin was checked. She eventually managed to move her arm so that she could look at her watch. To her astonishment she discovered that she had been sleeping for fifteen hours. She eased down the panel and luxuriated in the cool, fresh air that was wafting into the cabin before forcing her limbs to move. All that was visible through the porthole were the stars and the flashing silver of the *Sarania*'s wake. No lights. No sign of land. As best as her inexpert eye could judge, the yacht was punching into the swell at about sixteen knots.

She listened intently. No sounds from the galley. A quick dash along the passageway to refill her water canteen and grab a wine box, and she was back in the cabin. After a shower, a drink, and a meal consisting of a tin of peaches and a whole packet of biscuits washed down with a generous measure of wine, she felt a little more human. She tried calling Randall on the radio. As usual, there was no answer. She tidied up the cabin – disposing of the evidence of her occupation out of the porthole – and sat on the bunk, sipping wine, while trying not to think about cigarettes.

Dawn brought clear blue skies and no sign of land. At least she could obtain a bearing from the sun. The *Sarania* was heading south. Back to Istanbul? During the following ten hours she had to hide several times when there was activity in the galley. For tea, she opened a canned steak pie. The label said that it would serve four. She ate the lot with her fingers and drank about a quarter of the wine box. After a while the effect of the large meal, the wine, and the lulling throb of the engines caused her to break her rule by falling asleep on the bunk.

It was dark when she was woken by the sounds of the engines going hard astern. There was noise. Bustle. Ship's hooters. She cautiously drew aside the curtain and peeped out. The *Sarania* was tying up at Istanbul.

Assuming that the yacht still had a crew of three, she guessed that they would be busy on deck during the docking. She quickly cleaned her cabin – even wiping splashes from the washbasin – and packed her shoulderbag. The passageway was clear. She dashed past the doors leading to the engine room and crouched behind a ventilator duct, listening intently. There was the sound of a gangway being dragged into place above her head and then people were swarming onto the yacht, talking and shouting. About a dozen arguments broke out in Turkish. A bulkhead to the fore of the companionway that led up to the weatherdeck caught her attention. It looked new; she was certain that she had never seen it before. But getting off the *Sarania* undetected was more important than finding out what alterations the Soviets had carried out.

She poked her head above the companionway. The deck was crowded. Perhaps the massed boarding of all vessels arriving at Istanbul was an ancient Turkish custom. Whatever it was, it suited Jackie because no one noticed her as she pushed past about a dozen quarrelling chandlers all squabbling over who should have the

Sarania's custom. She had just reached the gangway when a woman's voice suddenly called out: 'Miss Morrison! How clever of you to find us!'

Jackie's heart sank. She turned. It was Elaine, looking very pleased to see her.

'Oh don't go,' Elaine begged. 'We'll be sorted out in a while. We're not stopping long so we'll be signing on a crew as quickly as possible and we'll need a cook. Isn't it amazing how the word goes round when a boat's coming in? How did you find out so quickly that we'd returned?'

Thinking quickly, Jackie said: 'Oh – I could see the *Sarania* coming in from where I'm rooming.'

Tony shouldered his way through the melee. 'Hallo, Miss Morrison,' he said genially. 'Welcome aboard again. Well – finding you is one problem less.'

Jackie returned the greetings and asked if the *Sarania* had been fitted with a new engine.

'Oh yes,' said Tony smoothly. 'She's running like a dream now. And we've had a new waterproof compartment installed for'ard. It'll be safer for long ocean cruises. I hope you'll sign on again?'

'So do I,' Elaine added with feeling.

'Do you know where you are going this time?' Jackie asked.

Tony smiled. 'Back to Alicante to pick up some friends and then through the Straits of Gibraltar for a cruise south. Ghana. The Caribbean maybe.'

'Sounds exciting.'

'If it wasn't for me, she would have scooted off,' said Elaine. 'Ah – there's Captain Owen!' She put her little fingers into her mouth and blew a piercing whistle at Owen who had appeared at the bridge rail, arguing with a customs officer. 'Captain Owen!'

Owen glanced down.

'We've found Miss Morrison! Okay if we sign her on again?'

'Hallo, Miss Morrison,' Owen called down. 'Yes – fine. Same duties. Same terms.' He resumed his dispute with the official.

Elaine looked seriously at Jackie. 'Is that okay with you?'

'And the same cabin, Mrs Karn?'

'Well – yes.'

Jackie had to exercise considerable self-control to stop herself bursting out laughing. 'That'll be fine, Mrs Karn. I hope the *Sarania* is stopping long enough for me to do some shopping?'

Jackie was in a noisy Turkish supermarket buying several cartons of cigarettes when she felt someone touch her sleeve.

'I carry them for you, Miss Morrison?'

It was Pepe – grinning hugely. She was genuinely pleased to see the diminutive Spanish boy. 'Pepe!' She gave him a hug and a kiss which seemed to embarrass him.

'I just sign on with *Sarania* again,' he explained, still grinning. 'They tell me you sign on.'

Outside the store, Jackie lit a cigarette and inhaled deeply. 'Pepe,' she said, tousling the boy's hair, 'you're the second-best thing that's happened to me today.'

93: The Aegean Sea Monday, May 20

The *Sarania* was six hours out from Istanbul, heading southwest for the Mediterranean at sixteen knots, when Jackie finally managed to contact Randall on her radio. His answering signal was strong.

'Where in hell have you been?' she wanted to know as soon as they had identified themselves.

Randall sounded aggrieved. 'I could ask you the same question, Angelica.'

Mindful of the new antenna on the *Sarania*'s bridgehouse roof, Jackie wanted reassurance that their signals could not be overheard.

'They're a hundred per cent secure,' said Randall. 'So where have you been? We searched Istanbul.'

'I stowed away on the *Sarania*. I've been to Odessa.'

'What? But they paid off the crew.'

Jackie outlined the events of the last few days. 'So we might as well call the whole thing off,' she concluded. 'It looks as if everything is as they said. The trip to Odessa was to have a new engine fitted and to have some refitting done. An enlarged watertight bow compartment. When we get to Alicante, I want to fly home.'

'I don't think so, Angelica.'

'Why not?'

'I'll talk to you about it in Alicante. But right now it looks like you're gonna have to hang on in there.'

94: Alicante Sunday, May 26

The *Sarania* completed the two-thousand-mile voyage from Istanbul to the Spanish port in six days, having maintained a credible average speed of fourteen knots. During that time the yacht had behaved magnificently.

It was late evening and Alicante was shrouded in the shadows of the mountains when she nosed into the harbour. The 150-foot Chris Craft that had shadowed the yacht most of the way across the Mediterranean and back again had arrived six hours earlier.

'She's a fine yacht,' Owen said to Tony in the bridgehouse, judging the distance to the quayside and throwing the engines into reverse. 'A quick checkover, bunkering and victualling, and she'll be ready for a five-thousand-mile trip. No problem.'

'The stay here will have to be quick,' Tony commented.

'Very quick,' Owen agreed.

The deckhand standing on the foredeck dropped the fenders into place and tossed a mooring line to a waiting harbour worker. The *Sarania* was made secure. Owen cut the throttles and signalled to the engine room that he had finished with the engines.

'There's Baldwin!' Tony exclaimed, pointing through the window.

Jackie was cleaning up the galley before going ashore when Pepe came in with the latest news. 'The guests come,' he announced. 'I carry their baggage to their cabins.'

'Any idea who they are?'

'Label on one bag say . . . Silvo . . .' He struggled with the name.

'Silvester?' said Jackie sharply.

Pepe grinned. '*Si*. Damion Silvester. And the other I think like Carlos. Charlie. They come with a Rolls Royce with chauffeur.'

Jackie hurriedly wiped her hands. 'Pepe – be an angel and finish in here for me.'

Jackie found Randall sitting at the customary table on the *Kon Tiki* floating bar. She sat opposite him and lit a cigarette.

'So why the hell didn't you stay in radio range?' she demanded.

'I'm sorry about that, Angelica.'

'It's no good being sorry. Why didn't you stick with me like you promised?'

'Angelica – there was no way that the craft I was on could go into Soviet-controlled waters. The Black Sea is strictly out of bounds. Besides – we thought you were in Istanbul. Stowing away was a pretty crazy thing to do. And you didn't learn anything.'

Jackie flared up. 'You sanctimonious creep! Do you have any idea of the misery I had to go through –' She suddenly shut up when she saw people at neighbouring tables looking at her.

Randall covered her hands with his and squeezed them affection-ately. 'Sure I know what you've been through, Angelica. And I'm proud of you. Really I am. But what did you learn about the *Sarania*? That it had a new engine fitted and a watertight bulkhead installed? And what else? What about the new microwave dish antenna on the bridge roof? What's that for?'

'A navigation system?'

'The yacht already has a satellite navigation system and a satellite television receiving system.'

'I think I know who Anton Suskov is acting as an agent for,' said Jackie.

'Who?'

'Charlie Rose. He and Damion Silvester are now on the *Sarania*.'

The news surprised Randall. He dredged in his pockets for his pipe and filled it with his dangerous-looking tobacco. 'Now how did they get here? We've got a guy watching the Alicante Airport arrivals computer.'

'They drove here,' said Jackie, pleased to have scored one over Randall. 'In a Rolls Royce that is parked not far from the *Sarania*. Its licence number is CR1. By a brilliant piece of reasoning that ought to leave you breathless, I have deduced that the car is owned by Charlie Rose.'

Jackie's satirical barbs were wasted on Randall. He lit his pipe and said slowly: 'That confirms his involvement.'

'Charlie Rose? Sure – he's the *Sarania*'s mystery owner. It's all above board and we've been wasting the taxpayers' money chasing our own imagination.'

'I only wish that were true, Angelica. Jim Hoffman – a private investigator – has been murdered in New York. From what was found out when the file access passwords were busted on his data base, he had been nosing around some ultra sensitive overseas bank

210

accounts owned by citizens of the United States who would do anything for America except bank all their money there. He had prepared a major report on just about every bank account throughout the world controlled by the mob. Some of the information will be passed onto IRS.'

'What has this got to do with us?'

'Hoffman was working for Charlie Rose. A large payment was wired him from Charlie Rose the day he was murdered.'

Jackie watched a bulk carrier leave the outer harbour. 'Maybe it was a straightforward credit check-up that Rose wanted?'

'A twenty-page report covering about five hundred bank accounts?'

'So how does it fit in with all this?'

Randall puffed thoughtfully on his pipe, exhaling clouds of poisonous yellow fumes. As usual, the local mosquitoes decided to go elsewhere. He slowly shook his head. 'Christ knows, Angelica. Everything seems to point to banking: the company owned by the Fleming girl's father; Silvester's knowledge of SWIFT software; the report Hoffman did for Charlie Rose. If they are planning a bank robbery, they're certainly going about it in a weird way. That's why you've got to stay with the *Sarania*.'

'And you'll stay in radio range all the time like you did last time?'

Randall smiled. 'I'll be wearing my shining armour every minute of the day – just in case you holler for me.'

'Well, if you do come galloping through the enchanted forest to rescue me from the evil baron, will you do me one huge favour?'

'Sure, Angelica. Anything.'

'Leave that pipe at home.'

Charlie eyed the *Sarania*'s swimming pool. 'It's under that?' he queried incredulously.

'That's right, Charlie,' said Owen. 'It will slide to one side and then the rocket rolls forward and is elevated automatically into place. When it does so, we're to clear the bridge and get everyone below aft. The blast won't harm the *Sarania* but it's enough to knock a man over the side.'

'And it's not under our control?'

'That's right.'

'I don't like it.'

'It stinks, Charlie,' Owen agreed. 'But what the hell can we do about it?'

Charlie finished his tour of inspection. The two men returned to the bridge where Damion was lying on his back, busy with a wrench. He was being helped by Tony. They had created a work station on the port side of the bridge against a bulkhead. The SWIFT terminal was screwed down to a table which Damion was in the process of bolting securely to the bulkhead. Mounted on the bulkhead, within easy reach of the table when sitting, was the control computer and the Westinghouse transceiver that would send and receive the encoded signals between the control computer and the duplicate SWIFT satellite when it was in orbit. Standing on a shortened camera tripod was the transmitter's folding dish antenna. Stacked on the floor was a pile of SWIFT servicing and maintenance manuals.

'How's it going?' Charlie asked.

Damion passed the tools to Tony and stood. 'I've just about finished,' he said. 'I'm not mounting the antenna outside until we're out in the Atlantic. This yacht's already got more than its fair share of dishes. Another might attract attention.'

He linked the units together with a set of interconnecting cables that Crick had made and powered up the entire system. He tuned the transceiver and then moved the dish by hand, aiming it south at an angle of about thirty degrees above the horizon. After some fine corrections to the dish's position, there was a sharp whistle from the transceiver. The monitor screen on the SWIFT terminal suddenly produced a meaningless jumble of madly scrolling garbage.

The five watched the display.

'That's SWIFT?' Charlie queried.

'That's right,' Damion confirmed, checking the transceiver's frequency read-out against an entry in one of the SWIFT manuals. 'You're looking at billions of dollars of encrypted electronic money.'

Owen stared in fascination at the screen for some seconds. 'We'll be ready to sail in fifteen minutes,' he reported.

Tony glanced at his watch. 'Elaine said she wouldn't be long.'

Damion looked up. 'Where is she?'

'She's gone into the town for some last-minute shopping and to phone her parents. Let them know that she's okay.'

'What's wrong with the yacht's phones?' Damion demanded suspiciously.

'She likes her calls to be private,' Tony replied, showing his irritation. 'Anything wrong with that?'

95: The Straits of Gibraltar Tuesday, May 28

The day after the *Sarania*'s departure from Alicante was one of those humid, overcast days when the slightest exertion produced prickly, uncomfortable sweat and a feeling of lassitude. Within sight of the yacht was a collection of carriers, tankers and assorted merchantmen – all converging on the Straits of Gibraltar: the gateway to the Atlantic Ocean.

At midday, Jackie finished preparing a cold buffet lunch and left Pepe in charge in the galley. She found a book in the *Sarania*'s small library. She was carrying an aluminium lounger to the foredeck where the breeze from the *Sarania*'s ten-knot progress was strongest when a Turkish hand took the chair from her and insisted on carrying it and setting it up for her. She thanked him and settled down to read with her feet resting on the raised lip of the circular swimming pool and her back to the bridge. She wished the pool was filled with water even if it were only two feet deep.

Two feet?

She stopped reading and looked at the pool over the top of her book. Like all empty swimming pools, it was a depressing sight and it attracted litter. She was certain that the pool had been deeper than that before the *Sarania*'s visit to Odessa. At least eighteen inches deeper.

On the bridge, Damion suddenly became alert and said: 'What's she looking at?'

Owen was taking a turn at the helm. He looked up from the radar screen. Despite automatic warning aids, in these busy waters vigilance was essential. 'Who – the cook?'

'Yeah.'

The two men watched Jackie intently. The American girl seemed to be more engrossed in the swimming pool than her book. She slipped off one of her sandals and ran her toe along a new welding seam. And then she appeared to have noticed the gap between the edge of the pool's rim and the surrounding teak deck planking. Certainly it seemed to the watchers on the bridge that she was

213

showing undue interest in the pool.

'What's her name?'

'Jackie Morrison,' Owen replied. 'She's probably wishing it was filled. It's bloody sticky out there.'

Damion grunted and continued to eye the American girl, his expression grim and suspicious.

Jackie watched the imposing bulk of the Rock of Gibraltar slipping past on the starboard bow for some minutes and returned her attention to her book. Damion went back to tinkering at the SWIFT work station.

Jackie's eye was caught by one of her cigarettes that had spilled out of its packet. It rolled back and forth on the teak planking, edging nearer to the mysterious gap. A gust of wind caught the cigarette. It rolled into the gap and disappeared. Jackie rummaged in her purse and found a coin. She reached down to pick up her cigarette packet and dropped the coin down the gap. She heard the metallic tinkle of the coin falling some feet below. She reflected that the *Sarania*'s new watertight bow compartment could not be all that watertight and that it was worthy of further investigation. Certainly it was a matter to be reported to Randall that evening.

She became bored with the book and leaned on the bow rail, gazing ahead at the leaden sky and the hazy horizon. The continent of Africa was receding into the mist on her left and the merchant ships were indistinct smudges, spreading out in a broad arc now that they had more sea-room. The laden tankers were swinging north-wards – bound for the oil-thirsty ports of Amsterdam and Antwerp.

The *Sarania*'s motion changed noticeably; it became more regular. The fine clipper bow was settling to a rhythm of plunging into a trough – hurling a fine, welcoming spray into Jackie's face – and then lifting itself clear before plunging into the next long, easy swell.

The *Sarania* had entered the Atlantic Ocean.

96: The Northern Atlantic Wednesday, May 29

Charlie was taking his customary afternoon sleep when Tony radioed the first report on the *Sarania*'s progress. Owen had sent the coxswain off the bridge and was at the helm. Damion and Elaine were watching a Dutch television 3-D movie with the sound turned down.

'*Sarania* to base,' said Tony into the microphone in English. 'This is Tony Karn on the *Sarania*. Do you copy? Over.' He was using the frequency-hopping scrambled radio that the Soviets had installed at Odessa.

'Base to *Sarania*. We copy you.' Damion looked up from the television in surprise. It was the same voice that had answered him when he had transmitted data to Moscow over the public telephone system. 'Good afternoon, Mr Karn. Is all going well?'

'We're now fifteen degrees west, thirty-five north. About thirty miles due north of Madeira. Over.'

A pause, then: 'Roger, Mr Karn. We confirm that. Over.'

'How can they confirm our position?' Elaine asked.

'They've got a satellite fix on us,' said Damion.

Tony keyed the microphone. 'Have you calculated our final position for us yet? Over.'

Another pause. 'Roger, *Sarania*. Please stand by for your instructions.'

'Take the helm please, Mrs Karn,' said Owen.

Elaine did not need a second invitation. She willingly left the television and took the wheel while Owen leaned over the illuminated plot table and entered on the navigation computer keypad the code that called up the North Atlantic display chart from the computer's memory. The plot table's screen suddenly flickered and cleared. Projected onto it was a large, computer-generated chart of the Atlantic with the meridians depicted as glowing lines.

'Base to *Sarania*,' said the voice. 'Are you ready? Over.'

'Go ahead, base,' said Tony. 'Over.'

The voice read out precise coordinates which Tony repeated and Owen entered on the navigation computer keypad. Forty degrees west, fifteen north. A spot of light appeared on the plot screen in the centre of the mid-Atlantic. It was almost exactly halfway between Dakar on the coast of northwest Africa and the West Indies. Down the side of the screen there appeared columns of figures showing the course the *Sarania* would have to follow to reach the point, the distance to be covered, and the likely fuel consumption figures for different speeds.

'Holy shit,' Owen breathed. 'Right smack in the middle of the

215

Atlantic! They couldn't have picked a more lonely spot.'

'*Sarania* to base,' said Tony. 'We will call you back in five minutes. Over and out.'

'Roger, *Sarania*. We will be standing by.'

'We've got to start operating the duplicate satellite by fourteen hundred GMT on June 3,' Damion reminded them. 'So we need to be on station by oh-eight hundred at the earliest.'

Owen entered the time into the navigation computer and studied the results. 'We'll never do it,' he declared.

Tony looked worried. 'Why not?'

'Because it's two thousand one hundred miles. To get there in five days means we've got to run nonstop at seventeen knots *into* the prevailing wind.'

'So?'

'Even if the weather holds, running at that speed means we'd finish up with empty fuel tanks – we'd be adrift smack in the middle of the Atlantic and away from the shipping lanes. Why the hell didn't those stupid bastards think of that first?'

Tony stared through the bridge windows. 'Hell . . . Look – does it *have* to take place on June 3?'

'Yes,' said Damion categorically. 'That's the day the telephone exchange in London is going to be fixed. We can't change the date.'

'Who is fixing the London exchange, Damion?'

Damion returned Tony's level gaze. 'Crick, of course.'

'How come you have not called him?'

'Security reasons. I would have thought that that was obvious.'

'But –'

'For God's sake, Tony – leave it alone,' said Elaine over her shoulder.

Tony was undecided for a moment. Eventually he keyed the microphone. '*Sarania* to base. Over.'

'We copy you, *Sarania*. Over.'

'This is very important,' said Tony. 'We are going to be out of fuel by the time we are in position. We will need refuelling after the operation. Over.'

'Understood, *Sarania*. We will call you back. Over.'

'No,' said Tony emphatically. 'Please listen to me. We need a guarantee of refuelling right now, otherwise the operation does *not* go ahead. Over.'

216

There was a long pause before the voice replied, 'Understood, *Sarania*. We will arrange for a ship to rendezvous with you on June 3. We will have an exact time and the name of the ship for you on the next report. Over.'

'Thank you, base. Over and out.'

Owen lifted the interphone telephone and told the engine room mechanic to stand by for maximum revolutions. He switched the telephone to public address and warned the crew that the *Sarania* would be increasing her speed to seventeen knots in five minutes.

97: The Northern Atlantic Thursday, May 30

A particularly sharp swell threw Jackie away from the porthole, causing her to drop the radio on the floor. She recovered it. Thankfully the red transmit light still glowed when she operated the microphone key.

'Mike!'

The *Sarania* heeled sharply, taking another heavy sea on her quarter. The sudden motion made Jackie bang her lip on the microphone.

'Still here, Angelica.' The background hiss accompanying Mike Randall's voice was louder than it had been the previous evening.

'Thank Christ it's still working.'

'What happened?'

'I dropped the radio. Mike – I don't think I can stand much more of this. How long can it go on for? She'll blow up her engines.'

'I honestly don't know, Angelica.'

'Can you keep up? Your signal's weaker than it was yesterday.'

'We're having a few problems,' Randall admitted.

Jackie nearly panicked. 'What's that supposed to mean?'

'As near as we can work out – the *Sarania* is heading for Puerto Rico,' said Randall. 'But at the speed she's holding, we don't see how her fuel is going to hold out. Are you sure that that watertight bow compartment doesn't house extra fuel tanks?'

'Well, I don't know! As I've already told you – it sounded empty.'

The *Sarania* heeled again. A cascade of water through the porthole drenched Jackie.

'Oh Christ – I'm soaked through!' she wailed.

'Listen, Angelica. It's important that you find out what's on the other side of that bulkhead.'

'How? By cutting a hole in it with a kitchen knife?'

'Galley knife,' Randall corrected.

'Listen to me, creep. When I get out of this mess, I'm going to use the sharpest *kitchen* knife I can find on this goddamned gin palace to hack your balls off!'

98: The Northern Atlantic Friday, May 31

The conversation around the breakfast table ceased abruptly when Jackie tottered into the dining saloon, pushing a laden breakfast trolley which she used to maintain her balance. The *Sarania* was now punching into a moderate sou'westerly gale and still holding her speed. The resulting rolling motion had made negotiating the trolley along the passageway a nightmare. She risked a glance at the repositioned panelled bulkhead – the reason why she was serving breakfast, and not Pepe.

'That smells good,' Elaine commented.

Jackie bid them good morning in turn as she unsteadily served up chilled orange juice. It was unusual for all of them to be present for breakfast. Charlie Rose was looking pale – obviously the *Sarania*'s heavy motion did not agree with him. Damion Silvester was his usual morose self. Rupert Owen looked indifferent. Only Elaine and Tony seemed cheerful. But then Elaine was always cheerful at breakfast.

'Where's Pepe?' Damion growled, his eyes following Jackie's every move.

'He's not feeling too good this morning, sir,' Jackie answered. 'I think it's the ship's motion.'

'He's not the only one,' Charlie muttered with feeling.

Jackie placed a silver salver in the centre of the table and removed the cover, exposing sizzling rashers of bacon and fried eggs.

'Marvellous,' said Elaine, grabbing a serving spoon and helping herself.

'Just coffee,' said Charlie weakly.

'And me,' Damion added.

As Jackie leaned over to pour Damion's coffee, she was embarrassed by the realization that her top blouse buttons were undone and

218

that his eyes were devouring her breasts. She was nearest the bulkhead when she was serving Tony, but she was still too unnerved by Damion's stare to take advantage of the fact.

Jackie returned to the galley deep in thought. She estimated that the dining saloon was about a yard shorter than it had been. With the loss of the billiards room, that meant that the watertight compartment, or whatever it was, was at least fifty feet long. She decided to try getting a good look at the bulkhead when she served dinner. Hopefully, Damion Silvester would not be present.

She forced herself to accept that she was very scared of the big man.

99: Tyuratam, USSR Saturday, June 1

The Central Satellite Control building at the giant spaceport was busier than usual because control room 101B was fully manned for the final stages of the delicate operation.

The senior controller activated the killer satellite's onboard slow scan television camera and switched the picture onto the main screen for the benefit of all the technicians sitting at their consoles.

The killer satellite was in orbit twenty-two thousand miles above the equator: the so-called geostationary orbit because satellites at that height orbited the earth once every twenty-four hours, matching the earth's spin, and so appearing to remain fixed in the sky. The orbit was popular for military communication and broadcast satellites because ground stations did not require steerable dishes. The geostationary belt was also infested with Soviet killer satellites such as the one that the controllers at Tyuratam had been 'walking' along its orbit for the past two weeks to bring it near the SWIFT III Atlantic satellite.

Several other Soviet killer satellites had also been moved and reparked during the past two weeks to fool the United States' tracking stations into thinking that they were observing yet another Soviet exercise.

The senior controller operated a joystick control set into his panel. The picture on the main wall screen transmitted from the killer satellite scanned once and cleared to show an indistinct image of a distant satellite.

219

'Range – four-zero-five metres,' a technician called out. 'Closing velocity – one metre per second.'

Four minutes passed on the control room's digital clocks. Another wall screen came alive and showed the position of the two satellites in relation to a map of the world.

The television picture scanned again. This time it was possible to discern various features of the SWIFT III target satellite such as its solar power cells.

'Range – one-eight-zero metres,' intoned the technician.

A number of faces looked expectantly up at the main screen.

'Range – one-zero-zero. Deviation zero.'

The killer satellite was precisely on course, closing purposefully on its target.

'Stand by for computer takeover and venier thrust cancellation,' instructed the senior controller, watching the screen intently.

'Standing by.'

'Range – zero-five-zero.'

The genuine SWIFT III satellite was now several times life-size on the main screen.

There was a brief spate of exchanges and confirmations between the senior controller and the assembled technicians. Control of the final approach was switched over to the killer satellite's onboard computer, because time delays due to the limiting factor of the speed of light would have introduced errors during the critical final stages when the killer satellite was 'parked' alongside its victim.

'Range – zero-zero-five metres. Approach cancelled?'

The SWIFT III satellite now completely filled the wall screen.

The senior controller relaxed and congratulated his colleagues. The killer satellite had been brought to a stop within five metres of the target satellite. The SWIFT satellite would be destroyed by the firing of a small laser-guided explosive charge from the killer satellite. The killer normally carried twenty of these projectiles arranged as a cluster of stubby muzzles. All but one of the charges had been used on previous exercises which was why the Soviet technicians were anxious to bring the killer as close to its target as possible to be certain of destroying the SWIFT III with the single remaining shot. Firing of the charge would be carried out by the controller flipping up a switch guard on his control panel and pressing the button underneath.

The time for that would be shortly before noon GMT on June 3. In two days' time.

100: Mid-Atlantic Sunday, June 2

At 15.00 the Soviet helicopter-cruiser, the *Minsk*, identified the *Sarania* on the warship's satellite plot of the mid-Atlantic.

Once identification had been confirmed, Captain Conrad Dalvanski realized that he was too close to the yacht. He took no chances and ordered an immediate change of course. The *Minsk* heeled sharply as she went about. Dalvanski ordered half-speed ahead. The revised course would ensure that his command would be at least five hundred miles away from the *Sarania* by noon the next day. His orders had been clear enough but nevertheless baffling: he was required to shadow the *Sarania* but never to get within three hundred miles of her. At 16.00 the following day, he was to not only destroy the *Sarania*, but also ensure that there were no survivors.

101: Mid-Atlantic Sunday, June 2

By early evening the weather abated. The skies cleared and the punishing swell gave way to a moderate sea.

Owen inspected the engine room. The two diesels were behaving magnificently. Even after 125 hours' sustained running at maximum power, they were showing no significant signs of stress. He took advantage of the improved weather conditions to increase the *Sarania*'s speed by one knot. The big worry was the fuel totalizers, which were now showing less than two tonnes of fuel left in the tanks.

He returned to the bridge. Charlie was at the helm.

'How's it going, Mr Rose?'

Charlie removed his cigar and grinned hugely. 'You can call me Charlie. You know something? This is great. Jesus – look at that sunset. Seems like running a yacht is something I could really get into. Maybe I will.'

'You already own fifty per cent of the *Sarania*,' Owen pointed out while consulting the navigation computer.

'Yeah . . . But I'd want something that hasn't been around as long as me. I'm gonna treat myself to the finest yacht afloat. Something to

221

make those West Coast hoodlums really sit up. Hey, Owen. How'd you like to be my skipper, eh?'

'Mr Rose,' said Owen seriously. 'After tomorrow, I hope to be looking for a skipper for *my* yacht.'

'Huh? Oh – yeah. Sure.' Charlie laughed good-naturedly and added, 'Maybe I'll sell you my share in this old lady. I guess she's okay for dukes and duchesses, but she ain't my class.'

'For an old lady, she's doing bloody well,' Owen commented. He checked the figures displayed on the navigation computer. 'Three hundred and ninety miles made good over the last twenty-four hours.'

'So it looks like we're going to make it?'

Owen hesitated. 'No reason why not.'

The uncertain note in Owen's voice alerted Charlie. 'What's the problem?'

'Fuel. We're down to two tonnes. We've enough to make it to the launch position by tomorrow morning if we maintain this speed. But our tanks will be dry.'

'Has anything been fixed up with our friends?'

'They've made a vague promise. But nothing definite.'

Charlie picked up the interphone and called Tony's and Elaine's suite. 'Tony,' he ordered. 'I want you on the bridge – like now.' He hung up without waiting for an acknowledgement.

Tony appeared two minutes later. 'What's the matter, Charlie?'

'Owen tells me we've still nothing definite fixed up with our friends over refuelling. You get onto them now and you tell them – tell them we want refuelling fixed up and we want it fixed up now.'

'They're working on it, Charlie.'

Charlie jabbed a thumb at the Russian radio. 'You find out now.'

Without argument, Tony picked up the microphone and called base. The voice in Moscow replied almost immediately. As soon as contact was established, Charlie grabbed the microphone from Tony.

'Listen, Moscow! This is Charlie Rose. Do you understand me okay?'

'We understand you perfectly, Mr Rose. Go ahead.'

'Our tanks are pretty well empty. We've enough fuel to reach the launch area but only just. I want something definite on our refuelling arrangements and I want to know now.'

'Stand by *Sarania*. We will return to you in a minute.'

'Stand by – nothing!' Charlie rasped. 'I want to know now, otherwise I pull the plugs on the deal *and* on your control gear. I put out a general call for assistance and sell your rocket to the highest bidder.'

'Please stand by for a few minutes *Sarania*,' said the voice calmly.

'Standing by,' said Charlie curtly. He returned the microphone to its hook. 'I think they've got the idea I mean business.'

'I think that's more than likely,' said Owen, smiling faintly at Tony's worried expression.

'That was an unfortunate thing to say,' said Tony.

Charlie shrugged indifferently. 'Not as unfortunate for us if we end up adrift in the middle of the Atlantic.'

Ten minutes passed. Charlie was muttering impatiently when the Moscow voice called the *Sarania*. Tony answered the call.

'We understand your problem *Sarania*,' said the voice reassuringly. 'A Soviet merchantman – the *Caspian* – will rendezvous with you at the launch position at sixteen hundred hours tomorrow. She is on her way now and has been for the past day. Over.'

Tony acknowledged the message and switched off the radio.

'Goddamned Ruskies,' Charlie muttered. Suddenly he no longer enjoyed being at the *Sarania*'s helm.

Elaine finished her fifth glass of wine. She threw herself naked across the bed and held her arms out to Tony. 'I don't want to hear any more moans about Charlie,' she admonished. 'What I want from you, my little Russian spy, is for you to make mad passionate love to me.'

Tony had just emerged dripping from the shower. 'I made mad passionate love to you this afternoon. And we've got a long day tomorrow,' he complained.

'To hell with tomorrow. That's another day. I'm talking about now.'

'Let me dry myself first.'

Elaine moved purposefully towards Tony on her knees. 'What's the point? I'll only make you all wet again.' She reached out for him. 'Especially this bit.'

Tony collapsed laughing beside her. 'It's true about sea voyages turning women into sex-crazed maniacs.'

'You mean I wasn't one before?'

Tony kissed her long and hard.

'I'm looking forward to this particular sea voyage turning me into a millionairess,' Elaine declared. 'I shall have my evil way with all the men who come panting after me for my money. I shall screw the more desirable ones senseless – let them spend all their money on me – and then drop them in the gutter like used French letters.'

'You won't,' said Tony.

'Why not?'

'Because you will be my wife and I'll be watching you day and night. Especially at night.'

Elaine became serious. 'You haven't proposed to me yet.'

'Well, I'm proposing to you now, you idiot.'

Elaine lay back with her head resting on Tony's knees. She hooked her arms around his neck and pulled him close until their noses were touching. She gazed into his eyes. 'That's what I like about you, Tony – you know how to say the sweetest things to a girl.'

Tony kissed her gently. 'Do you accept? After all – it's a great honour for you.'

'You're only after me for my nationality,' she replied drowsily, her magnificent jade-green eyes half-closed.

'Well, you haven't got much else to offer, darling.'

Elaine's eyes opened wide. 'Tell me what's worrying you.'

'Aren't you worried about tomorrow?'

'Not in the same way that you are. I can always tell with you – you start trying to match my flippancy. Spill.'

'Hundreds of things are worrying me,' Tony admitted.

'List twenty-six of them.'

'What will the crew make of the rocket launching? Okay – so we pay them to keep their mouths shut. But if one should talk –'

Elaine snuggled up to him. 'I've thought about that. I'm organizing a noisy do in suite six for them. Right in the stern. Loud music. Wine. They won't hear a thing.'

'A morning party?' Tony queried.

Elaine giggled. 'Don't worry. I'll sell it to them. Next problem?'

'Damion.'

'What about him?'

Tony sighed and idly stroked her hair. 'I don't know. Yes – I do. For one thing, he won't go into details of how Crick is getting on in London.'

'Oh, be fair, Tony. You know what a cocky little prat Crick is. He's probably not reported to Damion simply because everything's okay.'

'I suppose so.' He smiled down at Elaine. 'I suppose I am being very stupid.'

'You are,' said Elaine, kissing him. 'Now show me how very loving you can be.'

Jackie waited until 11.00 pm before venturing out on deck. She was wearing her nightdress and carrying a torch. There was the sound of a noisy card game coming from the crew's quarters but the rest of the yacht was quiet. She guessed that the easing of the weather after two days of pounding had decided everyone to catch up on their sleep.

The side deck was illuminated by the emergency lights. She glanced up at the bridgehouse and wondered who was standing watch. She hoped it was Damion so that he would be out of the way.

There was no point in further indecision: she entered the dining saloon and switched on the lights. Better to be open about everything. Besides – she had a contingency plan which was why she was wearing her nightdress.

A casual glance at the panelled bulkhead revealed nothing out of the ordinary, but a close inspection by pulling back the carpet showed a row of new clips that were holding the wood panelling in place. She discovered that it was possible to spring the clips away from a section of panelling and slide it to one side. A steel bulkhead with freshly welded seams confronted her. In the centre was a hatch that obviously wasn't meant to be opened because it was welded shut.

Damion was sitting at the SWIFT work station in the bridgehouse. He ignored the Spanish coxswain standing at the helm because he was busy running the final tests on the program disks for the following day's operation. Like himself, Tony, Elaine and Owen had opted for bank accounts in Switzerland. The program disk for their transactions was relatively straightforward. Charlie's requirements were complex: his program involved the raiding of several hundred accounts throughout the world and transferring the funds to a whole series of obscure accounts scattered throughout several countries. His mind wandered to the waiting bomb that he had planted in the

225

Mall, and the transmitter in his flat that would trigger it. Again, the unwelcome thought entered his mind that he had overlooked something incredibly trivial that would have a profound effect on the operation. It was a stupid thought; everything had been planned down to the last detail.

He forced himself to concentrate on Charlie's involved transfers. As he studied the lists of bank accounts, he realized that he would need the SWIFT directory which was in his cabin.

Jackie froze when she heard the cough. Damion! She hurriedly pushed the carpet back into place. She should have remained on her knees for her contingency plan to work. But hearing that cough and knowing that Damion was approaching made her panic. She dived under the long dining table and knocked one of the chairs over.

Jackie crouched in terror under the table, praying that the thick carpet had effectively muffled the sound of the falling chair. The dining saloon door opened. A pair of sandals approached the table and stopped. It was too late for her to do anything now: the lights were on; a chair was tipped over; and he was certain to hear her pounding heart. Damion knelt. She steeled herself but the preparation was wholly inadequate to deal with the nightmare that followed. Damion's face appeared. His expression of savagery forced an involuntary whimper of fear from Jackie. Powerful fingers closed around her ankle. He dragged her out from under the table, scattering chairs. She desperately tried to prevent her nightdress riding up over her thighs.

'Snooping bitch!' he snarled. He grabbed hold of her nightdress by the neck to yank her to her feet but the material ripped. She fell backwards, crying in terror and clutching her hands across her exposed breasts.

Damion pulled her brutally to her feet by her hair and held her face near his. 'What are you doing in here?'

Jackie tried moving her lips but could make no sound. Damion drew back his hand and struck her hard across the face. The force of the blow sent her staggering back across the table. This time she screamed out. And then Damion's hands were around her neck. His blazing eyes inches from her face. In despair she knew that he was going to kill her.

'Answer me, you bitch! What are you doing in here!'

Holding her by the throat with one hand Damion lifted his other hand to strike again, but he was suddenly spun around.

'I think it best if you left her alone,' Tony suggested mildly, his fingers around Damion's wrist.

Elaine was standing near the door. Her eyes wide with shock.

'You keep your fucking Commie nose out of this!' Damion shouted. 'I found her snooping about in here and I aim to find out why. My way.'

He tried to break Tony's grasp and was surprised to discover that he couldn't. He drew back his foot to deliver a vicious kick but Tony was too quick. An expert twist on Damion's arm spun the big man around. Damion was forced to release his grip on Jackie to prevent himself overbalancing. Before he realized what was happening, he found himself pinioned face-down on the table with his arm locked agonizingly into the small of his back.

Elaine rushed forward. She threw her arms protectively around Jackie, who by now was sobbing uncontrollably, and steered her to a chair.

'Oh you poor darling. It's all right. It's all over now.'

'Bastard!' Damion snarled, his face jammed against the table. 'I'll kill you. God help me – I will.'

'No one's going to do anything I don't want them to do,' said Tony calmly. 'I'm going to let go of you and I want you to tell me what happened. Now – do I let go or do I have to break your arm? Because I can, you know – very easily.' Tony demonstrated the point by increasing the pressure on Damion's arm.

Damion tried to struggle but the sudden stab of pain made him think better of it. 'Okay,' he muttered.

Tony released the big man and stepped back, watching him warily in case of trouble. Damion straightened up. He rubbed his arm and glowered at Tony, Elaine and Jackie in turn. Elaine was removing her nightgown and wrapping it around Jackie. The American girl's sobs were now under control.

'I found that bitch in here. Snooping.' Tony knelt in front of Jackie and gently turned her face towards him. An ugly bruise was already blackening the side of her face. 'What were you doing in here, Miss Morrison?'

'I . . . I . . .'

'Take your time,' Elaine said in a comforting voice. 'There's 'nothing to be frightened of.'

'I was looking for my wedding ring,' said Jackie in a small voice.

'At this time of night?' Damion's voice dripped sarcasm.

'It's been worrying me all day,' said Jackie, gratefully accepting a handkerchief from Elaine and wiping her eyes.'I couldn't sleep. And then I suddenly thought that maybe I dropped it in here when I was serving breakfast.'

'She was hiding under the table!'

'I was looking under the table,' Jackie protested.

Tony looked around on the floor. Something in the corner of the saloon caught his eye. He bent down and retrieved a gold ring. 'Is this it, Miss Morrison?'

Despite her recent ordeal, Jackie managed a smile of pleasure. 'Oh – yes.' She took the ring gratefully from Tony. 'Thank you so much, Mr Karn.'

'I'm very sorry that this has happened,' said Tony. 'Elaine – I think you'd better take Miss Morrison to our suite and see to her face.'

'I still say she was snooping,' Damion muttered to Tony when they were alone.

Tony regarded the big man with unconcealed dislike. 'You think what you want to think, Damion. And I'll think what I think. Right now it might be a good idea if we all got some sleep. We've got a busy day tomorrow.'

An hour later Jackie assured Elaine and Tony that she was all right and insisted on returning to her cabin. She locked the door and studied the throbbing bruise in the shower mirror. Her only consolation was that, thanks to her acting ability, it could have been worse. Also she had been touched by the kindness and concern shown to her by Tony and Elaine. The more she thought about it, the more she became convinced that there was an innocent explanation for the whole affair. The doubts returned when she remembered the look of fury on Damion's face when he had found her.

She recovered the radio from its hiding place behind the bunk panel and opened the porthole.

'Mike. This is Angelica. Do you copy?'

When Randall replied, she was horrified at just how weak and broken up his signal was.

'Mike! What's happened? I can hardly hear you. Over.'

The answer was a hiss of crackly white noise interspersed with a few words. '. . . trouble. Port engine . . . Making five . . . Sorry, Angeli . . . Notified US Coastguard . . . Navy . . . Interception . . . Puerto Rico . . .'

'Mike. Go again. Go again. Go again!'

Randall repeated the message several times, thus enabling Jackie to piece together the complete message. The surveillance craft was having engine trouble and was limping along at five knots. The chances that they could fix the problem were good, but Randall had managed to contact the US Coastguard and the Navy who would be intercepting the *Sarania* off Puerto Rico.

In despair and frustration, she hid the radio and tried to sleep.

102: London Sunday, June 2

The personal encryption terminal pad in the Soviet Ambassador's bedroom sounded its warning bleeper. Daniel Dvorkin was reading in bed. He looked at the machine in surprise. He had never heard the bleeper before except during the weekly test by the embassy's head of communications. He eased himself carefully out of bed to avoid waking his wife. The bleeper sounded again. He touched the mute key and then carefully pressed his forefinger on the fingerprint identification pad at the foot of the terminal's screen. The machine bleeped as it accepted the decryption command. Dvorkin watched the lines of Cyrillic characters gradually filling the screen. He stared in astonishment at the complete message.

> FROM THE OFFICE OF THE CHAIRMAN OF THE
> COUNCIL OF MINISTERS.
> MOSCOW. SUNDAY. JUNE 2.
> MY DEAR DANIEL,
> TOMORROW IS LIKELY TO BE AN EXTREMELY
> BUSY DAY FOR OUR AGENTS IN THE LONDON
> MONEY MARKETS. YOU ARE REQUIRED TO
> INSTRUCT THEM TO PURCHASE US DOLLARS
> IRRESPECTIVE OF HOW LOW THEY FALL DURING
> THE DAY'S TRADING. GOLD IS LIKELY TO RISE
> THEREFORE AUTHORIZATIONS ARE BEING ISSUED

TO OUR LONDON BANKERS AND ALL OUR UK
TRADING ORGANIZATIONS GIVING YOU THE
POWER TO TRADE ALL OUR LONDON GOLD
RESERVES DURING MARKET HOURS TO BUY ALL
THE DOLLARS YOU CAN. YOU ARE BEING PUT IN
PERSONAL CHARGE OF THE ENTIRE OPERATION.
AFTER TOMORROW, THE SOVIET UNION WILL
HAVE TOTAL ECONOMIC CONTROL OVER THE
WEST. PLEASE ACKNOWLEDGE BY PRESSING
FINGERPRINT PAD TWICE. MY WARMEST
REGARDS TO VALENTINA. GOOD LUCK.

The message ended with the Chairman's personal seal and his signature.

Dvorkin read and reread the amazing instruction. He pressed the fingerprint pad twice and reached for the telephone. This time he did not worry about waking his wife.

He had no way of knowing that a virtually identical message was on its way to the Soviet Ambassador in Washington. The difference was that the Washington ambassador was being instructed to buy European currencies even though the values of the British pound, the French franc and the West German mark were expected to plunge.

103: Andrews AFB, Washington Monday, June 3

Air Force Two – the supersonic Boeing emblazoned with the seal of the Vice President of the United States – reached vee one and lifted off from the runway. It climbed to ten thousand feet over the Atlantic before swinging northeast as soon as its captain received his oceanic clearance. He was assigned Track Charlie – one of the shorter, more southerly of the transatlantic air corridors and one that ensured that the big jet's arrival at Heathrow Airport would be not later than 9.00 am local time.

The passengers on the Boeing were Vice President Howard Penn, and Secretary of State Carol Weismann, plus a retinue of advisors, secretaries and journalists. Their mission – to finalize the contract for the sale and siting of anti-missile laser beam projectors in the UK – was of sufficient importance for them to have no wish to keep the

British Prime Minister waiting.

For Carol Weismann, the London visit was another milestone in her meteoric career. Elected to the Senate at thirty, she was now Secretary of State at thirty-nine while her youngest children were still at high school. She accepted that her cool, elegant good looks had played a significant role in her climb; they had assured her of plenty of press coverage which she had exploited wisely. Once she had reached the Senate, she had settled on a wardrobe of clothes that accentuated her image of brisk efficiency: well-cut skirts and jackets; flouncy dresses; nothing too glamorous and nothing too plain. And no matter what she wore, a knotted chiffon neckscarf always completed the ensemble. It had become her emblem and the press loved it.

But once in office, it was her formidable brain and undeniable charm that came to the fore and helped establish her reputation for getting things done her way.

She settled back in her seat and relaxed, wishing that her husband was with her. They had visited London together four years before. As Mr and Mrs Alan Weismann, they had been just another couple of American tourists peering through the railings of Buckingham Palace to watch the changing of the guard. And now, within a few hours she would be driving along the Mall and through the gates of that magnificent palace to have afternoon tea with the British Monarch.

It just didn't seem possible that the dream was about to become a reality.

104: Tyuratum, USSR

Satellite Control Room 101B at the spaceport began filling with staff shortly after 07.00 GMT.

The Senior Controller finished his coffee and tossed the plastic cup in his wastebin. He activated his monitor screen that provided the decoded slow-scan television pictures from the killer satellite. The target – the SWIFT III satellite – filled his screen. He transferred the picture to the main wall screen.

At 07.10, Yuri Grechko and Mikhail Grovanich entered the room accompanied by the director of the spaceport. The Senior Controller recognized Academician Grechko immediately. Once the introductions were over, the director withdrew, leaving the visitors in the Senior Controller's care.

'Everything is ready?' Grechko asked.

'Yes, comrade. There have been no problems so far.' The Senior Controller went on to describe the function of the various control consoles in the room and pointed out the picture of the target satellite on the wall screen. 'That picture is coming from the killer satellite now,' he explained. 'Everything is set.'

'What is the latest on the *Sarania*'s position?' Grechko wanted to know.

'We're just about to bring in the updates now,' said the Senior Controller. 'Your work station is ready. Everything has been thoroughly checked out.' He showed his visitors to a separate console that was equipped with a computer and a Winchester disk drive in addition to the normal telemetry monitoring equipment.

Once his guests had settled down before their consoles, the Senior Controller called for information updates from his colleagues.

According to the navigation satellite that was tracking the *Sarania*, the yacht was ten miles from the launch position.

Grechko produced a Winchester disk case which he entrusted to Grovanich. He used his electronic pad to call up the mission profile. It was a carefully documented checklist that detailed every stage of the delicate operation. He studied the first page of data and adjusted the position of his talkback microphone. 'We need a check on all the launch control telemetry channels to the *Sarania*,' he told the Senior Controller.

The Senior Controller acknowledged and issued the necessary orders. 'All channels checked, comrade. The launch vehicle status information is now on your monitor.'

Grechko thanked the Senior Controller and whispered to Grovanich. The two men examined the information that was being automatically radioed back from the remote control launch systems on the *Sarania*. All the systems were functioning correctly.

The Senior Controller was also satisfied with the progress of the countdown checks. Everything was going according to plan. There were no other changes to report. The picture of the killer satellite's intended victim – the SWIFT III Atlantic satellite – was still the same steady close-up as it had been the previous Thursday.

The final task was to aim the killer satellite's muzzle at its victim and wait for the *Sarania* to reach its launch position.

105: Mid-Atlantic

The two luminous dots on the chart display were very close together.

'Half speed ahead, both,' Owen ordered.

Charlie was at the helm. He eased back the throttle controls. The *Sarania* lost way. The rolling became more noticeable at reduced speed.

While Elaine and Tony looked over Owen's shoulder at the navigation computer, Damion was sitting at the SWIFT work station running through some final checks on the control disks. At his side was a portable television that was tuned into the BBC's World Service Direct Broadcasting Satellite breakfast programme. The volume was turned down.

The *Sarania* idled along at reduced speed, shuddering occasionally as she took a heavy sea on her foredeck. Charlie found it difficult to hold the yacht on course now that she did not have much way on her. The points of light on the chart display moved even closer together.

'Dead slow, both,' Owen called out.

Charlie pulled back the throttle levers until they were nearly on the stops.

Tony and Elaine stopped their small talk and watched the chart display intently. The two dots merged and became one.

'Stop engines. Finished with engines.'

Charlie repeated the command to the engine room. The muffled beat of the *Sarania*'s engines stopped abruptly.

'We're in position,' Owen announced. 'And we've about fifty litres of fuel left in our tanks.'

'We stop,' said Pepe, stating the obvious.

Jackie had been about to say the same thing. It was extrordinarily quiet in the galley without the regular thump of the diesels which had been running continuously since the *Sarania* had left Alicante.

'Why have we stopped, Pepe?'

The cabin boy shrugged. 'The engines – they sound good. Maybe

233

we have no fuel?'

'What!'

Pepe grinned. '*Si*. Max in the engine room tell me yesterday. He say, the *Sarania*, she will be out of fuel today.'

Tony reached for the microphone and called base. A different voice answered. A voice that Tony did not recognize at first.

'Yes – we are reading you, *Sarania*. Go ahead please.'

It was Grechko's voice!

'We're in position,' Tony reported.

106: Tyuratum

'We've just received verification of the *Sarania*'s last message,' said the Senior Controller. 'She is definitely now at the launch position.'

Grovanich frowned and looked at the computer screen in front of him and Grechko. Nothing concerning the *Sarania*'s position had appeared. 'Verification from where?'

'The controller's in voice contact with a surface unit that is monitoring the *Sarania*'s movements,' Grechko replied.

'What sort of surface unit?'

'Well, it won't be a research trawler – you can be certain of that.'

Grovanich decided not to ask any more questions. There were aspects of the operation, such as the sabotaging of the *Sarania*'s motor launches, liferafts and lifejackets, that he was not happy about.

'Launch minus fifteen minutes and counting,' said the Senior Controller. 'Final countdown from minus ten minutes will be under ALC computer control.'

Five minutes winked by on the digit clock in front of Grovanich.

A synthesized voice chimed in with: 'ALC control. T minus ten minutes on the tone.'

107: Mid-Atlantic

'Attention all crew! Attention all crew!' Owen's voice boomed from the *Sarania*'s public address speakers. 'All crew are to go below aft to guest suite six immediately to discuss a bonus payment. All crew to guest suite six and stay there until Mrs Karn sees you.' Owen repeated the announcement in his halting Spanish.

Jackie ignored the message. Owen's Spanish appeared to have been understood because several hands rushed past her on their way aft. She was carrying a tray laden with coffee and sandwiches. She climbed the steps to the bridgehouse and entered. All five were present. Elaine and Tony were examining the chart display; Owen was returning the public address microphone to its hook; Damion and Charlie were sitting talking by the new computer station that she had noticed on a number of occasions but had never had a chance to get a close look at. 'It's a shame I don't qualify for a bonus payment,' she commented ruefully to no one in particular.

A voice from a radio suddenly said, 'Base to *Sarania*.'

Damion looked up and scowled at Jackie. 'What are you doing? Didn't you hear the announcement?'

'My contract doesn't include bonuses,' said Jackie pointedly. 'It doesn't even include money. I only work for my food and board.'

'I ordered the coffee,' said Owen. 'Okay – thanks, Miss Morrison. That's all. You're to go to suite six.'

'But –'

'You do as you're told!' Damion snapped, standing between her and the computer station.

'Base to *Sarania*,' the voice from the radio repeated.

Elaine took Jackie's arm. 'We've decided that you should be paid, Miss Morrison. Plus an extra month's pay as a bonus – just like the rest of the crew. They've done marvels – we're making the crossing so quickly so far that I'm throwing a surprise party for all of you.'

'But we've stopped!'

'So that the crew can enjoy the party – silly!'

Jackie stared at her in astonishment. 'When?'

'Now, of course.'

'At this time in the morning?'

Elaine gave a gurgling laugh and steered Jackie out of the bridge-house and down the steps. 'Early morning's a marvellous time for a party.' She gave a conspiratorial wink. 'It's when men are fresh and at their best. Didn't you know that? Besides, no one ever thinks of having parties early in the morning which is why I want to try it. I love to be different, you know.'

Jackie knew only too well just how different Elaine could be. She

235

had often wondered if the English girl was slightly insane. Being unable to think of anything sensible or constructive to say, she allowed herself to be escorted below to suite six where the rest of the baffled crew were waiting. They stopped talking and looked expectantly at Elaine when the two women entered. The spacious suite was set across the stern of the *Sarania*. It was directly over the steering engine, and its windows provided only a stern view. For that reason, throughout the *Sarania*'s life it had been the least popular of the guest suites and the one that had suffered the least wear. Jackie noticed that there was a row of wine boxes and glasses already set out on a table.

Elaine clapped her hands and smiled seductively at the men. 'Pepe?'

'*Si*, Mrs Karn?'

'Pepe. You will translate for me. A month's bonus for everyone and a party now!' With that Elaine darted across to the suite's entertainment panel and called up some disco music. She turned the volume up to a deafening level. 'Jackie! You pour the wine! Someone close the curtains!'

Watched by the incredulous eyes of the crew, Elaine began dancing in time to the music. She grabbed a surprised deckhand, pulled him to his feet and gyrated her pelvis against his. Suddenly the rest of the crew were on their feet, clapping, laughing – eager for the same treatment. The wine started flowing.

Her senses numbed by the loudness of the music, Jackie was suddenly spun around and clasped by Max, the engineer. He lifted her off her feet as he whirled her around. And then Pepe was clinging to her, laughing hysterically.

'We go! We go!' he yelled excitedly. 'You and me! We go!'

Someone tried to pour wine down her throat. The mind-pulverizing barrage of the music pounded like a continuous rhythmic broadside. A joint was thrust between her lips. One lungful made her brain reel. She inhaled deeply. Another Spaniard grabbed her. He smelt overpoweringly of sweat and he held her roughly – but she didn't mind. While being spun around by what she thought was yet another crewman – she wasn't sure – she caught a glimpse of Elaine whooping delightedly as she was scooped up and dumped laughing on the bed. As she inhaled again on the joint, a rational corner of Jackie's mind wondered if she was going mad.

236

The music blasting from suite six was loud enough to be heard on the bridge.

'Go ahead, base,' said Tony into the microphone.

'We're about to begin elevation. Over.'

'Standing by,' said Tony.

The company on the bridge moved to the forward windows and stared down at the swimming pool. Occasionally it would partially fill with water when the *Sarania* took a heavy sea across the bow. But each time that this happened, the self-draining vents conducted the water away. There was a loud squealing noise – the sound of steel grating on steel. And then the swimming pool began moving sideways.

'Jesus,' Charlie breathed. 'Just look at that . . .'

Acting upon the radio commands from a control room six thousand miles away, the entire swimming pool was lifting and sliding sideways to expose a yawning hole in the *Sarania*'s foredeck.

Then there was the muted whine of powerful hydraulic motors. A pointed object appeared in the hole, thrusting outwards and lifting as it emerged into the early morning light. Slowly, the SS-49A rocket came into view – its length moving forward and elevating at the same time. First the slender nose cone and third stage with its spikelike radio antenna, and then the fatter second stage followed by the metre-diameter bulk of the first stage.

Even Owen muttered an expletive at the sight of the obscene birth that was taking place below.

The hydraulic motors slowed noticeably under their load as they laboured to thrust their burden to the upright position. And then the stunned watchers on the bridge were able to see the launcher's gleaming rams as they reached their maximum extension. At the end of two minutes, standing almost perpendicular on the *Sarania*'s foredeck, and supported by the arms of its launcher, were the shining, businesslike, ten metres of a Soviet SS-49A rocket complete with a cluster of sustainer boosters around the flared nozzles of its main engine.

'*Sarania* to base,' said Tony. 'She's fully elevated. Over.'

'Yes – we know that,' Grechko replied testily.

'ALC control,' said the voice. 'T minus one minute on the tone.'

'Are you all behind glass?' Grechko asked.

'Yes, comrade.'

'What is the music I can hear?'

'We're providing a distraction for the crew.'

Grechko grunted. 'Keep well clear of any windows in case they break. Also, turn your backs immediately before the launch.'

'Understood, comrade.'

'ALC control. T minus thirty seconds on the tone.'

'These windows are toughened glass,' Owen said quietly, unable to tear his eyes away from the gleaming rampant ugliness on the foredeck. 'Is that thing likely to cause damage?'

Tony shook his head. 'The SS-49A is designed to be launched from small ships.'

'ALC control. T minus fifteen seconds on the tone.'

'Let's get back,' Charlie ordered.

All four men moved to the aft observation area of the bridgehouse.

'ALC control. T minus five seconds . . . Four . . . Three . . . Two . . . One . . .'

The timeless phrases from the synthesized voice were drowned by a roar that quickly rose to a reverberating thunder that shook the entire bridgehouse. All the windows were suddenly enveloped in dense clouds of billowing white smoke. Charlie said something but his words were obliterated by the appalling uproar. Suddenly five receding points of intense white light were visible through the smoke. The four men dashed out to the bridge rail, letting fumes swirl into the bridgehouse when they yanked the door open. The heat, the hideous roaring and the choking, acrid fumes disorientated their senses. The wind whipped away the clouds of smoke and they saw the blazing lights lifting into the sky astride a column of thunder and smoke. The four sustainer boosters, having completed their task of lifting the SS-49A clear of the vessel, separated from the rocket and dropped lazily into the sea quite near the *Sarania*. Clouds of exploding steam marked their impacts.

Within seconds the rocket was a dwindling torch spearing a burning path through the low cloudbase. And then it was lost to sight although the fast-diminishing roar of its main engine continued for some minutes.

The four men remained silent while continuing to stare upwards in the direction of the muted thunder. The heavy beat of the music from Elaine's party could be heard again. Owen touched Tony on the sleeve and pointed to the foredeck. Without anyone noticing, the launcher had retracted itself and the swimming pool was back in place.

108: Tyuratum

There was a flurry of orderly activity in Satellite Control Room 101 B. Controlling the injection of a satellite into a geostationary orbit was something that the technicians had performed on many occasions. For several minutes there was a steady ebb and flow of orders and confirmations between the Senior Controller and his colleagues. Many of the operations were handled by computer and required only infrequent interventions from the technicians.

Grechko and Grovanich watched the proceedings with interest. The duplicate satellite that they had laboured over for many hours was about to be placed in orbit.

'Mission profile stage twenty has been attained,' announced the Senior Controller.

The final stage of the SS-49A – the nose cone with its precious cargo – had reached its orbital height of thirty-six thousand kilometres above the equator.

More orders and confirmations followed.

The Senior Controller moved from his console and conferred with a technician. The two men studied a monitor screen.

'What's the matter?' asked Grechko anxiously, sensing that something was wrong.

'The nose cone is not opening, comrade,' the Senior Controller replied.

Grechko suppressed the sensation of panic that had arisen in his throat. If the nose cone could not be opened, the satellite would be trapped inside – several million roubles' worth of useless electronics. 'Can you fix it?' he asked calmly.

'We have four backup channels,' said the Senior Controller. 'We're going to try them now.'

The buzz of conversation died away. Those technicians concerned with opening the nose cone hunched their shoulders over their respective consoles.

'Activate backup channel one,' the Senior Controller requested.

'Activated and standing by,' a controller replied.

'Response – negative,' a voice reported from the room.

'Backup channel two.'

'Activated and standing by.'

'Response – negative.'

Grovanich groaned. Grechko scowled at him but said nothing.

The silence in the room was nearly total when the third channel was tried. The result was the same: according to the instrumentation, the nose cone was still firmly closed.

'Activate backup channel four.'

'Activated and standing by.'

Grovanich closed his eyes and tried not to think.

'Response – negative.'

This time there was a collective murmur throughout the room.

'Stand by – stand by,' said the voice from the back of the room. 'Correction. Correction. She's opened. The nose cone has opened.'

Grovanich's eyes did the same.

'A sticky solenoid,' the Senior Controller reported, looking up at Grechko from the console he was bending over. 'These things happen. But we now have orbital injection. The new satellite is ten kilometres from the original satellite.'

Grechko nodded placidly. 'Don't do that to me again, please.'

The Senior Controller grinned. 'We usually get one gremlin on a launch. I can't see that anything can go wrong with the detonation of the killer satellite.

109: London

It was 7.30 am and already the traffic moving along the Mall was heavy, as if anticipating the time in a few hours when it would be closed to traffic.

'Okay. Hold it there,' Jason ordered into his lapel microphone. The cherry picker's platform stopped its upwards jack-knifing motion. Jason was now perched some thirty-five feet above the Mall. He aimed his television camera down the long, straight avenue towards the Admiralty Arch. Buckingham Palace was behind him. 'Four to OB. How's that, Rob?'

The outside broadcast director's voice answered in Jason's

earpiece. 'Yeah – that looks fine, Jason. How are you on a one-eighty?'

Jason panned his camera through 180 degrees. The director, sitting in the outside broadcast van, swore when he saw the tree obscuring the view of Buckingham Palace.

'Need five seconds to crank above it,' Jason commented, 'and then I've got the main gate dead centre.'

'Okay, Jason. The best thing is if I cue Bill on six from the top of the Admiralty Arch for a ten second loosen after your long approach shot. That should give you time to crank above the tree.'

'Right,' said Jason, making a note on his camera script. 'Let's try it on the dummy run.'

110: Mid-Atlantic

The *Sarania* rolled abominably. A strong sou'westerly had got up and was whipping spray off the crests of the swell.

Grechko's voice came through on the speaker in the bridgehouse. 'Base to *Sarania*. We are ready to neutralize the target when you are ready.'

Damion was sitting at the SWIFT station. Unencrypted hash from the genuine SWIFT III satellite was scrolling up the screen. He looked up at Tony. 'Tell them we're all set.'

Tony relayed the message to the control room at Tyuratum.

'Base to *Sarania*,' Grechko acknowledged. 'Stand by.'

'Who controls the switch-over?' Charlie asked.

'They do,' said Damion. 'And their timing is going to have to be spot on. They've got to switch over to the duplicate satellite at the precise moment they zap the original.'

111: Tyuratum

The Senior Controller watched the wall screen intently while he made a series of fine adjustments with his joystick control. The spot of light from the aiming laser roved over the SWIFT III satellite and stopped at the base of the solar panels.

'I'm going to hit the satellite's power supply,' he stated. 'Flying debris may cause us to lose our picture but that doesn't matter – the

241

killer is now at the end of its useful life. The replacement satellite will switch in automatically when the original goes off the air.'

'All systems ready,' a technician reported.

All eyes in the room were watching the doomed satellite on the wall screen.

The Senior Controller opened the switch guard and pressed the button. There was a slight blurring of the satellite's image. A hole appeared where the spot of light had been. And then the SWIFT satellite suddenly disintegrated. Bits of its casing hurled past the camera with such force that Grovanich instinctively blinked. The force of the blow sent the mangled wreckage of the SWIFT satellite tumbling away from the camera into a new orbit.

'Duplicate satellite now operational,' the Senior Controller announced.

112: Mid-Atlantic

'Base to *Sarania*. Target now neutralized. Replacement satellite operational.'

Damion looked at the monitor in surprise. The hash was still scrolling up the screen. He hurriedly entered a code on the keyboard. The screen cleared momentarily. The data reappeared. This time it was no longer scrambled and instead of scrolling, the screen was flashing rapidly – winking through pages of information that was too fast for the eye to follow.

Charlie, Owen and Tony gathered around the work station.

'What does it mean?' asked Charlie.

Damion touched a key. The display froze. Shown on the screen was a credit card authorization request from a twenty-four hour supermarket in Houston. A Mr A J Simpsons wished to make a $1,090 purchase to be charged against his United Kingdom Access card account.

As a hotelier, Charlie knew all about obtaining authorizations for large debits against credit cards. 'Jesus,' he whispered, awed by what he saw.

Owen was puzzled. 'What does that mean? Is that all we're about? A credit card fraud?'

Damion shook his head without taking his eyes off the screen.

'No,' he said slowly. 'It's not about that. What you're seeing now means that we've done it – we've broken into SWIFT. The duplicate satellite is working. It's taken over all the normal day-to-day transactions.' He produced his hip flask and took a long pull before carefully replacing the cap. 'We've done it,' he repeated, as though he could hardly credit the evidence on the monitor. And then he was shouting and thumping the desk. 'We've done it! We've actually gone and fucking well done it!'

113: Tyuratum

The Senior Controller hooked his hands together at the back of his neck and yawned. He swivelled his chair around to face Grechko and Grovanich. The atmosphere in the control room was in sharp contrast to the tension of the previous hour: technicians were standing around in groups or sitting on the edges of their consoles while animatedly discussing the strange information they were obtaining from the duplicate SWIFT satellite.

'I must congratulate you and your staff,' said Grechko, unable to take his eyes off his monitor. Out of curiosity, he had accessed the prices being beamed through the satellite from the Hong Kong stock exchange. He found it hard to accept that he could alter those prices by a few simple strokes on the keyboard. Not that there would be any point in doing such a thing without being able to block the landline validations.

The Senior Controller shrugged off the compliment. 'It's our job, comrade. And it's made a change from the usual routine.' He yawned again. 'So what's next on the agenda?'

'I think a few hours' sleep. We should all reassemble back in here at 13.30 GMT.'

The Senior Controller looked at his schedule. 'Ah – yes. That's when your agents block the transatlantic telephone cables?'

'That's right,' Grechko confirmed.

The Senior Controller keyed the talkback microphone. He thanked his colleagues for their efforts and told them to return to the control room at 13.30 GMT. He stood and was about to leave, but hesitated. 'Can I ask a question?'

'Go ahead,' Grechko invited.

'Why is the *Minsk* shadowing the *Sarania*? We don't need verifications on the yacht's position. Not with our tracking facilities.'

'The *Minsk* should be at least three hundred nautical miles from the *Sarania*,' Grechko pointed out. 'You can hardly call that shadowing.'

'She's approximately five hundred miles north of the *Sarania*,' the Senior Controller agreed.

'We considered it prudent to have her on hand in case anything goes wrong,' said Grechko coldly.

The Senior Controller sensed that he was being warned off. 'Okay. Just thought I'd mention it. Incidentally, there's another ship near the *Sarania*.'

This was news to Grechko. 'What? What sort of ship?'

'We don't know. Whatever she is, she's very small. Probably a cabin cruiser. Difficult getting a decent satellite resolution on her.'

'How close?'

'Two hundred miles east of the *Sarania*.'

Grechko relaxed. He had visions of a ship just over the horizon from the *Sarania* that might possibly witness events later in the day. 'It's probably a pleasure craft,' he reasoned.

'That's more than likely,' said the Senior Controller, moving to the door. 'I just thought I'd mention it.'

Grechko and Grovanich were alone in the control room. The academician remained silent for some moments. He seemed unable to take his eyes off the SWIFT screen. 'I don't think a small vessel two hundred miles east of the *Sarania* is a problem,' he said, as though thinking aloud. 'Not the real problem.'

Grovanich raised his eyebrows. 'What is then? We seem to be overcoming them all very successfully.'

'There's an aspect of this operation we know nothing about,' said Grechko. 'And that worries me. We don't know how our friends are going to block the transatlantic cables.'

'Why worry?' Grovanich asked. 'They've been remarkably efficient so far. Look at their operation to send us the data to build a duplicate satellite. Remarkable.'

Grechko gave a sudden laugh. 'You're right, Mikhail. I'm becoming like an old woman in my dotage.'

114: London

The City of London was coming to life.

Walter Fox made space among his six telephones on his desk in the huge dealers' room of Johnson Percival and studied his instructions for the hundredth time. Before him the SECQ monitors were displaying the usual frantic activities of the Tokyo and Hong Kong stock exchanges and commodities markets. Despite the madly changing prices, nothing exceptional had happened during the night in the Far East.

Monday morning was usually slow in getting started. Other dealers were wandering into the room, holding conferences around the beverage vending machine – where all the really important trading decisions were made – and occasionally grabbing their telephones when something caught their eye on the monitors. Walter ignored them all. Neil Jones dropped his huge bulk behind a neighbouring desk and called out a cheery 'good morning'. Walter grunted in reply. He was sorely tempted to confide in Neil about his weird instructions, but professional pride in preserving the confidences of clients prevailed and he remained silent. Walter had been a dealer for thirty years. In that time he had developed a sharp, reliable sixth sense that told him when something was about to happen. It was a sixth sense that was fed by international news: the trading performances of companies and countries; the snippets of information that he picked up in the Press Club; reading between the telexed lines of the news services; and even gossip in his local pub in the heart of the Surrey stockbroker belt. But today his sixth sense had deserted him. It was an ordinary day. It had been an ordinary weekend. Nothing had happened anywhere in the world that was likely to upset the delicate balance of the international money markets. No aggressive behaviour in the United Nations. Nothing. So why were the Russians suddenly so keen on buying US dollars? What was going to happen to the dollar after 3.30 pm when he was supposed to start buying? What did the Russians know that he didn't?

For the first time Walter experienced a twinge of fear. He looked at his watch. It was several hours before the New York markets opened.

115: London

Air Force Two touched down at Heathrow Airport at 8.55 am local time – five minutes ahead of schedule. A light drizzle prompted the British Airports Authority to wheel out their huge VIP canopy so that it straddled the Boeing and the waiting cars like a giant spider. Politicians did not generally favour the conventional jetties when disembarking from aircraft; they liked to be seen – to have batteries of waiting cameras to wave to.

Carol Weismann had managed to snatch only a few minutes' sleep during the flight. She would have welcomed the rain on her face as she confronted the whirl of security men and television cameras. The tiny, aspirin-size earpiece radio that her PR experts had provided obligingly whispered to her the names of all the British leaders just before she shook hands with them and before they were introduced. A junior defence minister was clearly flattered by her jumping the introduction and saying to him: 'Good morning, Mr Simmonds. I've been so looking forward to meeting you.'

The motorcade swept the visitors eastwards into central London. They passed a number of inevitable protest groups angrily waving placards that condemned the SDI deal. At 10 Downing Street there was a chance to freshen up and have a light breakfast before getting down to the business of the first meeting of the day – the clarification of a number of points concerning the finance of the anti-missile system that had not been fully covered during the earlier, lower-level negotiations.

The first meeting went well. Howard Penn dealt with the more difficult points with his customary bluff cheeriness. With her initial nervousness wearing off, helped by the charm of her hosts, Carol Weismann began to enjoy herself. She looked at her watch. 11.15 am local time.

In four hours she would be having tea at Buckingham Palace.

116: Mid-Atlantic

'Out! Out! Out!' Elaine yelled, dragging another deckhand to his feet and pushing him towards the door. 'It's over. Party's over!' She hauled Pepe to his feet. 'Come on, squirt. You too.' With that she bundled Pepe out of the door. Max was the only one left. He was sprawled across the bed. 'You too, Max.' She shoved him unceremoniously after Pepe, slamming the door behind him. She leaned against the door and watched Jackie sitting up on the bed. Her T-shirt was rucked up around her neck.

Jackie looked groggily around. She pulled down her T-shirt. 'What happened?'

'Nothing,' said Elaine, flopping beside Jackie on the bed. 'But it bloody nearly did. Some prat produced a merlin. I saw you take about three drags on it. Darling – don't you think that *three* drags on a merlin is just a tiny bit over the top?'

Jackie stood. She wobbled and nearly lost her balance while hitching up her jeans. 'Not as over the top as parties at the crack of dawn. Anyway, I didn't know it was a merlin.'

Elaine jumped to her feet. 'I'll tell Pepe to clear up in here.'

'Mrs Karn . . .'

'Yes?'

'I think you're either very clever or utterly insane.'

Elaine laughed and moved to the door. 'Let me know when you've made up your mind.'

As she mounted the companionway leading to the bridgehouse, Elaine glanced at the blackened decking around the swimming pool and wished that she had seen the launching. She pulled the door open. Charlie, Damion, Tony and Owen looked up from where they were gathered around the SWIFT work station. Their pleased expressions answered her unspoken question.

'So we're in?' she asked, joining them and looking at the terminal's screen.

Tony gave her a joyful hug and swung her delightedly around. 'We've done it, darling! We've done it! We've done it! We've done it!'

'Did the crew hear or see anything of the launch?' Charlie asked.

'Nothing,' Elaine answered. 'And nor did I. Judging by the messed-up paintwork, it must've been quite a spectacle.'

Damion grunted. 'It was more smoke and noise than anything.'

Elaine stared at the terminal's monitor. Nothing was happening because Damion had set the terminal to a stand-by menu. 'Have you tried out some experimental transactions?' she asked.

247

'What would be the point?' Damion asked. 'Manual transactions would be too slow. And any large sums will be automatically cancelled by the authentications. We can't do anything serious until the transatlantic phone lines are blocked.'

'Oh don't be so stuffy,' Elaine retorted. 'Let's have a little bit of fun first.'

'But there's no point.'

Elaine looked appealingly at Charlie. 'What do you say, Charlie? Just a little bit of fun with a few thousand dollars? Please? I know how to operate a terminal.'

Charlie grinned. 'Why not? It'll be great to see it all working.'

Damion shrugged and relinquished his chair. Elaine sat in front of the keyboard. 'Tony. The bank account you opened in Istanbul. I need full details.'

Tony produced his pocket memo pad. He called up on the miniature screen the information that Elaine requested and placed the pad by her elbow. Like his fellow conspirators, he had opened an account in Istanbul with ten thousand dollars – the minimum deposit required by the Swiss bank that he had selected to receive his break-in transactions.

'Fine,' Elaine commented, keying the data into the terminal's temporary buffer store. 'What bank account do you want to raid?'

Tony chuckled. 'How about Tass' London account?'

Elaine nodded without taking her eyes off the monitor. As she studied the menu, the enormity of the enterprise dawned on her: after months of planning, the impregnable SWIFT system and the countless billions of dollars that were entrusted to it by the world's banks and financial institutions were at the mercy of her fingertips. The impossible had become a reality. She clasped her hands tightly together for a moment in an attempt to stop them trembling before resting her fingers on the keyboard. She started by tentatively calling onto the screen a few 'pull-down' instruction menus. Everything behaved normally as if she were testing out a terminal in a London bank. Gaining confidence, she said: 'We'll need the Tass account numbers. Let's see if we can get into the central index. Normally it's protected by about a million passwords.'

'You'll have direct access,' said Damion shortly. 'Crick did a good job.'

An alphabetical index of London business names and addresses together with their sorting codes, bank account numbers and credit balances appeared on the monitor. Elaine sat back and stared. 'I don't believe it,' she muttered in astonishment.

Damion gave an indifferent shrug.

Elaine swallowed and hesitantly scrolled the screen through the thousands of entries, pausing occasionally so that she could see how far she had to go. The listings ranged from accounts that were a few pounds in credit to major accounts with several million pounds on deposit.

Owen felt his throat go dry. 'We could bust into *any* of those?' he queried in wonder.

'No problem,' said Damion.

'Ah – there's Tass' accounts,' said Elaine, freezing the monitor's display. 'My God – they've got enough of them. Why so many accounts, Tony?'

'I've no idea,' Tony admitted. 'Choose the biggest.'

Tass' largest account was nearly a quarter of a million pounds in credit. Elaine transferred its number to the terminal's buffer store. She returned to the main menu and called up SWIFT Message Text 400. MT400 was the payment advice routine. It generated a set of fields on the screen. None of the circle of watchers made a sound while she filled in the fields naming the paying bank and Anton Suskov as the beneficiary customer.

'Nothing over ten thousand dollars per transaction,' Damion reminded when she moved the cursor to the amount field. Even the normally phlegmatic Damion was unable to conceal a hint of excitement in his voice.

Charlie said nothing, but his black eyes glittered in anticipation.

Elaine looked over her shoulder. 'Don't worry, Damion. I know what I'm doing. Could you use six thousand pounds, Tony?'

Tony's nervous laugh did not break the tension. He nodded and managed an awed, 'Yes'.

Elaine completed the rest of the fields and called up the MT412 – the Advice of Acceptance routine. The monitor cleared again. The top half of the screen showed the details of Tony's account in Istanbul. The credit column was displaying his original ten-thousand-dollar deposit. The lower half of the screen displayed the Tass account in London.

'Nothing's happened,' said Charlie.

Elaine's finger was poised over the transmit key. 'Nothing will yet,' she replied. 'Watch.' She pressed the transmit key.

There was a pause. The screen remained unchanged.

'Now what?' Charlie demanded.

'Give it time,' Damion muttered. 'Now do you see why I've worked out all the transactions in advance on disk? Direct keyboard entry is too slow.'

Before he finished the sentence, the display changed. Although Elaine was expecting it to happen, it still seemed a miracle when it did: The Tass account suddenly decreased by six thousand pounds and simultaneously, Tony's Istanbul account increased by the same amount.

'Holy shit,' Charlie breathed.

Owen sucked in his breath and said nothing.

'Games,' Damion muttered disparagingly. 'Just a game with chicken feed prizes. You can't do anything serious until the London–New York cables are blocked.'

Charlie grinned. 'Maybe, Damion. But games are fun.'

During the next thirty minutes, Elaine made a number of minor transactions that did little to increase the wealth of the five conspirators but which did, with the exception of Damion, do much to further boost their morale.

117: London

Jason used a taxi that was bowling along the Mall towards Buckingham Palace to check the auto-zoom on his television camera. The sonic device kept the London cab perfectly centred on his screen.

'That's great,' said the director's voice in Jason's earpiece. 'Okay – I think we'll do it like this. You see that manhole? It must be about two hundred yards from you.'

Jason focused his camera on a manhole that was in the centre of the traffic lane. 'That one?'

'That's the one,' the director confirmed. 'I'll stay on you until the entire motorcade's cleared that point. I'll count to five from when the lead car reaches the manhole and then cut to Bill for his second long shot. I don't mind holding it for longer if you're not ready for your shot of the main gate. When you are, I'll want you to stay with the motorcade until the last car has passed through the palace's arch and then I'll take it over to camera nine in the central courtyard. How does all that sound?'

'Fine,' said Jason, scribbling notes on his camera script. 'How many cars are there and what's their order?'

There was a pause before the director replied. 'Apparently the PM's scrapped the usual protocol. Howard Penn and Carol Weismann will be in the lead car – the US Ambassador's Cadillac. Then the Secret Service. Then the PM's Roller, and the rest of the party will be following in three motor-pool Daimlers.'

'She's what I call a tasty piece.'

'Carol Weismann?'

'Why can't we find politicians like her?'

The director laughed.

118: Mid-Atlantic

Tony sat down beside Damion at the SWIFT work station. 'How's it going, Damion?'

'So so,' said Damion, continuing to watch the portable television. It was still tuned to the BBC's World Service coverage of the US Vice-Presidential visit to London.

Like all television sets designed to receive worldwide programmes, the name of the country originating the programme was shown at the top of the screen together with the station's callsign and the local time. Some studio pundits were filling in time between the outside broadcasts by discussing the implications of the impending treaty.

'Why the interest in that programme?' Tony inquired. 'You've been watching it all morning.'

Damion's hard eyes turned on Tony. 'Why not? My company's been involved in the production of a lot of SDI software.'

'I'd forgotten,' Tony admitted. He looked at the sleeves that held the program disks for the break into SWIFT. They were clearly labelled. 'Where's Crick's disk?'

'Crick isn't interested in making money out of the break-in.'

'You're joking?'

Damion showed that he was irritated by the questions. 'I never joke. All Crick wants is the satisfaction of busting in. Nothing else. Okay?'

'But I thought –'

'Look – if you want to find out about Crick's motives, I suggest you talk to him and don't go bothering me. He had a major row with SWIFT. This is his way of getting even.'

The picture on the television changed to the facade of the Savoy Hotel and then switched to the interior of the ornate main dining room that had been set up for the press conference. The Prime Minister led the way from the meeting room. He waved briefly at the cameras. There was a lot of milling about and firing of flashguns while the party of hosts and guests shook hands and swapped jokes with each other before taking their seats at a long table facing the assembled press. The camera moved in for a close-up of Carol Weismann, looking very attractive in a lemon skirt and jacket.

Damion turned up the volume. He looked at the bulkhead clock that he had reset to British Summer Time. It was 2.15 pm. 'We'll be breaking into SWIFT in fifty minutes,' he said curtly to Tony. 'At 3.05 pm by that clock. You'd better tell the others.'

119: London

Carol Weismann was thoroughly enjoying every minute of the visit. She shrewdly judged just how much charm to use, knowing that what went down well in America did not necessarily work so well in Europe. The second meeting at the Savoy Hotel after a buffet lunch had been less formal and had consisted mainly of an amicable discussion about the wording of the official press statement.

When the press conference got under way, she was a little embarrassed by the number of questions that were directed at her. She dealt with them with her customary skill and even exchanged some good-natured banter with an ITV man that went down well with the other journalists. And then the treaty was produced for the formal signing.

'Next stop, Buckingham Palace,' Howard Penn whispered to her as the party filed out to the waiting cars.

She glanced at her watch. It was 2.40 pm. Thirty-five minutes to go.

The police closed the Mall to traffic at 2.10 pm. From his perch on the cherry picker's platform high above the broad, tree-lined avenue, Jason kept one eye on the monitor that was sending him a programme feed while he watched the plain-clothes men and US Secret Service agents carrying out last-minute checks of the route. A police car stopped in the centre of the traffic lane beside the manhole cover. Two uniformed men got out of the car and checked the security of the four small metal plates that had been used to spot-weld the cover to its rim so that it could not be lifted. All the manhole covers along the route had been welded into place the previous week after the sewers had been carefully checked for bombs. Satisfied that all was well, the policemen returned to their car and drove off.

During his years with BBC World Service Television, Jason had covered many important events but none had been the subject of such tight security as this particular visit.

120: Tyuratum

It was 2.25 pm in London when everyone took their places in the control room.

'I take it that there's not much for us to do?' the Senior Controller commented to Grechko.

The academician took the program disks from Grovanich and loaded them into the computer drives that were before him. 'It's all up to the *Sarania* now,' he replied. 'Once we hear from her that the transatlantic cables are blocked, we can go ahead and transfer the transaction instructions on those program disks to the SWIFT satellite.'

'Are you going to tell us what the instructions actually do?' Grovanich asked.

'No,' Grechko replied empathically.

121: Mid-Atlantic

It was 2.45 pm in London. The television at Damion's elbow was showing the gathering outside the Savoy Hotel. Howard Penn shaking hands with everyone; the British Prime Minister chatting

253

with the Foreign Secretary; Carol Weismann looking stunning in the sunshine in her lemon outfit; waiting cars; security men – their eyes everywhere except on their charges.

Damion carefully inserted a new battery in his telephone answering machine transducer and slipped the unit into his jacket pocket along with the Pokketfone. For a moment he was again plagued with the notion that there was something that he had overlooked. He decided that if there was, it was so minor that it wasn't important. Next he removed the program disks from their sleeves and loaded them into the control computer's disk drives. The entire system was powered up and running. There was a SWIFT preliminary access menu waiting on the monitor screen. He didn't look up when Charlie, Tony and Elaine, and Owen entered the bridgehouse and locked the door behind them.

'Charlie,' Damion said. 'I don't want any distractions while I'm doing this. No one is to come near me.'

'Sure, Damion.' Charlie indicated to the others to position their seats some distance from Damion and the SWIFT work station.

'Why have you still got the television on?' Elaine asked.

Damion pointed to the time that was displayed at the top right-hand corner of the screen. 'I need the time in London. British Summertime – not GMT.'

'The picture's coming via a satellite,' Tony pointed out. 'That means there's about a second's delay.'

Damion grunted as he double-checked a menu guide in one of the bulky SWIFT manuals. 'I'm allowing for that. I'll explain in a few minutes. Now please – I have to concentrate. No one is to talk.'

Tony quietly moved his chair to one side so that he could see the television and Damion's face. The television screen showed Carol Weismann sliding elegantly into the backseat of the US ambassador's bulletproof black Cadillac, USA1.

It was 2.58 pm.

122

The Soviet helicopter-cruiser *Minsk* had been lying stopped for several hours, enabling Lieutenant Jan Valki to stand at the aft service deck rail and indulge his passion for killing. He took careful aim and fired. The soft-nosed bullet spread on impact and ripped across the porbeagle's back just behind its dorsal fin. Voiding blood and tissue, the stricken shark tried to dive. It thrashed the surface white and then went into its death flurry. Valki was about to fire again but a hammerhead intervened – guided to the scene by its superb sense of smell that enabled it to detect one part of blood in ten million parts of sea water.

Valki watched, fascinated, as the huge shark struck again and again at the dying porbeagle. The vicious jaws, with their triple rows of teeth, spooned crescents out of the porbeagle's flank as though its flesh was butter. Another shark closed in for a share of the kill, its dorsal fin cutting a sharp vee on the swell. Valki was aiming just below the speeding fin when a rating touched his sleeve.

'Lieutenant Valki. The captain's compliments. He wishes to see you in his day cabin.'

Valki thanked the rating and gave him the rifle. He made his way forward, past rows of Kamov Ka-50 helicopters with their rotors folded back over their tailbooms, and climbed the catwalk stairway that led to Captain Dalvanski's cabin overlooking the main flight deck. He knocked and entered when bidden.

Dalvanski stood and returned the helicopter pilot's salute.

'Good morning, captain,' said Valki, removing his cap and tucking it under his arm.

Dalvanski regarded the younger man with some distaste. He had selected Valki because he considered him the most cold-blooded of all the *Minsk*'s airmen. 'Lieutenant,' said Dalvanski brusquely. 'I have something to tell you that is most confidential. No one is to know about it except you and me. No one. Do you understand?'

Valkie came to rigid attention and clicked his heels. He stared fixedly over Dalvanski's shoulder at the bulkhead. 'I understand perfectly, captain,' he answered crisply.

'Five hundred miles due south of us is a ship that I have orders to destroy at sixteen hundred today.' Dalvanski pushed a facsimile picture of the *Sarania* across his desk. The pilot picked it up and studied it. 'A yacht, captain? I suggest an SS-N-35. It has the ran . . .'

'A missile is out of the question,' Dalvanski interrupted. 'My orders are that there must be no survivors. Nor must they be given the opportunity to identify and radio information on their attackers.

Suggestions?'

Valkie gave a thin, bloodless smile. 'I presume I will have the honour of carrying out the mission?'

'If you so wish.'

'Then I have several suggestions, captain.'

'Yes,' said Dalvanski almost regretfully. 'I thought you might have.'

123

Damion's television showed the motorcade leaving the Savoy Hotel and turning into the Strand. The time in London was 3.00 pm. Watched by the others, he entered the telephone number of his Putney flat on his Pokketfone's keypad.

He laid the Pokketfone on the desk. When the call was connected, it was possible for the others to hear the recorded announcement apologizing for Damion's absence and inviting callers to leave their message. Damion left the line open. Tony's suspicions were aroused but he had no clear idea as to what Damion was planning.

'Owen,' said Damion, turning round and giving a slip of paper to the skipper. 'Call up that number through the ship-to-shore.'

Owen took the slip of paper and crossed to the radio telephone set. 'What is it?' he asked.

'That number will give us the New York speaking clock via London. Set it for automatic recall every ten seconds or so. Once we can no longer get through, we'll know that the transatlantic lines are blocked.'

Owen entered the number and the recall instruction. After a few moments a woman's recorded voice said cheerfully:

'*Good morning. The New York temperature is sixty-five degrees. Eastern Daylight Time – ten three and ten seconds.*' The announcement was followed by a single bleep.

London's time was 3.03 pm. The motorcade, led by the gleaming black Cadillac flanked by police motorcyclists, was heading towards Trafalgar Square.

Tony was puzzled. Damion seemed more intent on the events on the screen than the time in London.

124: London

The motorcade skirted Trafalgar Square and headed towards the Mall. A knot of demonstrators, hemmed in by police, jeered noisily and waved their placards as the vehicles swept by. A speaker standing on top of one of the lions guarding Nelson's Column was shouting something indistinguishable through a loudhailer, but the general attitude of the crowds was one of good will.

The cars and motorcycles surged on, unconcerned and undeterred.

The last time Carol Weismann had driven under the Admiralty Arch had been in a London taxi. The shadow of the great edifice flitted by overhead and then they were at the beginning of the final half-mile of their journey along the dead straight Mall. She looked beyond the broad shoulders of the Secret Servicemen in the front seat and could see in the distance the gilding on the Victoria Memorial glinting in the sun. Beyond that was the sombre brooding elegance of Buckingham Palace. She felt queasy as the doubts she had been pushing resolutely to the back of her mind suddenly started clamouring for attention. Was her skirt too short? Would she fumble her curtsy? God knows – she had practised it enough times. And – horror of horrors – supposing someone else at the palace was also wearing a lemon outfit?

125: Mid-Atlantic

'Good morning. The New York temperature is sixty-five degrees. Eastern Daylight Time – ten four and ten seconds.'

Without taking his eyes off the television, Damion felt in his pocket and produced his telephone answering machine transducer. The Pokketfone was lying by his hand, its line still open to his Putney flat. The old worry about having forgotten something vital flitted across his mind.

Damion's actions puzzled Tony. How could an answering machine transducer and a Pokketfone serve in the blocking of the transatlantic telephone cables?

Tony caught Charlie's eye and realized that the hotelier was watching him carefully, a hand thrust casually into his jacket pocket.

'*Good morning. The New York temperature is sixty-five degrees. Eastern Daylight Time – ten five and thirty seconds.*'

126: London

The Cadillac's gleaming radiator grille was perfectly centred on Jason's monitor as the motorcade entered the Mall. Jason was a car enthusiast: he knew all about USA1 – the latest in a long line of Cadillacs to bear the famous registration number. USA1 looked sleek and graceful as it purred towards him. But despite its outward show of style, the car weighed nearly four tonnes due to a mass of sculptured armour-plating that was cunningly concealed behind its seat cushions and trim panels. The special tyres developed by Goodyear were reinforced with bulletproof titanium mesh and were filled with foam plastic instead of air. The low-ratio back axle and a turbo-charged General Motors ten-litre engine gave the vehicle the performance of a sports car should the need arise. The car was a veritable tank. Like all tanks, it provided excellent protection for its occupants against gunfire but was vulnerable to bombs exploding immediately beneath it.

Jason instinctively loosened the shot from a close-up an instant before he heard the director's request in his earpiece.

'Good, good,' said the director, as virtually the entire length of the Mall came into shot. 'Stay with it . . . Nice . . . Nice . . . There's the manhole coming up. Get ready to crank.'

Vice President Howard Penn took Carol Weismann's hand and gave it a reassuring squeeze. 'Don't worry, honey,' he whispered. 'They really know how to make a feller feel at home.'

'But I'm not a feller, Howard.'

'Don't I know it.'

She smiled and was grateful to him for slackening the knot of mounting apprehension in her stomach.

127: Mid-Atlantic

'*Good morning. The New York temperature is sixty-five degrees. Eastern Daylight Time – ten five and fifty seconds.*'

258

Damion picked up the transducer and held it near the Pokket-fone's mouthpiece.

Tony stared at the motorcade on the television. In that instant, everything suddenly made ghastly sense: the transducer; the Pokket-fone and its open line to Damion's flat; the television and the Vice-Presidential visit.

A bomb! It had to be a bomb!

'No!' he screamed. He launched himself at Damion, knocking the transducer from his hand. It rolled across the floor. Damion gave a bellow of rage and drove his fist into Tony's face. The big man tried to grab the gadget but Tony was upon him. The two men rolled on the floor, clawing wildly at each other.

A shot crashed out and smacked into the floor near Tony's head. 'Get back or she's dead!' Charlie yelled.

Through the blood coursing from his cut eye, Tony saw that Charlie was pointing an automatic at Elaine's head. She had half-risen from her chair. She sank back – her eyes fixed in a stare of blank terror on the barrel that was aimed unerringly at her.

'Get back! Get back!' Charlie's knuckles gripping the automatic were white.

Tony rolled away from Damion. 'Charlie – don't shoot!' he pleaded, choking the words out. 'Please don't shoot!'

Owen was riveted into his chair – staring in amazement at the unbelievable scene.

Swearing profusely, Damion snatched up the transducer and the Pokketfone. His chest heaving, he knelt at the desk. To his immense relief, the Cadillac still had fifty yards to cover before it reached the manhole cover.

'No one moves,' Charlie warned.

Forty yards.

'You can't do this,' said Tony desperately. 'Not this way.'

'Watch me,' Damion panted.

Thirty yards.

Owen recovered his senses. 'Someone tell me what's going on.'

'You'll find out. Now shuddup!' Charlie snarled.

Twenty yards.

'Good morning. The New York temperature is sixty-five degrees. Eastern Daylight Time – ten six and thirty seconds.'

Ten yards.

Damion quickly wiped the sweat from his forehead and pressed the transducer right into the Pokketfone's mouthpiece. His hand shook slightly as his finger rested on the transducer's slide switch. His eyes were fixed on the television as if hypnotized by the sight of the smooth tarmac disappearing under the Cadillac's grille.

Five yards! The grille was smack in the middle of the picture . . . .

Steady . . . ! Steady . . . ! There's the manhole cover! Think calmly. Think calmly. Remember – hit the switch just as the grille reaches the cover.

'Good morning. The New York temperature is sixty-five degrees. Eastern Daylight Time – ten six and fifty seconds.'

Three yards . . . Two yards . . . One yard . . . !

He thumbed the switch.

Nothing happened.

Nothing's happened!

He thumbed the switch again.

Nothing! Nothing! Nothing! For Chrissake – what's gone wrong!

He gave a cry of despair and was on his feet, staring dementedly at the long shot that showed the entire gleaming motorcade gliding gracefully along the Mall. He thumbed the switch frantically several times and then, through his bewilderment and rage, he suddenly remembered Crick's warning that the transducer's signal would also start the answering machine's tape in the normal way and that there would be only the one opportunity to detonate the bomb.

He resisted the temptation to hurl the Pokketfone and transducer across the bridgehouse. Instead he set them down carefully on the desk top and continued to stare at the television. The motorcade was passing through the gates of Buckingham Palace. The Royal Standard, fluttering from its mast on top of the building, seemed to mock him.

'Good morning. The New York temperature is sixty-five degrees. Eastern Daylight Time – ten seven and fifty seconds.'

Slowly, Damion turned to face the others. Charlie's face was white. He kept the automatic pointing at Elaine while his stare alternated between Damion and the television. Tony stood very slowly, holding a handkerchief to stem the flow of blood from his eye. He moved to Elaine's side. She reached out and clung to him. It was only when his arms encircled her shoulders that her courage and self-control deserted her. She started to tremble and then she was sobbing. Owen could think of nothing to say.

'So what went wrong?' Charlie asked, speaking very quietly.

Damion didn't answer. Charlie repeated the question.

Damion shook his head. 'I don't know. I just don't know.'

Charlie cast about in desperation, seeking an explanation. 'Maybe it did work and we're getting a delayed picture? Like those fast replays? Maybe the lines are all now completely block . . . '

'*Good morning,*' said the by-now familiar voice. '*The New York temperature is sixty-five degrees. Eastern Daylight Time – ten nine exactly.*'

'There's your answer,' said Damion woodenly.

128: Tyuratum

The Senior Controller looked at his watch and nodded to Grechko.

It was 3.15 pm in London.

Grechko picked up a telephone. 'Now for the crucial test,' he remarked casually to Grovanich. He punched out the number of the Soviet Embassy in Washington and waited. The dialling tone was repeated over an external speaker. Grovanich frowned. The sound of the dialling tone was hardly a good sign. There was worse to follow when a girl answered with a decidedly American accent. Grechko cut the line. He did not look up but consulted his electronic pad. He called another number and listened briefly to a recorded voice informing him what shows were running on Broadway.

There was total silence in the control room. All eyes were on Grechko. He waited a minute and then punched another number:

'*Good morning. The New York temperature is sixty-five degrees. Eastern Daylight Time – ten twenty exactly.*'

Grechko replaced the handset on its cradle. 'I'll try again in five minutes,' he decided. He turned and looked at Grovanich. His face was grey and haggard. 'But it looks as if something has gone very wrong.'

129: London

At 3.33 pm, Walter Fox was just about to start buying dollars on behalf of his clients when his emergency line telephone buzzed above the general uproar in the dealers' room. The day's trading was at its peak.

The voice gave a correct client identification code name and was much relieved when Walter confirmed that he had not started buying US dollars. Walter was told to disregard his instructions until further notice.

Walter acknowledged and replaced the telephone. He glanced up at the prices on his monitor. Nothing out of the ordinary was happening to the dollar in New York or Paris or anywhere.

He was secretly pleased that his professional sixth sense was not at fault and that his clients had eventually seen sense. All day he had been worrying, wondering how they could possibly know something that he didn't.

Another of Walter's senses was a rich sense of humour. He would have been highly amused had he known that a fellow dealer in New York had already been trading for five minutes, busily buying sterling when sterling was high and costing his clients nearly a billion dollars before he was contacted and told to stop. A Paris dealer did even better: he cost them nearer ten billion dollars.

130: Tyuratum

The blistering tirade from Moscow burned in Grechko's ear. He tried to interrupt several times and gave up.

Grovanich and everyone else in the satellite control room could hear every enraged word that was blasting from the telephone despite Grechko's efforts at pressing the handset tightly against his ear.

Grovanich wondered how he would be able to save his own skin by avoiding being dragged into the monumental row that was brewing.

Brewing? That was a joke. Judging by the near-hysteria erupting from the telephone, it sounded as if heads were not only rolling already, but being savagely kicked about and stomped on.

'Comrade Chairman,' Grechko managed to squeeze in when the speaker drew breath. 'Neither I or the *Sarania* know what has gone wrong. I will –'

The stream of sulphurous abuse resumed with renewed invective. Grechko's face became steadily paler. His hand holding the telephone was visibly trembling. He said: 'I shall present my resignation personally to you first thing in the morning, Comrade Chairman.'

'You won't!' the Chairman could be heard shouting. 'You will fly to Moscow this instant! I shall expect you and your resignation within two hours!' The line went dead.

For some seconds Grechko sat transfixed – staring straight ahead at the giant wall screen – the handset still held to his ear. Eventually he replaced it on the cradle. 'I don't understand it,' he muttered to no one in particular. 'What the hell could have gone wrong?'

Grovanich could think of nothing useful to say, so he remained silent.

131: Mid-Atlantic

The *Minsk*'s cooks and galley ratings were busy.

Valki watched as they opened several large, catering-size cans of offal and slurped their contents into a tough polythene bag. 'And the blood, please,' he requested.

The chief petty officer cook maintained a deadpan expression while pouring several litres of blood into the bag. It was not his job to question the outlandish requirements of officers. Besides, Valki was acting under Captain Dalvanski's authority.

'That's fine,' said Valki. 'I hope the bag won't leak?'

'It's a very strong bag, lieutenant,' the petty officer assured him.

Valki thanked the men. He looked distastefully at the bag's contents. The fifty kilogrammes of blood and ox organs swilling about looked quite disgusting. He doubted if he could ever eat liver again. 'Would someone please close it securely and take it to my helicopter on the flight deck.'

He left the galley and reported to Captain Dalvanski.

'Everything is ready, captain.'

'Very good,' said the senior officer. He paused and picked up a false-colour infrared satellite picture of the mid-Atlantic. A reddish coloured dot on the photograph had a bold circle drawn around it. 'When you've finished with the *Sarania* I have a detour I wish you to make. There's a ship just over a hundred miles due east of the yacht. It's too small to be a deep ocean fishing vessel and from the last three satellite passes, it is not following a recognized trade route.'

Valki took the offered photograph and studied it carefully. The positions of the *Sarania* and the mystery vessel were marked at the foot of the picture. 'A spyship?' he ventured.

'That's what I want you to find out,' Dalvanski replied. 'Make a low pass and come back with some pictures. If it is a US surveillance ship they must know we're in the area, therefore they won't be surprised to see you. In fact they might be suspicious if we don't show up.'

Valki clicked his heels and saluted. 'It will be done, captain.'

Twenty minutes later, Lieutenant Valki ran the turbine on his Ka-50 helicopter to three-quarters power and lifted off from the *Minsk*'s flight deck. He hovered for a few seconds, carrying out final checks, and then gave a thumbs-up signal to the aircraft ratings below. He turned his machine southwards in the direction of the *Sarania*. The leaden cloudbase was below two thousand feet but that didn't matter because this particular operation required a low-level approach to his target anyway. Slung between the ungainly fixed legs of his helicopter's trolley undercarriage was an AS-30 air-to-surface cruise missile with an armed warhead. Mounted on either side of the helicopter's fuselage were the ugly downward swivelling turrets of two rapid-fire cannons fully primed with belts of ammunition. Trembling and heaving like a living creature on the floor beside Lieutenant Valki was the polythene bag of blood and offal. He planned to scatter the bag's gory contents on the scene of the *Sarania*'s destruction. What the missile and cannons did not make certain of, the ever-hungry sharks of the mid-Atlantic most certainly would.

Lieutenant Valki was ruthlessly determined that there would be no survivors from the *Sarania*. He fully intended that the orders he had been given would be carried out to the letter.

132: London

At 4.20 pm the motorcade left Buckingham Palace and headed west to Heathrow Airport.

Carol Weismann sank back into the Cadillac's soft cushions and systematically pinned down her whirling recollections. Her husband and children would ask her the most searching questions about every

264

minute of the hugely enjoyable hour she had just experienced. The tea-and-biscuits encounter with one of the oldest families in Europe had passed off like a beautiful dream. Everything had been just right. Her curtsy had been perfect and no one else had been wearing a lemon outfit.

No one, she thought, could possibly match the consummate skill of the British Monarchy in the delicate art of putting people at their ease. Within a few minutes of being introduced to the Royal Family, she had been laughing and joking. Genuine laughter that had not arisen out of any observation of diplomatic niceties.

'It went well,' Howard Penn observed, smiling at her.

She nodded happily. Suddenly she was eager to be back home in South Carolina with her family.

133: Mid-Atlantic

The first thing Jackie noticed when she climbed up to the bridge-house was the blistered and blackened paintwork around the swimming pool. She tried the door. It was locked. Through the window she could see what was obviously a bitter argument in progress. Charlie was waving his arms and pacing up and down. Tony was holding a bloodstained handkerchief to his face. All of which gave her the distinct impression of having missed out on something interesting. She rapped on the glass.

Owen came to the door and opened it. 'What do you want? Can't you see we're busy?'

'Sorry to disturb you, captain. I've come to find out what the arrangements are for dinner. Only no one's answering the interphone.'

'You'd better come back later,' said Owen. 'Call up in about thirty minutes.'

'What happened to the swimming pool?'

'Call in about thirty minutes,' said Owen testily, and closed the door.

'I'll tell you what went wrong,' Charlie stormed at Damion. 'Crick fooled you –'

'For Chrissake, how many times do I have to tell you!' Damion

265

shouted back. I checked the bomb right before it was sealed! There was no way he could have switched off the detonator.'

'In that case you forgot something.'

The accusation stung Damion. 'Every detail was thought out in advance. Nothing was left to chance!'

'So what went wrong?'

'This is pointless,' Elaine broke in. 'You're just arguing in circles.' She helped Tony to his feet. 'If we'd known what you had been planning, we wouldn't have wanted any part of the operation.'

Charlie calmed down and looked cynically at Elaine. 'Yeah, that's right, kid. Easy for you to say that when things go wrong. But if money was flooding into your account right now –'

Elaine flared up. 'I wouldn't want it, Charlie! Neither of us thought you'd be getting involved in murder and assassination –'

'What do you mean "you"?' Damion demanded. 'We're all in this together.'

Elaine squared up to the big man and stared at him in contempt. 'Not us, Damion. We knew nothing about the murder of Crick or your crazy bomb plan.'

'May I say something?' Owen chimed in.

They all looked at the captain.

'It seems to me that we've forgotten something,' said Owen in a reasoning tone. 'The recriminations can wait. I'm as disappointed as the rest of you that everything's gone wrong. Our problem right now is that we're adrift with no fuel. As for the Soviets sending a merchantman our way, I think we can now forget that. The question is, what do we do now?'

'What do you suggest?' Tony asked.

'We've put out a general distress call for assistance. There's certain to be a ship within two days' steaming.' Owen managed to smile. 'The arguments we're going to have over salvage claims are going to make our present problems look like nothing.'

'I think we should discuss it first,' said Damion.

At that moment the radar warning set started bleeping.

Lieutenant Jan Valki was concerned about the oil pressure drop. His Ka-50's turbine was up to its old tricks again despite having had a new pump fitted. He was debating whether or not to abandon the mission and return to the *Minsk* when his forward target radar picked up the *Sarania* one hundred miles ahead – twenty minutes' flying time. He decided to continue. He primed the cruise missile's guidance computer with information on the *Sarania*'s position and lost height. Switching in the sea-hugging automatic pilot enabled his Kamov to fly with its undercarriage wheels barely skimming the swell. A minute passed while the machine's course held steady. A loud bleeping gave him five seconds' warning that the AS-30 cruise missile was about to be launched. Then the ignition lights winked rapidly. There was a sudden vibration and thunder from beneath his feet that drowned the sound of the explosive latches releasing their burden. The cruise missile streaked away from the Ka-50, blasting a trail of smoke and glare from its solid fuel rocket motor.

Relieved of its thousand kilogram cargo, the Ka-50 tended to leap upwards, but Valki anticipated the sudden lift. He swung his machine around and watched the AS-30 skimming across the wavetops like a flying fish as it hurtled towards its target at a steady eight hundred knots.

Owen spotted the exhaust trail arrowing at incredible speed towards the *Sarania*. He had just enough time to raise his arm and shout when the cruise missile struck the *Sarania*'s hull near the bow. The tremendous explosion burst open the foredeck like a mailed fist driven through a paper bag. Smoke and flames voided into the sky like the unexpected eruption of a volcano. As one, all the bridge-house windows shattered with a tremendous crash that followed the sound of the explosion. A sliver of flying glass ripped into Owen's chest, killing him instantly. Tony and Elaine were lifted off their feet and thrown backwards against the bulkhead. They were saved from the flying glass by the SWIFT work station that toppled over in front of them. A splinter sliced into Damion's calf muscle. Charlie was hurled against the bar. His head struck the counter. He crumpled to the floor and lay still. The *Sarania* began listing rapidly onto her starboard side as sea water roared through the gaping, jagged wound in her hull.

Jackie was busy in the galley, having just sent Pepe on an errand, when the missile struck. Her first crazy thought as galley utensils crashed around her was that one of the cookers had blown up and that dinner would have to be served late. Then she heard someone

267

screaming. Almost as soon as she recovered her balance she lost i
again, owing to the sudden alarming angle the floor was tilting at
Although confused, she pulled the door open and half-fell, half-slic
into the passageway, so steeply was the *Sarania* listing. Seeing the
whole length of passageway tilting told her that the *Sarania* was
sinking. The screaming continued. Someone was yelling in panic-
stricken Spanish. She stumbled along the passageway and was forced
to double back when she saw water foaming towards her. Confusion
gave way to fear when she realized that she was trapped. She forced
herself to think clearly. The porthole in her cabin! She ran to her
door and opened it. By now the *Sarania* was listing so steeply that
opening the door was like trying to push a hatch open. She pulled
herself up into her cabin. The padded wall panel had fallen out of
position. For some irrational reason, her first thought was for the
radio. She snatched it up and crammed it into her shoulderbag. The
Sarania gave a terrible shudder and settled, sending a small tidal
wave surging into the cabin. By now the porthole was nearly
overhead. She stood on the bulkhead and reached up to unscrew its
latches. She pulled. The porthole refused to open. Panic seized her.
Whatever had happened to the *Sarania* had warped the hull so that
the porthole was jammed shut. She pulled again, virtually hanging
onto the latches with all her weight. The porthole suddenly swung
down, causing her to lose her footing and fall backwards into the
black, surging water.

'Charlie!' Elaine suddenly cried out as Tony dragged her along the
side deck. 'We can't leave Charlie!'

Despite the blood pouring from his leg wound, Damion managed
to negotiate the tilting deck with surprising speed. He was several
yards ahead of the couple.

Tony stopped. 'Charlie!' he echoed, supporting himself and
Elaine against the superstructure. 'Damion! We've got to go back for
Charlie!'

'No time! He hit the bar. He's probably dead.'

The *Sarania* gave another shudder. The deck tilted over even
more.

'We've got to go back!'

'He's right!' Elaine shouted, pulling ineffectually at Tony. 'Let's
get the launches out first!'

268

The three managed to reach the port motor launch station. A Turkish and a Spanish deckhand had released the davits so that the launch was straddling the side deck. Damion yanked some lifejackets out of a locker and passed them out. Tony pulled one over Elaine's head and closed the Velcro straps. He broke the neck on the CO_2 bottle. There was a sharp hiss but the lifejacket refused to inflate.

'They all kaput!' the Spaniard called out.

'What? All of them?'

'Si.'

The *Sarania* settled deeper in the water. A swell broke across the listing deck, causing the launch to grate into a new position. The five climbed into the open cockpit. Elaine sat on the engine box and tried not to think about Charlie. The two deckhands cut through the davit ropes and threw the blocks clear so that they would not foul the launch's propeller.

'There's got to be more lifejackets in here,' Tony grunted, pulling out the contents of one of the launch's lockers. Like the other lifejackets, they were useless.

The launch tipped alarmingly. For a moment Elaine thought that something had snagged on the yacht so that the sinking yacht would drag the launch under with it. The *Sarania* was nearly on her beam ends. Air was bubbling and geysering all around the hull. It was inevitable that the yacht was going to sink. Suddenly the motor launch was floating free.

Lieutenant Jan Valki took his Ka-50 up to three hundred feet and coldly surveyed the devastation that his missile had wrought. Five miles away the *Sarania* was lying on her side, her hull surrounded by wreckage and nearly awash in the heavy swell. A motor boat appeared to have been successfully launched. He could see several people in the water struggling towards it.

Now to finish the job. He put his machine's nose hard down and headed towards the scene – the surface a blur as it disappeared beneath his canopy; the whirling rotors leaving a path of flattened water in their wake. His hand reached out and released the clip around the neck of the polythene bag and then he flipped the toggles that loaded the first rounds into the quick-firing cannons. So intent was he on the target racing towards him, he failed to notice the rapidly changing digital display on his oil pressure gauge.

Jackie's fingers scrabbled in desperation for a purchase on the *Sarania*'s hull while she frantically tried to wriggle her hips through the porthole. Her legs kicked wildly in the water beneath her that by now nearly filled her cabin. Someone was on the side of the hull – crawling towards her.

'I help you, Jackie! I help!'

'Pepe!'

The Spanish boy was less than twenty feet away. He was prevented from sliding down the slippery flank of the hull by a rubbing strake which he was gripping with one hand. He gave Jackie a reassuring smile and edged nearer her.

'*Momento*,' he panted, working his way carefully along the strake. 'Soon I help you.'

The throbbing, characteristic beat of helicopter rotors caught Jackie's attention. She saw the helicopter coming in straight and low. She was about to wave when the machine's cannons opened up – spewing a murderous hail of shells at the stricken yacht. She watched transfixed with terror as a row of holes hammered across the hull towards Pepe.

'Pepe!'

The boy looked up and screamed as shells tore through his spine and stomach. The force of the impact lifted his lifeless body off the side of the hull and tossed it into the water.

A shell ripped into the steel plating inches from Jackie's scrabbling fingers. She gave a cry and fell back into the flooded cabin.

Valki was a mile from the *Sarania* when he pulled the Ka-35 around in a tight, banking turn for his second pass. He levelled out. A strange noise from above caused him to look up in time to see the central rotor pylon disintegrate as the seized turbine tore away from its mountings. Valki fought the controls but he knew there was nothing he could do. The unbalanced machine reeled drunkenly about the sky. The entire gas turbine broke completely free and plummeted into the sea, throwing up a huge plume of white spray. Seconds later the Ka-35 crashed onto the surface and immediately started to sink. Valki's exhaustive training paid off: he kept calm, pulled the door jettison handle and jumped clear of the machine an instant before it hit the water. The impact knocked the breath from his body but his lifejacket prevented him from going under. As soon as he realized that there seemed to be no danger of a fire or explosion from the wreckage, he swam strongly towards the sinking machine with the intention of recovering its liferaft that was slung beneath the aft sponson. He was reaching for the liferaft's buoyant, day-glow release lanyard when he saw to his surprise that the sea around him was staining red. He came close to panicking, thinking that he had sustained a serious injury. When he saw the pieces of offal floating around him he realized to his immense relief that he was surrounded by the bloody contents of the polythene bag.

Something bumped his foot. At first he thought it was part of the Ka-35's wreckage. The second bump was more positive. There was a swirl of displaced water brushing against his legs. He caught a glimpse through the red-stained water of something moving away from him. A dorsal fin broke the surface. It moved slowly away and then turned towards him. He thrust his head underwater and yelled to frighten the creature away. He opened his eyes and saw the curiously misshapen head of a hammerhead shark preceding three rows of gleaming inward pointing teeth coming straight at him. He took a deep breath with the intention of yelling underwater again, but was too late.

The hammerhead struck twice: the first time tearing out a tentative crescent from his thigh; the second time closing its huge jaws across his pelvis. The creature went into a paroxysm – shaking its body violently – using the powerful spasms and the action of its jaws to sever Valki's torso from his legs. Suddenly the blood and gore surrounding the Russian officer included his own.

Jackie pulled herself free of the porthole's rim and sat on the *Sarania*'s hull. She grabbed instinctively at her shoulderbag and tried to collect her thoughts. She saw two bodies, twisting and tossing lifelessly in the swell as it surged across the hull that was now nearly awash. One of them was Pepe. She rolled onto her side and was violently sick.

The Turkish and the Spanish deckhand had been in the launch's cabin, tearing back the floor panels to get at the fuel tanks, when the helicopter had attacked. Both men were killed outright by a burst of

271

shellfire that ripped through the side of the hull.

'It's got to be contaminated fuel!' Damion shouted from the helm. Then he saw the two bodies lying on the cabin floor. He swore. The engine fired once and refused to do so again. His repeated attempts with the self-starter caused the battery to die. 'Fucking engine!' he yelled. Abandoning the self-starter button, he kicked the engine box aside and cranked the starting handle. 'Tony! Hold the throttle open while I swing her!'

At that moment Elaine forgot the horror of the helicopter attack when she spotted Jackie on the *Sarania*'s hull. She was crawling towards the exposed keel as the *Sarania* began turning right over. 'There's Jackie Morrison! Jackie! Jackie! We're over here!' She jumped up and down and waved frantically.

Jackie heard the cry. She looked up and saw Tony and Elaine standing in the cockpit of a motor launch lying fifty yards from the *Sarania*.

'I can't swim!'

There was no longer painted steel plate beneath Jackie's fingers. Instead she found herself fighting a losing battle to cling to a hull that was slimy and encrusted with marine growth. The inverted hull heaved sluggishly. She lost her grip and slithered helplessly into the water.

'Forget her!' Damion snarled. 'I need help with the engine! If that fucking chopper comes back, we're sitting ducks!'

'We're sitting ducks anyway!' Tony shouted back. 'It'll have to wait!' Without hesitation, he jumped into the water and struck out for the spot where he had seen Jackie fall into the sea.

'Elaine! Help me with this bloody engine! I can't swing the handle and hold the throttle open at the same time!'

'Please – Damion!' Elaine answered, without taking her eyes off Tony as he swam towards the whale-like humped shape of the *Sarania*.

Damion looked quickly around for a piece of rope or cord that would extend his reach. There was nothing. A handkerchief? He searched in his pockets and found the length of plastic strapping attached to its tiny servomotor. It was exactly what he needed. He hooked the plastic loop around the T-shaped throttle lever and his wrist. The murderous device that had ended the lives of three men gave him the additional reach he needed to hold the throttle open

272

while simultaneously cranking the starting handle.

Elaine ignored him. Her eyes were riveted on Tony. She saw him reach the side of the *Sarania*. Her hand went up to her mouth when a swell threw his body roughly against the hull. He dived under water. For a minute it was impossible to make out any details in the maddened foam that was churning and heaving around the hull. Something made her look down. Her feet were immersed. There was a good deal of water in the cockpit. She assumed it had been shipped when the boat was launched.

Damion gave a yell of triumph when his contorted ministrations persuaded the engine to fire erratically. It ran for a few seconds and then stopped.

'Christ! Where's all this fucking water coming from?'

'I don't know,' said Elaine, interested only in Tony's progress.

'Get this bloody thing started and we'll be able to pump out.'

Elaine didn't reply. She saw Tony's head break the surface some yards from the *Sarania*. He was holding something. It was some seconds before she realized that it was Jackie. Tony had an arm crooked around her neck and was swimming awkwardly towards the launch.

A heavy swell broke over the stern of the launch and partially flooded the cockpit. The sudden jolt threw Damion off balance. In addition to his swearing, Elaine heard a strange whirring sound but was too engrossed with Tony's progress to worry about the noise or to appreciate the danger that water reaching to her thighs represented.

'Fucking boat's sinking!'

This time Elaine turned around. Damion had stopped what he was doing and was staring at the rapidly rising water in the cockpit. At first she didn't notice the curious length of plastic strapping that was entwined around his wrist and the throttle lever.

'What?'

'Look at it, woman! I tell you the boat's sinking!' He was oblivious of the whirring servomotor that was inexorably drawing his wrist towards the throttle lever.

As though anxious to confirm the statement, the launch suddenly settled another foot into the water and listed sharply, enabling the swell to wash straight over the transom and into the cockpit.

Tony was ten yards from the launch. He stopped swimming and

shifted his grip on Jackie so that she could breath more easily. He stared horror-struck at the spectacle of the launch settling deep in the water. Elaine was sitting astride the coaming looking bewildered. Curiously, Damion was still wrestling with the throttle even though it was obviously too late to do anything about the engine now.

'Elaine! Jump!' Tony yelled.

'Tony! What's happening!'

'Jump!'

Jumping wasn't necessary. The vessel lurched and settled even deeper so the whole of the transom was submerged. Elaine had only to slip into the water and push herself clear. She trod water. 'Damion! Leave it!'

'I'm stuck!' Damion screamed. He seemed to be struggling to free his hand from the throttle. The water rose to his waist. 'The switch is jammed. A knife! Quickly!'

'What's the matter!'

'A knife! Anything! Please!'

It was the first time that Elaine had ever heard Damion plead. There was a note of hysteria in his voice. Baffled and helpless, she watched the water reach his waist. Then she saw the thin length of strap that seemed to be holding Damion's wrist to the throttle. He was throwing his whole weight dementedly backwards in a desperate attempt to break the strap. There was a sickening crack as his shoulder dislocated and still he continued the struggle to wrench himself free, bellowing in rage and pain as the muscle fibres holding his arm to his body began parting under the impossible strain. The water closed around his neck. He gave one final, despairing cry before the sinking launch dragged him underwater.

Death granted Damion Silvester two final mocking concessions before claiming him: the last earthly sound he heard was the product of his own ingenuity – the tiny servomotor that had wound his wrist against the throttle lever with an unstoppable thousand-pound force was still whirring contentedly despite its immersion.

And as the diminishing green light filtering down from the surface finally faded away to total darkness, he knew why the bomb had not exploded.

The three clung grimly to the *Sarania*'s overturned hull. Tony helped Elaine and Jackie into a more comfortable position, wedged

274

between the two propeller shafts and the slime-covered rudder skegs so that there was little danger of them slipping into the sea. Twenty feet of the sterngear section was the only part of the *Sarania* still above water. He noticed for the first time that Jackie's shoulderbag strap was partially around her neck. He carefully slackened it. She muttered a 'thank you' while continuing to stare straight with unseeing eyes at the restless ocean.

'It's air trapped in the hull that's keeping her afloat,' Tony decided.

Elaine nodded. 'I thought so. How long will it hold?'

'Listen.'

Above the sound of the surging swell could be heard a hissing sound. Tony carefully stood and steadied himself by gingerly holding onto the nearest of two multi-bladed propellers. The hissing was louder. He placed his hand near the gap where the propeller shaft emerged through the encrusted hull. He could feel the escaping air hissing against his palm.

'It's air escaping from inside,' he said laconically, sitting down again. 'I've no idea how much there is and how long it's going to last. It's under a lot of pressure because of the weight of the hull.'

The sun broke through the cloud. Tony's watch had stopped. He guessed that they had five hours of daylight left. At least the weather was warm, which was a blessing. The sun's appearance had a cheering affect on Elaine and Tony, but not on Jackie. Elaine shifted her weight so that she could put a comforting arm around the American woman.

'It's all right, Jackie. We're safe.'

'And the others?'

Elaine could not bring herself to reply.

'They're all dead,' said Tony, looking at the ocean because he knew Jackie was staring at him.

'Charlie?'

Tony nodded. 'All of them.'

Jackie was silent for a few moments while she marshalled her senses. 'Thank you for rescuing me, Mr Suskov.'

Tony gave an embarrassed smile. 'I'd better round up some of the wreckage before it drifts away. There might be something we can . . .' His sentence trailed into silence. He turned his head slowly to look at Jackie. 'What did you call me?'

'Why did the helicopter attack us?'

Tony was too astonished to answer.

'Miss Fleming?' Jackie asked, speaking quietly.

The use of her real name caused Elaine to give a faint smile. 'How much do you know?'

'I know it was a Soviet helicopter from its markings. But I don't know why it attacked us. My guess is that it was something to do with the alterations to the *Sarania* that were carried out in Odessa. Am I right?'

Elaine was the first to break the long silence that followed. She sighed. 'Tony – you're going to have to tell someone sooner or later . . .'

Elaine's phraseology puzzled Tony. 'Why me? Why not the both of us?'

'Oh hell,' Jackie exclaimed suddenly. To the surprise of her companions, she leaned forward, tugged her shoulderbag onto her lap and unzipped it. She produced the radio from the bag's sodden contents and looked sheepishly at the other two. 'I'd forgotten all about this thing.' She switched the set on and keyed the microphone. 'Angelica calling Mike. Do you copy?'

Tony stared at the radio and then at Jackie. 'Who is Mike?'

'A creep. I wonder if water's gotten into this thing?' She lifted the set to her lips again and was about to speak when Randall's voice answered from the speaker. His signal was strong and clear:

'We copy you, Angelica. Anything to report?'

134: Myrtle Beach, South Carolina Saturday, June 15

After a seven-hour nonstop flight from Brussels, Henri Brousalles' executive jet banked over the golden, crowded beaches of the Grand Strand and touched down at Myrtle Beach AFB – the home of the 354th Tactical Fighter Wing.

The video crew from WCOX 'Horry County's Local TV Station' paused in their task of making a documentary about the USAF's last airworthy A-10 Thunderbolt and watched the jet taxiing to a waiting knot of unmarked cars. They speculated about the curious logo of the world stencilled on the aircraft's passenger door and the meaning of the letters S.W.I.F.T.

Broussalles eased his overweight figure through the passenger door. He spotted the camera crew as soon as he stepped down from the aircraft. He paled.

'What are they doing! I was promised that there would be no –'

'There's nothing to worry about, sir,' a senior USAF officer assured him, exchanging a handshake with Broussalles while a Marine Corps driver held the door of the car open. 'They're here making a video about one of our museum pieces.'

The worried Belgian accepted the explanation and settled in the back of the car. He clutched his briefcase as though it contained his family heirlooms. At that moment, Henri Broussalles, executive chairman of the Society for Worldwide Interbank Financial Tele-communication, was probably the most worried man in the United States of America. And with good reason.

After a twenty-minute drive along pleasant, sunlit boulevards with occasional glimpses of the Atlantic Ocean, the Marine Corps driver turned the car into a private road lined with palm trees and stopped outside a ranch-style gatehouse. Two men in plain clothes carefully inspected Broussalles' passport card. The bar was raised and the car moved forward along a curving drive. It stopped outside a magnifi-cent timber-framed house built on stilts. The tastefully proportioned building, set amid a riot of subtropical plants, overlooked a private beach and what looked like an Olympic-size swimming pool. A butler came down the steps and showed the visitor into a large, air-conditioned sitting room with floor-to-ceiling windows that afforded a panoramic view of the ocean. The floors, walls and ceiling consisted of sanded and matt-varnished pine. The few pictures were all earlier twentieth-century original life studies that had not been selected by a prude. The furniture was simple but expensive: ten individual reclining chairs – each with its own table – arranged in a horseshoe around a fine Persian rug that easily accommodated the sprawled bulk of a slumbering Rottweiler. There was no television but there was a Steinway grand piano in a far corner. It was a room designed for people who were interested in each other; a room for conversation. Apart from the enormous dog, it was the sort of room that Henri Broussalles liked.

An attractive woman wearing an elegant white silk dress with a chiffon scarf knotted at her neck rose to greet him. She came forward smiling warmly, her hand outstretched in a gesture of welcome.

277

Broussalles recognized Carol Weismann immediately from her numerous appearances on television. The dog lifted its great head, decided that the visitor was either harmless or inedible, and returned to its sleep.

'M'sieur Broussalles, how lovely to meet you. I'm Carol Weismann. Please do come in and sit down. I'm sure you must be very tired after your flight. We have the guest suite already made up, so if you would care to rest and freshen up first . . .?'

Although the Belgian had other matters on his mind, he was pleasantly surprised at the correct pronunciation of his name. He shook the offered hand and explained that he would rather discuss business first.

'Of course. I fully understand.' She dismissed the butler and poured drinks for both of them.

'It's extremely good of you to see me, Mrs Weismann,' said Broussalles, lowering himself in a chair and sipping his orange juice when his hostess had sat down.

She smiled while gently caressing the sleeping Rottweiler's massive head. 'I'm sorry it's not in Washington. My seeing you here was the President's idea.' Her eyes twinkled 'Myrtle Beach does not receive the media attention that we're used to in Washington.'

'Thank you for your discretion.'

'Please understand, M'sieur Broussalles, that whilst the United States Government understands the need for discretion at this juncture, it is not interested in a long-term cover-up. Whether or not we decide to sit on this extraordinary story, and to what extent, is yet to be decided. The information we have released so far: that Charlie Rose – the motel chain owner – was drowned when an explosion destroyed his yacht and that a United States' ship picked up three survivors, is the truth and we don't want it any other way. As I told you on the phone, the President has tasked me with concluding this affair despite my personal involvement. I've been told to make it clear – no cover-up unless it is unavoidable.' She broke off and smiled. 'I don't propose using that let-out clause.'

The sudden show of decisiveness caught the Belgian banker unawares. 'I fully understand your desire to avoid a cover-up,' he said diplomatically. 'But Mrs Weismann, at this very moment millions of our daily transactions between North America and Europe are being routed over public telephone transatlantic cables.

The strain on international communications – clogged lines – is having a disastrous effect on trade and industry on both sides of the Atlantic. It is an impossible situation.'

'One that will be cured by the shuttle mission next month when your new satellite is launched,' said Carol Weismann drily. 'That is a self-repairing aspect of the situation, M'sieur Broussalles.'

Broussalles refused to be diverted from his principal concern. 'Please, Mrs Weismann. I beg you to consider the consequences should Anton Suskov's version of this leak out. The loss of confidence in international finance will have a disastrous effect on world trade. The EEC and the USA stand to lose untold billions! Third World countries will particularly suffer –'

Carol Weismann held up her hand. Similar points had already been put to her by experts from the Treasury. 'It was an attempt that failed. I think perhaps it will have a disastrous effect on SWIFT. But we're looking at the problem from different viewpoints. What primarily concerns us are the legal angles. Only when we've got those out of the way can we look at anything else. And of course – the legal issues will take us to the question of publicity. Let me set everything out as I see it. Firstly, we have now finished checking out all the details in the story supplied by Tony Suskov, Elaine Fleming, and the US Government agent who had infiltrated the *Sarania*. Those details –'

'Forgive me, Mrs Weismann. But I have not come all this way to discuss details.'

An icy note crept into her voice. 'The details include the brutal murder of Jeff Hunter at his home in Florida. A man who has provided your organization with many years of loyal service. Then there is the detail of the man who carried out that murder planting a bomb in London. A bomb which would have killed myself and any number of innocent people had it exploded. If you don't mind, m'sieur, I intend keeping the details in sharp focus.'

Broussalles realized that he had made a tactical error and remained silent. The Rottweiler yawned and regarded the visitor speculatively, as if the edibility question had yet to be decided.

'To continue,' said Carol Weismann. 'After a week of interrogation and careful checking, we are satisfied that every word of Suskov's and Fleming's story is true. We are also satisfied that they had no part in the bombing conspiracy and that they knew nothing of

279

the murder of Jeff Hunter. That leaves conspiracy to carry out a massive computer banking fraud – and here is where our legal experts are noisily divided: it is not immediately clear that Suskov and Fleming have actually broken the laws of this country. They are not US citizens; the planning was not carried out within the jurisdiction of the US courts; and the attempt itself was carried out in international waters on a non-US registered ship. One way to settle the argument is to put Suskov and Fleming in the dock in open court.'

'Heaven forbid,' Broussalles muttered.

'Of course, there is a possibility that they have broken Belgian law because they were instrumental in the destruction of a Belgian-owned satellite. If your government applies for their extradition, I doubt if the Department of Justice would refuse such a request. But the details of the case could not be heard in camera. Also, we would require a definite guarantee that they would stand trial in Belgium. Relations between our countries would be seriously damaged if we were to hand people over who were not accorded a fair and open trial.'

Broussalles shook his head vehemently. 'My society is most anxious that law-breakers should be brought to justice, Mrs Weismann. But SWIFT merely provides a service for its member banks. It is not responsible for the very powerful banking influences that will be brought to bear on the Belgian government. I know those influences. I will be frank with you – I believe that a trial in Belgium would not take place.'

She nodded understandingly. The Treasury had briefed her on the SWIFT society. A detailed analysis had stated that the society was an incorruptible organization that steered well clear of politics. 'Thank you for your honesty, M'sieur Broussalles. Well – that rules out extradition. Which brings us to yet another major problem. Suskov has applied for political asylum and we have a moral duty to give careful consideration to his application.'

'He is being held incommunicado?' Broussalles queried.

'Of course. Both of them are. In considerable comfort I might add. We have an arrangement for the security of VIP defectors while we examine their cases. We can easily decide that Suskov is an undesirable and put him on a flight for Moscow. But *is* he an undesirable? He speaks flawless English; he knows and understands his mother country. Reading the interrogation transcript leaves me in no doubt
280

that there is much we can learn from him. He would be extremely useful to the United States. My Soviet country desk officer would jump at the chance to have him on his advisory group.' She broke off. The warm smile returned. 'Also, one has to admit that his being involved in what could have been the greatest robbery of all time does demonstrate a willingness to embrace capitalism.'

The witticism was lost on Broussalles.

'Then there is the Fleming girl,' she continued. 'If we send her home to England, the British are certain to dredge up something to charge her with. If we let them both go, there is nothing to stop them selling their story to the highest bidder. And believe me, M'sieur Broussalles, the bidding would go very high indeed. If editors started checking the story, we would not be prepared to deny the facts. I stress that there can be no cover-up.'

The thought of the story being splashed across the headlines of the world's press made the Belgian visibly cringe.

'Suskov could easily emerge as a hero,' she continued. 'Remember – he saved the life of an American agent at considerable risk to his own. The plain and simple truth is, M'sieur Broussalles, we don't know whether to crucify Anton Suskov or give him a medal. That's our position. Now I'd like to hear your suggestions.'

'The girl is not a problem,' said Broussalles.

She raised her eyebrows. 'Oh? Why not?'

The Belgian removed a single typewritten sheet of paper from his briefcase and handed it to her. 'We would prefer it if as few people as possible learn of this, Mrs Weismann.'

As she read through the document, she was unable to prevent an expression of amazement spreading across her face. She gave a faint smile as she returned the paper to her guest. 'Unbelievable, M'sieur. Truly unbelievable. I congratulate you. But we still have the problem of Suskov and what to do with him. Do you mind if I make a suggestion?'

135: Tucson Ranch, Nevada Saturday, June 29

It was midday. The sun was scorching down, making the patio impossible to walk on. Tony was half-asleep on an airbed in the middle of the swimming pool. He was making lazy circling movements with his hands in the water to propel the airbed into the shade of the overhanging palms when a telephone warbled. He opened an eye and saw Elaine scampering naked along the swimming pool's white coping stones – the only place around the pool where it was possible to go barefoot. She picked up the handset, spoke for a few seconds and cut the line. A pair of swimming shorts landed wet and cold on his midriff. He sat up.

'That was the warden's office,' Elaine called out, wriggling into a beachdress. 'We've got company. He must be important company to be able to get in here.'

They were both sitting at a poolside table when an overweight figure dressed in a lightweight tropical suit appeared in the company of a warden. 'Mr Henry Brewsails to see you folks,' said the warden cheerfully, and withdrew.

Elaine gaped in astonishment at the new arrival. She saw Tony looking quizzically at her and the visitor so she covered her surprise by hurriedly positioning some aluminium chairs under the beach shade.

'My name is Henri Broussalles,' said the visitor. He smiled at Elaine as he sat. 'We have met before, I believe, Miss Fleming?'

'The Nice seminar,' said Elaine, glancing fearfully at Tony who was also sitting down. 'Mr Broussalles is the executive chairman of SWIFT.'

Broussalles smiled. 'I delivered a paper on the security of SWIFT. If you recall, Miss Fleming – it contained a statement to the effect that I anticipated that within five years a major but fruitless attempt would be made to break into our system. A prophetic statement as it turned out.'

Elaine looked embarrassed.

'Fruitless?' Tony echoed indignantly. 'But we actually *did* break in!'

Broussalles shook his head. 'You only think you did. You made a number of minor transactions that were cancelled as soon as they were made.' He turned to Elaine. 'Miss Fleming – I owe you an apology. It was my fault entirely. I was the one that refused to believe your father.'

'Wait a minute. Wait a minute,' Tony interrupted. 'What does all this mean?'

'Surely you have told him, Miss Fleming?' said Broussalles,
282

raising an eyebrow at Elaine.

She stared down at the flagstones. 'I've been putting it off and putting it off.' Her voice was very small and quiet.

'Putting what off?' Tony demanded angrily. He shook Elaine's arm, forcing her to look at him. There were tears in her eyes.

'I'm sorry, Tony. I really do love you, but . . . but . . .'

Broussalles folded his arms. 'Miss Fleming has been in touch with her father throughout your operation, Mr Suskov. She reported to him whenever she could, and her father passed on the details to me personally.'

The shock of the revelation drained the colour from Tony's face. He seemed unable to speak.

Elaine resumed her unseeing stare at the flagstones. 'Of course, I didn't know half of what was going on. You and me never knew what Damion and Charlie were really up to. And then being with you every waking moment, and with Damion watching everyone like a hawk – I hardly ever had a chance to get to a phone. What reports I did get through to my father were very sketchy.' She looked up at Broussalles. 'I don't blame you for only half-believing them.'

'Right from the beginning?' Tony whispered.

Elaine nodded unhappily.

'All that about wanting to run your own business . . .?'

'That's true enough. It's something I've always wanted.' Her voice became pleading. 'But not at the expense of betraying SWIFT or my father. Tony – my darling, the operation could never have worked. Please, Tony – don't hate me.'

'All the time you were seeing your father – reporting our every move. And at night, you and me . . .' His voice trailed into silence. When he spoke again, his voice was icy with contempt. 'I suppose you told him all about that as well?'

'I only saw him the once – when we got back to London from Chad. He was waiting for me at Heathrow. Remember how long I was being interviewed? Well, I was talking to daddy – alone – talking him out of doing anything until I had more positive information.'

No one spoke for some seconds. The sun beat down on the shade. Broussalles was embarrassed. He was anxious to say what he had to say and end the meeting. He ran his finger around the inside of his collar.

'Mr Suskov.'

Tony looked blankly at the Belgian.

'You have caused us a great many problems, Mr Suskov. A great many problems indeed. Problems that we are most anxious should never arise again.'

Tony shrugged. Elaine's hand stole across the table. She touched his arm but he jerked it away.

'I've been in contact with your previous employers, Mr Suskov.'

'So?'

'They seem quite indifferent as to what becomes of you. In fact there was an unwillingness on their part to admit that you had ever existed.'

'They can be like that,' said Tony coldly, while staring at Elaine with undisguised loathing.

'I have discussed this matter at a very high level in the US Government,' Broussalles continued. 'We are all aware that you played no part in the murder of Jeff Hunter and Hans Crick. Were that not so, I would not be here. I have come to offer you a job, Mr Suskov.'

Tony seemed not to have heard what the Belgian had said. Broussalles repeated his statement.

Tony transferred his icy stare from Elaine to Broussalles. 'What?'

'Our director of communication security services is due to retire within the next two years. I have offered him early retirement which he has accepted. I am offering you his job at the same salary – two hundred thousand dollars per year plus the same in expenses. There is a condition, of course. You must agree to live and be based in Switzerland for the duration of your contract with us. You will, of course, be bound by the company's rules of secrecy and, more importantly, by Swiss law.' He paused.

Elaine and Tony were staring at the Belgian with expressions of mutual speechlessness.

Broussalles pressed on. 'As I am sure you know, Mr Suskov, Swiss laws governing the discretion of employees in the banking industry are very strict indeed. Breathe a word of what has happened and you will find yourself in very very serious trouble.' He produced a card and slid it across the table. 'You can contact me there until seven this evening. You must excuse me, but I am a very busy man.'

Alone again, Tony and Elaine continued to sit at the table, but without speaking or looking at each other. Eventually Elaine marshalled enough courage to reach out and take hold of his hand. It felt lifeless. She looked for a flicker of emotion in his eyes and saw none but she continued to hold his hand.

Fifteen minutes dragged by. To Elaine it seemed like fifteen years.

'Tony . . . There was one thing I never lied to you about . . . I love you very much.'

At last there was a response from his fingers. They closed around her hand and gripped her tightly.

136: Washington, DC Monday, July 15

Randall breezed into Jackie's office.

'Morning, Angelica.'

'Good morning, creep.'

Randall looked hurt. 'You obviously fail to appreciate what a sensitive person I am. If you were my mother, I'd be emotionally retarded.'

'If I was your mother, I would have strangled you at birth.'

Randall dropped in a chair and proceeded to fill his pipe. 'Funny you should say that. She used to say something similar.'

Jackie ignored him and continued working.

'Anyway – congratulations, Angelica.'

She raised her eyes. 'What for?'

'I put your name down in my department for a special competition. You've won first prize.'

'Which is?'

'An all-expenses-paid-weekend in Geneva. I won the second prize.'

'Which is?'

'An all-expenses-paid-weekend in Geneva.'

Jackie sighed and closed the file she was working on. 'On the same flight as mine, I take it?'

'Yup.'

'And the same hotel?'

'You've got it.'

'You never give up, do you?'

'Nope.'

'Tell me something, Mike. Why is my prize the first prize and

285

your's the second prize when there's no difference between them?'

Randall grinned. 'Of course there's a difference. You get to have the pleasure of my company whereas I get stuck with you.'

Jackie looked around for something heavy to throw at him.

'What it really is,' said Randall, stoking his pipe, 'you and me have had an invite to a wedding next month.'

'Whose?'

'Elaine and Tony.'

Jackie stared. 'You've got to be kidding? Tony's being held.'

'Not now. They're in Switzerland. Tony's got a new name. New job. Everything. We can't breathe a word to a soul but we can go to the wedding.'

'Well I'll be damned,' Jackie muttered.

'Are you coming?'

'Yes – of course. But – Mike.'

'Angelica?'

'Separate hotel rooms.'

'Think of the money we'd save if we got married.'

'You think about it.'

He looked so genuinely crestfallen that she felt sorry for him. She reached out and took his hand. 'I'm sorry, Mike. But as I keep telling you – I can't marry you.'

'But you never say why.'

'You've got a major fault that I could never, ever come to terms with.'

'Being charming, handsome, debonair and modest is a fault?'

'It's not that.'

'It's my dazzling intellect?'

'No.'

He suddenly looked very worried. 'Not my pipe?'

'No.'

'What then?'

'It's just that I could never promise to love, honour and obey a Horace.'

He looked taken aback for a moment. 'Okay . . . Look, Angelica. I'm not sure how to say this, but supposing we skip the "do you take" and the "honour and obey bit" and just look for an apartment that we both like?'

Jackie rolled her eyes to the ceiling. 'Thank you, God. Now he's talking sense at long last.'

Randall looked startled. He broke into a delighted smile. 'Do we celebrate?'

'Why not?'

He stood up suddenly. 'Come on, Angelica. Let's take the rest of the day off.'

That night, after an enjoyable dinner, they were in a taxi taking them back to Randall's apartment when he suddenly remembered something that he had forgotten to tell her.

'We've found out why the bomb didn't go off,' he said quietly.

Jackie lifted her head off his shoulder. 'The Crick guy sabotaged it?'

'No he didn't. A couple of operatives in London managed to swap the cover without anyone noticing. They deserve a Congressional medal because they then defused the thing. When they took a close look at it, and the set-up in Silvester's apartment, they discovered that there was no reason why it shouldn't have worked perfectly.'

'Then why didn't it?'

Randall chuckled. 'It's amazing really. They plan the biggest hi-tech heist in history. Communication satellites. Killer satellites. Computers. You name it. And then they overlook something so incredibly obvious that any high school kid would've spotted it right away. The reason the bomb didn't go off was simple: as the Cadillac passed over the manhole, its mass and its mass of armour plating screened the bomb from the radio signal that was meant to trigger it. It was as simple as that.'

Jackie's head dropped onto his shoulder. She yawned and thought of Pepe. And then she fell asleep with Mike's comforting arm around her.